Walking on Mars
A Journey to the Red Planet

DAVID GATESBURY

Strategic Book Publishing and Rights Co.

Copyright © 2013
All rights reserved – David Gatesbury

This is a work of fiction. Names, characters, places, and incidents are the product of the author's imagination or are used fictitiously, and any resemblance to any actual persons, living or dead, events, or locales is entirely coincidental.

No part of this book may be reproduced or transmitted in any form or by any means, graphic, electronic, or mechanical, including photocopying, recording, taping, or by any information storage retrieval system, without the permission, in writing, from the publisher.

Strategic Book Publishing and Rights Co.
12620 FM 1960, Suite A4-507
Houston, TX 77065
www.sbpra.com

ISBN: 978-1-62212-044-4

Interior Book Design: Judy Maenle

To Matthew

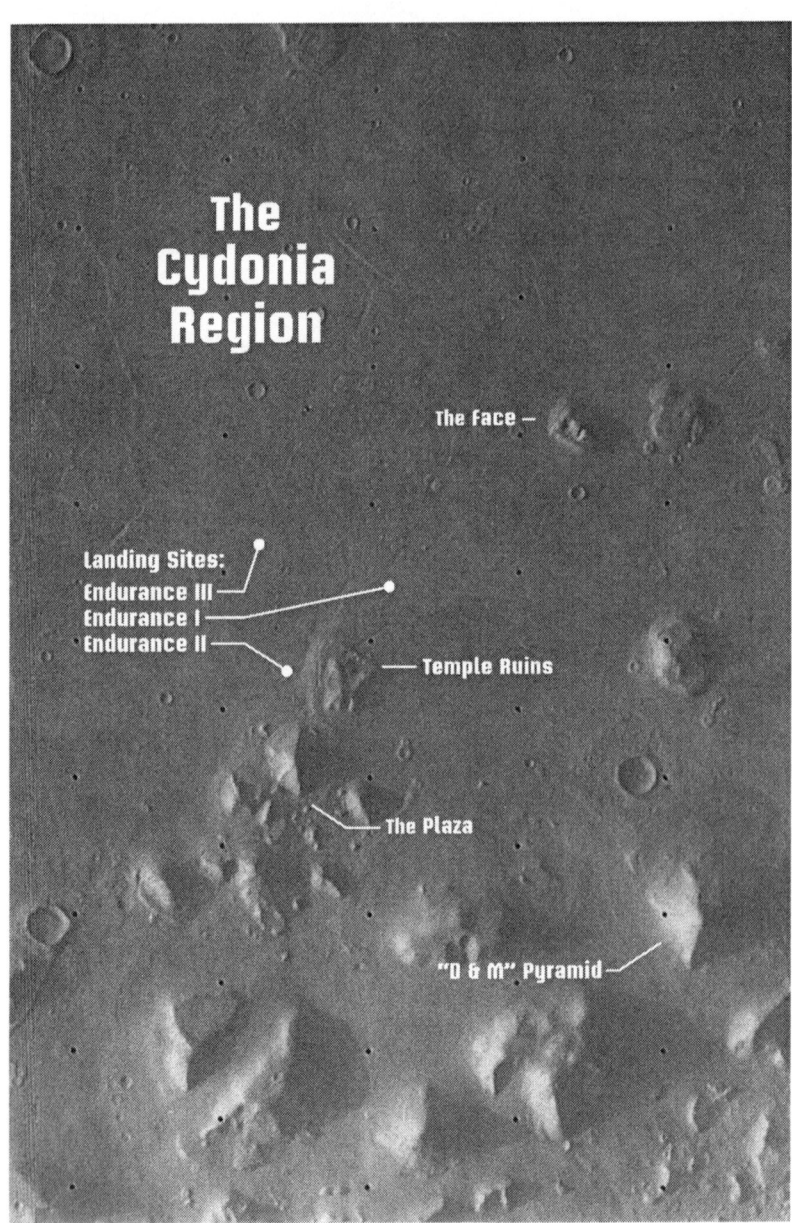

*A special thanks to NASA for supplying
the satellite photos for this work.*

Contents

	Introduction	1
CHAPTER 1	A Crew of Five	3
CHAPTER 2	Facing Complex Challenges	14
CHAPTER 3	The View Outside the Glass	21
CHAPTER 4	Getting Acquainted with an Alien Planet	29
CHAPTER 5	An Astounding Discovery	36
CHAPTER 6	Speculating about the Past	45
CHAPTER 7	The Alluring and Mysterious Eye Pyramid	51
CHAPTER 8	A Lost Architectural Civilization	58
CHAPTER 9	Essential Mission Priorities	67
CHAPTER 10	Lured to the Cydonia Complex	74
CHAPTER 11	An Eye-opening Experience	83
CHAPTER 12	Ambitious Thinking	92
CHAPTER 13	Work Commences	102
CHAPTER 14	A Pathway Long Since Closed	109
CHAPTER 15	Descending into the Depths of a Dark World	119
CHAPTER 16	Lights, Camera, No Action	127
CHAPTER 17	Perplexing Events	134
CHAPTER 18	A Desperate Night	141
CHAPTER 19	Where Is It Leading Us?	151

CHAPTER 20	The Grand Gallery	157
CHAPTER 21	An Unexpected Meeting	165
CHAPTER 22	What Do We Do to Treat It?	174
CHAPTER 23	Burying One of Our Own	184
CHAPTER 24	The Torrent Age of a Legendary Ruler	190
CHAPTER 25	Beasts of Mycuria	199
CHAPTER 26	Returning to the Pyramid	211
CHAPTER 27	What's Beyond the Wall?	217
CHAPTER 28	A Beast Surfaces	225
CHAPTER 29	A Late-night Visitor	235
CHAPTER 30	Threats to Our Survival Increase	244
CHAPTER 31	A Last-ditch Effort	255
CHAPTER 32	Jaws of Death	262
CHAPTER 33	Homeward Bound	269

Introduction

The United States has placed people on the moon and brought them home safely six times. Our shuttle program introduced space vehicles capable of launching from Earth and returning home for performing more space missions. We have sent probes and satellites to other worlds. There is no other country that can match these accomplishments, yet at this time, our endeavors in space exploration seem to have stalled. If we are to remain a technologically advanced leader of nations, we must invest in our space program and continue challenging ourselves. This is the pioneer spirit that made our country what it is today.

As soon as ancient man was able to think, he looked up to the heavens at the wondrous moon, stars, and planets. Where would man be without his dreams? What makes the idea of sending people to planet Mars so tantalizing is not only the fact that it is our closest neighbor in the solar system, but that this is a place that once had a surface quite similar to Earth's. Science has provided proof that the red planet once held surface water, lakes and streams, and perhaps great oceans. Since life takes hold in water first, there may have been vast jungles and an array of plant life.

How far did Mars go in supporting life before it changed into a desolate, lifeless planet? Does microscopic life still exist there today? I'd say there is a high probability that microbial life does exist there: There are traces of water beneath the surface; there's ice at the poles; and atmospheric conditions could support this type of life form. There's also a strong chance these microbes could be a threat to humans, for anything that can exist in Mars' poisonous atmosphere can potentially be a danger.

Technology continues to progress, and today we are able to send a manned spacecraft to Mars. However, what limits us are

David Gatesbury

those things needed to sustain the space travelers so they can survive the trip and return home. I don't know whether mankind will make it to Mars in my lifetime or not, for there are so many challenges to consider and prepare for, but I'd like to think that it will happen. When that time comes, I'm sure we'll make some amazing and fantastic discoveries that will impact our world for generations to come. It would be pure ignorance to believe that Earth is the only place in the universe where life can be found. When we contact intelligent life or find proof that intelligent life once existed elsewhere, it will change our lives forever.

CHAPTER 1

A Crew of Five

The year was 2037, and Stan Rhodes was captain of *Endurance III,* an aerodynamically designed, ninety-ton, V-shaped spacecraft traveling through outer space on the last leg of a 56-million-kilometer trip to reach planet Mars. An American of English, Irish, German, and Cherokee Indian heritage, Rhodes was a Navy captain and test pilot who flew jets from aircraft carriers. For six months, he'd commanded his crew of four in this self-contained vessel.

Rhodes occupied the middle seat of three spanning a broad instrument panel, and sitting to his right was Flavio Muret, a youthful Frenchman acting as second in command. In training exercises, under the most difficult circumstances, technicians watching Rhodes' body sensor readings said the sound of Muret's coolheaded voice had a calming effect on him. Suave and charismatic with dark, wavy hair, Muret gained favorable fanfare when competing for a spot on the Mars mission, distinguishing himself nicely. A member of the European Astronaut Corps, he spent six months aboard the International Space Station. When earthbound, Muret indulged his passion for skiing and was a mountain guide in the Alps near his home in Grenoble, France.

Far Hai Win, a petite female of Asian descent, sat to Rhodes' left. Born in Hong Kong and educated in the United States, she became an American citizen less than a year ago. Although every crew member received a crash course in medical training, Far was an M.D. and, having acquired the most extensive scientific training for the mission, held the rank of Science and Medical Director.

The next two seats staggered behind the first three completed a W formation, and seated behind and between Far and Rhodes was Jetha Karashan, an intelligent Indian-Pakistani. Jetha spent most of her adult life in London, where she received her education, and like Muret, she was a member of the European Space Agency. Although everyone aboard had some education in geology, she was the most qualified and had a great interest in history and archeology. Possessing a friendly nature, she had the most mysterious eyes, beautiful, golden-brown skin, and a healthy, voluptuous figure.

In keeping with the international composition of the crew, the last member of the team was a Russian cosmonaut named Aleksei Dimitri Polzinov. Occupying the chair behind and between Rhodes and Muret, Polzinov was a reserved man with rugged features, as well as the oldest of the crew at age forty. Like Rhodes, he kept his hair in a crew cut. A man of few words, he spoke with a slight accent. When holding rank as captain in the Russian Air Force, he complained to his commanding officers about inadequacies regarding safety equipment in the training of young cadets. As a result, his superiors reprimanded him in classical fashion, forcing him to undergo a punishing training course designed to break a person's mental and physical being, but he proved himself a resilient individual by completing and withstanding their exhaustive demands.

Even though there wasn't a raised deck at the nose of the ship, the seating area was still designated the bridge, and each chair had its own computer and monitor. Maintaining and overseeing the ship's status was a powerful computer that responded to commands whenever a crew member used the name Abe, a name that caught on fast with the scientists who programmed it. The unit communicated verbally using a male voice with the temperament of a studious assistant.

Caution held back the Mars mission for years. What helped turn interplanetary space travel into reality was the creation of the gravity simulator, which produced forty percent of Earth's gravity. Abe activated a pulsing pull of electromagnetic waves that in turn created a magnetic field encompassing the floor throughout most of the ship. There'd been various ideas thought up to compensate for weightlessness in space, but this technological leap transformed the design of a long-distance manned spacecraft by reducing some of the logistical challenges. Without some form of gravity, humans can suffer severe muscle atrophy, a 50-percent loss of muscle strength, and a reduction in bone mass.

The enormity and complexity of the Mars mission evolved at different stages as science and technology made advancements. Planning a trip to Mars demanded rockets with the capacity to deliver more thrust, and aerospace engineers developed a powerful, fuel-efficient nuclear thermal rocket engine that supplied those needs. Mission planners scratched a plan for a manned module to orbit Mars, as success in logistics relied primarily on vitally needed supplies going to those making the critical landing. Astronauts needed a backup ship in case the spaceship they landed in had technical problems that prevented liftoff when they were ready to return home, so planners decided instead to land an emergency ascent vehicle.

The plan actually involved deploying two ships to land on Mars before a ship carrying humans launched, and first to land was *Endurance I,* a bell-shaped emergency ascent vehicle that had two floors. This ship carried enough supplies for a trip home, but it would remain untouched during the travelers' stay on Mars. The emergency ascent vehicle ran on conventional rocket fuel, and over the next eighteen months, it would produce its own liquid fuel from Mars' atmosphere for a return flight. If this transport vehicle wasn't needed, it would stand ready for use by explorers on future missions. The second to land was *Endurance II,* a cargo ship and nothing more, and it landed about seven kilometers southwest from the emergency vehicle.

Two ships transported the supplies necessary to sustain a crew of five for a minimum of thirty months. *Endurance III* carried provisions for the trip to Mars and for a portion of the time spent on the red planet. *Endurance II,* the cargo ship, served to replenish them after they'd landed, but it also carried hardware and equipment, including the Mars Roving Vehicle (MRV).

Although these two ships had an identical body design, similar to that of an airplane, *Endurance II* didn't have a nuclear-powered rocket engine, nor did it have a nuclear power reactor. Both spacecraft relied on powerful rocket propulsion to make them airborne and provide flight control, using a revolutionary form of vector thrust to hover for vertical landings and a level descent.

The crew had recently fallen under Mars' gravitational pull and were checking coordinates through the main computer and the navigation and guidance system to track their progression for converging with the red planet. They could see Mars off in the distance to their right, often stopping to study its glow in the dark twilight of outer space.

The trip had gone smoothly thus far, and after making routine system checks through the computer, Rhodes unbuckled his safety belt and excused himself to take a short break. He hadn't moved far from the bridge when something rocked the ship. Rhodes became airborne, thrown against a wall before landing on the floor. Trying to get up, he became airborne again! Slammed onto the floor, he recovered quickly, but after getting tossed in the air once more, his head crashed into the floor.

Fearful his ship was coming apart, he gathered his dazed senses and tried making it back to his seat. Jetha extended her hand to him from her seated position, and catching hold of it, he pulled himself forward to his seat.

Chaos reigned: Lights flashed, alarms and buzzers screamed, and Rhodes stared wide-eyed at the instrument panel with a confused look on his face. After the initial quake, the ship continued to vibrate, and Rhodes was afraid that something onboard had exploded or that perhaps a meteor had struck the ship. They heard a loud pop, and sparks flew from a console on the port side. A second burst of sparks was unsettling, but they had to stay in their seats and endure the shaky ride.

Watching dashboard data changing, Rhodes couldn't be sure if the cabin pressure and oxygen levels were holding, nor could he get a fix on flight conditions to check the status of primary and backup systems. He said in a loud voice, "Abe, if you're still with us, shut off warning lights and silence alarms."

The lights shut off, the alarms silenced, and Far turned to Rhodes. "What do you think happened?"

"I don't know. Right now I just want to make certain cabin pressure and oxygen readings are holding."

The ship was still shaking violently. The vibration seemed to worsen and then peak before calming, and then the scenario was repeated.

"Abe, what can you tell me about the condition of this spacecraft?"

"The ship has undergone an abrupt change in course, resulting in a displacement of instrumentation, and data is changing as it is being recalled and rechecked. However, there are no fire indications onboard."

Flavio pointed into space. "We can no longer see Mars, but look how the star Regulus in the constellation Leo appears to be rotating in an odd way. That's a sign the ship is in a tumbling barrel roll."

Rhodes saw Regulus rotating clockwise. "We've had a course change, and we're in an unstable flight path. My best guess is that something struck the ship, probably a meteor or some space debris. While it's possible something onboard exploded, the computer should've reported pressure changes as they occurred through sensors."

Aleksei said, "You would think a collision with a meteor would've destroyed this ship. Even if it were pea-size, it would've breached the ship's skin and the computer would've reported pressure changes."

The next time the vibration settled down, Rhodes grabbed a fire extinguisher and rushed to the panel where he'd seen sparks fly, ready to put out an electrical fire. Removing a panel but seeing no immediate risk of fire, he resisted activating the fire extinguisher. Faint smoke rose out of a box containing delicate computerized components. Realizing the panel covered the communications box, he was concerned they may have lost their ability to trade information with Earth.

It took a short time for data to reach fixed numbers, and they were relieved to see atmospheric conditions inside the ship were holding. All the vital readings for survivability—cabin pressure, oxygen, and water supply—looked stable, and Rhodes' next concern was for the ship's course and what had jarred the ship in the first place.

"I want to keep an eye on these readings to see if there are any changes, but in the meantime I want you to split into pairs to inspect the ship and report anything out of the ordinary. Check the cabin, the cargo bay, and maintenance junctions on the starboard and port sides of the ship, and be thorough."

Jetha and Far linked up to survey the ship, and Aleksei went with Flavio, and when they returned they had nothing to report outside of the recurring wobble shaking the ship.

"I want all of you strapped in your seats, and we'll discuss the situation. While you were gone, I tried contacting Earth but didn't have any success, and I'm concerned we may not be able to restore communications. However, I'm certain technicians are aware we have problems through telemetry readouts they're receiving.

"In addition, I ran computer programs to determine the ship's location with regard to the timetable for catching up to Mars. Judging by data I've seen, the guidance computer is malfunctioning. Alignment updates and telemetry readouts aren't making any sense; the numbers are jumping around. At first, I thought it's because we're off course, but that's not it. As long as those navigation coordinates are plagued with inaccurate readouts, we've got problems correcting our course. In our training sessions working with computers, when we ran into an outlandish fluctuation in data, we had to shut down the computer and then restart it. It's just a guess, but the computer has probably gone into overload, and that's why we're not getting corresponding data."

"I agree," said Jetha as she studied the numbers. "The guidance computer's probably been in a type of emergency mode ever since our trajectory changed, and these readings are fallout resulting from that course change."

"It may be that the system is still computing information," stated Flavio. "We can't risk shutting down the guidance computer. What if we can't power it up again? That computer must be operating when we enter the Martian atmosphere to track the location of the first two unmanned ships that landed ahead of us on Mars. This isn't a vehicle we can land manually. To power down the computer at this stage may cause it to lose critical data. I don't want the controlled tracking and landing procedures to malfunction at the very moment we're preparing to land on Mars' surface. If we shut it down and it won't boot up, we'll have to abort the mission, so my suggestion is to give it more time to stabilize."

Aleksei spoke up. "We cannot attempt a landing with the guidance computer feeding distortions. We may land hundreds or perhaps thousands of kilometers off from our targeted landing site."

Rhodes nodded, taking a moment to think. "The main computer oversees navigation and guidance system coordinates. Listen while I ask Abe to advise us." He raised his voice slightly and said, "Abe, the guidance computer is not reading the data fed into it correctly. Seeing how it's not computing information accurately, we're considering a power-down to allow it to recalibrate itself. Do you find that advisable, or can you make those corrections?"

Abe responded, "The guidance and navigation system is on overload at this time. Data fed into this system is correct, but as the computer tabulates and unscrambles it, I'm reading distortions."

"If the guidance computer becomes unreliable, can you take over its functions?"

"No, I cannot, not for a long-term duration, and I am not able to interfere with the landing procedure, as my ability to override navigation and guidance functions is limited. Shutting down the navigation system and restarting it may allow it to tabulate the information correctly, but I urge you not to give the system any complicated commands for a short time after the restart. A few minutes should afford it time to reset and reprogram; otherwise, the computer may go into overload again. Shutting down the guidance computer will result in the loss of critical electric power. For the length of the shutdown period, you will barely have adequate power to run the ship, but your desk computers and their monitors will still work."

"While the guidance computer is off, do you have the ability and the data required to aid us in correcting our course?"

"Yes, a shutdown will not hinder my ability to perform this function, but you will have to power the ship manually to correct your trajectory. There will be sufficient energy to start rocket engines and thrusters to make a burn to correct the ship's course. By correcting the ship's course during this shutdown period, you'll take strain off the navigation and guidance computer that could otherwise throw it into another failure. I've concluded it's the ship's wobble throwing off this computer's ability to navigate, channel, and conduct our course. Directional finders cannot lay down a fixed trajectory, thus creating distortions in data."

Flavio's eyes squinted as he said, "Power the ship manually.... Don't tell me we're going to correct our course by navigating by the stars with a slide rule, doing calculations, conversions, and rudimentary computations."Rhodes shook his head no. "The main computer's going to do all of that for us."

Then Aleksei said, "How do we work that process? Will the computer give verbal commands on how to steer the ship to correct our flight path?"

"No, we use computer graphics to optically align our flight path, but first, we'll shut off the navigation and guidance computer. As soon as the main computer has made corrections in plotting our course of trajectory and we've performed the maneuver, we'll power up the navigation system and let it reprogram itself to take over again. I'm relying on this rocket burn not only to straighten out our flight path, but also to take us out of this tumbling wobble while smoothing out any other gyrations and myriad problems the ship has. After correcting our course in this manner, the navigation system's work should be made easy."

"Of course," said Far, catching on to the plan. "I remember doing something like that in flight class. This will be one of the rare times this ship will be flown manually."

"That's why the captain is the captain," Jetha remarked optimistically.

"Now I don't see that we have any choice but to shut down the navigation and guidance computer," said Rhodes. When no response came, Rhodes gave Abe the order to shut it down. A warning light indicator for the navigation system brightened before shutting off, and then some of the other lights dimmed, including cabin lights, giving him an eerie feeling.

The ship began to shake and shudder. Rhodes was breaking the rules, as the crew was supposed to be fully suited and wearing helmets when performing this procedure. "Flavio, prepare to fire up the engines and, after I give you the signal, start a countdown from ten."

After coordinating a short system check between Far and Flavio, there was quiet, and then Rhodes brought up a computer graphics program on his monitor for initiating manual guidance of the ship. His monitor screen turned a bright shade of blue, and a pulsating tunnel appeared by way of white, throbbing, arched lines that kept blinking in a recurring inward fashion. Adjusting the steering column by pulling it up and toward him, he shifted the steering wheel until it fell into a comfortable, locked position. He then threw switches to establish manual control of the ship. An image in the shape of a plane took center on a level line on the monitor, and he controlled the little plane with the steering wheel. Turning the wheel slightly to the right and left tipped its short wings to one side and then the other. This would also influence change in the tunneling effect too. Rhodes then addressed Flavio, "Ready for countdown to begin."

Flavio responded, "Ten, nine, eight, seven, six, five, four, three, two, one, ignition," and with the flip of a switch at his fingertip, the engines fired.

Placing his hand on the power lever, Rhodes slowly moved it forward. The firing thrusters made the ship lurch forward with a burst of speed. The shake and shimmy of the ship worsened as power increased and symptoms persisted, but soon engine thrust and speed delivered a smooth, stabilizing motion while propelling them through space. As he manipulated the spacecraft, he watched the computer-generated imagery as the plane shifted within the dancing, pulsating lines. The plane tilted from right to left as he steered to center it and level it off. In executing the maneuver, he coaxed the ship one way and then the other while steadying it to alter their course. The pulsating arched lines slowed to indicate the ship was closing in on its true flight path, and after the lines locked to hold steady, he'd successfully redirected their trajectory for Mars.

Believing they were back on track and had straightened out their trajectory, they could see Mars in the distance again. Rhodes eased back on the power lever and said, "Engine power stop." With the ship cruising smoothly, he no longer sensed any vibrations, and flipping a few switches to take the ship off manual control, he then adjusted the steering wheel into a downward position. He last addressed the computer, saying very plainly, "Abe, as soon as you think it's safe to power up the navigation and guidance computer, do so."

Easing back in his seat, he remarked, "Let's just sit tight till the navigation and guidance computer resets itself." A short time later, the computer made a chattering sound, the light indicator for the navigation and guidance system came on, and he heard sighs of relief.

After waiting a few minutes, Rhodes ran computer program files to ensure the guidance computer was in control of the ship, and leaning back in his chair, he reviewed the information. The navigation and guidance system was actively receiving tracking from range finders, assimilating data to calculate their position.

"Before doing anything else, let's make certain the guidance computer readouts are accurate and confirm that data through the main computer. We accomplished a lot getting this ship back on course, and with a little luck, the trip will go smoother from here on, but we're not out of the woods yet. We still have a communications breakdown, and when we orbit Mars later, we'll have to inspect the ship's heat shield before considering a landing."

The crew spent hours checking systems and making repairs, and when Rhodes inspected the electrical box, a blackened area revealed that they had nearly had an electrical fire. Replacing two bad circuit breakers, he noticed that the breaker that gave power to communications kept kicking off. Sensitive elements burned up inside the box kept triggering the breaker. Rhodes knew receiving stations on Earth constantly disseminated telemetry data with a seven-minute delay while actively receiving tracking from range finders for calculating their position. However, mission planners would be concerned about losing contact with their ship, and as much as Rhodes hoped to soon overcome these system failures, there looked to be little chance of reinstating communications with Earth.

CHAPTER 2

Facing Complex Challenges

Finding no damage to controls or instrumentation, Rhodes concentrated on repairs connected with the communications box. Roasted circuit panels that were part of an integrated system sequential for sending and receiving communications were a major concern. They carried a micro-size network of field-effect terminals and transistorized circuits that controlled conductivity of voltage-to-frequency and frequency-to-voltage conversions. Inductor coils and other components channeled pulses from emitters and collector currents as audio and video frequency signals independent of other onboard telemetry equipment.

Rhodes saw that damage to sensitive circuit boards left them beyond repair. Manifests for their ship and the cargo ship *Endurance II* showed they lacked replacement parts, as it was highly unusual for this equipment to fail. They had only one other way to communicate with Earth: After landing on Mars, they could use communication equipment on *Endurance I*. However, mission planners had stressed time and time again that this emergency ascent ship was off-limits and designated solely to get them home in an emergency. Carrying on this expedition without exchanging ideas and information with aerospace engineers on Earth would be a great handicap, not to mention a huge responsibility for Rhodes.

Fortunately, Far had a keen sense for electrical circuitry, and she and Rhodes had some success using soldering techniques to achieve ship-to-Earth communications. As far as they could tell, they were again sending out a signal, and the others congratulated them joyously on their success. They all made a showing in front of the dash camera in the instrument panel to express problems they'd experienced and to communicate messages to family members. Rhodes last communicated concerns he had about making a landing on Mars, making mention that they'd have to first perform a spacewalk when orbiting Mars to inspect the ship's fuselage and heat shield for damage.

Rhodes looked haggard from combating the ship's problems, and Far mentioned he had purplish bruising on the outside of his left eye from having hit the floor when the ship was initially jarred.

Not knowing what had rocked his spacecraft worried him, as a collision with a meteor would almost certainly destroy a spaceship, leaving him to wonder what damage they'd sustained. His main concern was still for the condition of his ship's heat shield, and he hoped that when they rendezvoused with Mars, their space walk would confirm the heat shield was intact. A breach in the ship's skin could cause a catastrophic explosion when they encountered the intense heat of Mars' atmosphere.

He also wondered about the navigation and guidance system's computing capacity as well, for it controlled the landing sequence. It had to be fully operational when they entered the Martian atmosphere to track the location of the first two unmanned ships. Their survival rested upon the reliability of this spaceship, but while technical failures cast doubt and uncertainty on the future, Rhodes wasn't ready to abort the mission. Regardless, it was absolutely necessary that they reached Mars, for the only way to change course and turn back to Earth was by orbiting the red planet.

Long under the red planet's gravitational pull, they saw a panoramic view of this mysterious world through the spacecraft's windshield. Though little more than half the size of Earth, Mars looked enormous, and huge quantities of iron gave the planet its rusty-gold color with amber highlights. Scarring its surface was *Valles Marineris,* or Mariner Valley, a vast canyon six miles deep and long enough to stretch from Los Angeles to New York City. *Olympus Mons,* a 90,000-foot-high volcano, the largest known volcano in our solar system, stood three times the height of Mount Everest, and *Tharsis Montes,* a volcanic region, showed the dark-brown bruising of a string of volcanoes. The mountain ranges were astounding, and the crew saw clear evidence of drainage gullies running to dried-up lake beds in low-level plains of white sand that may have formed as early as the last decade. This was a reminder that for a period of at least a billion years, Mars had surface water and a climate similar to Earth's.

They fired a retro-rocket burn to bring them into an elliptical orbit for swinging widely out and away from the planet, falling into a more circular orbit on their second revolution. Accompanying them in the twilight celestial heavens were Mars' moons, Phobos and Deimos, two weirdly contorted, rogue asteroids captured in low orbits around the planet.

Rhodes periodically ran computer program files to confirm the navigation and guidance computer was in control of the ship, while reviewing readouts to be certain they were accurate. Scheduled to perform a spacewalk during their third orbit around Mars, he contemplated the risks with entry into Mars' atmosphere. At one point, the navigation and guidance computer was going to take control over the landing sequence, and once that happened, there was no turning back. Their lives would be in the hands of a computer system.

Far tapped into a geographic information system through her monitor that presented high-definition satellite images of Mars, and running through these photos she saw evidence of Mars' watery past. Valley networks and gulley erosions collected to form streams and rivers, cutting channels to what looked like a long-running shoreline where a vast ocean once existed.

Flavio, Jetha, and Aleksei gathered around her monitor to view a series of excellent regional photos, some taken years earlier by a Mars global surveyor, others by satellite orbiters more recently.

Flavio said, "Stan, what do you say about taking another look to see what's in the vicinity of the landing site?"

"I've looked at those photos a million times."

"Yeah, I know, but it'll take only a few minutes to survey the area."

Rhodes switched his monitor to view what Far's monitor was showing. Just then, she brought up an image of the face on Mars, which had long before whipped up so much controversy and speculation.

"As you well know, that face is a trick of nature made up of light and shadows—angled sunlight reflecting off natural, sloping formations to create distortions that resemble a face,"

Far explained. "We're merely looking to see what's in the outlying area, and to me, that land formation looks like an island in a vast ocean."

Rhodes took a deep breath. "I have little interest in that outcrop of land, but those other land formations located southward will be reachable on foot. That's if this spacecraft lands where it's supposed to."

Far now brought up a recent orbiter photo that pinpointed exactly where *Endurance I* and *Endurance II* had landed just north of a cluster of anomalies, and there was little change in the outlying imagery.

Aleksei gazed at the monitor screen. "The intricate geometric shapes of those anomalies in what's called the Cydonia Complex are intriguing. Some look to have true pyramid shapes, do they not?"

"That idea has been run into the ground by theorists, but those are what scientific researchers refer to as a yardang, meaning they're formed by wind erosion."

Jetha commented, "These regional photos remind me of when I spent six months in Egypt studying lavishly decorated royal tombs in the Valley of the Kings."

Rhodes then switched back to reading computer program files for assimilating data, ignoring the chatter of his crewmates.

While making preparations for the space walk, Rhodes chose Flavio and Jetha to accompany him to inspect the ship's heat shield, and they suited up to enter the vacuum of space. On his way to an alcove where a number of doors branched off at the rear of the cabin, Rhodes passed by pod enclosures in a starburst pattern that were the capsules they slept in. One door led to a lab containing sensitive, scientific instruments and refrigeration boxes for specimens found on Mars that might contain life. There was a door to the cargo bay and another for a lavatory where two private stalls stood adjacent to a shower room with lockers for storing personal items.

Rhodes joined Flavio and Jetha in the cargo bay. Their newly designed, slim-fitting spacesuits were easier to maneuver in than those they'd trained in. They were all equipped with backpack life-support units and jetpacks, and they switched on their ventilation fans and warming systems. A door on the chest of their suits opened from the top down to expose software, making it easy to read the condition of the suit's components. The backpack assembly was the most vital part of the primary life-support system. Dual oxygen tanks fed air for a maximum of seven hours with a thirty-minute reserve emergency air supply, and two rechargeable 16.8 volt batteries powered the suit's electrical system.

Flavio, Jetha, and Rhodes donned helmets that read MARS, adjusting them to a sealed, fixed position on their suits' neck ring to secure them. Each person's designated monitor picked up the view he or she had from the helmet's camera; these were images they'd be transmitting back to Earth. Knowing it would take time to cover a ship this size, Rhodes worried about their multi-laminated suits, which provided little protection from cosmic radiation. He underscored the importance of finding damage to the ship, however, saying, "The length of entry into the Martian atmosphere should be under eight minutes, but the temperature outside this ship will be more than twenty-five hundred degrees. Our survival may depend on our finding something as small as a scratch or a pinhole."

The cargo bay chamber's door was actually two doors in one, with the main door holding an inner hatch in the shape of a bulging, fish-eye window. The circumference of the fish-eye window gave adequate space for one to enter and exit the ship. The inside of the main door was flat, as it opened as a ramp, having smooth-fitting, reinforced crossbars with durable panels for walking across when entering or exiting the ship with cargo.

Rhodes was last to exit the ship, and he closed the hatch behind him. Next to the cargo door, the wing began protruding as a streamlined fin running outward as it angled toward the back of the ship. The three astronauts spread out from the midsection with their jetpacks propelling them into space. Jetha moved forward to check the roof section while Flavio inspected the hull. Rhodes would scrutinize the port side before giving the wings a look-over.

The striking brightness of this wondrous, celestial sphere called Mars left Rhodes momentarily spellbound, but he proceeded with his systematic inspection of the port side and its wing. He then moved beneath the ship's underbelly to get to the starboard side. Controlling his movement with his jetpack was awkward, and he used his hands and feet to skim the hull while pushing off it. Stopping at the midway point to view the expanse of the vessel, he caught sight of Flavio scanning the ship's underside and went on.

Arriving at where the starboard wing connected to the ship, he'd yet to see anything odd until sunlight reflecting off Mars' surface exposed a deviation in the straightness of the starboard wing. Moving out with the front of the wing a few meters to get a closer look, he saw an indentation and scrape marks. He felt uncomfortable examining what appeared to be minor damage from the glancing strike of a meteor moving at tremendous speed.

"I've found it. Come over to the starboard side, and you'll see where a rogue meteor grazed and deflected off the wing."

Almost a minute went by before Flavio and Jetha showed up, floating in space above the wing. Flavio maneuvered closer to make an inspection. "Wow, it's nothing less than a miracle that the ship wasn't destroyed. Can we replace this piece?"

Rhodes rubbed the sleeve of his suit against the curved section of the wing, "No, and I'm not certain it won't present a problem on entry into Mars' atmosphere. Any imperfection in the heat shield raises concerns. Even a scuff mark may cause enough friction to ignite the ship."

Jetha gave close study to the scrape marks. "What may have made the difference between survival and disaster was the angled incline by which the meteor ran with the ship to skip off the wing." She used her hand and arm to demonstrate how she imagined the meteor's direction and trajectory caused it to graze the edge of the wing to put the ship in a tumbling barrel roll.

Returning to the interior of the ship, Rhodes sent a transmission to technicians on Earth to let them know what they'd found, mentioning he'd keep them abreast of his decision to make a landing on Mars.

CHAPTER 3

The View Outside the Glass

After his next sleep period, Rhodes approached the window to look out upon the dazzling spectacle of this strange world called Mars. He took his seat up front, and the others soon joined him, wearing the baggy pants and sweatshirts they wore while sleeping. They knew their captain was concerned about technological failures and potential hazards that may come with attempting a landing.

"We've just crossed fifty-six million kilometers of space to reach Mars, and now we've come to the moment of truth. The next step is the prized landing. However, there are risks not only to entering Mars' atmosphere with regard to the heat shield, but also to landing this spacecraft. We're dependent on the computer system to get us down safely, and the success of the mission and our very survival hinge on our landing as close as possible to *Endurance I* and *Endurance II*. Since the landing process is entirely out of our hands, you have to consider that the success rate of landing unmanned probes on Mars is less than fifty percent.

"At one point, the guidance and navigation computer is going to take control of the landing sequence, and another important aspect about our vertical landing is that we need four parachutes to deploy at just the right time. Our fate will be essentially in the hands of a preprogrammed computer command system that has already malfunctioned. In the event that this computer doesn't perform well and we miss the landing site by a great distance, we're going to be in big trouble. What if the computer fails to allow us to take off again and we're hundreds of kilometers away from the emergency ascent ship? We'll be marooned and doomed to die on planet Mars.

"Having touched on these points, I still see no strong reason to abort the mission. Once we've broken through Mars' atmosphere, we're committed, our lives are completely in the hands of the computer system, and God help us if something should go wrong.

"We'll start performing system checks while comparing each other's tabulations, and I'll inform Earth of our plans to land. I'll also be checking other critical data, including landing coordinates with the guidance and navigation computer. Abe continuously tracks weather conditions on Mars, as dust storms sometimes encompass the red planet, and static electricity and lightning produced by them could create electrical problems."

Seeing Flavio already beginning to make preparations, Rhodes said, "Flavio, we want to set the time for firing up the rocket engines for ninety minutes from now. Hold the countdown at the number ten."

Rhodes then addressed the main computer. "Abe, we are preparing to enter Mars' atmosphere. Can you check all primary and backup systems, and give verification that everything is ready?"

"Affirmative. All ship's systems are ready."

"We need to know if weather conditions on Mars' surface are suitable for performing a landing."

"Mars surface conditions are calm. I show no ground activity at the landing site that can threaten or affect your landing."

"Can you do an analysis on the guidance and navigation system's tracking ability to locate *Endurance I* and *Endurance II* to make certain that landing procedures are followed?"

"Since the guidance and navigation computer's restart, all data I've read has coincided with the computer's readouts. There are no data distortions to alter the computer's ability to track the landing sites of the first two spaceships. Landing coordinates are thirty-five degrees north, two hundred twelve degrees east. There's no sign of wind, and unless those conditions change to cause interference, we should land within a range of ten kilometers of that locale."

Eager to explore this alien world, they soon began suiting up at the rear of the cabin in preparation to land, and Rhodes ascertained the ship's readiness from an army of automated microprocessors.

Taking their stations, they put their helmets on and fastened their seatbelts, and Flavio said, "Flight controls register okay. All systems are go."

Far acknowledged, saying, "All systems check out here."

Rhodes' monitor showed color-coded, wire-frame imagery of geological features presented by the thermal emission imaging system, evolving with the ship's changing movement. He read areocentric data coming in from the navigation and guidance system across the bottom of the screen while he flipped switches. The ignition of rocket engines gave the ship a slight surge.

"Commencing landing procedure," remarked Rhodes.

Placing their fate in the hands of the navigation and guidance computer, they could feel the roll of the ship's pitch as the ninety-ton vehicle turned toward Mars. This maneuver brought the ship into contact with the searing heat of entry, with steaming clouds forming outside the window before roaring flames appeared at the nose of the spacecraft.

Thundering into the Martian atmosphere at a six-to-seven-degree wedged angle as an unsettling firestorm raged outside, Rhodes felt this was the longest six minutes of his life. The ride was rough and getting rougher fast. The cabin took on a strange luminosity during the worst vibration, and then the ship suddenly broke through the upper atmosphere. Turbulence lost its grip on the ship, and flames dissipated to enable them to catch a glimpse of the Martian landscape beneath a clear, blue-gray sky. Drawn to tracking signals from *Endurance I* and *Endurance II,* the ship swerved to the right, lurching as rocket engines gave thrust in pursuit of the targeted landing area. Tracking the flight's progression on their monitors, they saw that the topography showed regional land formations they passed over patterned as hills, ridges, and anomalies in quick-changing, wire-frame configurations. The ride smoothed as they felt deceleration, and Flavio said, "Approaching altitude of descent at sixteen thousand meters, fourteen thousand meters, twelve thousand meters . . ."

Then came a sudden jerk as the engines made a retro-rocket fire to slow the ship down, followed by vector thrust to ease their descent. Rhodes glimpsed changing sequential data at the bottom of his monitor screen before looking out the windshield to see how the ship had begun sinking to gravitate toward the Martian surface. He heard the activation of landing gear dropping into position, and the ship shuddered while sets of massive parachutes above the cockpit and at the ship's tail section deployed to bring them down gently.

"Four thousand meters, two thousand, one thousand, five hundred meters . . . Brace yourselves. We're landing."

In the final stage, the roar of engine thrust delivered a rocking motion to slow their descent while leveling the ship, stirring a swirling dust storm outside as the footpads softly settled into Martian soil.

Flavio finalized the sequence: "Touchdown!"

The engines stopped, the dust cloud outside the ship slowly began to settle, and Rhodes removed his helmet before unbuckling his seat belt. The others removed their helmets and seat belts before rising from their seats and gathered at the window. Filtering through drifting and settling dust was a clear, blue-gray sky over a wide-open plain, an inhospitable world that didn't look much different from a desert scene on Earth.

Seeing this barren, destitute wasteland with more clarity as dust continued to settle, Rhodes believed the landing was a success. However, he knew that a safe landing was only half of it, and he now wondered if they'd landed at the programmed site where *Endurance I* and *Endurance II* had previously landed. He looked at his monitor and said, "Abe, can you provide imaging to show us the location of *Endurance I* and *Endurance II?*"

Appearing on their monitors was an overview, indicating the location of their ship as a blinking red dot, the surrounding landscape a sketchy, wire-frame outline. The computer signified the locations of the other ships with Roman numerals: I with a dash pointing to a black dot southeast of their ship; II with a dash pointing to another black dot located directly south.

"Can you give us distances?"

The computer acknowledged, "*Endurance I* is approximately seven point five kilometers southeast of *Endurance III*, and *Endurance II* is approximately four point two five kilometers south of *Endurance III*."

Flavio nodded at his monitor. "That pyramid-shaped anomaly south of where we've landed has striking primary alignments."

Rhodes looked at the anomalies south of their landing site, and one in particular held geometric symmetry in its five-sided axis points. He now saw warning lights flashing and began running computer programs to determine what problems they had.

Abe's voice came through the ship's intercom. "I'm reading pressure changes through sensors in the port side junction compartment, but there are no fire indications in that area."

Rhodes ordered Flavio to survey damage in the port side maintenance junction, and he entered the junction through a forward access door in the cargo bay to make the inspection. Finding a slushy coating of ice covering everything, he first checked a gauge showing their oxygen supply was holding. He then saw that the water tanks had lost almost all their liquid volume as a result of a tubular connection bursting, raising concerns about their water supply. Aleksei teamed up with Flavio to vacuum icy water from the junction and they made repairs to make the plumbing serviceable. Afterwards, the two ran icy water extracted from the junction through a filtering system to be returned to the water supply, but a large volume of water had been lost.

After notifying technicians that they'd made a safe landing, Far then offered a schedule for beaming back signals showing the first Mars walk they'd make the following morning so it could be televised worldwide. At the same time, Jetha forwarded to Earth photographs she'd taken earlier through line scanning cameras on the sides of the ship to show the surrounding desert plain and gently rolling sand dunes. Rhodes was still concerned about communications but knew technicians could pinpoint their exact location on Mars by referencing the first two ships by two unmanned satellites orbiting Mars. One orbiter monitored weather conditions while searching for subsurface water;

the other sought out seismic activity, and either one could show their landing position.

As soon as Flavio and Aleksei finished repairs in the port side maintenance junction, they rejoined the others in the cabin. Aleksei used a management program to access the status of their water supply. Rechecking the figures, he mentioned, "I've confirmed that with the water we've lost, we have enough to last for only two months aboard *Endurance III*, but there's water in abundance stored on *Endurance II*."

Next, the crew sent live images of themselves to Earth. Communicating their joy at having landed on Mars and expressing heartfelt messages to loved ones livened up the crew, and no one showed signs of being the least bit tired.

The northward angle of the ship didn't allow them to view the sunset, but they watched through the windshield as sunlight slowly dimmed and darkness engulfed the landscape. There wasn't any alcohol aboard the ship, but they did have an assortment of beverages and fruit juices, and they clinked their glasses together to celebrate a successful landing. Wearing a big grin, Rhodes raised his glass and said, "It's exhilarating to know we've made a safe landing, and I'm proud to share this accomplishment with you all. This is truly a momentous and historical achievement. Tomorrow we walk on Mars!"

During their journey to Mars, Rhodes saw his crew bond and form a strong sense of camaraderie. To help combat boredom on such a long trip, they had various forms of entertainment on their computers: DVDs of movies; science, nature, and history documentaries; music and the arts; and novels. They usually wore headphones so not to disturb others who desired quiet. Another form of amusement was watching Flavio and Aleksei clown around, trying to get a laugh out of everyone. Flavio once frightened Far and Jetha by putting on a rubbery alien mask.

Seeking to liven up their first day on Mars, Flavio pulled up news footage they hadn't yet seen, announcing, "Hey, everyone, take a look at this." They gathered around his monitor to watch recordings of themselves amid people they'd competed against for a place on the mission. The first segment caught a relaxed interview as a newscaster approached contestants in street clothes after a training session.

The camera focused on Aleksei, and the newsman said, "Aleksei Dimitri Polzinov, you are one of the oldest candidates competing for a seat on the Mars mission spacecraft. Do you think your chances are good for clinching a spot?"

"I don't see why not. There's a high probability that at least one Russian will earn this high honor, and I have a huge advantage over my countrymen, as years ago I swore off drinking vodka."

The reporter smirked as others chuckled.

"Of course, being that I am pure Russian, this can also be a great disadvantage, so I worry."

The newsman broke out in laughter, surprised by the response. Then he regained his composure and asked, "Seriously, though, do you see your age as a disadvantage?"

"I am a distinguished captain in Russian Air Force with countless hours flying Mig fighter jets and a veteran cosmonaut with six months aboard International Space Station, but you ask if age is against me, and I say no. A man of my years of experience should be considered an asset, as an experienced man is more likely to keep a cool head under highly challenging circumstances."

Everyone clapped, and Aleksei grinned. Flavio clapped loudest, saying, "Bravo. Well-spoken." The camera picked up Flavio's face, and the interviewer approached him next. "Here we have a Frenchman, Flavio Muret, a man held in high regard by the European Space Agency. Flavio, you've also spent six months aboard the International Space Station, but a trip to Mars is sure to be much different. What is one of your biggest concerns about this trip?"

"I understand there will be women aboard the space flight to Mars, and my hope is that they aren't bad to look at."

The newsman asked, "Are you serious?"

"I do not mean that in a derogatory sense, and I mean no disrespect to any of my colleagues. So that my remark is not taken out of context, let me plainly state my feelings on the matter. The way I see it, if I'm going to be cooped up with the same people for two and a half years, it will be helpful if the females are not bad to look at."

"I'm glad you expanded on your answer," said Far, grinning. "So what do you think about the females they chose as your crew members?"

Flavio glimpsed at Far and Jetha. "I have no complaints whatsoever. The two of you are charming, but seriously, some women in the running were a little scary to look at."

Jetha swatted Flavio on top of his head in mock anger.

Time passed, and a starry-eyed Far looked out across the moonlit Martian landscape and said, "For years we've entertained the contention that life exists outside our world, and our curiosity has taken us to neighboring Mars to seek answers to that question. Robotic rovers and probes couldn't provide a definitive answer, but in the days to come, we'll perform scientific tests to either prove or disprove the presence of life on the red planet. Does anybody think we'll find life out there?"

After a moment of silence, Rhodes replied, "I believe we'll discover microscopic organisms. As inhospitable as Mars is, the building blocks for life do exist here. Mars was once a blue planet just like Earth. It held surface water, and if favorable conditions took hold for life to flourish for just a few hundred thousand years, who knows what life forms developed here? Life may have taken hold on the red planet first, and there may be fossilized remains waiting to be discovered beneath sedimentary layers.

"It's important that you all think of something important to say to the people of Earth tomorrow when we're outside the ship. My advice is to jot down a few words or comments relating to our first Mars walk, preferably something about our mission, our goals, or the future of space exploration. I'd like to see what you propose to say so we don't repeat ourselves. Far will choreograph a sequence giving you all a few minutes on camera, so as soon as you put together something, let us know."

CHAPTER 4

Getting Acquainted with an Alien Planet

In the morning, Rhodes saw the glory of a sunny landscape outside the viewing window, a stark contrast to the infinity of space he was used to looking at. After all the hoopla made about this Mars mission, he was only now beginning to understand how this expedition may be awfully boring. Isolation was one of the negative aspects of the trip that psychiatrists had warned them about, but his crew gave him no reason to think they didn't have the mental toughness to see this through.

Standing at the bridge reading atmospheric conditions outside the ship, Flavio jokingly commented, "I don't know what the UV index rating is out there, but we may need some sun block. The temperature is minus sixty-three degrees Celsius; surface pressure is calculated to be fewer than seven millibars; and radiation levels are about three points into the red, but that's nothing significant."

Far read information displayed on her monitor. "Chemical elements in the Martian atmosphere read as follows: 95.32% carbon dioxide, 2.7% nitrogen, 1.6% argon, 0.13% oxygen, 0.07% carbon monoxide, and about 0.03% water vapor, showing additional traces of nitric acid, neon, krypton, xenon, ozone, methane, and ammonia."

Approaching the time of the scheduled Mars walk, the crew presented pieces of notepaper to Rhodes with what they'd written and expected to say on camera. Not wanting to make a big production out of it, he turned the project over to Far, who organized the amateur choreography, putting together a smooth working program for them to follow.

They soon gathered in the cargo bay wearing suits equipped with life-support backpacks, and they switched on their ventilation fans and warming systems. Jetha found it difficult to adjust hers to a sealed, fixed position on the suit's neck ring, and Aleksei gave her assistance. Far made sure everyone's helmet-mounted camera and voice communications equipment worked. She had a remote control device for switching to the camera of any crew member's helmet. The remote let her zoom in and out and had its own visual screen, which allowed her to view what they were recording. In addition, she could switch to an adjustable port side line camera that would extend from a door outside the ship so they all could be in the picture at one time.

Far filmed Rhodes from the camera in her helmet, viewing him as a silhouette ready to face deadly extremes in the Martian atmosphere. Holding a still position, she announced, "Our captain, Stan Rhodes, will be the first human to step on Martian soil."

Rhodes pressed a button to engage the door to drop down as a ramp and air jets bellowed like a spray of steam meeting freezing cold temperatures for repelling atmospheric airflow. Far switched to the camera in Rhodes' helmet to view the sunny landscape ahead of him, and then switched to the ship's exterior line camera to get a side view of him crossing the ramp. When he came to its edge, Far's push-button expertise sharpened the focus for a close-up of his boot making an impression in Martian soil. Rhodes said solemnly, "As I walk on the surface of Mars, I do so knowing that many will follow in my footsteps to find out whether there was, and still is, life on the red planet."

The camera followed Rhodes walking to gently rolling dunes of white sand stretching as far as their eyes could see. Then he stopped and turned around to face the ship. "There are many unknowns awaiting us. What future generations accomplish here will reflect on humanity, for we will terraform Mars in the hope of one day seeing plant life in abundance here."

As Rhodes stood facing the ship, Far switched to the camera in his helmet to show his crew of four walking out of the cargo bay's shadowy interior. They emerged in twos, avoiding the fish-eye glass in the middle of the cargo door to veer off in different directions.

Flavio approached Rhodes while moving out onto the Martian expanse. "I am Flavio Muret, second-in-command aboard *Endurance III*. From what we've gathered, *Endurance I* and *Endurance II* are south and southeast of our landing site, both less than ten kilometers away. Mars is a world of deadly, hostile extremes in the form of a poisonous atmosphere and a merciless climate. Air density here is equivalent to that of Earth's atmosphere at seventy thousand feet altitude, and gravity on Mars is only about one third of what we experience on Earth. Since Mars no longer possesses a magnetic field like we have on Earth, exposure to cosmic radiation is a deadly hazard we'll face on this mission. I now give you to my colleague, Aleksei Dimitri Polzinov."

Far switched to Jetha's helmet camera, Aleksei in her viewfinder. He addressed the camera by saying, "People of Earth, I wish to take this moment to salute the early pioneers of rocketry whose efforts, trial and error, and foresight paved the way to make this day possible: Konstantin Tsiolkovsky, Robert H. Goddard, Valentin Glushko, Wernher von Braun, who designed the *Saturn V* launch vehicle that enabled man to walk on the moon, and Sergei Korelev, chief designer of the first rocket-space exploration systems in Russia. Under Korelev's leadership and calculations, the first man was propelled into space—Yuri Gagarin. I have named but a few, but there are many others whose contributions and accomplishments made this mission successful. We thank you."

There was a pause before Far switched to the camera in Rhodes' helmet, and she stepped into the picture, "Hello, I am Far Hai Win, science and medical director for the Mars mission. The ultimate question posed in interplanetary exploration is, does life exist on planetary bodies besides our Earth? Scientists believe this landing site is an ancient ocean basin, and we hope to find evidence of organic materials supporting the theory that life forms once existed here. Our goal is to perform an outlined study of rock formations. Any signs of life, fossilized or otherwise, will be a stunning discovery. Organic molecules are even scarcer here than on Earth's moon, but trace amounts of ammonia and methane give some indication for the presence of life on Mars. It's not likely that our home planet is the only place in the cosmos where life's taken hold, so we'll keep you posted on whatever evidence of life we find here. Now I give you Jetha Karashan."

Far moved her thumb to press a button on the remote, and the view changed from Rhodes' helmet to Flavio's to show Jetha turning to him. "We will be searching for sources of water that may play an important part in future missions, and we hope to discover rare mineral ores. A serious threat from Mars' iron oxide dust are swirling dust devils, and major dust storms can grow to global proportions. This dust is ten times finer than talcum powder, and it can clog machinery and air supplies. In the fury of these storms, the rubbing of granules and dust particles can produce electrostatic charging, creating enormous static electricity sparking up to twenty thousand volts. These electrical charges can destroy the ship's electric components and threaten life-support equipment."

Far now switched to the ship's line camera to show them filing into a line. Rhodes took a step forward from the center. "We stand on this planet as a testament to the will and determination of the human spirit and to the technological expertise and talents of scientists and aerospace engineers. Their work has allowed us to fulfill man's dream of interplanetary exploration, and for the efforts of those men and women, we thank you. Let me also say that this historic day wouldn't have been possible without the courage and discipline of this brave crew, who traveled across fifty-six million kilometers of space to reach this goal. We will try to send a transmission back every day to give you insight into the discoveries we'll make with pictures that we hope will dazzle you."

With that, they waved, and Far cut off the transmission. Amid giggling and laughter, Rhodes said, "I don't know what you're all laughing about. I thought it went pretty well."

Jetha poked fun at Aleksei by saying in a deep voice, "People of Earth . . ."

Flavio laughed but then patted Aleksei on the back. "You did all right."

Aleksei shrugged, "It is not every day I talk to millions of people, so I approached them as people of Earth."

"Why didn't you just refer to them as earthlings?" commented Far. Then she backhanded his arm. "You were supposed to introduce me before you finished."

"I knew I left something out, but it is not every day that I take the podium."

The crew gathered the massive parachutes that aided them in touchdown, cutting them free and bundling them up before placing them inside the ship's cargo bay. After grabbing a toolbox he'd left in the cargo bay chamber, Rhodes gave Abe the command to secure the ramp, and cables pulled the access door up into place. From a pocket in his suit, he removed a remote control device he'd need to open up the cargo door on *Endurance II*. He made sure it had power by pressing its button and seeing a red light come on; he then returned it to his pocket. While the others encircled him, he looked at the watch and compass connected to the forearm of his suit in preparation to lead his team across the desolate frontier.

"Let's start footing our way south to locate *Endurance II*. That's where most of the goodies are, including the MRV. Why walk when you can ride?"

Ahead lay a frigid, desert wasteland composed of gently sloping sand dunes sterilized by intense, cosmic radiation. As Rhodes' eyes swept across this barren plain, he understood this area was once below sea level, and it didn't look much different from what he'd seen in the movies of the Sahara or Kalahari Desert. In photographs of Mars' surface, he'd seen rocky rubble composed mostly of lava rock that, by comparison, would've been much tougher to travel across than this terrain.

It wasn't long before walking in spacesuits grew tiresome, and scanning the wide-open flatland, Rhodes saw that the ground made a gradual ascent. The rise of this sloping incline met an uneven ridgeline running across the south and southwest. Wispy clouds in a hazy mist obscured outcrops of anomalies in these elevated regions, and he believed the gray haze may have been all that remained of a dust storm that occurred in the not-too-distant past.

He thought *Endurance II* shouldn't be much farther than that ridgeline, and his eyes searched the horizon straight south for the craft. The pointed, triangular shape of one anomaly, with a sweeping sand dune smoothly ramping up its northwest side, stood out to draw his attention.

"Look what's coming," said Flavio, pointing in a westerly direction, where two swirling columns of dust were coming toward them. They stood little chance of avoiding the ghostly dust devils running as a pair, and Rhodes feared for their life-support systems. A storm of abrasive dust particles pelted their face shields, and as fast as they'd appeared, the whirling dervishes were already out of sight. The crew shook loose dust from their suits, and Rhodes said, "I'm hoping *Endurance II* isn't much further than that ridge up ahead, so let's make tracks."

When they finally reached a ridge peak, they met a valley in a wide, winding ravine that had remained unseen from the plain they'd tracked across. The descent of this gorge had blended with the wide, stretched, terraced bank that lay on the other side of the valley that was of much higher elevation. This far ridge looked like a natural barrier, marking a change in the land, and the cap of a mountain or anomaly lay beyond—the one with that triangular shape. Rhodes believed water may have shaped this valley.

Rhodes looked eastward and saw the cradled wreckage of *Endurance II*. The other crew members followed his gaze and stared at the damaged supply ship. It had a crunched nose and a bowed belly, and its tail lay propped on a slope.

"My God, what went wrong?" asked Flavio, a look of disbelief on his face.

Seeing parachutes lying at the tail end of the ship and not at its front, Rhodes said, "It looks like the parachutes at the front of the spacecraft failed to deploy. The ship's systems couldn't level off the spacecraft on its descent. It could've easily exploded and caught fire on impact."

They started down the ridge and made a visual study of the wreckage as they approached, noticing that the ship's landing gear had collapsed. Rhodes pressed the button on the remote control he carried, but the ramp door didn't open, and seeing the ship's body twisted out of alignment made him wonder if they'd be able to open it.

The spacecraft held little importance; its contents were what they valued. Jetha remarked, "I can't imagine all the supplies being ruined."

"What's most important is the water," said Rhodes. He moved to the ship's nose to view the badly broken windshield, with cracks running in every direction, and decided this was the best way for them to get inside the spacecraft.

Far had the same thought and added, "If we open the ship up and leave its interior exposed to the elements, there's a chance of indigenous Martian microbes getting into our supplies. Ancient microbial life immobilized by extreme cold in this freeze-dried world may pose a threat when brought into our ship."

Rhodes replied, "We'll worry about sealing the ship later. The packaging should protect the provisions anyway. Right now we need to get inside that ship."

CHAPTER 5

An Astounding Discovery

The crew gathered at the front of the ship. The crushed landing gear brought the ship's nose closer to ground level, but climbing it wasn't going to be easy. After sizing up the situation, Rhodes placed the toolbox he carried on the ground and said, "Flavio and Aleksei, clasp your hands to give me a boost."

As he was lifted onto the nose, Rhodes was careful about how he pulled himself up into a standing position. Taking aim at a spider web of cracks in the windshield, he kicked the glass in and slipped through the opening to enter the ship's dark interior. He flipped a few switches on the instrument console to power up the electrical circuits, but everything was dead.

Switching on his helmet light enabled him to see a spacious, open area in disarray. Crates, cartons, and canisters of various sizes sat on skids, wrapped in plastic. Many items had broken free and shifted forward. Most of the canisters were blue and contained water, but they weren't completely full to give the water room to expand in case it froze, which it undoubtedly did.

This ship's cargo door didn't have a window, but off in the shadows Rhodes saw the faint image of the Mars rover, its front end facing the cargo door. The vehicle sat high with a lot of clearance between its frame and the floor, and even though it was readily accessible at the door, it appeared to be pinned. The first challenge would be to get the ramp down to provide an open exit to drive the land cruiser out, and he had an idea for how to get the cargo door open. Seeing Far getting ready to enter the ship through the windshield, he said, "I left a toolbox out there that we'll need. Have someone hand it to you before following me back this way."

Creeping over and between crates, he noticed the floor felt slippery and looked down to see a layer of ice. Immediately thinking they'd lost a portion of their water supply, he knew water was going to become crucial to their survival.

He approached the open-top, American-built, six-wheel-drive Mars rover to find its passenger's side flush against a jutting wall where a control panel for the cargo door was located. He then came around the vehicle's left side where the steering wheel was located. When he reached the cargo bay door, he exposed one of the rover's fuel cells to generate electrical power to open the access door.

The light on Far's helmet beamed about until she finally showed up to hand over the toolbox. Fishing through its contents, Rhodes located an electrical tester, wire cutters, and a screwdriver to remove the control panel's cover. He cut the wires that formerly supplied power to the door and then extracted a length of wire from inside the wall to telegraph electricity from the rover's power cell to the switch. By hooking up these leads, he hoped to deliver power to the mechanism to open the door.

Far worked her way closer. "I don't know if you've noticed, but the floor's all iced up."

"Yeah, the blue canisters hold water, and some of them burst on impact, leaving me to think water's going to play a critical role in the mission."

Grasping what Rhodes was attempting to do, Far said, "Ooh, you are a smart cookie."

"Hold the praise until we've gotten the door open."

Flavio's helmet light kept changing direction as he joined them, and having heard them talk about water, he looked down and saw ice. He was apparently the last one to enter the ship, as the others couldn't make the climb without getting a boost, and he watched Rhodes connect wire ends and twist them together securely. When Rhodes hit the switch, a clicking hum commenced, but then the noise stopped and he realized the door was jamming because the ship's body was misaligned.

"The door may be free, but we'll have to use the rover to force it to open."

Holding the vehicle in place were four ratcheted straps attached to its axles and floor anchors, and Flavio took a box cutter from the toolbox before scooting beneath the vehicle to cut them. Disconnecting wires hooked up to the vehicle's fuel cells, Rhodes then flipped a switch on the dashboard. Instruments lit up, but even though its motor had power, it didn't make a sound.

Not wanting to crush the others while maneuvering the vehicle, Rhodes allowed them to climb into the rover before taking the driver's seat and turning the headlights on. The front seats were awkward, designed for passengers wearing life-support equipment, but Flavio had plenty of room in the back, and he placed the toolbox in a hollow compartment beneath his bench seat.

Putting the gearshift in drive, Rhodes applied light pressure to the accelerator. A grinding sound reminded him that the right, front fender was pinned against the protruding wall where the door controls were. He then shifted into reverse and applied pedal pressure again. The wheels reacted as he turned the steering wheel, but the vehicle was still jammed.

He kept shifting from drive to reverse, applying acceleration while turning the steering wheel one way and then the other, and the vehicle finally started moving. He placed the gearshift in reverse once more and backed up, causing a wide, protective, metal plate spanning an upright corner on the wall to tear free. The vehicle shoved skids and crates up against one another, giving him space to plow forward, but he stopped before shifting back to drive, thinking someone may be on the other side of the door.

"If anybody's anywhere near the cargo door, move away from it. I'm going to force the door down using the rover."

"All clear on this side," said Jetha.

With that, he pressed the accelerator down gently, and the rover crept forward until the front end bumped the door. More foot pedal pressure easily brought the door down. He drove the rover out onto the sunny Martian soil before switching off the headlights and putting the gearshift in park.

Jetha and Aleksei came over to admire the machine, and Jetha remarked, "At least we won't be walking back to the ship."

Rhodes insisted on inspecting blue canisters to get a count of those that hadn't ruptured to estimate their water supply, and sunlight streaming into the ship's interior was helpful for finding intact containers. Tallying their numbers, Rhodes estimated they had enough water to last sixteen months on Mars. Basing this calculation on their current consumption of water and including what water they had stored on *Endurance III*, they were obviously facing a water shortage, as they wouldn't have enough water for their return trip home.

"Only with great sacrifice can we conserve enough water to last out our mission here and still have a sufficient amount to get us home. We have two choices, as we can make it a short stay of three weeks, or commit to the full course of the mission, but that will mean conserving water stringently. Staying the course means remaining on Mars for eighteen months, as we'll have to wait for the orbits of Mars and Earth to close in for allowing the shortest approach for a return spaceflight home."

Deciding to take four water canisters back to the ship, after loading them in the rover, Rhodes looked for a way to prop up the cargo door for securing it. He examined the wide metal corner that had ripped free from the wall when the rover first began moving, and believed its V-shaped bend for wrapping around a corner gave it sufficient strength to brace the door. Asking the others to raise and hold the door, he then jammed one end of the metal corner up against the door while wedging the other end down in the soil and it held the door closed.

Aleksei scooted a stone up against the metal corner piece, seating it firmly in the soil for giving added support for propping the door up in a fixed position. They then discussed placing plastic over the windshield later to keep windblown contaminants out.

Jetha had grown bored with what they'd accomplished so far and, pointing to the steep, terraced bank running south along the valley, said, "I want to see what's beyond this valley. I'll be right back." When she reached the crest, she began waving her arms excitedly. "Hey, you've all got to come up here and see this."

Flavio looked at Aleksei. "She wants us to climb up to that rim, and all I can say is the view had better be worth it."

The two started up first with Far and Rhodes following, and Jetha kept flagging them anxiously as though something of great importance lay beyond their field of vision. Flavio slipped in the shifting sand but regained his footing to continue his ascent on an angle to reduce the steepness of his climb. "What do you see: beaches, hotels, swaying palm trees? Does it look like the Riviera?"

Aleksei laughingly slapped Flavio on the shoulder. "I can hardly wait to see it—motorboats, girls in bikinis . . . and a waiter awaits our arrival with a tray of bubbly champagne."

The humor abruptly ended when the two reached the ridge to join Jetha facing southward, and the silence stirred Far and Rhodes' curiosity all the more. Continuing to climb, Rhodes held Far's arm to steady her while leading her toward the others, who remained mysteriously still.

At the top, a stunning spectacle came into view. Built along what must have once been the shoreline of a great ocean was a colossal pyramid. The course of sand trailing up its northwest side had disguised its true shape, but having moved east to reach their cargo ship, they now had a clear enough view of an amazing, recessed eye on the northeast face. The masterfully sculpted eye was awe-inspiring artistry on a grand scale. The skill necessary to contour the stone to smoothly meet the shape of the eye was astonishing.

"Somebody, pinch me," remarked Far with perfect timing.

Spellbound and without breaking his stare from the hypnotic eye, Rhodes said, "Far, can you record this?"

Far fidgeted with the controls on the chest of her suit to activate the camera in her helmet.

"It's the most astonishing thing I've ever seen in my life," said Jetha, "partly because it was so unexpected. Who'd have dreamed we'd discover a megalithic superstructure on the surface of Mars? And unlike the Great Pyramids at Giza, this one still has its smooth outer casing."

Aleksei's face was expressionless. "A profound discovery of intelligent design. To build such structures with incredible precision is a wondrous thing, and we aren't even sure exactly how the Egyptians did it. Certainly, it took a concerted effort to place one course of stone on top of another, but the enormity of such backbreaking work must become far more difficult as you reach greater heights. And here the Martians took it a step further by erecting a pentagonal-shaped pyramid."

"Yes," said Flavio, "the satellite photos indicated a five-sided structure, a much more complex design to build, but how is it that we didn't see even the slightest hint of that eye?"

"The eye is recessed," explained Jetha, "and its receding contour smoothly blends with the pyramid's outer casing in overhead satellite photos."

Wanting to say something to mark this discovery, Rhodes said, "This moment captures the splendor of an ancient Martian civilization, and standing here with the sun overhead, we have a cosmic drama. This inspiring monument with its beautiful, mystic eye, in a strangely astrological sense, almost seems to pull together our link to the infinity of space, time, and the stars. The sight of it projects wonderment, as if filling a single ray in the spectrum of the universe, and one can't help knowing there must be other worlds in other solar systems where life has flourished."

Aleksei then commented, "This Cydonia Complex has spawned much study, speculation, and controversy. I suggest we immediately begin exploring this site."

Rhodes glimpsed the sun. "I'm sure you all want to get a closer look, but we've already used up a fair portion of our oxygen supply and I'm concerned about the rover. It's important to get back to the ship to fully charge its fuel cells so we know it's reliable. We can visit the pyramid tomorrow and spend the whole day studying it, but for now we can take a quick spin through this valley to make certain *Endurance I* landed safely."

Before starting back down to the rover, Rhodes gave the pyramid a last look. "I'm trying to envision it the way it was when waves pounded that beachhead over there and this land supported life. From this ridge, you can see how this shelf gently slopes up to the shoreline, and the valley where *Endurance II* landed is the drop-off depth zone that served as a breaker for waves. What would be your best guess for the latest date this planet could've supported life? How long ago does earth science estimate that life could have existed here?"

Far replied, "Scientific estimates place Mars as a warmer, wetter world as late as three billion years ago. However, what we find in that complex may challenge that estimate."

Aleksei raised a brow. "Their monuments have transcended time, but I wouldn't be surprised if life on this planet surpassed that time span, more like three million years."

They started back down the terraced bank to return to the rover. Far took the passenger's seat while the others found a place in the back with the water canisters. Rhodes drove through the valley in an easterly direction until he encountered a gentle slope that gave passage to the elevated shelf and shoreline. From this level, the crew had a clear view of the pyramid's northeast face. It was as though the eye was observing their every move. Below the scrutiny of the eye, they noticed what appeared to be sprawling ruins, but it was difficult to make out what these intriguing ruins represented.

After traveling about seven kilometers, they saw *Endurance I,* a vertical, bell-shaped space vehicle nestled in a sloping, sunken area, and Rhodes stopped the rover. While the others gazed at the pyramid, he walked down to inspect the emergency ascent vehicle that had landed months earlier. A short robot probe had exited the ship to travel a few meters before parking on the Martian surface. Cables and hoses extended from the ship to the robot, which functioned as part of the ship's ability to convert chemicals from the Martian atmosphere into fuel. The only ingredient the ship carried to add to the mixture was hydrogen. Over the next twelve to fourteen months, the unit would be making fuel for a return trip home, but they didn't expect they'd need to use it.

Opening a panel on the robot, Rhodes pressed buttons to enter a code that verified the ship's system was functioning correctly. The craft had a long way to go before creating its fuel reserve. Closing and securing the panel, he then went around the vehicle to inspect the ship's exterior. All seemed well. Returning to the rover, he said, "As best as I can tell, everything's fine. We'll come back to check it again in about four to six months, if we're still here. In the meantime, I can monitor its status from our ship."

Far studied the carved vestiges of the eye and said, "Stan, I'd be willing to guess the eye is a different mineral from the pyramid's white limestone casing."

Rhodes took notice of the eye's faint rosy appearance, saying, "It may be granite."

Traveling back the way they came, Rhodes followed the rover's tire tracks. The mystifying stare of that eye etched in the pyramid periodically drew his attention. Steering the vehicle down into the valley, he lost sight of the monument, and soon passing the wreckage of *Endurance II,* he saw the climb they had ahead of them to reach the ridge.

Aiming for the rim they'd descended to drop into the valley, Rhodes gave everyone a warning when he punched the accelerator. "Hang on!"

The tires dug in, churning up soil as they climbed to the crest of the ridge, and after that the vehicle delivered a smooth ride as they took to the flat plain they'd crossed on foot.

Rhodes glimpsed Far. "It's important that we keep a constant vigil on our air supply when we're outside the ship. If we're in the vicinity of the supply depot and our air is getting low, we can retrieve fresh oxygen tanks before starting back to the ship. Do you all understand?"

Everyone acknowledged by saying yes.

After returning to their ship, Rhodes showed everyone how to hook up accessories from the ship to the rover to charge its fuel cells. When he rechecked his figures for the water supply, he found his numbers to be correct. He expected they could easily conserve enough water to last the eighteen months they'd be on Mars, but they'd lack water for the six-month trip home. He knew the crew would be willing to make sacrifices by drastically cutting back on water usage. At the first sign that water was becoming a matter of survival, they wouldn't be able to use any water whatsoever for washing. Even to consider a lengthy mission on Mars meant rationing water immediately, but any unexpected shortages could lead to their deaths, leaving him to believe their stay would be a short one.

Rhodes intended to send a daily report to mission planners, and with today's report, he let them know the condition they'd found the cargo ship in. He pointed out that after *Endurance II* landed, there was a delay before it sent back photos of the surrounding terrain to Earth, but those pictures didn't give a clue to the ship's condition. In addition, he sent the recording they'd made from Far's helmet of the five-sided pyramid. Thinking of the genius and inventiveness it took to erect such a structure, he believed Earth's scientists would be abuzz about this astounding discovery.

CHAPTER 6

Speculating about the Past

Rhodes joined his comrades on the bridge as they looked at overview shots of the sector where the pyramid was located. As they studied high-resolution satellite photos of the area designated as Cydonia Mensae on Far's monitor, other intriguing, dome-shaped structures drew their attention, but they soon turned their focus to the fascinating pyramid.

In quality digital enlargements, they found the eye on the pyramid's slanted northeast face virtually invisible as the smooth outer casing took the contour of a deep recess. The eye escaped detection in daytime photos as it blended with light reflection, and much the same happened when the pyramid's northeast face fell into a shadow. Upon close inspection of the structure, they saw how some of the pyramid's corners had worn unevenly as a result of wind erosion.

Even to the trained eye, many details of these anomalies blended into their natural surroundings from the distance satellite cameras had taken the photos. The light, sandy color of the landscape wasn't much different from that of the monuments themselves, concealing and obscuring many of their features. Jetha pointed out that below the eye, at the base of the northeast facing, an extending compartment of sorts existed. Moreover, opposite the eye engraving, on the southwest side of the pyramid, which they saw as the pyramid's backside, the angled rise of a corner was distinguishably different from the other more sharply angled corners of the monument. If this particular corner wasn't a true corner, it was difficult to see why because of the sand that had collected on the pyramid.

The Viking mission discovered the Cydonia region and the "face" in 1976, and satellite photos of these anomalies were an instant sensation as a broad field of investigators studied them. Some photos had nametags labeling sections of the complex, and the crew shared ideas and did their own fair share of speculating. For instance, some of the photos they saw had the "City" connected to the Cydonia Complex. Even though there probably had to be a densely populated metropolis on the outskirts of this complex, it didn't seem likely that this cluster of anomalies was an urban center.

At the heart of these monuments, located at the southwest edge of the eye pyramid, was an area designated the "City Square," where indistinguishable, knobby objects that could be boulders were scattered about. The crew didn't think this was a proper identification for this area either, as it wasn't likely that a so-called public square would be in the midst of these colossal structures. Instead, they saw this plaza as a place for ceremonial gatherings.

Researchers had designated the sprawling ruins located in front of the northeast face of the eye pyramid as a "Fortress." These ruins looked to be on the jutting point of a wedge-shaped peninsula. It seemed more likely to the crew that this was all that remained of a palace or temple at the edge of a coastal zone, but they acknowledged they could be wrong. At different times, there must have been a huge workforce gathered to build these structures, but it wasn't likely there was a permanent population center at the heart of these pyramids. If a multitude gathered at the site to pull together in an effort to erect a monument, they most likely dispersed afterwards. Of course, all the crew's ideas were based upon conjecture.

This newly discovered alien civilization fueled speculative ideas, but there was no doubt that a long, long time ago a highly sophisticated culture organized to build colossal monuments, probably close to a port. The crew had no way of knowing the purpose for which these monuments were erected, but they reasoned that there had to be a strong motive for building such immense and elaborate structures. Most pyramidal shrines on

Earth honored a god or a supreme monarch, although some had astrological significance. This fact left most of them to visualize the complex as sacred ground, a religious or holy sanctuary that entombed dynastic kings.

Satellite photos indicated another five-sided pyramid a few kilometers southeast of the complex, and researchers designated this anomaly the "D and M Pyramid." It appeared to be substantially larger than the eye pyramid but lacked its sharp angles, and Rhodes believed it had formed naturally like a yardang. He thought this formation may have served as a model in designing the eye pyramid. Structures and formations were numerous in this complex, but they couldn't tell from the photos if they were artificial or not.

They went on sharing thoughts and ideas about the Cydonia Complex and the eye pyramid, and Jetha commented, "Just think, a rapidly advancing culture grasped a high level of mathematics and geometry to build aspiring monuments. To build on such a scale took organized planning and a huge workforce. Located on the outskirts of this complex must have been an economic center, a great city. These structures in all probability reflect the golden age of a once-powerful and prosperous nation. I may be wrong about what I'm envisioning, but I see exotic plant life along this coastal area, an oasis, a paradise lost.

"What we're seeing is the remnants of a well-organized society with traditions that could've included worshipping a godlike ruler. There may have been a privileged ruling family, a dynasty of sorts carried on by birthright. To exert his will and keep his kingdom manageable, he must have performed religious rites that gave him divinity over his people."

Aleksei then stated, "They must have had either ruthless, tyrannical rulers or a deep-seated faith they adhered to that pulled them together to build these collective, cultural projects. Their religion may have taught them to believe they'd be well-rewarded in the afterlife for their participation in the building of these architectural wonders. However, pyramid design and construction aren't unique. The pyramid shape is the ideal design, and pyramids of varying sizes and shapes are scattered all over the earth. Nevertheless, a five-sided pyramid would be much more challenging to design and build. The Egyptians were experts on building pyramids, but they never built a five-sided one, at least not to my knowledge."

Further discussion brought about more speculation, and Flavio carried on the conversation, "If these were pyramids for dead kings, then there may be mummified bodies of ancient Martian rulers inside them."

"That's an enticing thought," began Far, "but even if they used the best techniques to preserve their remains, what would be left of them after thousands of years? It's also possible we'll find untold treasures entombed with their remains, and diamonds and jewelry wouldn't have deteriorated through the ages."

"It's evident that Mars had liquid water, and life, for a time, flourished here," began Jetha. "It is mesmerizing to think about it, that when humans were merely entering their primordial stages of development, here on Mars there were kingdoms where the inhabitants were erecting pyramids."

There was a pause before Far expanded on these thoughts, "The concept of evolution could've been far different here than we can imagine, for they may have been of a species we cannot even begin to comprehend. We're basing the idea that they were humanlike on the eye engraved on that pyramid and the fact that they engineered pyramids, but these things tell us nothing about them in a physical sense. Whatever they were, at one point they took on an intellect that enabled them to build cities and monuments with precision that may have brought about a cultural revolution to influence other civilizations on Mars."

Flavio commented, "They may have been more like lizards than mammals, or insect like creatures. There's no telling what the climate was like here, although I imagine it must have been very cold."

Then Aleksei said, "Perhaps not, when you consider that this planet may have gone through a greenhouse period, making it favorable for plant life to take root and spread. The atmosphere could've warmed up through geological activity in the form of volcanic eruptions; there are plenty of volcanoes here to suggest that scenario. Any number of circumstances may have helped bring about a warming trend that raised temperatures in the atmosphere, promoting conditions for these beings to multiply and, over the course of time, develop into a civilized society."

Rhodes contributed to the conversation, "For some time we've believed that life exists on other planets, and here on Mars we've discovered evidence of an ancient civilization. In all probability, life took hold here in much the same way as it did on Earth, and in an essence, another Genesis took place here. Life may have come from the depths of space, hitching a ride on a comet, and the cosmos also delivered the means for its demise. A huge asteroid, or collection of asteroids, must have obliterated Mars' surface to turn it into a raging fireball, remaining a strange, spherical inferno visible in the night sky from as far away as Earth. The ravages of time and dust storm erosion have erased the hellish horrors that befell this land and engulfed this planet to leave Mars the desolate place it is now."

Aleksei added, "My guess is that the occupants of this Cydonia Complex were almost in every sense of the word people, but we may never know if they resembled us. They must have lived through catastrophic cataclysms and mass extinctions. Natural disasters, along with disease, famine, and starvation, may have decimated their numbers many times, but they started all over again. This race struggled to survive to dominate the planet, and for a short time, they populated this region and built structures until they reached the climax of their civilization.

"Humans essentially went from the Stone Age to the age of pyramids over a few thousand years, but how long did man exist before advancing to a civilized species using language and math? Did these creatures follow a similar path before a superheated shockwave from an asteroid impact wiped out everything once and for all? You know, it's even possible this species of Martians survived meteor impacts before the last apocalypse changed their world into the barren wasteland it is now.

"Over the span of man's reign, meteors have struck the surface of the earth and brought devastation many times without exterminating us. One of the best-preserved craters is in your state of Arizona, and it occurred a mere fifty thousand years ago. This impact was equivalent to about one hundred fifty times the yield of the atomic bombs used on Hiroshima and Nagasaki. Then there's the mysterious Tunguska explosion over Siberia in 1908 that may have been the blast of a comet nucleus, which leveled nearly eight hundred square miles of forestry. Mankind survived those impacts, so I suspect these beings must have seen the same kinds of catastrophes and outlasted the results."

These observations inspired Flavio to say, "It is evident that Mars was once a living planet where there were oceans, rivers, and abundant plant life with geological activity in the form of volcanoes. Those who walked this land may have been very similar to you and me in that they had a language and customs, and they must've experienced many of the same emotions and problems that we humans have faced. They probably studied the stars and eventually organized to build cities and pyramids. Most important of all is that they had the ability to think, love, hate, and dream as we do."

Taking time to magnify the satellite imagery to give them further study, they looked forward to exploring the ruins. As their imaginations stirred, they turned in to get some sleep. Some of them dreamed about what awaited them at this ancient site called the Cydonia Complex.

CHAPTER 7

The Alluring and Mysterious Eye Pyramid

With the new sunrise, they saw frost on the ship's windshield, giving evidence there was minimal moisture in the Martian atmosphere. They were all looking forward to seeing the eye pyramid close up, and after breakfast, the crew stepped into their suits to venture out in the fully charged Mars rover. Far activated and tested the camera in her helmet to make certain it would record what they'd see at the complex.

Upon exiting the ship, Rhodes announced, "I'd prefer the expedition last no more than six hours, and it's important that we stick together. From now on *Endurance II* is our storage depot, and whenever we're out and about we should stop by there to pick up either water canisters or food supplies. We'll take turns driving the rover so we can all say we drove on the Martian surface, and this time Flavio will take his turn behind the wheel."

"Do you mind if I take a different route to get to the pyramid?"

"What do you mean by a different route?" asked Rhodes, turning to look at him from the front passenger's seat.

"I just thought we could travel eastward to survey the Martian terrain while taking a roundabout course to reach the pyramid."

The rover's windshield contained a digital compass, which Rhodes made note of before saying, "I don't mind, but that's time we'll lose exploring the pyramid complex."

Flavio stomped on the accelerator, and the rover's tires dug into the soft soil, stirring up dust as they passed a series of sloping hills. The rover got great traction on the Martian surface, and they were soon traveling across a vast plain, leaving behind a dust cloud as they moved in a northeast direction. They rode the crest of a long-running sand dune, and Rhodes had an idea of where they were going but refrained from making a comment. After riding a long distance, he saw a hilly land mass on the horizon and envisioned it as an island.

Flavio slowed down. "The land formation up ahead made the face we saw in those satellite photos."

Far raised her voice a few decuples higher than normal, saying, "I for one would like to see the pyramid."

Then both Jetha and Aleksei said in unison, "Pyramid."

Flavio punched the accelerator to head in a southerly direction.

Rhodes motioned to Flavio, "Since we're out this way, I want to get a look at a meteor crater a few kilometers south of here."

"We are losing time," Far said insistently.

"I know, but it's rare that we'll explore this far out from the ship, so I want to take this opportunity to see it."

Far nodded disappointingly and leaned back in her seat.

Minutes later, they saw the rim of a crater, but Rhodes signaled for Flavio to keep going. "That's not it. We're looking for one much bigger."

A short time later, they saw the immense bulging rim of an impact crater, and they stopped to approach the fringes of its massive, fog-filled interior in an awesome bowl shape. It was much larger than the first crater they'd seen, and impressions of faint channels running down its sides gave indications of water erosion.

"Hey, look," said Aleksei, "that must be the D and M Pyramid," and in the distance they saw a mountainous pyramid shape that appeared considerably larger than the eye pyramid.

Rhodes replied, "Yes, I thought we'd be able to see it from here, but this is as close as we're going to get to it." Far recorded the crater's expanse and then took a long look at the distant pyramid shape, footage they'd be sending back to Earth.

Flavio kept gazing at the anomaly. "From this distance in this hazy atmosphere, I can't tell if it's natural or artificial, but photos have shown it to have five sides like the eye pyramid.

I've closely studied photos of it, and it doesn't have the sharp, angled corners the eye pyramid has, so it likely formed naturally." Rhodes then stated, "I know you're all curious, but to put any more distance between us and the ship invites danger. Can you imagine the situation we'd be in if the rover broke down out here? I don't know how many hours it would take to walk back to the ship, but we have only a seven-hour air supply."

"The captain's right," said Far. "We can't make good time walking in these suits, and we're probably maxed out on the radius we can venture from the ship. At least we've had an opportunity to view this anomaly, and it'll be there for the next Mars mission to investigate."

Skirting the rim of the crater in the rover to head northwest, after a short while they approached the Cydonia Complex to see it from an entirely different angle. A strange, domed pyramid with a curious, elongated shape tapering from north to south appeared on their left, drawing their attention until the eye pyramid came into view.

The eye was mysteriously hypnotic. They all agreed that the monument's casing was limestone, but the alluring eye had a rosy-buff color, differentiating it from the rest of the pyramid. They'd touched on the idea that the eye may be of a mineral unknown to man.

Rhodes flagged Flavio to get his attention. "I want to swing around the point where we saw ruins, and then skirt the shoreline along the northern edge of the complex. That will take us to the spot where we first saw the pyramid yesterday and bring us to within walking distance of both the eye pyramid and the storage depot."

The enduring superstructure with its staring eye silently awaited their arrival. As they rounded the point and surveyed the ruins sprawled across the peninsula, they weren't able to tell much about what these ruins were. They soon recognized tracks made by the rover the previous day. The edge of the shelf line blocked their view of the escape ship.

Nearing the pentagonal-shaped pyramid, the structure looked like nothing less than a majestic mountain, and he parked near as he could to the cargo ship located in the valley down below.

"We should have sufficient air supply to explore this network of structures to get a general idea of what's here. When we were studying the photos, someone identified a jutting housing compartment on the northeast face of the pyramid below the eye that could've been an entrance to the pyramid. Who pointed that out?"

Jetha raised her hand.

"Okay, Jetha, you lead the expedition."

As they passed through a causeway to reach the northeast face of the monument, Rhodes kept glimpsing to his left at the spread of buried ruins across the jutting peninsula. "Hold up," he said and stepped out of line to identify what this huge mess was. He located a large, partially exposed, rounded stone in a half-moon shape. He knelt to clear away loose sand and saw that the shape looked like a gigantic checker cut in half. Others like it lay in disarray in clustered layers. Two of these stones combined were approximately a meter thick and five or six meters in diameter, and seeing some strung out in rows enabled Rhodes to see they were sections of fallen pillars.

"These are massive columns that must've staggered before falling every which way to form this colossal heap, maybe toppling as a result of a powerful quake."

The others converged on the huge stone pieces, their boots sinking in loose sand and soil as they spread out. Fascinated by how many there were, Flavio said, "There must have been well over a hundred columns standing here. As we discussed, this could be the site of a temple."

Aleksei could see how those erecting this temple did so by stacking one slab of stone on top of another to create very high columns whose smooth facing displayed no writing or images. He came alongside Rhodes as Rhodes pondered, "How tall would you say these columns were when they stood vertically?"

"They may have stood as high as sixteen to eighteen meters, perhaps more," Aleksei answered.

Jetha appeared dazzled by the toppled collection of columns. "At the Karnak Temple near Luxor in Egypt, there's a dramatic, man-made forest of more than one hundred thirty stone columns standing in sixteen rows. Defining a processional aisle where ceremonies took place are twelve central columns sixty-nine feet high, and in its day, the temple was roofed. Even though ritualistic ceremonies were held there, Egyptian temples didn't provide for congregational worship, as only kings and priests were permitted to attend."

Rhodes looked up at the monument, unable to detect the eye's contoured recession in the sloping angle of the pyramid's face. "This temple must have been a striking site at the water's edge, especially with the eye pyramid overlooking it. It would've extolled the opulence of an empire and forewarned enemies of a great power. They may have erected this lavish, pillared hall as an offering temple or a shrine. I'd like to picture its construction as similar to that of the Greek Parthenon, the most important surviving building of ancient Greece. Its columns stand eighteen meters tall."

The team moved on from the pillared ruins to the pyramid's immense, smooth-sloped base, high-stepping through mounds of sand and silt to reach it, as though walking in snow. They came to a stone structure extending from the pyramid, its roof supported by an archway. Blocking the mouth of the entryway was a sand dune. However, above this mound was a dark, recessed entry. Jetha led the way, crawling on all fours to make her way inside.

Rhodes was next to enter the enclosure, studying an arched ceiling made of stones set tightly in mortar, and there were massive stones sealing off the pyramid's entrance. Examining the impregnable stones, Jetha said, "This extension of the pyramid must have once served as a decorative entranceway for the monument, the stones placed here after a ruler was laid to rest."

Flavio then commented, "This pyramid isn't much different from those on the Giza plateau, and probably all the pyramids in Egypt have been broken into by thieves. Where there's a will, there's a way."

Departing the pyramid's original entrance to continue around its base, they found the pyramid's proportions impressive. When they cleared the next angled, buttressed corner, the strange, dome-shaped pyramid southeast of the eye pyramid came into view, the one they'd passed riding in the rover after stopping at the crater. Not much more than a mound of lofty circumference with a crust of silt and sand, it lacked an elaborate design and had an artificial look.

Following the pyramid's base, they approached the second corner and came to a huge, open mall or ceremonial plaza they'd seen in orbital photos. Rhodes saw obelisks scattered about and realized these were the knobby objects seen in satellite photographs. Seeing them for what they were—stone obelisks standing ten meters above ground—he could understand why these iconic stones looked like knobby objects in the photos. Engraved in them were artistic designs and weird symbols that had meaning only to the Martian culture that created them. Other surrounding structures of the same crude shape and design as that of the domed pyramid gave the appearance they were from an older kingdom.

At the next corner they froze in amazement at the sight of a staircase that ran all the way up to the pyramid's peak. The staircase was set where a sharp, angled corner of the pyramid should've been, shooting skyward like a stairway to heaven. The land seemed to slope up to the base of the stairs, which was nearly two and a half meters wide, and if the stairs narrowed on the way up to the top, it was difficult to tell.

Rhodes quickly realized these stairs were set on the pyramid's southwest end, directly behind the eye, and he remembered thinking something was odd about the angled ridge of this southwest corner when he studied the photos. The distance of the satellite camera and sand cluttering the stairs made for a distortion he couldn't then perceive.

"Let's continue through this plaza," said Rhodes, "and by circling around the monument we'll return to the northern end of the complex where we left the rover." Then, noticing he was missing a crew member, he asked, "Okay, who's missing?

Flavio? Flavio, I thought we were going to stick together. Where are you?"

"I'm still with you. I haven't left the area."

They all looked around but were unable to catch sight of him. Rhodes said, "Okay, we still can't see you, so clue us in."

"I've begun walking the staircase of the eye pyramid."

Looking toward the pyramid, they saw him steadily marching up the steep staircase, already one third of the way up.

Rhodes shook his head. "If you fall, there's nothing for you to grab on to. You're certain to get killed."

"I'm not going to fall, and I'm not going to get hurt either. Just stay there for a few minutes and don't give me any distractions until I've returned."

Watching him climb the stairs, Aleksei smiled. "It must be the mountaineer in him that couldn't resist the challenge. Apparently, it's in his blood to do such things."

"If he falls, he's dead," said Rhodes. "There's no way he can survive a fall from that height."

"I suggest we don't say anything that might draw his attention," remarked Jetha.

Not wanting to watch Flavio scale the pyramid, Rhodes moved to the center of the plaza, where obelisks encircled him. He caught sight of a broken obelisk, and what grabbed his interest was that the chunk of stone that had broken free wasn't resting next to the obelisk. He walked over to the stone to inspect the ground around it, thinking the broken-off piece may be lying buried in the soil.

The missing part of the obelisk wasn't a great mystery for Rhodes. He was merely trying to keep himself occupied until Flavio returned, but thinking about it made him wonder.

CHAPTER 8

A Lost Architectural Civilization

Inquisitively attracted to the broken obelisk, Rhodes circled the upright stone's base while looking for any sign of the missing piece. His interest aroused, Aleksei came to watch Rhodes move about searchingly and asked, "Looking for something?"

"I noticed the top half of this obelisk is missing, and what's curious to me is that the broken chunk of stone isn't lying here. If it fractured when this civilization existed and the stone held any significance, religious or otherwise, it seems they would've gone through the trouble of replacing it. However, if the obelisk fractured after the demise of these Martians, then the missing chunk ought to be lying here next to the obelisk."

Jetha and Far overheard the conversation and came over to watch Rhodes drag his boot sideways in the soft sand to see if the missing chunk of stone lay beneath the surface. He soon discovered two large stones barely hidden: one, the broken chunk from the obelisk; the other, a smooth, round granite column lying horizontally. Clearing away loose debris from the column's facing, he found it to be ten meters long and less than a meter in circumference with a decorative cap. It became apparent that the pillar had struck the obelisk, both snapping in the middle as they fell. He knelt to scoop away sand to find the footing that supported the pillar when it stood upright.

Rhodes uncovered a second pillar only a meter away, then a third, all evenly spaced apart, and further excavation uncovered a stone floor. Rhodes stood and observed, "There must have been a palace or temple located in this open courtyard. Instead of the random collection of obelisks we see now, there may have been others evenly spaced, encircling this columned structure, and when the palace collapsed its columns knocked down some of the obelisks. There may be dozens of granite columns buried here beneath the sand, and their toppling probably came at the same time the other pillared temple came down, during a worldwide apocalyptic catastrophe."

Looking back at the stairs leading down from the pyramid, Rhodes saw Flavio reaching the bottom, and as soon as his feet touched the ground, he approached the others. "More columns?"

Aleksei responded, "Yes, it seems our captain's discovered the remnants of another palace or temple buried here."

Flavio turned to point at the peak of the pyramid. "At the pyramid's summit I found something I didn't expect. The peak is flat and just inside its rim is a recess in the form of a round basin with a shaft maybe a half meter in circumference. It drops straight down into the depths of the pyramid, making me wonder what purpose it has. Did these Martians hold ghastly sacrificial rituals like the Aztec, Inca, and Mayan civilizations?"

"That may very well be," said Jetha, "but that shaft may have had spiritual or astrological importance."

Rhodes looked at Flavio. "I never would've thought you foolhardy enough to pull a stunt like climbing that pyramid staircase. If you'd lost your footing and fallen down those stairs, you would've broken every bone in your body."

"Yes, but we're here to make discoveries, and perhaps part of the reason I was chosen for this mission is because I'm an agile and physically fit person. If there's any way possible to explore the interior of this extraordinary eye pyramid, then we must do so. I also think we ought to make a study of the eye to learn the makeup of the mineral they carved it from. It's obviously different from the limestone construction of the rest of the pyramid. It may be granite, but it may also be something not in existence on our Earth."

"I agree," said Far. "This stone could've been the core of a meteor found buried in a crater, and thinking it had mystical powers, the Martians carted it off to make use of it as the eye of their pyramid."

Flavio's eyes brightened. "We have an almost inexhaustible supply of durable, nylon rope, and I brought some climbing gear with me. To simplify things, I can go up those steps and rig up a line at the top, so I won't actually be climbing the pyramid. I thought about placing a tube-shaped object inside the shaft at the apex of the pyramid and attaching it somehow to keep it from dropping into the shaft. After tying a rope to it, I'll hang from the line to walk across the pyramid's limestone casing to get to the northeast face. From there, I can chip away a few fragments from the magnificent eye."

Rhodes thought the idea was insane. "Are both of you crazy? If somebody gets killed falling from that pyramid, it isn't likely we'll be transporting his body back to Earth."

Flavio calmly responded, "Stan, everyone knows I'm a very capable individual, and what I'm proposing to do is far less dangerous than climbing a mountain peak. Anyway, I think making an examination of the properties of the eye is quite important, don't you? The most significant feature at this site is the eye of that pyramid, and I want to go up there to find out what makes it so intriguing."

"I could order you to forget the idea."

"Yes, but I don't think you will. After all, how can I forget the eye when it stares at me every time I'm in the sight of it? This is what we're here for. The purpose of this mission is to explore and investigate, and it is my passion to accomplish such feats. It's what I was born for."

"If you're that bent on doing it, I want you to write something exonerating me of the responsibility, because I think it's a dangerous and unnecessary risk. I don't want you to type it on your computer either. I want it in your own handwriting so I've got something to show to your grieving family. That way they'll know I tried to discourage you from doing it."

Rhodes wore a perturbed expression as he led the way around the eye pyramid. The crew surveyed more of these strange, domed anomalies in the Cydonia Complex. Moving away from the eye pyramid to avoid a sand dune ramped up its northwest face, they then moved east. Having completely circled the pyramid, they returned to the rover and rode a short distance down into the valley to get to the storage depot. They collected six water canisters and then covered the cargo ship's broken windshield with plastic and duct tape. Flavio caught sight of a wide spigot handle, and insisting he had a use for it, he got a socket wrench from a tool set kept in the rover to disconnect it and took it with him.

Returning to the ship, Rhodes felt as though they'd accomplished a lot by walking through the Cydonia Complex. The eye pyramid was a testament to the creative ingenuity of these architectural builders, who were probably the most highly developed culture on Mars.

The next morning, the team made plans to return to the eye pyramid, as Flavio was determined to make a close examination of the eye to learn what mineral comprised it. Per Rhodes' request, he had submitted a handwritten letter explaining his reasons for wanting to make the study and that he was taking the initiative. Flavio explained a plan he'd formulated: Take an empty oxygen tank and modify it to insert it inside the shaft at the pyramid's peak. He removed the head of the tank and then welded the wide spigot handle he'd gotten from the supply ship to the head. The handle's circumference was bigger than the shaft he was dropping the tank into. Taking a length of nylon rope, he intended to tie the rope to the spigot and hang from it while making his way from the steps to the location of the eye on the northeast face.

Rhodes didn't think finding out what type of stone the Martians sculpted the eye from was worth such a risky endeavor, but he understood that mission planners might want to know the eye's mineral composition. Not wanting to make a big fuss out of it by objecting to Flavio's plan, he merely stayed behind to address other projects that needed his attention. They were required to drill into the Martian surface to try to find water, and he wanted to gather the drilling equipment so they could get started the following day.

At one point, Flavio approached Rhodes. "Stan, what I'm doing isn't going to cause a rift between us, is it?"

Rhodes shook his head. "Far and the others agree that investigating the eye is important, and I suppose if I were a young man with your talent I'd have thought of it myself. However, it's going to cause me a whole lot of grief if you get injured, so be careful climbing around up there. When you climbed the Alps, you weren't wearing a spacesuit, and it can make a person awfully clumsy."

Flavio proceeded to leave the ship with a collection of tools, and since the zippered pockets in the pant legs of his spacesuit weren't very big, he wore a wide climbing belt around his waist. The harness belt had a pouch to carry a rock hammer and a chisel and an attachment that held a looping length of rope.

Rhodes spoke to his crew before they placed their helmets on. "Flavio is an experienced mountain climber, and if he wants to break his neck that's up to him. I don't want the rest of you taking any chances. No matter what happens, he's on his own. Far and Flavio, I want you both to have your cameras switched on so I can track your movements from the ship, and remember to bring back another six water canisters."

The crew entered the cargo bay chamber. Aleksei cradled the empty oxygen tank in his arms, while Far and Jetha carried additional tools and equipment Flavio wished to have available. They were soon off in the rover, stopping at the supply depot to load six water canisters, and then they moved on to the Cydonia Complex.

Rhodes watched the view through Far's camera on her monitor as Aleksei handed Flavio the oxygen cylinder. He let the cylinder rest against his shoulder, gripping the spigot out in front of him while balancing the tank at an angle as it slanted forward.

Splitting the monitor screen to observe Far's and Flavio's viewing perspectives at the same time, Rhodes kept watch on the side showing Far's camera to see Flavio climbing the steps of the monument alone. He walked rigidly to offset the weight of the tank, his left hand carrying the bulk of its weight while his right hand clasped the spigot tightly.

As his eyes danced back and forth between the camera views, Rhodes was more concerned for Flavio's safety as Flavio climbed to a higher elevation. He could hear Flavio's breathing as he made steady progress up the stairs. In a surprisingly short period of time, he came to the pyramid's summit, and the view from his helmet's camera was stunning. Rhodes now had an opportunity to see the strange recess capping the pyramid, and he saw a nearly perfect round shaft in a sunken basin as Flavio had described.

Flavio gently fed the cylinder into the shaft, and a hollow, metallic sound clanged as the tank came to rest securely. Moving to uncoil the rope, he tied it to the spigot and walked partway back down the stairs before tugging hard on the rope to take out its slack. Glancing up to the peak, he made sure the rope was tight and then stepped off the staircase onto the pyramid's limestone face.

Rhodes was fascinated by the slanted angle of the pyramid as seen from Flavio's helmet, and looking at Far's view from ground level, he watched Flavio traverse the pyramid's casing in a sure-footed stance. With his right leg stiff and straight and his left bent, he kept his head up, wrapping the rope around his waist with one turn. He displayed his climbing skills by the smooth way he adjusted the rope, continuously shortening it as he drifted step by step to the middle of the face. He remained level with a joint running along the stone slabs, and from the midway point, he began to give more length to the rope while moving toward the upcoming corner.

Watching one side of the monitor and then the other, Rhodes kept pace with Flavio's progress. Far was doing a good job, walking around the base of the pyramid and keeping up with his movements. Moving his attention again to the view from Flavio's camera, Rhodes watched as Flavio passed one corner and went on to the next, making good time reaching the northeast face to close in on the eye. Rhodes focused on the smooth, contoured curvature of stone as it sloped to meet the great eye, and Flavio was careful how he crossed the slanted limestone in his approach to the sunken area.

No longer in view from Far's camera, Flavio had dropped out of her sight to scrutinize the features of the mystifying eye, whose reddish color stood out from the surrounding limestone. Making a looping knot with the rope as a means of securing it around his waist, he then brought forward the chisel he had tucked away. When he scraped the chisel against the eye's course surface, the sound clearly indicated that the eye was not stone but a metallic substance.

"The eye isn't stone but a type of metal, and hard enough that I won't be able to get any specimens off it with the tools I've brought with me." Continuing to scrape the stone with the chisel, he finally took out his hammer to smack it, and it sounded like a solid metal plate. "I certainly wasn't expecting this. It must be fairly thick, and it sounds like there may be hollow space behind it. Wouldn't it be something if all we had to do was cut a hole in this plate to get inside the pyramid? We need to get a cutting torch up here to cut into it or maybe a grinder, and I wouldn't mind removing the entire eye to give us something to take back home."

Having accomplished all he could for the moment, Flavio started to backtrack across the pyramid's face to the staircase. Rhodes watched him as he made his way past the first corner, and then he began logging data in his computer while checking their list of supplies.

Rhodes listened to the others jabber excitedly about the prospect of penetrating the eye to enter the pyramid. He thought it couldn't be that simple to get inside the monument, but his imagination kept him wondering. Suddenly hearing gasps from his crew, Rhodes turned to see Flavio had slipped on the pyramid face, and he watched as the climber regained his footing. He returned to the stairs and then came down safely to ground level, but this incident convinced Rhodes that he didn't want Flavio climbing the pyramid a second time.

Flavio addressed Rhodes, saying, "Captain, we would like to stay at the complex a little longer if that's okay. There's plenty of time left on our oxygen supply."

"I don't have a problem with that, but stick together and don't do anything dangerous or strenuous—you, especially—and after ninety minutes begin heading back to the ship."

Resuming his work on the computer, Rhodes listened to the crew members as they traveled south through the plaza, moving deeper into the complex. As they came upon another immense, dome-shaped pyramid significantly larger than the first they'd seen at the southeast end of the eye pyramid, they noticed it had the same elongated, tapered appearance.

Far commented, "I still can't tell if these odd-shaped mounds are artificial or natural. Have time and the elements distorted their true shape? The only monument that's relatively clear of silt and sediment is the eye pyramid, and that's because of the steep angles of its design."

Jetha replied, "I suspect that a good many of these obscure anomalies are pyramids, but it's hard to recognize them for what they are because the builders didn't use limestone in their construction. Many of the pyramids in Egypt and some gargantuan pyramids in Peru were made of mud brick, and now they're not much more than piles of rubble. What's strange is that all of these domed pyramids have a long, sweeping slope, and although most stretch south, not all do."

Rhodes detected uneasiness in Jetha's voice as she continued. "Sometimes I feel a foreboding sense, as though we're being watched. From the very outset, I've thought of this area as an ancient burial site. Ingrained in these monuments and even in the land is an enduring spiritual presence."

Flavio grinned. "Does the sensation make you feel as though the spirits of these ancient ones are overseeing our presence?"

"Something like that. I feel a resonance of those who once reigned over this land, as if their spirits are keeping watch over this complex, and it gives me a creepy feeling."

"Are you superstitious?" asked Far.

"No more than the average person, but breaking into that eye pyramid seems like a terrible thing to do. It's a sacred, splendorous shrine, and by breaching it we'll be desecrating it."

"You're probably a person with religious convictions," began Far, "and you may be linking this place to your own ancestry, comparing it to religious shrines in your native homeland. The Taj Mahal is a tomb or mausoleum, yet people visit it every day.

The pyramids in Egypt too, and those monuments don't hold any greater importance than the structures in this complex. I don't see why we can't enter the eye pyramid with respect and admiration for the ruler for whom it was built."

"The monument will be plundered, just as the others have been plundered, and when we're finished it will never be the same. Just wait and see."

Flavio responded, "If we aren't the ones to breach it, then the next expedition is sure to. Do you want the fame to go to those arriving on the next mission? They won't have any more respect for the former occupants of this Martian civilization than we do."

Then Aleksei said, "Now is the time for this discovery; this is the purpose for our being here. What kinds of explorers would we be if we didn't strive to breach its outer casing? However, I don't think entering it is going to be as simple as removing that eye."

Flavio had the final word. "If we decide to stay on this planet for the next eighteen months, there's no doubt in my mind that we're going to see the inside of that pyramid. We can't stay here without making an effort to break into it, and besides, it's our duty. We wouldn't be human if we didn't try."

They returned to the ship hours before sunset and had their evening meal before settling in at the end of the day. They viewed recordings made since their arrival, including footage already sent back to Earth. Images of the eye pyramid and even those weird, domed pyramids made them curious, leaving an indelible imprint on their minds while stirring their imagination.

CHAPTER 9

Essential Mission Priorities

The following morning, Rhodes reviewed tests essential to the Mars mission. The length between Earths and Mars' orbital alignments was increasing every day, and since they expected their stay on Mars to be brief, it was important to complete the tests. They had ten days before they'd have to depart, or they'd have to stay for the full course of the mission.

Rhodes sat at his computer monitor, and Flavio broke his concentration by saying, "Stan, I'd very much like to return to the pyramid. I'm going to take a cutting torch and a grinder with me to remove the eye, and I'd prefer that you accompany me and lend assistance. Not only would we acquire a metal that has retained its strength and appearance for millions of years, but we'd be returning with tangible evidence of a once-great Martian civilization."

"Tell me, did you see any deterioration in the metal?"

"None whatsoever, not even any rust around the edges where the stone rests flush with the metal. That's the primary reason I think we may have found a new type of metal. Its outer surface was course, as though they'd sprinkled something on it during its final stage of firing that makes it look like stone. Up close, you can see a dull glaze covering its outer surface, and this may be what helps preserve the metal."

"The revelation that these structures are artificial is a profound discovery, but it still doesn't take priority over the primary goals of our mission," said Rhodes. "Drilling for water is a mission requirement. Right now, discovering water is extremely important, as we can't risk staying here for eighteen months without finding more water. If we don't discover water over the next ten days, we'll have to return to Earth. It's going to take us six months to get back to Earth, and we have only enough water onboard to carry us for about four of those months."

"Yes, but in perhaps only a few hours I can go up there with a cutting torch and remove the eye from the pyramid. Think of what it would mean to science. Nothing we're bringing back with us can be of greater value."

In a more assertive tone, Rhodes said, "I didn't like your following your impulse to climb that monument in the first place, but I didn't want to make an issue out of it. Dragging equipment up there is dangerous, and what if a cutting torch doesn't do it? You're pressing your luck every time you go up on that pyramid. I don't want to be remembered as the captain of the first Mars mission mainly because there was a fatality and you were it."

"But, Stan, we can't ignore the fact that these ancient monuments are out there. Surely you haven't lost your sense of curiosity."

"I don't want to consider transporting your body back to Earth in a body bag. For the rest of my life I'll be defending my reasoning for allowing you to go up there. Your family will blame me and demand answers for why it happened. Besides, as I said, we have to drill for water."

"It's going to take nothing less than a miracle to find water on this planet."

"Nonetheless, it's a primary goal to attempt to extract water from the subsurface. From here on, the Cydonia Complex is off-limits. Neither you nor anybody else is to venture south of the supply depot. Look at it this way: If we start drilling and over the next ten days we find water, we're going to stay on Mars for the full term of the mission. That means we'll have plenty of time to do all the things that you and the others want to do, including climbing up to remove that damn eye if that's what you're determined to do.

"If we don't complete the necessary tests, this mission is going to be a complete failure. There are soil tests. We have to collect an abundance of rock samples from the surrounding area, and they have to be processed to find out if life forms have taken hold in them. While Far, Jetha, and I perform these tests, I want you and Aleksei to set up drilling equipment and begin efforts to find water. I've gathered everything you need and left it in the cargo bay. All you have to do is keep the drill bits plumb as they're fed into the soil."

Rhodes was short with his crew members the rest of the day. He, Far, and Jetha rode around in the rover gathering specimens, while Flavio and Aleksei began drilling into Mars' rock-hard surface. The last location where they picked up stones and soil samples was near the supply depot. Before picking up another six canisters of water to take back to the home ship, they managed to free two large cartons that Far wanted to make accessible for the next morning. She didn't say what the cartons contained but insisted they use care when sliding them over to the cargo door.

After returning to the ship, Flavio displayed his disappointment by ignoring Rhodes. He and Aleksei had penetrated almost a meter into the soil, but the equipment had begun bogging down in the rocky subsurface.

Later that evening, Rhodes sat down with the crew to delegate the next day's work. "Tomorrow Jetha and I will take a turn at the drill. Aleksei and Flavio will go with Far. She has two projects she wants to accomplish, which includes setting up some equipment. One can be erected at the site of the supply depot, but the other must be situated at a higher elevation."

Rhodes turned to Flavio. "Far thought the best place would be the high ground where the face is located. While you're at the site, study rock formations and investigate whether that area holds any geological significance. If so, you'll be able to collect specimens under Far's instructions.

Aleksei interrupted Rhodes. "For a moment I thought you were going to say the equipment needed to be set up on the pyramid."

"The pyramid is off-limits. It would've been ideal, but we'd have difficulty arranging secure placement for it. For what it's worth, in the event that we find water, I'll be the first to accompany Flavio up to that eye on the pyramid."

Far said, "If that eye is a metal plate and you remove it and take it back to Earth, it would be a big feather in your cap."

Ignoring the comment, Rhodes said, "I'll be listening to monitor your movements in case you need help, but if something should happen at that remote area, it would be next to impossible to reach you on foot. So let's be careful out there tomorrow."

Early the next day, Jetha and Rhodes stayed inside the ship's cabin to monitor the situation while Far, Flavio, and Aleksei set out in the rover to go to the supply depot. The trio opened the first carton and began assembling a compact, hi-tech, robotic, Swiss-made helicopter. Flavio and Aleksei connected the blades that would give it flight while Far knelt to activate a computer program on the unit for it to fly through Mariner Valley. Far aligned a cockpit camera that would record a bird's-eye view of the aerial trip; after completing the journey it would automatically retrace its flight course to the ship before landing.

The main reason Rhodes had remained behind was to ensure the main computer's hard drive picked up the helicopter's signal. Far made sure she had the correct coordinates, and Rhodes gave an okay that the computer was receiving a sharp picture. Then Aleksei and Flavio fueled it up, and after Far pressed the ignition button on a remote control device, its motor immediately started. Pressing a start button engaged the blades, and after a few revolutions, they were buzzing. She last pressed autopilot, and with that, the blades went into high gear to lift the helicopter, stirring up dust as it soared skyward and flew away.

Having accomplished Far's first project, they now loaded another carton onto the rover and started off across the Martian landscape to reach a hilltop at the face where they'd set up the equipment. The unit they arranged at the site had to remain there for forty-eight hours, and after getting it operational, they collected rock specimens. Rhodes listened to their movements throughout the day, and he and Jetha went outside to crank up the drill to resume drilling for water. When the others returned, they saw Jetha and Rhodes had achieved little, as the rocky ground put up tough resistance against the cutting edge of the carbide-tipped drill bit.

Near sundown, the unmanned drone returned, and Flavio and Aleksei suited up to see it circling overhead until it crash-landed about forty meters from the ship. It wasn't important to retrieve the disk that recorded the flight because they had it on a hard drive, but they did so anyway. That same evening, nibbling on popcorn, they enjoyed viewing what the drone's camera recorded, finding it tremendously entertaining, as if they were actually winging it over the land. The remarkable aerial photography showed an extraordinary view of the Mariner Valley canyon, various craters, and the sprawling Martian landscape in high-definition clarity. When they watched the unit's return to the ship, they shared a panoramic view of the Cydonia Complex, with the pyramid's mystical eye seemingly awaiting the drone's return.

The equipment they'd placed on a hilltop at the face had been there for the recommended forty-eight hours when Far, Jetha, and Rhodes went out to get it. Rhodes and Jetha followed Far until they came upon a plain, gray box with a rotating disk still actively circling from its top. Far checked to make sure it had operated fine before switching it off, and Rhodes and Jetha took notice of the words stamped on its top surface before picking it up:

Geographical Information Systems Data Base
Electronic Radar Infrared Scanner and
Microwave Imager with Laser Altimetry

Far explained the unit's purpose, saying, "The unit sends out a piloted frequency of ground-tracking radar that fans alternating profiles of primary land formations. Geo-referenced acoustical sensors read geometric, dimensional representations modeled mathematically into range measurements. By detecting and translating these descending and ascending waves, it builds a topographical environmental shape of the land to forge a precision simulation of geological surfaces."

"I may be wrong," Rhodes began, "but didn't the ship's main computer read the land's topography as we were landing?"

"Yes, but this unit is more sophisticated, and we're going to integrate the work done here with what the main computer has already ingested. I'll be able to refine and enhance land proportions and incorporate artificial products to make a 3-D virtual-reality world. With a little luck we'll have it done this evening, so have the popcorn ready."

Upon their return, Far and Jetha started work on computer graphics at the leading edge of 3-D modeling animation and virtual reality with interactive visualization techniques. While they put it together, Flavio, Aleksei, and Rhodes overheard them fidgeting with computer images. At one point, Far overran Jetha on her keyboard, making adjustments, and Jetha said, "Why don't you sit down here and take this over? You know the system best."

Far shook her head. "I just wanted to add more color, but from here on it's yours."

The entertainment began later as their monitors came to life. At first, the landscape appeared much the same as footage from the unmanned drone: an aerial view of a sun-drenched, desert wasteland. They saw it as a bird would, circling over the outcrop of land designated as the face, the ground appearing dry, parched, and destitute, and the surrounding plain just as desolate. Blue water suddenly overtook the surrounding spaces, transitioning to lively waves splashing against the shore of this island landmass where lush plant life began sprouting up all over. This fascinating transformation accelerated as leafy, green palm trees and a menagerie of exotic plants sprung up across the island. A big wave careened into a rocky ledge before dispersing into white foam, and then they began to travel as though swooping over a vast, churning sea.

Off in the distance, they saw the Cydonia Complex as it must have appeared all those eons ago when life flourished here. At the windswept wedged point of the peninsula, stirring waves crashed onto the shore where exotic palm trees swayed in the breeze before a colonnade of pillars. This awe-inspiring, pillared hall resembled the Greek Parthenon, with tall, massive columns, and behind this structure was the majestic eye pyramid. The land looked arid, and other monuments in the complex had more distinctive characteristics than before, but they still appeared as structures from older kingdoms. The aerial view dipped, taking a sweeping turn into the plaza where a grand, royal palace with columns and red banners stood, and colorful images on obelisks caught the eye.

After circling this network of structures once more, the aerial view soared while turning southward along the seashore. They could hear lifelike waves, and sometimes a seagull would appear. Following the coastline, they soon glimpsed the five-sided D and M pyramid on the horizon before the picture faded to black.

Aleksei and Rhodes clapped, and Flavio said, "That was excellent."

They went on to transmit the footage to Earth along with what the unmanned drone had recorded after Aleksei and Jetha first added classical music to them. The next evening they sat back and viewed these recordings with the music they'd added and found it very relaxing.

CHAPTER 10

Lured to the Cydonia Complex

The upcoming days went by without their discovering water, dashing any hope of staying on Mars for any length of time. Staying the full term of the mission would leave them no water for the trip home, and while Mars and Earth are in relatively close orbit, they had little choice but to prepare to launch. The crew sided with Flavio, trying to convince Rhodes to remove the eye from the pyramid, pointing out how mission planners would demand an article of proof of this ancient civilization. However, Rhodes stood firm on his decision not to return to the Cydonia Complex. He kept sending the crew back to the supply depot for canisters to replenish their water supply, and he knew on occasion they couldn't fight the temptation to climb the ridge to look at the alluring eye, but he felt certain they wouldn't challenge his authority by going any closer.

The day before their designated launch, Aleksei, Jetha, and Rhodes rode in the rover to the storage depot to put the vehicle back onboard the wreckage of *Endurance II*. Thinking it may be years before humans will set eyes on the monument again, the three went up to the ridge to view the pyramid for the last time. Admiring the eye while wondering what was behind its silent gaze, Rhodes understood that by failing to bring back archeological proof of this discovery he may be failing in his mission. He had sent a transmission to Earth explaining their situation, letting mission planners know it wasn't worth endangering his crew by spending more time at the Cydonia Complex. He'd given a projected liftoff time and confirmed the course they'd take to return to Earth.

The following day, as the scheduled time to launch neared, Rhodes checked systems through the main computer, and everything was set to go. The minutes passed by, and when the count down was less than an hour off, they suited up while proceeding with final tabulations in preparation for liftoff.

Rhodes looked at Flavio before putting his helmet on. "In six months you'll be back on Earth with the media swarming all over you, and just think of all those girlfriends you left behind."

Flavio grinned. "You've got a point, Stan. As much as I wanted to do more exploration on Mars, I miss Mother Earth."

"What's in your favor is that you're young enough to make another trip to Mars, and maybe on the next mission, you'll hold the rank of captain. The most valuable asset for space travel is experience, and you also have the skills mission planners want."

Far added, "Upon our return to Earth, we'll be hailed internationally as heroes and remembered for generations to come as the first humans to land on Mars."

Fast approaching liftoff time, Flavio and Far reaffirmed data showing that all systems were set to go, and Rhodes said, "Everyone, put your helmets on and fasten your seatbelts. Flavio, start the countdown from number ten."

"Ten, nine, eight, seven, six, five, four, three, two, one, ignition," said Flavio and flipped a switch, but all they heard was a hollow thump.

"Hit it again," Rhodes said, but all they heard was the same sound. Obviously irked, Rhodes let his elbows rest on the arms of his seat, clenching his hands together in a big fist. "There's always the unexpected." He then addressed the computer. "Abe, engines didn't fire. Can you give an account for this failure?"

"I'm aware of that, Stan, and I've isolated the problem to the ignition system."

A wiring diagram popped up on their monitors, and while any number of components could've hampered the engines from firing, an electrical failure or a short was most likely the culprit. Aleksei and Rhodes removed two panels in the floor to begin testing a group of components. Flavio, Far, and Jetha checked switches and electrical circuits in the engine compartment. Everything was in working order, which helped isolate the problem to the bridge.

Far sent a message to Earth explaining the delay in liftoff and then joined Flavio and Jetha at the back of the cabin. The three remained out of sight for some time before Far returned to the bridge. Rhodes' head was sticking out of the floor space as he studied a printout of the ignition system stretched out on the floor. Far knelt in front of him to get his attention. "Look, Stan, this is a job for two people, and Aleksei and I can handle it. We're going to be stuck here for at least twenty-four hours, so it might be a good idea to consider going back to the pyramid with Flavio to extract that eye. You know as well as I do that if you let this chance go by, you'll always regret it. Bringing back that eye will be pivotal in weighing the success of the mission."

"The rover's parked in the storage depot, which means walking all the way there carrying equipment we'd have to lug up on that pyramid, and that's exactly what I've been trying to avoid," Rhodes replied.

Far said, "Flavio and Jetha are suited up in the cargo bay. They have the equipment ready on a makeshift sled to transport the load, and they're waiting for you."

Rhodes resumed studying the diagram for the ignition system, ignoring Far, and she walked off without saying anything more.

Aleksei changed positions as he lay in a crawl space beneath the floor. He turned to look at Rhodes and said, "Testing the parts in this system is a relatively simple exercise, but it takes time. There is no shortcut. I have seen the pyramid, and I have no desire to climb up to that eye, but why don't you go ahead with the others and work to remove the eye?"

"I'm trying to get this ship launched to get us back to Earth. Climbing up that pyramid in our suits is dangerous, and cutting out that metal plate will be difficult," replied Rhodes.

"Far has a point, though, as you may have misgivings later. That eye's perplexing allure may haunt you for some time to come. If you and Flavio can remove it, it will attest to the ingenuity of this Martian civilization, giving the scientific community something to examine firsthand. If we brought back three times as many stones as we have now, they would not equal the value of that eye."

"That may be true, but if something goes wrong up there, it's been nice knowing you. You're not going to be satisfied until somebody falls from the face of that pyramid."

"Don't let anything go wrong then. Flavio is a very capable individual, so you don't have to worry about him. Just look out for yourself. You've done everything you can to convince everyone that this is a bad idea. You Americans hold democracy so highly, so you can always tell them you handled it democratically."

"Don't kid yourself. We Americans also hold responsibility high, and when things go wrong we commonly look for someone to hang for it."

Aleksei grinned while nodding. "It's much the same in Russia."

After his chat with Aleksei, Rhodes suited up to venture out onto the Martian surface with Flavio and Jetha. Joining them in the cargo bay, he looked at Jetha and commented, "I know he wants to go through with this crazy stunt, but I thought you might be the one person who'd object to plucking out that eye. I suppose mission planners will want to see proof that what we've seen here is real, never mind that somebody could get killed in the process."

Flavio had taken a sheet of fiberglass from a wall in the lab that served as a backsplash to make a sled. Two holes in the corners supplied the means for tying a rope to pull it.

Before putting on his helmet, Rhodes noticed short welding tanks and welding masks designed to hook onto their helmets for eye protection, and he asked, "Are you sure we've got everything?"

"I've got the cutting torch, a grinder with four, diamond-edge disks, and more rope so you'll have your own length of rope supporting you."

Rhodes gave a nod. "Let's get it over with before I change my mind."

The three soon exited the ship and began their march to the pyramid with hours of daylight ahead of them to remove the eye. Flavio and Rhodes dragged the sled behind them. Jetha kept pace, the camera in her helmet activated to record the climb. They spoke little, and the walk seemed long since they'd grown used to riding in the rover.

Passing by the storage depot, they climbed over the next rim to reach the shelf where the majestic monument came into full view. Looking up at the eye, Rhodes wondered what he was getting himself into, but he knew the others were right. Mission planners would want definitive evidence of what they'd seen and photographed, and they'd never let him live it down if he didn't return with something scientists could study.

Arriving at the pyramid, they took the corridor in front of the northeast face that ran alongside the temple ruins. Asking Jetha to wait near the original entrance to the pyramid below the eye, Flavio attached one bundle of rope to his belt, holding the other length of rope in his hand.

"Once we've made it to the eye's recess, we'll throw down a rope. Tie the rope to the bundle with the torch tanks first, and we'll send the rope down again for the other bundle."

Leaving her behind, Flavio and Rhodes rounded the pyramid's base to reach the southwest corner where the stairs were located. Looking up the long staircase, Rhodes saw the loose end of rope Flavio had used days before lying on the stairs one story above.

"I'm going to walk to the top first to tie a rope to the spigot so we'll both have our own supporting tether. When you see me at the peak, begin your ascent. I'll descend to meet you on the stairs at the same elevation as the eye." He then gave Rhodes an inquisitive look. "You have such a serious expression, Stan. Where's your sense of adventure?"

"I left it back at the ship. Let's get on with it."

Flavio made the climb look easy, moving like a mechanical figure, keeping a steady stride all the way to the apex. At the top, he fastened the rope to the spigot, tugging on it hard to make certain it was secure.

Seeing Flavio begin his descent, Rhodes started climbing the stairs, and when he reached the loose end of the original rope lying on the stairs, he bent over to pick it up. Continuing his slow, steady climb, he glanced up to see Flavio waiting, the additional length of looped rope still attached to his belt, and they met on the stairs at a staggering height.

"From here on, I advise you not to look down," cautioned Flavio. "Keep the rope loose around your waist to make adjustments easier, shortening it as we approach the middle and lengthening as we near a corner. I find it best to grip the rope with both hands, one hand in front of you and the other behind you while short-stepping your way across." After Rhodes nodded, he added reassuringly, "I'll go first. Just do what I do."

Rhodes waited, poised to follow while keeping tension on the rope from above. He watched Flavio loop his length of rope around his waist before beginning to walk across the pyramid's slanting surface. After distancing himself from the stairs, Flavio signaled for Rhodes to follow.

Staring wide-eyed at the daunting angle of the pyramid, Rhodes took a deep breath and thought, *I can't believe I'm going through with this.*

"Don't be such a wimp, Stan," said Flavio as he waved again for him to follow while leading the way.

Feeling nervous and uneasy, Rhodes wrapped the rope around his waist as Flavio had done, tugging hard on it before stepping forward onto the pyramid's slanted surface. Never looking down and trying not to think about the elevation he stood at, he realized he'd done more daring and difficult things in his life. Taking one step at a time, he made progress by imitating Flavio's moves, adjusting the rope while side-stepping his way across the pyramid. Beginning to think the task was getting easier, he saw Flavio pass the first corner to move out of sight and didn't see him again until he arrived at that same corner. By then, Flavio had already reached the following corner at the far end, and he waved to give Rhodes encouragement before moving around that corner, which interceded with the northeast face. Upon reaching it, Rhodes caught sight of Flavio ducking into the sunken area where the pyramid's facing stones met with the eye. Seconds later, Flavio stuck his head out to check Rhodes' progress before disappearing again into the recess.

Rhodes soon reached the curve of the recess, and Flavio lent him a hand to take a crouched position in front of the giant eyeball. Stone etched around the eyeball created creases that gave it a more lifelike appearance when viewed from below.

No longer able to see the northeast face from where they huddled on the sloping cheek of the eye's recess, they realized there was plenty of space to stand up, should someone dare to do so. The downward slope from the eye was gentle for the first couple of meters before dropping off dangerously. Rhodes watched as Flavio gave himself plenty of slack to allow him movement before knotting his rope securely around his waist. Rhodes did the same, and then Flavio took hold of the other rope attached to his belt, hanging on to one end while flinging the wadded rope out so it would drop down to Jetha. He'd already knotted the inside end of the rope to a spare chisel, which helped the rope unwind as it rolled down the steep slope of the pyramid. After giving her time to tie the end of the rope to the first bundle, they received a couple of gentle tugs to let them know she had it ready. They pulled up the first bundle containing the cutting torch and tanks, and then they repeated the process to bring up the rest of the equipment.

They donned their lightweight welding masks, and it took only a minute for Flavio to hook up a tank to the cutting torch and light it. He directed the flame to the base of the eye before increasing the heat, but it didn't take long to see it had no effect on the metal.

Flavio shook his head. "This torch isn't doing anything."

Eager to get the job done so they could get off the monument, Rhodes said, "Let's try the grinder."

After Flavio shut off the torch's flame, they removed their welding masks, and then he set up the grinder with a thin, diamond-edge cutting disk. Flavio held the grinder firmly with both hands and switched it on. As soon as the disk hit the metal, sparks flew. It was plain to see the disk was gouging the metal, cutting as it left an open trench, and he stopped to change his position.

Flavio stood and reached up to begin at the one o'clock position on the eye and continued cutting clockwise along the eye's perimeter. The cutting disk didn't last long, but he went on using it until it could no longer cut into the metal, and he then changed to a new disk. They only had two cutting disks left, and he wondered if they would last long enough to cut all the way around the eye.

Pausing long enough to remove a chisel tucked into the pocket of his pants leg, Flavio used the tool's thin side to penetrate the gouged hole he'd made with the grinder. It passed through, letting him know that the cutting disk had cleared the depth of the metal plate, and he gave Rhodes a nod to show they were making progress. He then resumed his work from a stooped position, maneuvering the grinder with a steady hand while skillfully following the outer shape of the eye.

Curious as to how deep the metal eye set into the surrounding stone, Rhodes looked forward to seeing what lay beyond the metal plate, as he suspected there was a stone wall behind it. He could do little except watch as Flavio went on cutting a gouge around the eye, and he knew he'd soon have to get out of Flavio's way by trading places with him. As sparks flew, the cluttered space provided little working room, and Rhodes was afraid of falling when scooting around Flavio.

When Flavio changed from the second to the third disk, he was almost at the six o'clock position, not quite halfway. When he changed from the third to the fourth, he'd barely reached nine o'clock. He stood up to continue. Rhodes silently questioned whether they would be able to get the job done. Both men guessed there'd be only a small amount of the metal left holding the eye in place when they finished—the uncut area would be from twelve to one o'clock.

The last disk had worn down so that it no longer cut with any depth, and the grinder's battery pack had also begun to lose power. Flavio reached high to gouge a track across the remaining metal to weaken it before finally shutting off the grinder.

David Gatesbury

He'd ended up about eighteen centimeters short of his starting point but believed the little bit of metal still supporting the eye wouldn't keep them from removing it. Using his chisel to hook the metal while prying and pulling it out from the bottom, however, he found the metal wouldn't give. With little leverage to pull outward, they tried to push it in, leaning against the eye with their shoulders. The giant eye just stared them down, not giving way.

CHAPTER 11

An Eye-opening Experience

Stumped, they continued their efforts by lying down on their sides and kicking the eye, and it began tilting inward from the bottom. The force of every hammering kick opened more space at the bottom, and when Flavio signaled to stop, they had finally breached the pyramid!

Sunlight reflected off the smooth, contoured limestone surrounding the eye, making a stark contrast to the darkness of the pyramid's interior, and Flavio rose to a stooped position to peek inside. Seeing nothing but sheer black, he pushed the eye with his shoulder to give him more space to look in, and with Rhodes helping to push, the gap around the eye widened as it slanted inward even further. Flavio leaned forward to look inside and then gasped, throwing his hands back before rising as he backpedaled. He stepped on one of the welding masks and slid backwards off the eye!

"Aah!"

Shocked by what had occurred, Rhodes was slow to act. Immediately noticing tension on Flavio's rope angling stiffly down from above, he scrambled to look down the slope, while clinging to his own tether, and saw Flavio a few meters below on the pyramid's slanted face. The rope tied around his waist had stopped his fall, but he was having trouble finding stability to work his way back up to the level of the eye. Reaching to catch hold of Flavio's rope to pull him up, Rhodes couldn't tug with his full strength without losing his footing, although by now Flavio had begun pulling hand over hand on his tether to climb back up.

A pale Flavio dropped to his knees when he reached Rhodes, and Rhodes checked his life-support system. "You almost got killed, falling back that way."

"Are you okay up there?" asked Jetha anxiously.

Then they heard Far's voice, saying, "Is everyone okay? Do you need help?"

"Everything's okay," replied Rhodes. "Just be still for a minute."

Flavio raised a shaky, gloved hand to point at the eye. "I saw a pair of glimmering eyes in the darkness."

Seeing the fright on Flavio's face, Rhodes turned to peek inside the opening, and goose bumps crawled up his spine as he saw two gleaming eyes looking back at him!

The eyes were a shimmering white, and whatever this thing was it kept its distance, holding still as if ready to strike! Time stood still as it held a stationary position across a wide expanse of floor, and a bulging, shadowy form began to take shape that appeared quite large. Rhodes noticed that the eyes had a faint, flickering sparkle, and sensing no movement from the being, his feeling of fright diminished, for he believed it was a statue glaring back at him.

"I'm telling you there's something there!"

Rhodes said calmly, "It's a statue."

Bound by amazement, Rhodes remained kneeling at the rim of the eye to view the tomb of an ancient Martian ruler, and Flavio came forward to peer over his shoulder. Their eyes adjusted to the darkness of the pyramid's interior, and they saw what appeared to be two great statues inside. They turned on the lights on their helmets while loosening their ropes to be free of them, and the statue with those unusual, gleaming eyes continued to seize their attention. It stood straight across a spacious chamber—a substantially large, sculpted figure that looked like the bust of a person with a base in the shape of a pyramid.

"This is Far. If you guys don't let us know you're okay, we'll have to suit up and start for the pyramid."

Neither Rhodes nor Flavio responded as they stared in wonderment at the glittering eyes, which were unmistakably white-blue diamonds. They took positions on each side of the eye to lift and lower the metal plate until it came free. It took some muscle to lean the giant eye against a wall, where they left it to begin studying their surroundings.

The chamber now showered with sunlight, they could see the second statue, the larger of the two, stood to their right to leave an unobstructed view of the bust facing their point of entry. It was hard to determine what this sprawling, jumbled form depicted.

Far shouted irritably, "Stan and Flavio, this isn't funny. One of you has to respond. Jetha, can you see those two?"

"No, I can't."

Rhodes finally replied, "I'm slow coming back to you because we've just entered the pyramid through the eye, and what we've found is astonishing."

Far's voice turned soft. "You're inside the pyramid?"

"Yes, we are, so just keep your shirts on for a few minutes while we familiarize ourselves with what's here."

Flavio said in amazement, "I . . . I can hardly believe this. Can you, Stan?"

"I never would've believed we could enter this pyramid through that eye. I expected a wall of stones to be behind it, yet here we are."

"Are those real diamonds in the eyes of that statue? If they are, then they're the biggest diamonds I could ever hope to imagine. They're the size of my fists!"

Far came back, commenting, "I don't know if I can believe the two of you or not. Are you really inside the pyramid?"

"Yes, we are, and if you'll keep quiet we'll describe the objects we're seeing."

"Okay," replied Far, "but the two of you should activate your cameras so I can record this as it's happening. You left the ship without switching on your camera equipment."

After switching on his helmet camera, Rhodes said, "Far, you and Aleksei may be watching this now, but I know Jetha isn't able to, so I'm going to go on describing what we've discovered. Before us is a bust made of limestone, an enlarged scale of a ruler watching over his domain. The ruler is a brawny hulk with humanlike characteristics, and those large diamonds you heard us speak of represent his eyes, giving him an ominous appearance. A well-rounded head bears a fanciful headscarf, and he's clad in a ceremonial robe that drapes down in front. His carved face has a pronounced brow ridge, high cheekbones, and a brooding expression with a somewhat sinister smile that leaves deep creases in his cheeks.

"Behind the bust is a sunburst beautifully etched into the wall, with rays raining down in all directions like a relief. This wall must stand at the midway point in the pyramid, leading me to believe there may be space for another compartment on the other side of it.

"The architecture of this chamber is unique in that the ceiling is fashioned as a huge arch running from left to right as you come in. Sloping at a wide angle to meet the floor, this arched construction must provide strength to support the weight above it. The majority of the ceiling is a heavenly night scene with stars scattered all over it or something that looks like stars, and the floor is painted aqua-blue, the paint cracked and peeling."

Rhodes turned to his right to examine the other intriguing statue of a life-size man battling a monstrous lizard, motioning for Flavio to carry on describing their surroundings. Flavio said, "The sun disk behind the bust showers a broad area with its rays, and I believe I'm facing the southwest, which is how the sun would be setting. A few of the stars that were once attached to the ceiling have fallen. Hang with me as I examine one to describe it to you."

Most all of the fallen stars were broken, but Flavio picked up one that was intact. "These stars look like albino starfish, and they're similar in shape to those we have on Earth. Since this complex was located near coastal waters, it may have been common to find them off these shores, and they dabbed a thick adhesive in the center of its underside to hold it to the ceiling."

Rhodes had been studying the sprawling statue of what looked like a man balanced on the back of a giant lizard, thrusting a spear into the base of the animal's neck. Erected on a pedestal, the statue ran lengthwise from the pyramid's entrance to nearly as far as the location of the bust.

Flavio interrupted his concentration. "Stan, wouldn't you describe this as a starfish?"

Taking his eyes from the menacing creature to glimpse the starfish, Rhodes commented, "I don't think starfish are technically a fish, but like our starfish, it has five arms or rays radiating outward to give it the star shape."

Flavio started to chuck it aside and Rhodes stopped him. "Bring it back to the ship with us. The others will want to see it."

Flavio stuck the object in the pocket of his pants leg and then gazed at the statue Rhodes had been examining. Rhodes began to describe it. "In my examination of the second statue, I'm seeing an abstract art form made of a rusty, red metal. I'm no art critic, but as much as it's unique, for me its features aren't quite complete. My guess is that these Martians must've just entered their Iron Age to forge such an artistic achievement, a fascinating depiction of a life-size man taking on an awesome, reptilian creature. I'm describing him as a man because he has a humanlike physique, masculine with a robust, athletic build and a well-rounded, bald head. He's wearing nothing but raggedy trunks. He stands balanced on the back of this giant lizard, an animal that must be ten meters long with its jaws open wide and a whipping tail. It has powerful jaws and formidable incisors for ripping apart meat. It's turning its head as it twists to snap at its attacker, who's ramming a spear into the base of the beast's neck."

"Wait, Stan, look behind the statue there. Etched into the wall is cryptic writing, the first writing we've seen." Flavio marveled at the primitive but complex writing form spanning a broad area behind the statue. "Stan, we have no way of knowing for certain what this inscription says, but it may tell of this ruler's courageous fight with the menacing creature as seen before us. Perhaps by slaying it, he won the hearts and minds of those who lived in this region, and for that, they made him their king. This writing, so long mute but destined to speak to us from across the ages, calls out to us to be deciphered and understood." Flavio gripped Rhodes' arm excitedly, a giddy expression on his face as he spoke passionately. "We can translate it, Stan. The computer covers dialects of ancient civilizations, including Sumerian, Semitic, Phoenician, Coptic, Hebrew, Egyptian, Babylonian, Syrian, Ionian, and Greek. All we have to do is transfer the writing or duplicate it somehow so we can feed it into the computer."

Rhodes turned to scan what first looked like a bare wall on their left as they'd entered the pyramid, noticing inscriptions etched into its surface as well. This was the wall opposite the statue of man and beast, and the combined inscriptions made for a lengthy text.

Drawn to the perplexing lettering, Rhodes reached out to touch the wall with his glove, imagining the time it took Martian scribes to do it with such precision. He directed his next words to the others. "I expect the writing on these two walls contains a wealth of information about a race of beings that once dominated this planet." Pausing to gaze about at these newfound discoveries, he added, "If you're sure you've recorded all we've seen here, Far, we're going to start back to the ship now."

"It's all been recorded," acknowledged Far.

Rhodes turned to Flavio. "We'll have to get the rover out of storage to transport the eye back to the ship. We can't launch to return to Earth for at least another forty-eight hours to give us time to fully investigate what's in this chamber."

Flavio excitedly shook his head no. "We can't leave now that we've breached the pyramid. It'll take weeks to completely study what we've found here."

"Flavio, if it weren't for our water situation, I'd be happy to stay."

Flavio's eyes widened "We'll keep looking for water, and somehow we'll find it, but we can't leave now. Don't you see? Just like the chamber we've discovered here, there must be other vaults in this pyramid, and this Martian ruler must have horded a vast treasury of untold riches. Can you imagine the scientific importance of finding the skeletal or mummified remains of a Martian?"

Rhodes was skeptical. "It'll probably disintegrate into dust the very second we touch it. If we're lucky enough to find a mother lode of stashed diamonds and jewelry, I hope we'll be able to use it to buy some water, because without it we're certain to die here."

"Stan, you've got to think positively! There's no way we can leave Mars now."

"We'll discuss it with the others, but I don't see how we can possibly stay on here and expect to survive. When the water runs out, you'll all blame me for the outcome."

Going back to the opening where sunlight streamed in, Rhodes was uncertain about how to get the eye down from the monument, and they lifted it to move it closer to the opening. Rhodes knew that what made this metal eye manageable was that gravity on Mars is one-third of what it is on Earth. He remained inside the pyramid as Flavio stepped onto the outside ledge. Looping and tying their ropes around their waists, they gave themselves liberal slack to allow them mobility. Lifting and maneuvering the eye to turn it horizontally, they kept the eye image face up so as not to scratch or mar its surface.

They held it waist-high with their arms spread as though they were handling a broad table, keeping it level while moving in short steps. Flavio backed up, and they turned the eye so it easily passed through the widest angle of the opening it previously occupied.

Flavio moved outside the chamber to stand precariously at where the pyramid's angled facing began, and they gently let the eye rest on the slanting slope. He hung on to his rope as he came around to reenter the pyramid to join Rhodes, and then they both squatted in position to push the metal plate. "Now what?" he asked.

"We're going to let it slide freely down the limestone casing on its own," said Rhodes. "Jetha, keep your distance," he called out. "We're going to let this giant eye slide down the pyramid, so get clear of the northeast face."

"Okay, all clear," she said.

Flavio and Rhodes gave the metal plate a shove and heard the crunch of metal grinding against stone, but this push wasn't enough to get it sliding down the pyramid's sloping face. They tipped and tilted the plate to let it sag at the far outside end, and Rhodes was confident another driving push would send the eye plunging down the monument. They pushed again, and it took off sliding while immediately picking up speed. They heard an amplified grinding sound and metallic pinging, followed by a pounding thud as it sank in a sand drift near the original entrance to the pyramid.

After collecting their tools, Rhodes and Flavio strapped the bundles to their backpacks. They began the perilous journey back to the stairs, using the ropes as their lifelines in the same fashion as before. Rhodes was relieved when he reached the stairs and even more so after reaching the ground, where Jetha stood waiting for them.

"The two of you looked pretty good up there," she said.

"Yeah, except for the time Flavio nearly fell off the pyramid."

"Well, nobody got hurt, and you've made an amazing discovery."

Then Flavio blurted out excitedly, "There's a chamber inside the pyramid where there are two impressive statues, and one statue has the biggest, knockout diamonds I've ever seen for eyes! We can only speculate on what the text reads that covers two walls inside that chamber, but it may speak of Martian history and give insight into their ways of life." He removed the starfish from his pocket, finding it broken. He handed her what was left of it. "This is a starfish that had fallen from the ceiling."

Jetha said, "It looks like a starfish with those fine, rippled indentations on its underside, but we'll be able to learn more about it after examining it under a microscope."

"Okay, we'll have to get the rover out of storage to transport the eye back to the ship, and later I'll send a transmission to Earth updating our situation here."

After getting the rover out, they closed up the storage depot and drove the vehicle up close to the pyramid. Gathering their gear and placing it in the rover, they then spaced themselves evenly around the eye to carry it horizontally, moving slowly in heaps of sand that bogged them down. Laying it flat on the rover, its diameter ran over the vehicle's sides and back end. They used rope to secure it to the rover.

As they left the Cydonia Complex, they looked up at the monument and the gaping, black hole previously occupied by the eye. Jetha barely fit in the front of the vehicle between Flavio and Rhodes, riding high with her rump resting on the eye, her boots nestled on the console. She hung on to the seat's headrests for balance, saying, "It's sad that we removed the eye, for we've stolen the pyramid's mystical grandeur, and it will never be the same."

"It's a little late to cry about it," remarked Rhodes.

"Yes," began Flavio, "I'm certain that whoever that powerful ruler was, his spirit is now very angry that we've come here."

Rhodes drove slowly to prevent the metal plate from shifting, riding the brake as they descended into the valley, and the rover strained as it climbed to the rim of the next ridge. They stopped on the level plain to tighten the ropes and then resumed their trip back to the ship without any trouble. Upon their return, they carefully brought the huge eye into the ship, turning it diagonally to get it through the cargo door and standing it on end sideways to clear the ceiling. Using rope and cords to secure the eye against a wall, they closely scrutinized its indented features before measuring and photographing it. They sent these images back to Earth along with what Rhodes and Flavio had recorded inside the chamber. They also let mission planners know that they'd be staying on Mars for at least another forty-eight hours.

CHAPTER 12

Ambitious Thinking

Aleksei informed Rhodes that he'd replaced an automatic relay switch that had blocked the engines from firing. He also cleaned the engine's fuel injectors to be certain they weren't clogged, and a systems check showed they should be able to start the next launch sequence anytime. The team then watched what the cameras in Flavio's and Rhodes' helmets had recorded when they were inside the chamber. They were convinced this discovery meant they must stay for the entire length of the mission, but Rhodes' concerns about a water shortage stopped him from making that commitment.

As Far looked at the statue depicting the ruler attacking a giant lizard, the size of this animal mystified her. "I'm not convinced that statue is life-size. I mean, the artist who designed it may have exaggerated its size to please his king. Many ancient kings portrayed themselves as larger than life to feed their egos, and this sculptor may have stretched the size of this dinosaur-like creature to embellish the kill."

Jetha responded, "That may be so, but no one's going to give praise for a statue hidden from the publics' eye, so what would he gain by enlarging the creature's proportions?"

Far zoomed in for a close up of the spears angle, studying how it pierced the creature's neck, "The wound must've caused serious injury to nerve cell bodies, and vertebrae in the animal's spinal neck column."

They talked about returning to the pyramid to remove the diamonds from the statue's eyes, as well as other plans. Flavio expressed his desire to erect some sort of walkway from the stairs to the entrance of the pyramid to make the chamber opening more accessible, but Rhodes thought the idea outlandishly dangerous. Jetha and Far were eager to transfer the Martian dialect inscribed on the chamber walls to the computer so it could begin translating it. Their discussions fueled their dreams of staying on to penetrate deeper into the pyramid. Instead of Rhodes' admonition about a water shortage cooling these ideas, it seemed as though the crew was getting a fever, and they were more determined than ever to remain on Mars.

Rhodes felt strongly opposed to staying on any longer than another forty-eight hours but was trying to be diplomatic about the situation. He wanted to give his crew a chance to convince him they'd be willing to make great sacrifices rationing water, but even at that, the odds were stacked against their survival. Not wanting to force the issue that night, he waited till the next morning to see how the crew acted. They started the morning enthused about exploring the pyramid.

Sipping his morning coffee, he interrupted their chatter. "Before we do anything else, I think we need to take our seats and intelligently discuss the future of the mission." As soon as they sat down, he continued. "The temptation to stay on Mars is greater than ever now that we've breached the pyramid, and that's why I think we need to have this meeting of the minds. Apparently, I'm not getting through to you people about the dangers involved in staying on here. It's extremely unlikely we'll find water in the upcoming months, and I don't want this mission to end disastrously. I believe we can stretch our stay here another two weeks, and after that, we will have lost the window of opportunity to head home, leaving us committed to staying for the long haul. I don't want to pull rank by insisting we have to launch and start back to Earth, but we have to look at this situation realistically. If we should somehow stretch our water supply to last our entire stay, it's still unlikely we'll have enough water to sustain us on our six-month trip home." He fixed his gaze on Jetha. "Jetha, I was really relying on you to be one of the few sane ones. You were against plundering the pyramid, but you're ignoring the risks just like the others."

"The archeological artifacts we'll find inside the pyramid will be of great value to our mission," replied Jetha. "There's something about that pyramid that draws me to it. I suppose part of it is curiosity, but I'm with the others on this. I know water is going to be critical, but we've already begun rationing, and there is a possibility we'll find water."

"Whatever we find inside that pyramid is not worthwhile risking our lives for."

Flavio joined the conversation. "Stan, we can use the emergency ascent vehicle's communication equipment to talk to mission planners. They may have some ideas to help us, and they'll tell you straight up if they want us to stay or go, which will simplify matters for you. You're struggling with yourself about whether to go on with the mission, but even you yourself know that if there's any way possible for us to carry on here, then we must try. In addition, the emergency ship has water, so in case water takes us to a life-and-death struggle, we do presumably have enough on that ship to get us home. In the here and now, these discoveries warrant investigation, and what it comes down to is whether these discoveries outweigh using that emergency ship."

"Disturbing that ship is out of the question. It has a special purpose, and just like today, when this ship's engines failed to start, we may come to rely on it for lifting off from this planet. While we may have to turn to that vehicle in an emergency, we cannot interrupt its computers while it's creating fuel for a return trip home. Using its communications isn't going to be much help to us either, because no matter what people on Earth say, their advice isn't going to be much good when we're dying from lack of water.

"We'll be banking on the fact that no water deficiencies will arise. In the final analysis, we have to ask ourselves if the discoveries we'll find here equal the risks, and I say they're not worth dying for. We'll have to break down our intake of water to a science, and if we die before reaching home because we didn't have enough water to sustain us, what will it all have been for? If we start taking water from the emergency ascent ship before the end of this mission, we won't survive the trip home. That's the alarm warning us we're doomed."

Rhodes then turned to Aleksei to try a different approach. "Alek, I respect your point of view, and I have to wonder what you would do if you were in my shoes. If you were captain and you were faced with aborting the mission and heading home, do you think the leaders of Russia's space program would want you to risk your life and the lives of your crew by staying here?"

"I sympathize with your dilemma, Stan. It's a difficult question to answer, but judging from these discoveries, I surmise my people would want me to make the maximum effort. Each time we feel the G-forces generated to escape the earth's gravity, there are risks involved, but we've already established a foothold on Mars and can't let go now."

"But even if we could talk to Earth, and they told us that they wanted us to go the distance, it's our necks that are sticking out, and if we die here, what did we accomplish?"

"We do it because we can and we must. We do it because we as humans accept challenges. We do it because it is man's destiny to explore other worlds."

Rhodes saw he was getting nowhere with Aleksei, and he turned to Flavio. "You're second in command so you're partly responsible for the lives of these people. I heard you talking about building a platform from the stairs to the pyramid entrance, and I imagine you're thinking about using materials from the supply depot. With audacious strategizing like that, how can we possibly cut down on our water consumption? The more physical work we do, the more water our bodies are going to require. You're an experienced mountain climber, but these people aren't. You're not thinking about the welfare of your fellow crew members."

"Listen, Stan, I stayed up almost the entire night pondering it, and it's not the monumental task you may think it is. It'll take time to build a platform, and it will entail physically demanding work, but I can do the bulk of the preliminary setup on the pyramid myself.

"I'll have to predrill two horizontal rows of holes into the pyramid's face to set plastic sleeves to anchor fasteners to hold the platform's framework. These sets of holes will align vertically and repeat at half-meter intervals, while serving to attach one leg at a time on the angled slope of the pyramid. After attaching the legs to the pyramid, there will be tie-ins stabilizing the metal framework to support the platform's decking made from wall and floor panels from the supply depot.

"I'm not dictating any kind of arrangement, but Aleksei is a good candidate to fabricate the support legs inside the storage depot. After making the first leg, we'll have grasped how to pattern and precision-cut pieces to assemble identical leg supports before taking them up on the pyramid, and they will be lightweight for easy handling. After that, it will be simple to align the holes.

"Like you said, we'll have to use materials from the supply depot to build the platform, which helps because it's not far from the pyramid. It's going to take maybe ten days to construct the leg framing, but I'll have finished the drilling in perhaps two, so I can start installing the first group of legs on the pyramid immediately.

"Vertical posts should be placed along the platform connected by a support cable to improvise as a handrail, and we can do the same on the stairs. In fact, I should first install handrail posts on the stairs and run a cord from the pyramid's summit to give us added support when we climb up with a load or descend from the platform. The framing legs won't weigh much so we may be able to carry two at a time, and if we have enough material, I'd like to broaden the platform at the pyramid chamber's entrance. I know it sounds dangerous, but I've hung off cliffs and crevices mountaineering, so it's not like I'm doing this for the first time."

"An undertaking like that requires planning, and two people may be required to work on the pyramid," interjected Rhodes.

"You've already proven you're not afraid of heights, so it's merely a matter of getting used to working on the angled slant of the pyramid. I can rig up a network of tethers to serve as our lifeline, and we'll devise hangers and clasps for making it a snap to change positions. The point is that once this platform is finished, it'll be much easier to explore the pyramid."

"What do you intend to use to assemble the skeletal structure of the platform?" Rhodes asked.

"Both this ship and the supply ship were designed for easy assembly, and the guts of our supply depot should disassemble fairly easily. Framing uprights consisting of two hollow, steel rods with metal zigzagging tie-ins connected by spot welds essentially act as supports to give the ship its body strength. By removing these uprights, we'll get two rods for every support taken out of the ship to create the leg framing, and as I've said, wall and floor panels are lightweight and durable to use as the platform's decking."

"The rods you'll procure from the ship may not provide enough material to assemble legs stretching from those stairs all the way around to the opening of the pyramid," argued Rhodes.

"That's true. As a last resort, we may have to get some materials from our ship, but the removal of an interior wall shouldn't compromise this ship's integrity."

"If you're all serious about this, you need to submit a plan of design, and we need to determine whether we have the materials available."

Rhodes then looked at Far. "Okay, what are your theories about this, and are you and the others willing to haul materials up the steep stairs of a pyramid?"

"I'm willing to do my fair share," Far replied. "Once Flavio rigs up a handrail, it'll make the climb safer and easier. However, I have some other projects I'd like to get off the ground as well. First, breaching the pyramid has prompted me to think about using a robotic, hi-tech, ground-penetrating radar instrument. It has its own computer brain, emitting electromagnetic pulse strikes as it scans a surface—in this case, the floor space of the chamber. These pulses bounce back to the machine's receiver while recording underground abnormalities on a disk, and I expect it may take the better part of a day for the instrument to cover the space inside that chamber.

"Something else mission planners want us to do is perform soil tests. They sent along a plant observatory we're supposed to build, and with a climate control unit we're to attempt to grow plant life. They were adamant in their desire to try to grow something in the soil. It's considered a very important experiment."

Flavio then asked, "So why didn't we start it sooner?"

"For the short amount of time we would've conducted those experiments, we wouldn't have seen any results, but since we're considering staying on here, these are viable tests that need to be done."

Aleksei commented assertively, "We'll never grow anything in that Martian soil. The land here is dead."

"I'm not so sure that's true. After we've initiated nitrogen and an assortment of additives into the soil to make it more fertile, with some tilling and nurturing, the results may be surprising. Of course, as I've said, to get any seedlings to take hold in the soil and sprout, we'll have to introduce climate change in the form of an observatory."

Aleksei raised his index finger. "As important as these tests are, we cannot waste a valuable resource like water on them. We'll trade off water used for the soil tests for raising the chances of our survival, and for time to investigate the pyramid's archeological importance. Stan, did you figure into your water-conservation equation the water needed for these soil tests?"

"I cut back on the water usage required for the soil tests, but eliminating those tests won't save a significant amount of water."

Aleksei concluded, "Whatever little amount of water it saves may make the difference between life and death for us, and I don't believe these soil tests are crucial for two reasons. Number one, scientists already know farming in this sterile, freeze-dried world is the same as trying to raise a crop on top of Mount Everest. Second, I've hatched an idea to make better use of the climate-control observatory: I propose that we use the climate-control device to control the climate inside the pyramid."

"Wait," began Far, an amazed expression on her face, "can that be done?"

Rhodes responded, "We can try it, and provided it works it's an absolutely brilliant idea. We'll have to expand on the concept by making some modifications, but it is possible that we can make the pyramid's interior a closed ecosystem. We'll have to set up a generator at the mouth of the pyramid for electricity and arrange some kind of ventilation system to circulate the air."

Far commented, "If this concept has any chance of working, I think we ought to give it consideration. It'll mean working without our suits when we're in the pyramid. The climate-control unit can convert carbon dioxide into oxygen, but it's a very slow process. One thing in our favor is that the unit requires little maintenance: simple servicing and a periodic filter change. The plant observatory would've had heat ducts running from the ship to bring up the observatory's temperature, so we'll just have to wear the appropriate clothing to combat the cold."

Aleksei gave a nod. "Now you're getting the picture."

Then Rhodes said, "Yes, barring any unforeseen circumstances, it can be done. We'll have to set up safety devices to monitor air quality, and we have plenty of those. We can rig solar panels designed to help provide power for the climate-control unit for an additional source of energy. The generator has a power cell to store energy in case it runs out of petrol, and those solar panels will extend the power cell's ability to store energy. The pyramid's angled slope is ideal for catching the sun's rays, and we can hang the panels above the entrance where they won't take up space." Rhodes paused before adding, "I've yet to check the manifest for straitjackets, for the construction of this platform will be an appallingly dangerous and ambitious undertaking—in a word, crazy. I'm not comfortable with the risks involved, as the dangers we're facing in order to survive this trip are already bad enough."

Flavio then added, "There will be a handrail on both the stairs and the platform to give us added support, but we'll have to be careful. Never try to carry a load heavier than you can handle. We're a capable crew, and I for one feel confident we can achieve this goal. We have the will and determination to make this project work. Surely if these Martians can build a gigantic, five-sided pyramid, we can erect a simple platform."

Jetha said, "It's stimulating to talk of such things. Mission planners had no idea we'd find such great discoveries here." Her bright eyes showed that her mind was sparking with great expectations. "Pumping oxygen into the pyramid so we can work without our suits is a fantastic idea. We may find the remains of a Martian ruler and an unimaginable wealth of artifacts from the time of his reign that will give us insight into his world and life."

"Something I've forgotten to mention," remarked Far, "is that we have water pellets that should help us combat dehydration as we ration water. The supply may last two months, more than enough time for us to erect the platform."

Aleksei addressed his crew mates. "Our water supply is going to be critical. If we stay on and the water runs out, we cannot place any blame on our captain. He's done everything possible to convince us of the dangers. With that aside, we have something spectacular to investigate at this site. Exploring the pyramid and the Cydonia Complex will make our mission pass by quickly, and I'm not altogether certain landing at this site was an accident, but we may never know the truth."

Rhodes stood before his crew and said, "I'm going to hold off committing to a long-term stay for forty-eight hours. In the meantime, I suggest you work on those plans. If just one of you comes to me and agrees with me that what we're doing is too dangerous, we're launching to return home. You're all so bound and determined to raid that pyramid, but you're going to be damn sorry if we run out of water later. In the event that we choose to stay on Mars, we'll have to overcome whatever unforeseen challenges we're faced with one at a time."

The next day, after a brief consultation with Rhodes, Flavio returned to the pyramid to extract the valuable white-blue diamonds from the bust. There was no question the stones had tremendous value. He also brought the ground-penetrating radar device, or GPR, up to the chamber. A trio of spectators—Far, Jetha, and Aleksei—accompanied him, and Rhodes monitored Flavio's movements from the ship via the camera in his helmet.

After Flavio made his way up to the chamber, he flung a wadded spool of rope out for one end to drop down to the others, and they tied the rectangular shaped GPR to it. He began pulling it up the pyramid's face, and the heavy instrument rolled on large wheels across the limestone casing smoothly. When he got it up to the chamber, he followed Far's instructions to place it in a corner and then open a small door on its top to ensure the compact disk inside hadn't dislodged. He activated the unit, which caused its motorized drive train to crawl along a wall under its own power. Sensors adjusted its wheels to avoid stationary objects so it could cover the entire floor.

After leaving the GPR operating, he used the hammer and chisel he'd brought to chip around the mortared-in white-blue diamonds in the bust. Rhodes watched him work for a few minutes, then turned his attention elsewhere, not wanting to see the sculpture defaced. Flavio spent a lot of time chiseling the limestone to remove the diamonds, which he tucked inside the zippered pockets in his pants legs. Upon the crew's return to the ship, he bought them out for all to admire, and then Rhodes put them away in storage for safekeeping. The crew wondered what else they'd discover inside the pyramid.

CHAPTER 13

Work Commences

The size of the white-blue diamonds captured their imagination, and the idea of finding more treasures made them all the more eager to return to the monument. Flavio went back to the pyramid to retrieve the disk from the GPR with Aleksei and Jetha, and the two waited at its base as he went up to enter the chamber. Far and Rhodes watched on a monitor as he found the mechanical device in the corner opposite its original position, and they saw signs it had disturbed the flaking, aqua-blue paint on the floor.

Returning to the ship, Flavio gave Far the disk. When she inserted it into her computer, an outline of the chamber popped up on her monitor. The floor space of the chamber appeared in gray with the outer perimeter black, and the bases of the two statues were white. Centered before the larger statue was a highlighted oblong track in a deep shade of pink, and this track ran parallel to the statue but was shorter than its base. A second, narrower track, shown in a paler shade of pink, connected at the end of the first one and extended to the southwest, skirting the bust on the right as it ran to the wall behind it.

Rhodes studied the outlines, estimating the darker pink track to be less than two meters wide and roughly six meters long. He also guessed the narrower extension of pale pink to have more depth as it ran beneath the wall.

Far glimpsed the expressions on the others' faces and then looked at Rhodes, and asked, "What do you make of it?"

Rhodes raised his eyebrows. "They must be tunnels, and perhaps the paler of the two drops in elevation, but it's going to take some excavating to learn the true meaning of these highlighted images. My suggestion is that we let it go for now and begin acquiring the materials we need to erect the framework for the platform. That's if Flavio is still determined to go through with it."

Flavio responded by going to a storage room to gather tools and equipment to dismantle the guts of the storage depot. The others assisted him. It was going to take a lot of work, and everyone seemed to be for it, but Rhodes was still concerned about their water supply. He sent a transmission to Earth explaining their plans to stay on for the full term of the mission, knowing this decision had to be causing calamity back home. Exploring the pyramid made him wonder what fate had in store for him and his crew, but these discoveries must have stirred the curiosity of the planners, who were probably hoping they'd stay the course.

In the upcoming days, the team dove into dismantling the inner walls of the wrecked ship. A generator was set up to provide electrical power, the same generator they intended to use to provide electricity to the pyramid after the platform was finished. They found the work to be more complicated than they first expected, partly because creating space to work in the supply depot wasn't easy. There were many more water canisters and a horde of food rations that they'd either have to transport to their home ship or resituate to make room for tear-out work. At the end of each day, they had to find room for the supplies they'd brought to their ship and stacked up in the cargo bay.

The rover proved to be a valuable asset, and it didn't take long to learn they could save time by taking a different route to reach the steps of the pyramid to make deliveries. By driving southwest along the ancient shoreline to enter the Cydonia Complex, they were able to drive around the pyramid and directly up to the staircase.

After they removed wall panels they intended to use for the platform's decking, they then started on the wall's skeletal framework. These framing stud supports consisted of two hollow, metal rods with metal, zigzagging tie-ins connecting them. The rods would serve as the primary assembly pieces for the platform's framing legs. They went on to remove floor panels whenever possible to use as additional decking for the platform.

Screws used to install these panels were recessed and capped with a plug that sat flush with the outer surface. Among other fasteners, they acquired a plentiful supply of screws with a seventeen-millimeter hex head. They intended to use this common screw fastener to attach the legs of the platform to the pyramid.

Flavio drilled to anchor upright posts on the stairs, connecting them with a nylon rope that ran from the pyramid's apex to create a secure handrail. They had planned to begin building the platform on the southeast half of the pyramid. However, to stay level with the chamber's entrance, they first had to go to the pyramid's opening to determine a starting point. Rhodes and Flavio discovered that the ancient stones making the monument's casing fit together precisely, and more importantly, the straight mortar joints were level and true. Making their way over to the chamber's opening, they targeted a horizontal joint line lower than the base of the eye that ran completely around the pyramid and chose this line as the height of the decking. The sloping, contoured area outside the entrance didn't have much immediate pitch, and the line they'd chosen left some of the stones outside the entrance exposed.

Flavio began striking the chosen mortar joint with a chalky stone, tracing it all the way back to the stairs to give them a guide for which joint to follow. The next step was to drill a series of level holes to anchor the platform's framework. They measured to set the holes at half-meter intervals eight centimeters below the chalked joint line. After drilling the first series of holes, they followed up with a second row running parallel to and vertically level with the first, one and a half meters below the first row of holes. They attached a level to a template patterned to the first leg frame assembly to create a reliable tracing tool, ensuring the distance between the holes was exact.

The first leg frame Aleksei assembled served as the prototype. Aleksei had mentioned that he had gained experience working with sheet metal in his youth, and it showed in his metal-working abilities. He turned the supply depot into a workshop, and they'd formed an assembly line under his supervision to cut, fit, and weld pieces together. Making the leg assemblies out of the storage depot's framing supports wasn't difficult for him, and he was careful to maintain quality control while manufacturing many of them. Because of the precise measuring techniques they adhered to, they were confident that the holes set in the leg frames would align with those drilled in the pyramid. Removing the framing supports from the walls of the supply depot weakened its shell, and on one occasion, it creaked and swayed under a gust of wind but remained standing.

The finished framing legs were lightweight and triangular; when seen from the side, each leg consisted of three bars welded together. The top bar was the shortest and would support the platform decking horizontally. A second bar anchored to the pyramid's slanted stone casing. Set on an angle, it was the longest piece and the base of the leg frame. The third bar tied the other two together and was the outside vertical support bar to hold the top bar that supported the deck level.

Ready to start attaching the leg frames to the pyramid's casing, they inserted plastic sleeves made from tubing into the holes they'd drilled in the stone. The idea was that when a screw was affixed, the plastic sleeve would expand as it compressed to provide a firmly seated hold that would resist loosening and absorb shock. When they installed the first leg assembly off the stairs, they anchored the top screw first, and the lower screw fell into perfect alignment with the hole in the limestone. Rhodes kept a socket wrench in the pouch of his pants leg, using it to tighten the screws and applying ratcheted pressure until the screws' hex heads seated snugly. The installation went swiftly as the leg frames fell into place, one after another, and the prototype had made for a near-perfect match every time.

Rhodes made sure he always had tension on the rope attached to his waist, and he usually knelt on the slanted facing, looking up at the pyramid's peak. Once the first course of leg frames running from the stairs to the pyramid's first angled corner was completed, they appeared shaky and unstable by themselves. But the tie-ins reinforced them, giving the legs stability and strength to support a substantial amount of weight. The decking installed on this first run made the framework sturdier yet, and they assembled this platform with high expectations and enthusiasm.

Aleksei made his first climb to the platform, and the height didn't seem to bother him. He met Flavio and Rhodes at the first corner to trade ideas to pattern framework so they could proceed. He attentively showed them how to make modifications at the corner so they'd understand how to join with the next run of assembly legs.

Everyone had a hand in erecting the platform, but Rhodes made the best use of Aleksei's expertise by having him manufacture the platform's leg supports. At one point, Aleksei expressed having little desire to climb about on the monument, and Rhodes thought the Russian may have a fear of heights. Far and Jetha did not fare well working at great heights on the slant of the pyramid either, and were reluctant to do so for any lengthy period of time. The three made countless trips up the pyramid's staircase carrying the lightweight leg assemblies and stacking the pieces along the newly installed walkway to one side which served to keep Rhodes and Flavio busy installing them. Unified in their purpose, they remained persistent in their drive to accomplish this feat. There were times Rhodes wasn't sure if his crew was up to such an immense undertaking, but they made steady progress, and the assembly came together as a strong, sturdy piece of engineering. There were moments when nothing but stubborn determination kept them going. For Rhodes, and perhaps some of the others, Flavio's words were a driving inspiration: "If the Martians could meet the challenge of building this colossal, five-sided pyramid, then we should be capable of erecting this platform."

After they installed the last course of framework to reach the pyramid's opening, the decking fell into place like a breeze, and seeing this encouraged them to continue to completion. The walkway was about one and a half meters wide, but they extended the framework at the mouth of the pyramid almost double that. They set up vertical posts to complete supports to attach a steel cable placed under tension to act as their finished handrail.

As the walkway neared completion, crew members would briefly enter the chamber to feast their eyes on the statues. Jetha photographed the Martian dialect etched on the walls, and when she turned the photographs into negatives, she found the lettering was more pronounced and easier to identify. This technique speeded up the transference, and when the symbols were fed into the computer, it recognized and digested them. However, she knew it may be weeks before the computer chucked out something in the form of a translation.

In the meantime, they carried up additional electrical equipment, including the climate control unit. They also lugged up an electric generator that contained a power cell that stored energy for up to forty-eight hours after the generator stopped working. They'd torn out anything from the supply depot that could prove useful, scrounging up plastic pipe and electrical wiring. They found a case of hose sections in the storage depot, a lightweight, slinky, corrugated plastic pipe that compressed lengthwise for easy transport. These lengths of hose snapped together at the ends, and they intended using heavy-duty tape to attach one kind of pipe to another when needed.

Aleksei framed a wall at the pyramid's opening, fitting an entrance door that was formerly an electrical equipment compartment door. He left sufficient space on one side to set up the climate control unit, constructing a large shelf to support the generator above it.

They brought up three large solar panels that were originally supposed to help power the plant observatory's climate control unit but would now provide a boost to the generator's energy storage cell. Flavio practiced his acrobatic skills, hanging the solar panels above the pyramid's entrance, using nylon rope to raise and support the solar panels from the pyramid's apex before securing them level on the stone facing. Aleksei had welded together a ladder out of an assortment of leftover rods and used it to assist Flavio. The panels hung evenly above the entrance, and they dramatically transformed the ancient pyramid's appearance, making it look futuristic.

Far and Jetha helped Rhodes finish the duct work for the climate control unit, but when they switched on the unit, strong airflow created pressure, forcing air to escape from the chamber entrance when it was open. To counterbalance this pressure, they needed to create a compartment inside the pyramid. In a small way, this air pocket would perform as a decompression chamber to allow pressure to subside, requiring a door that would remain closed when the exterior door was open. This compartment didn't require much strength to stem airflow, and they threw together a flimsy skeletal structure formerly designated for the plant observatory. They used a roll of tough, plastic sheeting to encapsulate the enclosure, and even the door was a loosely made framework reinforced with this plastic, but it worked satisfactorily.

The climate control unit now drew carbon dioxide through an intake and converted it into breathable air, and they had devices to monitor the chemical composition of the air. These devices gauged oxygen levels and gave a warning if harmful gases seeped into the pyramid. They also read moisture levels in the air. A working generator meant they had electrical power, and they assembled three, tall post lamps to provide lighting inside the chamber. The post lamps were like trees of lights with adjustable fixtures, and Far and Jetha pointed some of them at the statues, stopping to gape at the awesome, reptilian beast.

Almost from the very moment they saw this alluring pyramid, they were infatuated with its existence. They shared in the success of building the platform, and as work on the pyramid consumed their time, they felt as though they were giving this monument life.

When the ship's devices read high doses of radiation entering the atmosphere from outer space, they took a break from their work and caught up on much-needed rest. They had many months ahead to investigate the megalithic structure. When radiation levels ran high, Rhodes made as few trips as possible to the pyramid to fuel up the generator and get it running again, but for now, work at the pyramid site came to a standstill.

CHAPTER 14

A Pathway Long Since Closed

Stretched to the limit rationing water and with the days of radiation subsiding, they'd made two short excursions outside to resume drilling for water in the Martian soil. These efforts yielded no success, and they were anxious to move ahead with the next phase of investigating the pyramid. Those highlighted, oblong images indicated by the GPR were on everyone's mind, and they had yet to make a thorough examination of the floor space in the chamber.

The team suited up and went to the pyramid, where they found the generator humming and the quiet climate control unit operating perfectly. They filled the generator's tank with petrol. Rhodes entered the pyramid and waited for the others to enter before closing the outer door, and after the atmospheric pressure balanced out, he opened the flimsy compartment door to enter the chamber. They switched off their helmet lights as the post lamps' lights put out sufficient light.

Rhodes read a digital device on the wall that registered atmospheric conditions and said, "Oxygen levels haven't changed much, and I have my doubts about succeeding in this climate control experiment. Once atmospheric readings show the air is breathable, the system must maintain those conditions for a reasonable amount of time before we won't need to wear our suits. We're in search of a way to explore deeper into the pyramid, and should we discover newfound territory, the placement of oxygen is going to change, as levels are certain to drop as the volume of airspace changes. If and when we do shed our suits, for safety's sake, we must keep them readily available. Your life may depend on your being able to get into your suit at a moment's notice."

The bust looked far different without the glittering diamonds. Its dark, gouged-out eye sockets gave it a gruesome appearance. The other statue drew Rhodes, Far, and Flavio toward it. As much as it showed the Martian ruler to have courage, the depiction of the manlike Martian trying to slay such a huge beast with only a spear didn't quite sit right with Rhodes. Studying the creature's jaws and teeth, he thought it didn't seem possible that an individual could kill a menacing monster of this size with just this one weapon.

Jetha joined them, remarking, "I hope that when this historical record is deciphered, it tells us about the action portrayed in this statue."

Meanwhile, Aleksei had been closely studying the face of the bust. He called out, "Hey, everyone, I see something about the features of this Martian ruler that tells me something about him." Lured to the bust to learn what Aleksei was referring to, the group watched as he pointed to the individual's cheeks as though bringing their attention to the ruler's smile. "I've been looking at his wide grin, and I believe these deep depressions or dimples in his cheeks represent gill slits he breathed through. This was not an oxygen-rich atmosphere like we have on Earth, and more than likely this Martian breathed carbon dioxide just like we do oxygen. This is merely an observation, of course, as the composition of Mars' atmosphere was probably different in his time than it is today."

Rhodes gazed at the creases in the Martian ruler's face and then went over to the second statue. "Those creases are a prominent feature on this statue too, so it is a possibility that they are gills he breathed through. Then again, they may just be creases."

Jetha went back to examine the beast's brawny chest and shoulders. "Is this an enormous lizard, or would you call it a dinosaur?"

Far replied, "I believe lizards and dinosaurs fall under the classification of reptiles and are alike in that they both have scales. The head and long, serrated teeth of this enormous lizard remind me of a downsized *Tyrannosaurus rex* with canines, and there's no doubt it was a bloodthirsty creature. It has the proportions of a predatory dinosaur with long, powerful front legs, but it also reminds me somewhat of the Komodo dragon. Before nineteen twelve, giant lizards were long since thought to be extinct, but reports of an enormous prehistoric creature drew expeditions to the island of Komodo in Indonesia. The Komodo dragon was a startling discovery: a ten-foot-long lizard capable of killing water buffalo."

Flavio asked, "I've often wondered if they attack people."

"Attacks on people are rare, but prowling Komodo dragons are a threat, and although they prefer wild boar or deer, they'll devour almost anything they come across, including humans and other dragons. Most prey die from a single bite, but if they don't die instantly, the dragons have venomous bacteria in their saliva that can kill a wounded animal quickly. The thick skin of a Komodo dragon is like a suit of armor, and its huge jaws allow it to swallow large chunks of meat. They usually ambush their prey, using a sharp sense of smell. They actually smell through their slithering tongue, which enables them to detect prey up to several kilometers away. They are usually slow moving but can be incredibly fast for short sprints, able to scramble up a hill as fast as a man can run on a level path."

Jetha remarked, "This monster is immense. Just look at those teeth and brawny claws."

"Fossil discoveries have determined that the Komodo dragon once had a much larger cousin, *Megalania prisca,* meaning 'ancient giant butcher,'" replied Far. "Its size may have been more proportional to this creature's, as with its elongated tail, it may have been as long as thirty feet and weighed an estimated sixteen hundred pounds. It's said to be the largest lizard to ever walk the earth. Some Nineteen thousand years ago, it disappeared, but it lived at a time when humans were present and it was undoubtedly a man-eater. Aboriginal cave paintings less than ten thousand years old have depicted them. In modern times, according to eyewitness accounts, people have claimed to have seen these giant creatures along the isolated Australian outback. One may not consider it to be such a preposterous claim when you think how the crocodilian family survived the extinction of the dinosaurs, and ancient ancestors of the crocodile grew to over fifteen yards in length."

Rhodes knelt in front of the statue to search for any signs of the oblong track the GPR had detected there. The aqua-blue paint on the floor made it difficult to see anything, but much of the paint was peeling. Brushing away loose paint with his gloves, he found indentations in the floor, and further examination enabled him to see three large, square slabs. Each slab was approximately two meters square, and their combined length formed the deeper pink track in the GPR diagram.

Rhodes spotted four evenly spaced circular plugs in the surface of one stone recessed with great precision to make them difficult to locate, and then he noticed the other two slabs had four plugs inset in the same manner. He grabbed a short, metal rod lying on the floor in a corner and began scraping around the plugs to discover their purpose. One of them moved slightly so he kept digging around it until it loosened enough for him to pluck it free from the massive stone.

The plug was a funnel-shaped stone that must have taken a stonecutter much time and effort to make it fit perfectly in the slab. Seeing an open hole at the bottom of the cavity, he jabbed his gloved index finger into it and pulled it back out.

"Let's dig out the rest of these plugs," he announced and then turned to Far. "Among provisions in the supply depot is a large box containing a lift-hoist that can raise these stones, and I want you, Flavio, and Aleksei to bring it here in the rover. The pieces to assemble it are an interlocking plate steel in square, hollow tubes consisting of legs and cross-member pieces that can adjust to take on all kinds of dimensions and shapes."

"Yes, I'm familiar with that lift equipment."

"Be sure to bring all the accessories—there's a motorized compressor that comes with it, and wheels, chains, cables, and steel pins that I expect we'll need."

Far nodded, "The GPR proved surprisingly accurate in marking this spot."

Jetha and Rhodes stayed behind to chisel out the plugs in the three stones. Some were stubborn, but they had them all out in less than an hour. They then went to wait at the bottom of the stairs to meet the others and haul up pieces of the lift-hoist assembly to the chamber. They interlocked a good many pieces to form two cross-members that were long enough to straddle the first slab nearest the entrance, and the bottoms of four supporting upright legs were fitted with wheels.

There were various methods for the hoist to lift an object, and they were going to use a hydraulic system to raise the extendible legs to remove the heavy stone using four cables dangling from cross-members. They attached a motor to charge up its compressor to hold a high percentage of air pressure, and the upright legs would extend upward through a system of sleeves as they increased pressure by turning a valve. To make the lengths of these four cables comparable, they either wrapped these cables around the cross-members or unwrapped them the same way for adjusting their lengths individually. They left them long to feed the pins at the ends of the cables through the funnel-shaped holes of the stone nearest the entrance. After the pins passed through the holes, the pins relaxed and became horizontal in preparation for catching the stone's underside when the hoist began lifting the cables.

Releasing pressure in the lift's hydraulic system caused the legs to slowly extend vertically to draw tension on the cables. The pins caught hold of the stone's underside, causing the cables to stiffen as the weight they carried increased, and the lift's wheeled framework shifted as it centered over the oblong stone. The crew heard the stone grinding against others as it rose from its seated position in the floor as the lift raised the twenty-five-centimeter thick stone.

With the stone hanging above the floor, Rhodes unplugged the compressor and they worked together to roll the lift away from the hole by pushing and pulling it by its legs. The stone swung like a pendulum as they moved the lift ever so slowly away from the opening to the wall opposite the larger statue. Before they released pressure from the system to lower the stone, they stacked scrap pieces of leftover panels under the stone to keep it elevated so they could remove the pins.

They returned to gather around a dark pit running toward the wall with the sunburst on it, an opening that had been sealed for millennia. The pit looked to be four meters deep and contained a recessed ledge that had supported the stone they'd just moved. They saw a grouping of spears at the bottom made of the same rust-colored metal as the statue of the giant lizard that would prove lethal if someone were to fall and become impaled on them.

Gazing at the collection of spears, Rhodes said, "The GPR indicated a second faint track leading southwest from the end of this pit to the wall with the sunburst etched into it. That track may be a hidden passageway leading to the innermost sanctums of this pyramid, and just like we're seeing spearheads awaiting us here, there might be other booby traps. They designed this shrine to thwart thieves who'd come to plunder it, and we're the thieves they intended to stop."

Aleksei eyed the spears below and said, "If one of those spearheads tears through your suit, it poses a risk to your survival. Also, the spears may have been dipped in a lethal poison."

They proceeded to remove the other two stones using the lift, placing the second slab alongside the first and stacking the third to straddle them. They moved the post lamps closer to the edge to rope the area off, and the lights showered an oblong pit similar to the highlighted dimensions indicated by the GPR.

Rhodes took a position at the northeast end of the pit. "Aleksei, how about that ladder you used to help Flavio hang those solar panels?" Aleksei had left the ladder lying horizontally against a wall, and Rhodes gave him a hand sliding it down into the pit from the northeast side. They lowered it until the base of the ladder knocked down some of the spears, and then they let the ladder lean on an angle at the edge of the pit.

Flavio descended the ladder, using his outstretched boot to knock over spears. The ends of the spears were set in a bed of mortar and had deteriorated to such a degree that it took little pressure to make them fall. Once they were all down, Flavio moved them aside, and the others moved the lift to straddle the opening once again, locking its legs to arrange a hanging basket made of crumpled sheet metal. They lowered the basket for him to stack the spears on, and then they raised it from the pit. It took several loads to empty the pit.

Flavio now inspected the wall at the pit's southwest end. "All I see here are large stones in a staggered pattern—nothing to indicate an opening—but this is where GPR showed the start of that next track. Send down a sledgehammer and a crowbar and I'll start hacking into this wall."

Aleksei came down the ladder partway to hand Flavio a crowbar and a sledgehammer, which Flavio used to hit the wall a few times to loosen stones before using the crowbar to pry the stones from the wall. Driving the crowbar from different angles caused a stone to move outward, and it fell to the floor, spilling sand and dry mortar into the pit in a dust cloud. He pulled and tugged on other stones, sliding them one way and then the other to free them, and tossed them to the floor behind him.

Waving his hand to clear the air of a dust cloud, Flavio straddled the hole he'd made to peer inside, seeing nothing but sheer black on the other side. He resumed the task of removing more stones, letting them hit the floor with a pounding thud to form another dust cloud, and then he took another long look inside.

"Stan, there is definitely a corridor here, a passageway descending at maybe seven degrees that's plenty wide enough for people to walk through, and I can see a turn not too far off."

Rhodes looked at Far and Jetha. "Are we all going down in the passageway today, or would you rather wait until tomorrow and start fresh?"

Far looked at Jetha. "Do you want to go down there now or wait?"

Jetha shook her head no. "I can wait until tomorrow."

Far then looked at Rhodes. "Jetha and I are going to wait, but anyone entering that passage ought to switch on his camera."

Taking Far's advice, Rhodes immediately switched on his camera, and then he turned to Aleksei. "How about you?"

Aleksei grinned and replied, "I see no need to go down there just now. I can wait."

Flavio kept removing stones to form an opening in the shape of a wide doorway leading to a corridor squared off with large, stone slabs making up the ceiling, walls, and floor. Stacking the stones to one side in the pit, he stopped to look up at Rhodes. "So just you and I are going to comprise the first expedition, Stan."

Rhodes climbed down the ladder to join Flavio. "If you're that anxious to go exploring, I'll let you lead the way."

"I have no problem taking the lead," Flavio announced, picking up the crowbar. "I don't anticipate running into any Martians, but I feel more comfortable with a weapon in my hands."

Flavio led the way into the passageway, which had plenty of clearance to maneuver through.

The lights from their helmets illuminated the walkway, and following it as it turned to the left, they heard Far say, "Keep talking, and describe what you're seeing."

"There's not much to tell," replied Rhodes. "It's an enclosure of stone with a downward slanting pitch and a series of left turns, and as we descend, the pathway seems to get longer. It's as though as we drop deeper into the monument, the passageway runs longer with how the pyramid widens dimensionally near its base."

The grimly forbidden nocturnal world left Rhodes wary of what lay beyond, making him feel insignificant. He felt as if the souls of high priests had arisen to hum a ritual chant on behalf of their king. They finally came to a place where the slant of the passageway became more subtle and saw a fork where they had to decide whether to keep going straight or turn right.

"We've come to a junction where we can turn right or keep going straight, and I'm following Flavio as he turns right. Either way, these extensions of the passageway expand in width and height. If we'd gone straight, it appears the passage resumes a downward slope, whereby the pathway we've taken is level."

They soon came to mammoth stones blocking the way, and Flavio said, "This must be the original entrance to the pyramid where that jutting structure is located at the base of the northeast face beneath the eye."

"I guess you heard what Flavio just said. Four colossal stones block the original entrance, and it's remarkable how they moved such massive stones in here. Anyway, we're turning around to return to the descending passageway."

Coming back to the junction, Rhodes saw a large, round stone set in the middle of the floor that had engraving etched into it. "Flavio, look at this."

They knelt down and brushed away the dust and an image began taking shape.

"We've stopped to examine a large granite floor stone to see what's carved in it. . . . It's the giant lizard. The reptilian beast is standing alone in a frontal stance, its head posed as though turned to one side and its broad chest and shoulders bulging."

Flavio asked, "Do you think they placed this stone here to frighten intruders?"

"I'm sure such a creature would've been a flesh-eating animal, but we'll understand more about the ruler and the significance of this creature once that text's deciphered."

They continued on a downward slope at a steeper grade than before, and they marveled at the precision used to form the labyrinth complex.

The limitations of their lights made it impossible to see far. Flavio stopped and asked Rhodes, "Should we keep going?"

"That's up to you. You're the leader of this expedition."

"Okay, let's go a little further."

Soon they encountered an angled turn to the left, and Jetha addressed Flavio, saying, "Flavio, we haven't heard much from you. Tell us what you're seeing."

"The passage has expanded to be roomier, but it's pretty much more of the same, a far-reaching walkway taking us deeper into the pyramid, and there are occasional turns. We're getting a creepy glimpse into the unknown, as all we see ahead is black infinity. It's as if we've entered the catacombs, and venturing deeper into the monument inspires a superstitious fear, giving me a feeling of abandonment and impending doom."

The passageway went on and on, but at one point the wide, subterranean passage changed from stone to cut rock tunneling through natural barriers. Flavio acknowledged this by saying, "We're seeing bare rock-cut excavation dug into the depths of the planet. Instead of the walls, floor, and ceiling being stone, it appears that workers cut through solid bedrock. We are no longer inside the monument but beneath it."

Far responded, "Don't you think you ought to stop now before you've gone too far?"

"Flavio," began Rhodes, "maybe we shouldn't go any further. This passageway may go on indefinitely, and I don't like being cut off from the others."

"Okay, then, let's head back. I wasn't expecting to go this far, but I wanted you to be the one to halt the search."

When returning to the upper chamber, Rhodes checked the oxygen readings, and as expected, the oxygen level had dropped substantially since oxygen was now seeping into the passageway. Not knowing how far the descending corridors ran, he believed it was impossible for the climate control unit to condition so much space. Before ending their day, he draped a sheet of plastic over the labyrinth's entrance to impede the loss of oxygen.

Upon returning to the home ship, Rhodes sent a transmission updating their progress and expressing how awesome an experience it was to enter the labyrinth. His crew members were thrilled about the idea of exploring the depths of the pyramid, as they hoped their quest would lead them to the Martian king. However, exploring the cavernous passageway left Rhodes concerned about his crew's well-being, as he was responsible for their safety. Inasmuch as he was getting a charge out of searching for archeological evidence of a Martian culture, he also knew they were evoking dangers contained within the pyramid.

CHAPTER 15

Descending into the Depths of a Dark World

They'd been on Mars almost six weeks now, and except for being concerned about their water supply, Rhodes was looking forward to further exploration of the pyramid. His speeches about dying from a lack of water were sinking in, as they'd made progress in water conservation—they now only took sponge baths—and this was encouraging. They had reduced their water consumption to less than three gallons per person per day, which was about the minimum amount of water that could sustain a human for any extended period of time.

The next morning at breakfast the team talked about how oxygen levels in the chamber had dropped after they had opened the labyrinth, and they hoped that by now oxygen levels would have rebounded. They discussed installing a door at the labyrinth, since isolating the upper chamber would give them a place they could escape to in an emergency where there'd be a survivable air pocket.

Another topic of conversation brought up was how the lighting in their helmets, though sufficient for close work, faded in the long tunnel. Needing as much light as possible in these unexplored areas prompted Far to locate a powerful searchlight that conveniently plugged into their suits, and she had it with her when they left the ship.

It wasn't long before they were huddled in the upper chamber of the pyramid. Oxygen levels had rebounded some, but they were still short of breathable levels. Ready to descend the ladder to explore the labyrinth, they gathered at the edge of the pit. The camera in Far's helmet would record every aspect of the adventure, and the searchlight she carried sent out a powerful beam to show the way ahead. Sharing a feeling they were about to embark on what may be a dangerous expedition, they went down the ladder one at a time. Flavio carried the crowbar, while Aleksei and Rhodes carried spears shoulder high.

Carrying a length of rope, Rhodes gave one last word of warning. "Before we enter the labyrinth, I want you to keep in mind that the beings who built this pyramid showed intelligence in its design. They constructed it with the idea of stopping looters, and I've mentioned that there may be booby traps, so you're all aware of the risks inherent in entering the labyrinth. As a precautionary measure, I'm going to tie us together, leaving about three meters of rope between us to give us all a little breathing space.

"Eventually I want to set up lights down here with closed-circuit television cameras to monitor goings-on inside the pyramid. Perhaps we'll be able to strategically arrange three or four cameras hooked up with motion sensors, and we'll have the ability to switch at will from one viewpoint to another from the ship. It's important to be able to see what's happening in certain areas so we can respond quickly in an emergency. A person can get seriously injured in any number of different ways, but like I've just said, this monument almost certainly contains booby traps designed to kill and maim. Having had my say, I wish us luck in finding the resting place of this Martian king, who I'm sure never would've imagined people from another planet invading his shrine. Flavio, you'll have the honor of leading the expedition, and I'll be behind you. Far is next, then Jetha, and Alek will bring up the rear."

Rhodes tied the rope around their waists snuggly starting with Flavio, stretching his arms three times to measure enough rope to separate one person from the next. Then, one after another, they stepped inside the labyrinth to begin an excursion into the unknown. Rhodes knew they wouldn't be human unless they found this experience eerily disturbing.

Moving along in single file, they followed the slanting maze that Flavio and Rhodes explored the day before and soon came upon the junction. They followed the level passageway to show the others the impenetrable stones that sealed the entrance. Upon returning to the junction, Flavio directed their attention to the round, granite stone with the image of the giant lizard inscribed on its surface.

Flavio proceeded with caution down the descending passageway, which gave them space to walk three abreast. The rope that bound them together hadn't presented much of a problem. They made adjustments as needed when spreading out or stopping to huddle, sometimes carrying the slack that otherwise would drag and present a tripping hazard.

The stone enclosure soon turned to the rock-cut subsurface, and it seemed they'd entered a strange realm. Keeping a steady pace, they followed the passageway, perpetual darkness absorbing their projected lights. Before long they saw something tantalizing, a prelude to coming change. As Far steadied the searchlight, they could see a junction or antechamber up ahead, and they came to a hall consisting of four pillars carved from the same rock that made up the cavernous passageway. At the center of this pillared hall was a round stone in the floor nearly identical to the stone at the first junction, holding the same etched image of the giant lizard.

The passageway had come to a T, and they had to either turn left or right. In either direction, the pathway stayed level. Flavio turned left and led them to a wide-open chamber where they saw a mound of odd-shaped granules in a gritty, rustic-brown dust. The round room had a domed ceiling, but they couldn't go any further without climbing over the heap in their way.

Rhodes jabbed the granules with his spear, and a minor dust cloud formed when he pulled the spearhead out. "Does anybody have a clue what this stuff is?"

Alek forced his spear deep in the granules, moving the handle in a circular motion to churn the particles. He then looked up and said, "There's enough headroom that I can climb this mound. Do you want me to see what's on the other side?"

"That's okay with me, but I wish I knew what this junk is first," said Rhodes as he jabbed his spearhead into the granules once more, looking closely at the particles in an attempt to identify them. "It looks like a substance that's been here a long time. I don't think it presents any danger to walk on it, so if you want to climb it, go ahead, but be careful."

Rhodes untied the rope from Aleksei's waist to allow him to step forward. Far handed him the searchlight while plugging it into his power pack, and he held the light in his left hand and the spear in his right. As he began to climb the mound, his legs sank into the dune of dusty granules, and he stopped to retain a stable position. He kept moving in the same way, jabbing the spear into the debris as he made strides and stalling periodically to regain his balance. When he reached the top of the heap, he stood erect, holding the spear horizontally as he placed his gloved knuckles against the ceiling and shone the searchlight's beam all around to survey the room's circumference.

"The room is circular and there are no other doorways that I can see, but dead center in the ceiling is a circular opening," he reported. Moving to look up into this hole, he added, "I think I'm standing at the bottom of the airshaft that runs through the center of the pyramid. I can't say I see any light up above, but if you recall, the summit of the monument is blocked by the oxygen cylinder Flavio placed in it."

Rhodes glimpsed Flavio using the curled end of his crowbar to probe the mound of granules and saw him lift something free of the debris. When Rhodes saw the object, he said to Aleksei, "Okay, come on back carefully and watch your step."

Aleksei was barely able to remain upright as he started back, using his glove to graze the ceiling as a way to keep his balance. Rhodes extended the handle of his spear to catch hold of, and Aleksei came to stand on the level floor, noticing a Martian skull resting close by.

"I didn't want to mention what Flavio pulled out of the mound until you'd gotten back down."

Orange with a red hue, the skull looked somewhat human. Like the statues depicting the ruler, the specimen had a pronounced brow ridge, which must have been a characteristic of this race of beings. The skull and the teeth were larger than normal human size, and some of the teeth were crooked and chipped, but it didn't appear that any were missing.

Aleksei gave the skull a brief inspection. "This heap of rubble must be deteriorating bone fragments, which is evidence they used the shaft running down from the apex of the pyramid for sacrificial purposes. They may have believed that offering body parts nourished the spirit of their once-great king as a way to ensure regional domination. This skull is wider than an ordinary human skull, and I'm guessing the one who carried it on his neck and shoulders may have been a large male who, I suppose, was a defeated enemy of this empire."

Aleksei handed the searchlight to Far as Rhodes retied him to the rest of the group, and they moved on. No one realized it, but Aleksei had left his spear behind in the mound.

Rhodes looked at Flavio and said, "Use the curve of your crowbar to hook the eye of this skull to take it back to the ship."

Flavio hooked the skull through its eye socket and said jokingly, "I don't mind hooking up with a passenger."

Far and Jetha were quiet for a time. When they passed among the four pillars, they saw what appeared to be an open, intact funerary chamber at the far end of the junction. A strange calm befell them when they entered the chamber.

Everything in the room was white; rather, the walls, ceiling, and floor were simply raw limestone without any painted markings or inscriptions. At the room's center stood a waist-high, rose-colored block of stone with decorative carvings, and resting on top of it was what looked like a basket. Closer examination disclosed that the basket was actually a tilting chest made of some type of wood that had deteriorated over the course of time.

Rhodes sifted through scattered fragments lying near the chest to find ornamental decorations that once embellished its outer casing, discovering two large rubies and a collection of other gems in brilliant colors. As Far and Jetha started to collect the stones, he said, "Jetha, I'd like you to document all the stones and jewelry, and when we return to the ship they'll be placed in safekeeping." Jetha used the zippered pouch in her right pants leg to carry the stones.

Rhodes carefully removed the chest's lid, letting it rest next to the chest, and saw what may have once been a living thing cradled inside. He soon decided it was the remains of a fetus, presumably a son or daughter of the ruler for whom the shrine was built. The others gathered about, and their lights brightened the bottom of the chest to give the shriveled, mummified remains a closer examination.

Far expressed her maternal instinct, saying, "Aww, it's a baby, probably a prince or princess who died not long after birth and was perhaps an heir to the throne. The chest may crumple to dust the very second we disturb it, so we must handle it with great care and somehow stabilize it for the trip back to the ship."

"Hey, everyone," began Aleksei, motioning from the wide doorway of an adjacent cubicle. "Come and take a look at this. It looks like an offering room."

They walked over to survey a room smaller than the one they stood in. A winged idol was perched on a wide altar against a far wall facing them. It looked like a bat with the beak of an eagle, and it held its webbed wings spread wide as if making a landing. The floor was uneven and sunken. Aleksei moved toward the altar, saying, "Look, before that statue on the altar is a marble vase holding diamonds and sapphires."

There was a sudden crackling sound before the floor caved in beneath Aleksei and he vanished from sight, pulling Jetha toward the opening on the rope! Far dropped the searchlight as she and Rhodes braced themselves and hung on to the rope. Flavio, at the far end of the rope, had caught hold of the stone block supporting the Martian fetus, clutching its corner in an effort to stop Jetha from going over the edge.

Momentarily holding their positions, Rhodes asked, "Alek, are you all right?"

Aleksei's breathless voice came back. "Yes, but don't let me fall any further. There are more of those spears down here, and I don't want to get impaled."

"Okay, just hang on and we'll pull you back up."

They regrouped, joining together in a coordinated effort to pull Aleksei back up. Soon the top of his helmet appeared, and then one of his hands reached out to grasp hold of something to pull himself up, but the floor provided nothing to grip. They kept tugging until he emerged from the pit, shaken and out of breath, and they dragged him away from the edge of the pit before Far made certain his life-support system was still functioning.

The experience left him exhausted, and after taking a deep breath, he said, "I thought I was done for." He then turned to Rhodes. "I have to admit, I first thought the idea of tying us together was silly, but your simple safety technique is the only thing that saved my life."

Flavio crept on all fours to the edge of the pit and looked down. "It's just like the first pit in the upper chamber, a cluster of spearheads, ready to deliver death to anyone who falls in."

They understood how the labyrinth's builders had cleverly arranged the offering room to draw looters to the diamonds on the altar so they'd fall into the pit just as Aleksei had done. The idea of one of the crew nearly dying had left them all somber and shaken. Far moved to examine the searchlight she'd dropped and was relieved that it worked when she plugged it in. She said downheartedly, "I think we've had enough excitement for one day, and I might feel different tomorrow, but right now I say forget this place. Like you've said all along: Is finding the tomb of this Martian king worth dying for? Next time we may not be so lucky."

"What we're doing is dangerous," countered Flavio, "but we've faced risks from the very minute we launched from Earth. Don't tell me that after the many days we spent hanging off the facing of this pyramid building that platform that we're going to let this one incident destroy our ambitions." Flavio then pointed into the pit, "What we're after may be on the next level below. We can't stop now. Yes, the designers of this monument shook us up, but in the end we're going to find the king's burial chamber and the treasure trove it holds."

Rhodes then commented, "I know what we're doing is something of great importance, but my main goal is to get us all back home safely. When you're captain on a mission like this, the prospect of losing one of your crew members is a horrible thing to consider. You blame yourself, especially if it's something that happened needlessly, and here we are taking all these chances. I'll say this, though: Those Martians had a pretty clever way of luring us to that altar, and Aleksei was just one step away from buying himself a burial plot here on Mars. Well, let's pull ourselves together and head back to the ship. Tomorrow we'll start again."

Flavio then asked, "What do we do about the bowl of diamonds and gems on that altar?"

Rhodes replied, "I suggest we leave them where they are. Remember that when we return to Earth, we're going straight into a quarantined facility for an unspecified period to ensure that we're not carrying any Mars pathogens or viruses. Mission planners will use that opportunity to account for all articles we find. Everything is subject to inspection, and, technically, there are few things that belong to you personally. Anything we find here is the property of those nations that have contributed to the mission. You should all know that I'm not the type of person who likes his patience tried, and I hope I don't have to say this again."

The marble bowl full of diamonds and gems remained untouched on the altar, and they left the pyramid thinking they were tempting fate. Not only did they not find the tomb of the Martian ruler, but the pit that had almost swallowed Aleksei sent a strong message about the dangers they faced in exploring a uniquely designed pyramid.

Rhodes dwelled on the mission, thinking how Mars fell into oblivion as a result of asteroids pummeling its surface, and not until five space travelers from a neighboring planet came to explore it had there been any life here. He felt fortunate to be one of the visitors who'd found evidence of an ancient civilization, but after what had almost happened to Aleksei, he wasn't sure if he'd made the right decision about staying. That was all behind him now, though, as he was committed to staying for many months, but his first goal was to return home with the same number of people he left with.

CHAPTER 16

Lights, Camera, No Action

Late that same night, the sound of whimpering awoke Rhodes. Realizing Jetha was having a nightmare, he woke her from a deep sleep. She explained that she had dreamed of exploring the labyrinth when the floor suddenly caved in beneath her and she fell into a pit. As crew members tried frantically to pull her back up, the long fingers of Martians living beneath the floor tried to pull her down. The battle was lost, but she awoke before falling into the hands of the beings. The dream seemed real, as many do, and the experience of Aleksei falling into the pit may have triggered the episode. After a few minutes, she was all right and went back to sleep in her pod.

Rhodes half expected Flavio and Aleksei to make comic remarks about the incident, but there wasn't anything funny about it, and in the dead of night, no one saw fit to make a comment. Exploring the pyramid and adventuring into the unknown meant they were treading on thin ice, and no one mentioned her dream the following morning.

In the upcoming days, they carried more supplies to the upper chamber, including wiring, light sockets, bulbs, and a few more floor panels. Hanging a string of lights at intervals throughout the labyrinth dramatically lit up the passageways, and they also installed a light inside the funerary room where they'd discovered the fetus. They could now move around without needing their helmet lights, thereby conserving the energy powering their suits' life-support systems. They also installed various safety devices in the labyrinth to monitor atmospheric conditions, as these devices could sense a range of harmful gases that might seep into the pyramid.

Flavio climbed into the pit that nearly took Aleksei's life and knocked down the spears. However, this pit didn't have any passageways running off it, and no one could find the next hidden passage in any of the areas they'd already explored. Although they found no other tunnels in the pyramid, they knew there had to be a passageway leading to the Martian ruler's resting place.

Flavio and Aleksei transferred a portion of the debris in the domed room to the pit that Aleksei had fallen into, filling it by way of a useful handcart wagon. They'd begun this task partly to sift through the debris for more archeological evidence, and they found a few more skulls, which they later took back to the ship. They also found pieces of arm and leg bones. They packed the remains of Martians into the pit until it was almost as hard as concrete, but this did little to shrink the mound of rubble in the domed room. If the king's tomb was beneath the mountain of debris, it was safe for now, but it seemed unlikely a king would allow the remains of his enemies to rest on top of his tomb.

Far and Jetha went to the pyramid to retrieve the marble bowl containing precious stones and the wooden chest containing the Martian fetus. They slowly slid the crumbling wooden chest off the stone and onto a flat, rigid panel, which they then gently placed in a cardboard box. Finally, they tucked flimsy plastic around the chest to reduce the chances of damage during transport.

Wanting to determine the timeline for this ancient civilization, they took a chunk of wood from the chest, but reliable results required testing another article. They chose to pluck an already loosened tooth from one of the skulls they'd found. The tooth still had a root, which they thought might prove significant in determining the skull's age. After pulverizing the items, they let the ship's computer brain test them, though they didn't expect to receive results for some time.

Rhodes knew the climate control unit was capable of conditioning a space twice the size as the upper chamber, and he continued monitoring oxygen levels inside the room. Seeing that the oxygen level hovered at levels short of breathable air, he believed that either oxygen was seeping out or carbon dioxide was somehow seeping into the chamber. Talks resumed about installing a door at the bottom of the pit where the labyrinth began, but for now they had other priorities.

The crew placed four cameras with connecting lamps activated by motion sensors at various locations inside the pyramid to monitor operations. In the upper chamber, they aimed one at the statue of the giant lizard, and anyone going to and from the chamber had to pass by it. They attached the other camera to a post lamp to give an overview of the pit and the entrance to the labyrinth. The third camera was in the pillared hall, catching the movements of anyone coming down the passageway. The fourth motion detector was situated in the burial chamber on the stone that had supported the wooden chest containing the remains of the Martian baby. Far aimed the camera paired with it at the offering room to pick up the altar with the statue of a deity perched on it.

They had adequate lighting, but when their presence set off a motion sensor, a light connected to the camera would go on to provide additional lighting. All four cameras could record simultaneously, and the ship's computer hard drive would automatically record whatever activated the motion sensors. In addition, every time the cameras began recording, they'd set off a faint signal from Jetha's computer, so all day long these weak signals sounded as the crew journeyed throughout the pyramid triggering sensors. If someone were at the ship, however, he or she could hardly detect the faint signal, so it wouldn't be bothersome.

Days turned into weeks, and it struck Rhodes as odd that they were seeing swirling dust devils more frequently and in greater numbers. They'd seen them occasionally, but recently it seemed like they were their constant companions, strange visitors accompanying them on trips to the pyramid or to the ship. They'd spring up out of nowhere to surprise them and cut across their path, and one afternoon it seemed as though one was chasing them in the MRV. Some were kilometer-high cyclones that were a sight to behold, and they wondered why these curious, ghostly whirlwinds were springing up like never before.

They lost exploration time when outside radiation readings rose to dangerous levels, and it took a long time for this to subside. While radiation levels were high, the crew couldn't venture outside without the risk of receiving high doses of radiation, so they remained inside, documenting their findings. Examining the four Martian skulls, they compared their shape to that of primitive man's. One had a big hole in its forehead, a good indication of how the individual died. One cranium was pitted with holes, which Far claimed was the result of a nutritional deficiency, and one had a tooth abscess.

Cooped up for days inside the ship, they kept themselves occupied. Flavio and Rhodes went to the pyramid twice, but they weren't there for long and didn't enter the pyramid. They'd gone there strictly to refuel and restart the generator.

One evening, Aleksei approached Rhodes as he sat at his computer. "Stan, I'm often up late, and recently I've heard the cameras inside the pyramid activate. No one besides me is up any later than ten o'clock, and the last three nights at just before eleven o'clock I've heard the signal go off. The first couple of nights it happened I wasn't quite sure, but last night I heard the signal at precisely ten fifty-seven."

"That's very interesting. If you're right, then the camera should've recorded what set it off here on the computer's hard drive. Once activated, the camera will record for a minimum of three seconds, so let's see if it picked up anything eye-catching."

Rhodes brought up the network file to see what the cameras had recorded thus far. He split the monitor's picture into four quarters to show the viewing angle of each camera. They hadn't entered the pyramid during the past few days, and viewing the most recent recordings taken during the past seventy-two hours, they saw the date and time shown in the upper right-hand corner of each recording. They discovered still photos taken by the camera in the burial chamber. Far had aimed this camera into the offering room where the bat god was, but there was no activity shown in these recordings, and that was unusual.

When they randomly checked previous recordings, those showed someone passing by, which triggered the motion detector and camera to record. Some recordings were merely three to five seconds long, but those taken in the past seventy-two hours all ran for about one minute even though none showed any movement. The first was taken three days earlier at 10:56 p.m. The second recording was taken almost exactly twenty-four hours later at 10:59 p.m.

The last recording was taken at 10:57 p.m. the previous night.

Curiosity drew the rest of the crew members to band around Rhodes, and Jetha asked, "What's going on?"

"Over the past three nights," Aleksei began, "I've heard the motion detector sensors activating a camera to record. Each time it's happened it's been the camera in the burial chamber, but we haven't seen any action in those recordings."

Isolating the footage to take three quarters of the monitor, Rhodes left one quarter of the screen blank in the upper right-hand corner. The three shots were identical in every sense, showing the view of the offering room with the altar and statue. He was now able to bring up the present viewing angle of the offering room, where just one light was operating. When the motion sensors had activated a camera in the other three recordings, the additional light came on, so those photos were brighter.

Rhodes remarked, "For some inexplicable reason, this one motion detector is sensing movement to set off a camera and a light, and the lengths of these recordings are all more than a minute long. Something triggered that motion detector, which in turn touched off the camera to record nothing the naked eye can see."

Far listened to Rhodes' comments while studying the recordings on the monitor. "Could a crawling or flying insect have set it off?"

"We haven't encountered one living thing since landing here, and it would be outlandishly uncanny for an insect to have set off the motion detector at almost the exact same time for the past three nights. I'm more apt to think it's a glitch in the system. I don't know anything else it could be."

Jetha spoke up, saying, "You don't think . . ."

"C'mon, Jetha," began Far, "you're among friends here, so go ahead and finish what you were going to say."

"We were just throwing out ideas. Working in a funerary complex inside a pyramid that has burial chambers... You don't think that it's some sort of paranormal activity, do you?"

Flavio grinned. "Ghosts from Mars. I've been waiting for someone to say he's seen the spirit of a dead Martian." Then he shrugged. "It's as good an explanation as any, and even if it was a glitch somewhere in the system, what could account for it to have happened at the same time three nights in a row?"

Rhodes replied, "Well, one thing is sure: We'll be waiting to see if it happens again tonight, and if it does, it's definitely worth checking out."

Aleksei asked, "Are you thinking about staying inside the pyramid all night to investigate? All of this time we've been here, not once have we been outside this ship after dark."

"No, I'm not going to spend the night in the pyramid. I just have to stay there till after eleven o'clock. Let's just see what happens tonight, and if the motion detector doesn't set off the camera, then it was merely a glitch or a fluke, like I said, and there'll be nothing more to say about it."

Abe interrupted them, saying, "Far, the age of those items you sent through for testing has been determined."

"That's wonderful. What is their age?"

"Both items are nine hundred fifty thousand years old."

Rhodes squinted at the others. "Nine hundred fifty thousand? How can that be?"

Then Abe said, "To be most accurate, more tests have to be performed, but we do not have the means at our disposal to conduct those tests."

Aleksei said, "If that's true, then this Martian civilization was still here when man was at the dawn of his existence. It's as if at the moment of the Martians' demise, a new species with similar characteristics was forming on a neighboring planet. Their world must have ended in a terribly violent cataclysm when a shower of asteroids vaporized everything on the surface of Mars in a raging firestorm."

Far interrupted to say, "That timeline makes for intriguing supposition and conjecture, but we may never really know what brought about these Martians' extinction. It probably was a shower of asteroids that annihilated everything here. I agree with that in theory because the asteroid belt lies between Mars and Jupiter and there are craters all over the surface of Mars."

That same night, they gathered at 10:30 p.m. to see if the incident repeated itself, and as the time approached 11:00 p.m., everyone's eyes were on the monitor. At 10:59, the camera mysteriously switched on. They heard the signal and saw the light connected to the motion sensor go on. The recorded sequence lasted just over one minute—one minute and nine seconds, to be precise—and they reviewed the recording several times. Studying the footage of all four recordings, they watched them in slow motion and periodically checked them frame by frame, zooming in to carefully examine every detail. They saw no traces of life, nothing but the stationary objects in the room, yet the motion sensor had detected something moving in the deepest confines of the pyramid.

"This is awfully weird, Stan," said Far. "Maybe Jetha wasn't so far off when she said it could be paranormal activity."

"Well, I'm not saying it is or isn't something supernatural, but tomorrow night I'll be in that burial chamber before eleven o'clock to see what's causing this strange phenomenon, and it'll be interesting to see what happens." Rhodes shut down his computer and stood. "Very well, then. Tomorrow night we'll see what extraordinary presence is triggering the motion detector."

"Are all of us going?" asked Far.

"I haven't had time to consider taking company, but I don't think all of us need to make a trip to the pyramid for this."

Rhodes later thought it unwise to go down into the depths of the pyramid alone, but he wasn't certain whom he would ask to come along. Of course, while he was there he intended to top off the generator's fuel tank.

CHAPTER 17

Perplexing Events

The next evening at 6:00, Rhodes and Flavio, always eager for adventure, prepared to suit up to go to the pyramid. Before leaving, Far picked up high-pressure readings that could indicate a change in Mars' atmosphere, but when she checked the radar, there was nothing visible on the screen. Less than a half hour later, with less than two hours of sunlight left, the two started for the pyramid in the rover. Wind coming in from the northwest stirred up a smoky dust that crossed the land in foggy waves as it danced along the Martian surface.

Travel this late to the pyramid was unusual. They'd always returned to the home ship long before sundown, and Rhodes had never seen the sun angled so far southwest. A purplish-red sky portrayed a colorful dusk, and seeing two dust devils crossing their path, Flavio slowed down and steered clear of them.

The level of radiation outside was dropping daily, and it was possible they'd return to work on the pyramid the next day without risking exposure. Investigative progress at the pyramid had become stagnant because they hadn't found another hidden passageway leading to the ruler's tomb, but they believed a burial chamber of such existed, and it may contain a great treasure.

They learned the generator at the pyramid must have stopped working sometime during the night, but the climate control device was still functioning from power stored in its fuel cell. A look inside the pyramid told them the lights were still operating, and when they refueled and restarted the generator, the lights brightened. They entered through the air pocket enclosure to set off the first motion detector and a light. Oxygen levels inside the upper chamber were near a safe, breathable level. Rhodes thought it promising that the unit was holding these conditions while regulating air in such a broad space, and he was convinced a door at the labyrinth was the answer to sealing off the upper chamber.

The post lamps near the pit provided plenty of light to go down into the labyrinth. A string of electric lights along the passageway guided them. They set off another motion detector and light along the way, as well as the one in the pillared hall. Then they heard Far's voice through their helmets.

"Stan and Flavio, do you read me?"

"Yes, we're picking you up fine."

"I hope I don't lose you. Communication on this end sounds fuzzy and broken up. I've been watching changing weather conditions, and radar shows what looks like a huge, crescent-shaped wave coming in from the northwest that may be a major dust storm. I can't imagine what else this wave can be, and changes seem to be accelerating outside the ship as the wind is stirring up dust. To best determine what this disturbance is, I'd have to go outside to make an observation, but I thought I'd better check with you first . . . Do you read me?"

"I want you to stay put! Don't anyone leave the ship under any circumstances tonight. Do you read me?"

"Yes, I read you, and we'll stay put as advised. Considering you have about three hours to go before your eleven o'clock rendezvous, you might want to think about starting back now before conditions get too bad. Finding your way back after dark in a dust storm could present serious problems. . . . Do you read me?"

"Yes, we made it as far as the pillared hall, and we're leaving now, but it's going to take time for us to make it out of here and get back to the rover. We may be able to see something from the elevation of the platform once we're outside the pyramid. We'll let you know the minute we're out."

Moving at a brisk pace, they came out of the labyrinth to climb the ladder to the upper chamber when they heard Far's voice amid crackling static. "We just got hit by a dust cloud that turned visibility to zero. The outside world is black as night."

They stepped outside onto the platform to view a colossal wall of red dust coming their way. Rhodes had heard of such things occurring even on Mother Earth but had never seen anything quite like it. Knowing it was coming toward them at a fast clip, he said, "Yeah, we see it—a wall of dust a kilometer high. Just remember to stay put. Do you read me?"

"Yes, but unless the pyramid has breathable air inside, you won't have enough oxygen to get you through the night, and if this storm continues to gain strength, visibility may be just as bad tomorrow. It's my place to remind you that this dust storm could turn planet wide and obscure the surface of Mars for months, so get back here as fast as you can."

The wind kicked up dust around the pyramid as Rhodes said urgently, "Just stay put. Whatever happens, stay put!"

Communications went dead, and now Flavio and Rhodes raced along the platform to get down from the monument before the dust storm hit. Winds were brisk, and sunlight was dimming in the west as they quickly descended the stairs with Flavio in the lead, but as soon as they hit ground level, a swirling dust cloud engulfed them.

Visibility turned to zero as blinding dust pelted Rhodes' face shield, and he grabbed Flavio by the arm and said, "Forget the rover! We'll get lost driving in this pea soup and run into something."

They saw a bright flash as lightning struck the ground nearby!

"Lightning! What are we going to do?" asked Flavio.

"We have no choice but to return to the pyramid. It's our only way to escape the electrical field generated by this churning dust."

"I can't see the pyramid."

"Stay close to me. We'll find it."

Rhodes thought he'd have no problem finding a monument as big as a mountain, but the sandstorm smothered the landscape, making it nearly impossible to see where they were going. Switching on his helmet light didn't help, but he spotted their footprints and followed them, only to lose the prints in the blurring sand, leaving him confused about which way to go. Just as he caught sight of the stairs, lightning struck a second time, and this threat to their life-support systems worried him.

Moving speedily up the stairs, Rhodes gripped the rope handrail, and he slowed to glimpse Flavio hot on his heels, nearly ramming him from behind. Lightning kept striking all around, and pressing on until he reached the platform; he resisted grabbing hold of the steel cable used as a handrail. They followed the decking around the pyramid, and as they passed each corner, the wind's velocity worsened with a fury of swirling dust colliding in crosswinds. Just as they came to the pyramid's entrance, another bolt of lightning struck close by, and they ducked inside, Flavio slamming the outer door behind him. They breathlessly hit the floor of the upper chamber, and the plastic enclosure of the first compartment rustled from the wind. The first motion detector set off a camera and the light connected to it, but since there was a communications breakdown, no one back at the ship saw this.

"Wow, I thought that last bolt of lightning hit me," said Flavio, squatting on his knees and the toes of his boots. "That was a little too close."

Catching his breath while on his hands and knees, Rhodes said, "I hope the lightning will subside."

"Yeah, but this dust storm isn't likely to settle down for hours, possibly even months, and we don't have any air tanks at this site. We've got only enough air to last us till one o'clock in the morning. Seven hours is the longest we can rely on our oxygen to last, and we left the ship at about six o'clock."

Rhodes took a deep breath. "I know, but no matter how you look at it, we can't leave the pyramid just now. If we're lucky, the lightning will settle down during the next couple hours. Oxygen levels inside this shrine have been hovering around safe, breathable levels, and I'm guessing that if we don't exert ourselves, we may be able to shut off our suits' life-support systems to save our oxygen. That way if there's still lightning going on outside later, we'll have additional oxygen with our spacesuits' tanks in case we have to stay in here a few hours longer than expected."

"Do you really believe it's safe to shut off our oxygen?"

Rhodes stood up and entered the upper chamber with Flavio following him. "Oxygen levels inside the pyramid have been nearly safe enough to breathe for days now. To breathe this air for a prolonged period of time can be dangerous, and if we relied on it to get us through till morning, we may even suffocate, but I'm not saying that we do that. What I'm saying is that it would be wise to conserve our air supply, and it may not bother us to breathe the air in the pyramid for two or maybe three hours. After that, we'll power up our life-support systems to breathe oxygen supplied by our air tanks. Shutting off our oxygen now should leave us with five hours of air from eleven o'clock on."

"Stan, aren't we going to be guinea pigs? The oxygen we'll be breathing will have contaminants and impurities from the Martian atmosphere."

Flavio's worried tone showed he was concerned about the storm's potential, but Rhodes remained calm and relaxed. "We've talked about making the interior of the pyramid a closed ecosystem for some time, so sooner or later we'd have committed to breathing this air, and besides, I don't think we have any choice."

Flavio nodded his head. "Are you suggesting that I be the first one to remove his helmet?"

Without replying, Rhodes turned off his life-support system, shut off the oxygen to his suit, and removed his helmet after switching off the light.

Seeing Rhodes without his helmet, Flavio did the same. "Hey, I don't believe it! The air is breathable in here."

Rhodes' warm breath expelled as steam in the cold air. "We're still breathing contaminants, but I think we're safe for two or three hours at the most. After that, we'll start feeling ill effects, as there's barely enough oxygen to sustain us. Why don't you just stay here and relax? Take a nap if you like, but keep your helmet close by, and if you start feeling lightheaded or dizzy, put it on and power up your life-support system. In the meantime, I'm going to use this opportunity to go down to the burial chamber to find out what's setting off that motion detector."

"Whatever's setting it off isn't expected to occur until eleven o'clock. You want me to stay here by myself until then?"

"Yes, remain here to conserve your air intake, and don't leave this spot until I get back."

"Your three-hour time limit of breathing this air will be maxed out at eleven o'clock, and air quality in the depths of the pyramid isn't as good as it is here."

"If I feel any ill effects, I'll put my helmet on and switch on my life-support system, but a few minutes after eleven I'll be back here, and then we'll suit up to check conditions outside. Then we'll consider our options again, but we'll still have roughly five hours of oxygen left because we shut off our oxygen for the time that we did."

Flavio nodded. "Are you sure you don't want me to go down there with you?"

"I'd prefer that you come with me, but we need to do everything possible to conserve air, so its best that you stay put."

"What if you don't return shortly after eleven o'clock, then what?"

"Don't worry. I'll be here, and whatever you do, don't leave this chamber."

Rhodes started down the ladder into the pit carrying his helmet, and the second motion detector activated the next camera and a light from a post lamp in unison. Flavio stood at the edge of the chamber floor, watching him enter the labyrinth. Soon after he entered the passageway, Rhodes felt a strong sense of isolation. Moving down the lengthy corridor, he had the weirdest feeling, and it wasn't long before he wondered if leaving Flavio behind was such a good idea after all. Realizing the weird feeling could be from the lack of oxygen in the air, he felt as alone as a person can be, for he'd never ventured this far down into the monument by himself.

Lights clearly showed the way ahead, giving depth to the gigantic mausoleum erected to withstand the test of time, built by the toil of thousands. He sensed the ancients were watching, as if their eyes were in the walls, seeking to deliver death to anyone who dared trespass on this hallowed ground. The spirits of the ruler and his most trusted high priests were at bay, compelled to wreak their vengeance upon him for having breached the pyramid.

It was very cold inside the pyramid, but walking in his suit generated some heat as he passed the first junction leading to the original entranceway. All he saw down the passage was black infinity. Nearing the pillared hall, another motion detector activated a camera and its light, and then he turned right to enter the burial chamber and adjacent offering room. The motion detector there immediately sensed movement to activate the camera and light.

Whatever had set off the motion detector before in this room was undetectable to the naked eye, leaving him puzzled to the point that he had to try to find out what it was. Keeping his helmet within arm's reach, he lay on his side on the floor in front of the large stone pedestal supporting the motion detector and camera. He faced the same direction as the motion detector and let his head rest on his right forearm to view the connecting offering room and the altar supporting the godlike statue that resembled a bat. Keeping still for a few minutes to try to slow down his breathing, the motion sensor no longer detected movement, and the light went out. There was a light that stayed on constantly, but it didn't illuminate the room very well, and after a short while in these dim surroundings, he began to doze off. It was quite possible he was getting oxygen starved because little oxygen from the climate control unit was reaching this far down into the pyramid. Staying awake became difficult, and he soon drifted off to sleep.

CHAPTER 18

A Desperate Night

The tomb's frigid cold awakened Rhodes to unintentionally set off the motion detector, and the light came on from behind him to brighten the room. He felt the cold creeping into his bones and powered up his suit's life-support system to generate heat, but he kept quietly still. Looking at his watch, he saw the time was 10:45. Surprised he'd slept so long, he moved as little as possible, and the light soon went out to make the room dim again.

Breathing air that barely contained enough oxygen to sustain him for almost three hours had left him disoriented, and he thought that if the cold hadn't awakened him, he may not have woken up at all. But he was determined to stick it out, though it was taking forever for the seconds to tick by. Finally, it was 10:55. Just as he glimpsed the time again at 10:58, the light went on behind him to signal the motion sensor had picked up movement of some kind! Petrified by the idea he wasn't alone, he scanned the area in front of him and suddenly caught sight of a tiny, glowing red sphere that appeared in the offering room near the base of the altar. He watched this mysterious orb floating toward the ceiling with barely enough movement to register, slowly drifting upwards as it made a subtle, side-to-side dance. The strange and wondrous object was an absorbing phenomenon, and his eyes followed it all the way to a crack in the ceiling where it disappeared. He didn't know what else to expect, and a second later the light behind him went out, which clued him in that the entertainment was over.

Anxious to return to the upper chamber, Rhodes stood up, causing the light to come on again to brighten the room. At first, he felt lightheaded and dizzy. He immediately attributed these sensations to breathing the pyramid's air and realized it wouldn't be safe to breathe it for much longer. He put his helmet on and pulled up his life-support system. Taking in pure oxygen and feeling his suit heat up, he moved into the labyrinth to find his way back to the upper chamber.

He'd just entered the pillared hall when everything in the pyramid turned pitch black! The nightmarish realm of perpetual black took him to the brink of sheer terror. Paralyzed with shivers running up his spine, he gasped but was unable to draw air into his lungs. A powerful sense of vulnerability caused him to fumble with his instruments until he switched on his helmet's light, which enabled him to take in air again.

Deducing that lightning from the dust storm had finally knocked out the power grid they set up with the generator, he spoke softly, saying, "Flavio." He then called Flavio's name louder and, hearing no reply, concluded that if Flavio didn't have his helmet on, he couldn't hear him.

He had never felt as fearfully infinitesimal as he did in this nocturnal world, and deliverance from this place would come only with his return to the upper chamber. Passing through the pillared hall in a brisk walk to start up the inclined labyrinth, a lack of oxygen blunted his mind's ability to think clearly, while fear fueled paranoid delusions. Pushing on, in the back of his mind he feared losing the light from his helmet, and coming to the junction leading to the original entrance, he went by it without looking down the passageway. After that point, his mind began working at its full capacity, and he kept telling himself the most frightening part of his journey was behind him.

He made it to the pit to climb the ladder to the upper chamber's floor and momentarily faced off with the bust displaying those awful, gouged-out eye sockets. The statue seemed to be looking for vengeance. Then his light hit the form of the lizard beast, and the animal looked as menacing as ever. Unable to find Flavio, he was unsure where he may have gone before he spotted him lying on his side on the floor, sleeping. He shook his friend to wake him up, but when Flavio didn't show any signs of life, Rhodes worried he had suffocated. Then his eyes opened.

Rhodes could tell by his slow movements that Flavio was succumbing to a lack of oxygen and helped him to a standing position to put his helmet on. He spoke loudly enough for his voice to carry outside his helmet. "We need to attach your helmet and switch on your life-support system to feed you oxygen and get some heat into your suit."

Flavio grumbled sluggishly, "What happened to the lights?"

"The dust storm knocked out the power," replied Rhodes. Not getting much help from Flavio, Rhodes struggled to keep him on his feet while trying to attach his helmet. He shook him and said sternly, "Flavio, pull yourself together. We have to get out of here."

"You said you'd be gone only three hours. How long has it been?"

"Not much more than three hours. At eleven o'clock I started back up here."

Rhodes finally got Flavio's helmet on but was now having trouble switching on his life-support system. He was able to turn it on and, thinking Flavio was at least getting oxygen, let him stand on his own. But Flavio began to flounder, slipping to the floor, and he caught hold of him to lend support.

"Stan, can't you come back and get me in the morning?"

The communication in Flavio's helmet was working, and grabbing hold of his suit, Rhodes shook him again. "In the morning, you'll be dead!"

Flavio was in terrible shape, shivering as his eyes focused on Rhodes. "I feel so weird. What's the matter with me?"

"You'll be okay in a few minutes. Breathe deeply to get some of that pure oxygen into your lungs."

Checking digital readings on the display door at the front of Flavio's spacesuit, Rhodes saw his life-support system was malfunctioning. A series of system checks led him to believe the suit's electrical system wasn't working properly. The ventilation fans and warming function weren't performing the way they should, but what concerned him most was that he couldn't tell how much oxygen was reaching Flavio's lungs. He thought perhaps that last burst of lightning must have short-circuited the suit's backpack. This could explain why his suit could no longer produce heat.

Caught in a life-threatening situation with his options running out fast, Rhodes let Flavio sit down to rest and went to the pyramid's exterior door. He opened it to see blackness in the fury of a raging dust storm. Standing there, the only thing he could think to do was try to get Flavio back to the spaceship, but finding their way in this swirling dust would be almost impossible. Without Flavio's life-support system operating the way it should, Rhodes didn't know if his partner would make it, but he had to try something or Flavio was sure to die. He had no way to communicate with the crew, but even if he could, they'd probably get lost in this dust storm, just as Rhodes expected he and Flavio would.

Just now realizing his primary life-support system was malfunctioning, Flavio said, "I'm not getting any heat in my suit."

"I know. I think lightning knocked out that function."

"If I don't suffocate, I'll freeze to death."

"You're getting air so you're not going to suffocate."

Flavio's complexion looked pale. "Yeah, but I'm feeling dizzy, and maybe it's not circulating the way it's supposed to."

"Look, we have to start walking back to the ship, which will help generate heat. I see no other way. We've got to try this."

Seeing a five-meter-long piece of rope lying on a stack of material in the corner, Rhodes grabbed it and tied one end around his waist and the other around Flavio's waist. "We're losing precious time. At least with this rope connecting us, I won't lose you. I'll provide some pull. All you have to do is stay on your feet. If we get anywhere close to the ship, I should be able to reach help to get you the rest of the way there."

Switching on the light on Flavio's helmet, Rhodes noticed it was dim and switched it off to preserve power in his suit. Leading him to the outer door to look out once more, he saw nothing but swirling dust. "I don't see any more lightning, but we're almost certain to encounter more of it along the way."

Flavio then spoke in a weak voice, "How are we going to find our way in that muck?"

"We're going to use the pyramid to get our bearings and get us pointed north, and after crossing the valley where the supply depot is located, we'll climb the next ridge. From there, we'll find the rover's tracks, which will lead us back to the ship. We're going to make it, but you'll have to push yourself."

Flavio gave a reluctant nod and mumbled, "Follow the rover's tracks."

They stepped outside onto the platform and into the howling wind, and Rhodes shut the door. Following the platform by the handrail cable was the easy part. At the first angled corner of the pyramid, their visibility turned to zero, with crosswinds colliding in a whirlwind of dust.

Just as Rhodes removed his hand from the steel cable, lightning struck the cable and sparks flew. "That damn lightning's likely to take us both out with one strike!"

Feeling the tug of the rope, Rhodes turned to see Flavio lying crumpled on the platform, his face looking a pale white.

"I can't make it, Stan. I feel as weak as a newborn baby. Just leave me here."

Rhodes pulled him up from the platform to get him to his feet. "Let's get you back inside." Rhodes guided him back to the access door, and as soon as they were inside the pyramid chamber, he closed the door and helped Flavio lie down on his side. Seeing his friend's condition steadily deteriorating, he removed the length of rope from their waists and inadvertently tucked it inside the pouch in his left pants leg.

"Please don't let me die, Stan," Flavio pleaded, his body shivering and his teeth chattering.

"I'm not going to let you die."

"What are we going to do?"

"Let me worry about that. I'm going to leave, but I'm coming back for you. Just hang in there and don't give up hope."

Flavio's expression was blank as he lay on the floor, and there was no question he was slipping away, with as little as two hours left before he'd expire. Rhodes knew he didn't have much of a chance to make it to the ship to return with help, which left him few choices.

Stepping out into the storm, Rhodes was worried that the electrically charged atmosphere would knock out his life-support system the same way it had Flavio's. Walking along the platform, he kept his distance from the cable to avoid electrocution from the lightning. As he started down the stairs, he remembered there being air tanks inside the supply depot, and the manifest had shown two extra spacesuits there as well. He recalled seeing the air tanks but not the suits, but it was imperative to find at least one of them to replace Flavio's life-support system. He now wondered if his crew had transported those suits to the ship. Regardless, he had to at least try to find the equipment and return to the upper chamber as quickly as possible.

At the base of the stairs, the swirling dust was blinding at times, but going to the supply depot was Flavio's best chance for survival. He decided the shortest route to the supply depot was to cut through the causeway that ran around the pyramid's northeast face. Keeping close to the pyramid's base so he wouldn't lose his way, he kept looking to the spread of temple ruins extending as far as the northeast tip of what once was a jutting peninsula, but he saw nothing out there. Passing by the original entrance to the pyramid told him he didn't have much further to go before coming to the ancient shoreline.

Moving away from the foot of the pyramid to leave the Cydonia Complex, he ventured out into the brunt of the dust storm, trying to walk in a straight line with sand pelting his face shield. Thinking he must be facing north, he walked across the shelf leading to the drop-off where the valley lay and began descending the terraced slope.

Reaching the valley floor, he thought the supply depot couldn't be far, but unable to see much of anything, he feared losing his way. Holding one hand up to shield his face shield from pelting sand enabled him to see the ship's tail section, and walking alongside the ship's body took him to the cargo door. He removed the brace propping it up to find it terribly dark inside, but after his eyes adjusted, he was able to see his surroundings and moved about carefully to avoid tripping. Finding the oxygen tanks readily available at the back of the ship, he gathered two and placed them near the cargo door. Now he needed to locate the spacesuits.

Rhodes fumbled around inside the supply depot for half an hour looking for the suits, stumbling once and bumping his knee. Becoming weary, he checked a number of boxes and crates without success. Deciding to search up front near the bridge, he finally located them. Two suits were packaged individually in a box. He set aside the helmets to pull out the suits and separate them. He removed a backpack life-support assembly from its clear plastic bag. He inserted two 16.8-volt batteries into the backpack to complete a brief test to ensure the system was operable. He then hooked up two oxygen tanks to the backpack so it would be ready to replace the bad unit the moment he returned to the upper chamber.

Unsure of how long they'd be stuck in the pyramid and not knowing how much oxygen he'd need to wait out the storm, Rhodes decided to assemble a second backpack life-support unit. Then he gently placed both fully assembled backpacks out onto the Martian surface. Closing the ship just as a bolt of lightning struck nearby reminded him of the deadly threat.

Trying to decide the best way to distribute the weight of the backpacks, he thought about reentering the wreckage for a length of rope, only to remember the rope he'd stuffed into the pouch of his pants leg. He tied one end of the rope to the harness of one backpack and the other end to the harness of the second. There was rope left over, which he tucked inside the pouch of his pants leg to keep from tripping on it. Crouching to take hold of the rope, he placed it over his helmet to hang from around his neck and shoulders, and, standing with the weight evenly distributed, he began walking toward the terraced bank.

Trudging up the hill was a challenge, as shifting sand slid down against his legs, and the added weight caused him to bog down, but fearing Flavio could die if he failed, he pushed on. Summoning the strength to carry him to the crest, he made slow progress on the steep slope, and when his eyes cleared it, all he saw was swirling dust.

A streaking bolt of lightning struck nearby, compelling him to muster more strength, striving to make a few more steps until he came to stand on the gently sloping shelf. He moved toward the beachhead encompassing the Cydonia Complex, but visibility was so bad that he still couldn't see the pyramid, and it worried him not to be able to see such a colossal monument. He could be walking right next to it and not notice it in this blinding storm, and he began looking for the footprints he'd made a short while earlier on his way to the storage depot.

Catching sight of the temple ruins told him that he needed to move further westward, and he soon found the causeway separating the ruins from the pyramid. His boots sank in the soft sand, and mired in it, he fell to his knees near the pyramid's base where sand dunes collected to ramp up its slanted face. Tiring fast, he took a deep breath as the outline of the original entrance to the pyramid came into view, inspiring him to rise to his feet again.

Rhodes knew he'd never forget this night, nor the fury of this Martian dust storm. The entire evening had been a nightmare, and it still wasn't over. The flurry of dust impeded his sight throughout the night's journey. Following the base of the pyramid around to reach the stairs, he heard another bolt of lightning strike behind him, which quickened his pace. The steps finally came into view, but he could see up the stairs but a short distance before they disappeared into a rampaging cloud of dust.

He took a deep breath before starting an ambitious march up the staircase while shouldering the weight of the backpacks. At first he ignored the rope handrail, and only after he'd become tired did he grab hold of the rope to help pull him upwards. Winded from the seemingly never ending struggle, he felt his heart pumping rapidly, and his legs felt the strain like never before, but then he saw the platform and decking. Reaching the platform, Rhodes hoped he wasn't too late to help Flavio. As soon as he stepped on the decking, he fell clumsily forward and nearly tumbled down the stairs! He grabbed hold of the first handrail post to keep from falling to his death and then clung to the post in a stooped position.

Looking behind him to see if a loose line from a backpack had caught on something, he realized the excess rope he'd tucked into the pouch of his pants leg had snagged on the edge of a step. He reached to yank it free, but it resisted, for the rope had stubbornly pinched at a joint where stones came together, requiring more effort to free it.

Rhodes lifted the rope connecting the backpacks above his helmet to let the equipment rest stably on the platform's deck. Then he squatted to free the rope from the stones. After gathering the excess rope in his clenched, gloved hand, he lifted the rope attached to the life-support systems to place it around his neck again and stood up. Walking on level decking now, he kept his distance from the steel handrail. He finally reached the entrance to the upper chamber. Closing the door behind him, he placed the backpacks on the floor, and seeing Flavio lying curled up on his side, he moved swiftly.

He thought Flavio must be getting some oxygen through his suit's life-support with his helmet attached because his face had some color. In his motionless condition, he probably didn't need much oxygen to stay alive. Rhodes untied the rope from the backpacks to free them, tossing the rope aside.

Rhodes now wrestled with Flavio to bring him around so he could get his backpack off in order to put the new one on him. He received little cooperation, as Flavio was groggy and rigid, but he finally managed to get him to stand on his own to make the switch and left the faulty backpack lying in a corner. He immediately powered up the new primary life-support system and saw the display panel on the front of the suit light up. Fresh oxygen tanks would carry Flavio for the next seven hours, and the ventilating fans and warming system were operating to help him rebound.

Helping Flavio find a somewhat comfortable position to rest on his side on the floor, Rhodes now felt exhausted and even woozy from a horrendously trying night. His strength zapped, he switched off the light on his helmet to conserve his suit's power and sank to his knees before lying on his side. He felt bad enough to worry that he and Flavio had ingested an airborne Martian virus while breathing air in the pyramid. He was afraid the tainted air may contribute to lowering their resistance against germs. He gave into ill feelings that weakened him and less than a minute later fell asleep.

CHAPTER 19

Where Is It Leading Us?

Rhodes woke up sometime later in pitch blackness, an annoying buzzing sound bringing him to consciousness. He realized the noise was his primary life-support system warning that he was running out of oxygen, and he needed to change over to a thirty-minute emergency oxygen supply. Fumbling around in the black abyss, he couldn't see his hand in front of his face. He finally switched on his helmet's light to find and press a button to halt the warning buzzer.

Getting up off the hard, stone floor of the upper chamber, he looked over to see Flavio sleeping restfully. Realizing he must have slept for a few hours before exhausting his air supply, he looked at his watch to see it was almost four o'clock in the morning. When he had exchanged Flavio's faulty life-support assembly for a new one, Flavio received seven full hours of oxygen, while Rhodes was still breathing oxygen from his original air supply, and it had finally run out. He did notice, however, that he felt much better than he did when he lay down hours earlier. The rest helped regenerate his strength.

He entered the air pocket enclosure to reach the outside door to the pyramid and opened it to view a dust storm still raging in the night. Then he closed the door to check on Flavio's condition.

Flavio appeared to be resting quite comfortably. His life-support system showed everything working properly, and he had four hours of oxygen left. The gauges showed plenty of juice in the batteries. In another four hours Flavio's current oxygen supply would run out, so he'd switch the empty tanks for those tanks in the faulty backpack Flavio wore before, which still contained about three hours' worth of oxygen. By then it would be daylight, and, provided the dust storm wasn't so dense that it wouldn't allow sunlight in, they could try to return to the ship. He hoped that atmospheric conditions would have improved enough by then for them to ride back in the rover; otherwise, they'd have to walk back to the ship, and finding their way would be a challenge. The storm may have wiped out all traces of tracks leading to the ship, but he still had a compass. Most important, however, was Flavio's physical condition and whether he'd be able to walk.

Exchanging his backpack for the other one he'd brought from the storage depot gave Rhodes a full seven hours of oxygen. Lying back down and turning off the light on his helmet, Rhodes tried to get some rest while rehashing in his mind the experience he'd had in the offering room. He remembered seeing that extraordinary red orb ascend from the floor, watching it until it disappeared into a crack where the wall and ceiling met. Pondering the incident made him wonder if there was another passageway on the other side of the wall behind the altar. Trying to comprehend how the red orb materialized, he couldn't discount some supernatural energy had produced it, and he thought about it until dozing off.

Rhodes had gotten little rest, and he was awake when Flavio began to stir four hours later, his life-support system warning that he was running out of oxygen. He was slow coming around but gained his composure to stand under his own power, which made the job of changing his oxygen tanks easy.

Afterwards, Rhodes stepped outside to see the dust storm receding and sunlight breaking through the atmosphere, but he still couldn't see the stretch of temple ruins down below.

Both stiff from sleeping in their suits, the two men said very little when leaving the chamber, and after closing the access door to the pyramid, Rhodes felt relieved watching Flavio walking under his own steam. Seeing little of the land area down below, they began to descend the stairs. They made it to ground level and started digging the rover out of a mound of sand that had collected during the storm, Rhodes scooping sand from the vehicle's floorboard to get to the foot pedals. Rhodes then switched the vehicle on to drive it forward, and Flavio hopped in the passenger's seat. They rounded the monument to leave the Cydonia Complex, passing through the valley before traveling on the wide, open plain on their way back to the home ship. Almost halfway there, they met three travelers on foot. Far, Jetha, and Aleksei must have left the ship at daybreak to offer their help in the pyramid.

Rhodes pulled up to greet them. "What are you people doing out here? I thought I gave orders for you to stay put in the ship."

Far responded, "You gave orders not to leave the ship last night, so we waited for sunrise to leave, and thinking your air supply should've run out long before now, we didn't expect to find survivors. So how did it go?"

"Let's just say that last night made for an interesting but strenuous experience. Lightning from static electricity knocked out power to the pyramid. Flavio's suit malfunctioned and he became so ill that he couldn't even walk. I had to go to the supply depot in that nightmarish dust storm to get two life-support systems with fresh air tanks to hold us over, and I somehow managed to do it without getting lost."

Flavio commented, "I remember our making an unsuccessful attempt to leave the pyramid and returning to it. If you hadn't gone out to get that equipment, I probably would have died."

Rhodes replied, "If we didn't have oxygen tanks stored at the storage depot, neither one of us would've survived the night."

"We saw bursts of lightning outside the ship throughout the night," said Jetha.

"It's a little more exciting when you're outside and lightning's striking all around you, but we can talk about it more back at the ship."

The others got in the rover, and when they returned to the home ship, Rhodes and Flavio slept for a few hours to catch up on their rest. After they woke up, Far massaged Rhodes' neck and shoulders while Jetha worked on Flavio in the same way to relieve the stiffness from sleeping in their suits.

Sitting down to eat a meal with the others, Rhodes said, "We're lucky this storm didn't upgrade to encompass the entire planet as some have done in the not too distant past. We wouldn't have made it if it weren't for the additional spacesuits and oxygen tanks we had in the supply depot, so we learned the importance of storing extra gear there. In addition, Flavio and I breathed air in the pyramid for about three hours, but low oxygen content and airborne impurities probably brought on some ill effects we both experienced. The climate control has the capacity to condition the air in that upper chamber, and it's important that we set up a door at the entrance to the labyrinth to give us an air pocket in case emergencies arise."

After finishing their meal, they continued their discussions, and eventually they got around to talking about the motion detector going off in the funerary room the past few nights. Flavio glimpsed at Rhodes. "Stan was in the burial chamber till eleven, but I've yet to hear if he saw or experienced anything."

Rhodes then said, "I went down to the funerary room positioning myself facing the same way that the motion detector and camera were aimed. The altar with the winged bat-god was in plain sight before me in the adjoining offering room. I had taken off my helmet and was breathing air in the pyramid to conserve my oxygen, and I must've become drowsy because I soon fell asleep. I woke up just before eleven o'clock and shortly thereafter, the motion detector went on. After a second, I caught sight of a tiny, red orb floating near the base of the altar and watched it slowly drift up to the ceiling. Then it disappeared into a crack where the wall met the ceiling."

Glimpsing the expressions of the others, Rhodes remarked, "I don't believe in the supernatural, but that red orb was a strange sight. You be the judge and make of it what you want. I was oxygen starved at the time, and maybe I'd become delusional."

Aleksei then commented, "Even if we thought you were delusional, we know the motion detector isn't."

They sat around looking at each other and then Far said, "So what do you think it meant?"

"I don't know, but it's possible there's another passageway beyond that offering room."

Flavio had an inquisitive look on his face. "What if we come to find the labyrinth continues beyond the altar? What are we supposed to believe? It'll have to be investigated, but we must move ahead cautiously."

Jetha said, "It is only natural for us to want to learn more about this civilization, but remember, the offering room is where Aleksei nearly died falling into that pit. If we find another passageway there, it's not going to sit well with me. Could a spiritual entity be manipulating us while luring us to explore deeper in the pyramid? What reason would it have for showing this to us other than wanting to endanger us and bring harm to us. I think it's leading us into another trap."

"That's exactly what I was thinking," Rhodes agreed. "Exploring deeper in the pyramid may be dangerous, but, of course, we won't know there's a passageway until we've tried excavating that wall. If there's nothing there, then perhaps I merely dreamed the episode while being deprived of oxygen. However, my encounter with the strange orb brought to mind that lengthy text etched into the walls in the upper chamber, and I thought it may be helpful to know what it says. Jetha, can you tell me if the computer has made any progress in deciphering the text?"

"The computer has compared the dialect to various ancient writing forms and has made progress deciphering it. It did indicate the writing may be a curse or a warning, but in a text that long there has to be more being told, and I expect it will give us insight into the king's life. I have it pegged for high priority, so the computer should let us know the moment it's translated."

"I suggest we return to the pyramid and get the generator and climate control unit up and running again," said Rhodes. "That way we can start pumping oxygen back into the structure. We'll have to check the electrical system to see what damage the storm did to it and make repairs so we have lighting throughout the structure again. The climate control never worked efficiently, but after we've installed a door at the entrance to the labyrinth and isolated the upper chamber, we may succeed in creating a safety zone with survivable conditions. It's important to keep the supply depot replenished with additional air tanks and at least two suits available there in case there's another emergency. After we've accomplished this work, we can find out if there's anything behind that wall in the offering room. From now on, we must be careful about monitoring weather conditions before going to the pyramid, and we won't be going there again after nightfall. It's simply too risky."

On their way to the pyramid, they saw that the dust storm had settled to a mere haze in the atmosphere, leaving the sky a purple-gray at midday. They had little trouble getting the generator and climate control unit running again, but they found a short in the wiring they needed to trace down. They'd gotten a late start, but before finishing for the day, the motion detectors and cameras were all operable, and devices for monitoring atmospheric conditions in the passageways were working too. Aleksei hung a functional door in the pit at the opening of the labyrinth made from a panel taken from the storage depot. This door sealed off the opening well enough to stop the escape of oxygen from the upper chamber, and in time they hoped to turn the upper chamber into a safety zone with breathable conditions.

Before leaving the pyramid, Rhodes went down to glimpse the bat-god statue on the altar in the offering room. Looking up at the crack where the ceiling and wall met, he thought about the strange orb. That same night, they stayed up to see if the motion detector device would pick up any activity. At 10:54, the motion detector sensed something to activate the camera and light, yet they observed nothing on the monitor. This was another surprisingly perplexing event, and although it made Rhodes uncomfortable because he didn't understand it, he wanted to believe something electrical was causing it. The others made little comment about the incident, as it left them spooked.

CHAPTER 20

The Grand Gallery

The next morning, intrigued by a series of motion detector activations, the team returned to the offering room and examined the wall behind the altar. They quickly learned the wall was made of stone with a layer of mortar smoothing its outer surface, and there was ample space on either side of the altar to begin excavating. Flavio pounded the ancient wall with a sledgehammer, and cracks began to form. Then he used a crowbar to pry at the joints until loosened stones fell to the floor. They soon discovered the cubicle's wall concealed a continuation of the labyrinth spanning the full width of the offering room.

They continued dismantling the wall, and Rhodes stepped forward to shine the searchlight's beam into the passage to see a bleak and descending rock-cut tunnel. Once they had the wall down, they reconfigured the lift-hoist to move the bat-god statue from the altar, making the legs taller to lift the statue from the altar's counter. Within two hours, they'd moved the deity into a corner in the funerary room, and afterwards they dismantled the altar to completely open up the passageway.

Inasmuch as Rhodes wanted to see where the passage would lead them, he felt hesitant, as the mysterious red orb gave him reason to suspect there were dangers awaiting them. It was as if something had invited them on this leg of the expedition for unknown reasons. Watching Far check her camera, he put these superstitions aside.

Rhodes tied his team together in the same manner as he'd done before. He led the way into the depths of the passageway, Flavio behind him carrying the crowbar in one hand, and the others followed as they walked twenty meters to meet a wide, descending staircase. Noticing an archway above with flaking gold paint and an inscription, they took a few more steps to an open hall, which was a wide and long gallery.

Mystified by a chamber he perceived to be as much as five meters wide and eight or ten meters long, Rhodes wondered if this eerie underground region was the ruler's tomb for which they'd built the pyramid. Far failed to hold her powerful searchlight beam steady long enough for anyone to recognize anything, and their lights reflected dimly off indiscernible objects. The artistically decorated walls had bright, colorful, geometric patterns, but closer examination showed these designs to be flaking paint. The arched ceiling resembled the upper chamber's ceiling, painted dark blue with starfish scattered across it, and on the floor were fanciful mosaics in bright colors.

Drawn to an enormous figure shrouded in perpetual night at the far end of the chamber, Rhodes approached the strange shape slowly and carefully.

"Okay, I want to get a look at what's ahead of us, so let's all converge and concentrate our lights."

Far aimed the searchlight beneath the wide arch spanning the width of the room where they saw not one figure but two large statues. In the background against the wall stood the guardian of this strange realm, a bigger-than-life statue of the winged bat-god, its great beak open wide as if shrieking. The spectacular sculpture had manlike arms, shoulders, and legs, and its webbed wingspan extended to nearly span the distance of the arch. It was difficult to tell at first, but instead of being connected to the statue, the masterfully carved, webbed wings were part of the wall behind it.

They saw before this deity a life-size statue of the divine ruler regally seated on a throne-like chair carved from a single block of stone. He looked proud, as if holding court and boldly delegating his will over loyal subjects. The crew recognized his distinguishable facial features from the statues in the upper chamber: the sinister grin, the creases in the cheeks, the well-rounded head.

Jetha said, "They must have had strong faith in their bat-god, believing this winged figure would protect them in the afterlife."

After staring at the two amazing statues for a minute, Rhodes turned his attention to the broad pillars on each side of the gallery near wide steps. The image on one pillar looked to be that of a Martian queen, and he untied himself from the others to move in closer and study her features. She looked like a long-haired woman wearing a feathered headdress, smiling with a casual gaze, and a broad, flaring, jeweled necklace covered her chest. An artist had originally painted her etched image to make her more life-like, but the paint had faded, and he also noted a textual inscription beneath her.

The others joined Rhodes, their lights reflecting off the same pillar, and Far said, "This must have been the funerary chamber of the queen."

They ventured up the steps to enter the midway point in a tomb containing a sleek, pink granite sarcophagus. It's gently flowing lid had elegant, rounded edges. There was text painted on a wall in bold lettering, but so much of it had flaked away the message was likely incomplete. Standing around the sarcophagus, they couldn't resist caressing its smooth, contoured shape, and Rhodes said, "Let's see what's in the chamber on the other side of this gallery before we run out of time."

Exiting the queen's burial chamber, they crossed the gallery to see pillars devoid of inscriptions. This funerary tomb looked coldly artless, implying they'd found the resting place of someone who held no notoriety, was inconsequential, or preferred anonymity. They went up the few steps leading into the chamber to see a simple, oblong sarcophagus made of limestone. The lid of the sarcophagus was eight centimeters thick and there were no inscriptions anywhere.

"Do we open this one?" asked Flavio.

"We're pressed for time, but I suppose we can. Let's all gather around it to get a grip on the lid, and then we'll see if we can get it to budge."

Flavio went around the sarcophagus, prying the lid with the crowbar to loosen it, and then they tried to shift the stone slab.

Moving the lid at one end and then the other, they heard stone grinding against stone, and as it began sliding off the sarcophagus, Rhodes started to feel its weight.

"Wait, wait everyone," said, Aleksei. "This lid is extremely heavy, heavier than we may think, and we'll have difficulty putting it on the floor without smashing somebody's fingers. Give me a few minutes and I'll get two stones from where we took down the wall so we'll have something to rest the lid on."

Rhodes untied Aleksei and Flavio, who quickly returned with two reasonably flat stones of similar size. They placed them on the floor a short distance from the sarcophagus. The team then resumed shifting the lid, sliding it to get it teetering off the edge of one side. Changing positions, two of them stood at each end now, and Rhodes held the middle with his arms spread wide to better equalize the weight. Their combined strength enabled them to tilt the lid while sliding it off the sarcophagus, and Rhodes dropped to his knees to take on as much weight as he could. It scraped against the side of the sarcophagus as they let it come down to rest on its side against the pair of stones, and they left it leaning stably against the crypt.

They now gazed upon the thin, frail remains of a mummified male whose clothing had dramatically deteriorated over time. His slightly raised bald head nestled in a withered pillow, his gaunt and narrow face so smooth and well-preserved that he appeared to be sleeping peacefully. The shape of his head differed from that of the skulls they had found in the mound of rubble, which had well-rounded craniums. The other skulls also had a protruding brow ridge, but this emaciated head made him look more human. Lying with his forearms crossed over his chest, he had a serene, dignified expression, giving the impression he'd lived to an old age. His skin was almost black, which may or may not have been because of his age or the burial process.

"This cannot be the king," stated Jetha, "for his tomb would be meritoriously opulent, but it must be someone of nobility or great importance to hold a place in this funerary chamber. His physical stature doesn't resemble the features of the robust king either, whose physical build was much stockier and whose head is rounder. I think we can presume that he may have been a general who led an army to glory, a deceased brother, or an eldest son who passed away before his father."

"Some of the skulls we've found remind me of Neanderthals," remarked Far, "but this person makes me think these beings had begun to evolve to look more like modern man."

Aleksei pointed to his cheeks. "Look, he has those creases in his cheeks like the ruler in those statues, so they may really be gills used for breathing air in the Martian atmosphere."

Rhodes noticed the creases, only in this person's solemn expression they weren't as pronounced. "Until these remains have been X-rayed, we won't be able to conclude whether these creases represent gills."

Flavio then remarked, "The computer stated these beings may be nine hundred fifty thousand years old, making any mummies we find quite fragile and delicate. We are obviously not equipped to move them, as they may crumble to dust. We can also assume the frigid cold in this funerary crypt has helped preserve their encapsulated remains, halting their decay. If and when this being is brought back to earth, precautionary measures must be taken so an oxygen rich atmosphere won't accelerate his deterioration."

Far reached inside the sarcophagus to probe in the cloth-like materials the corpse rested in, removing a gold staff capped with a cluster of rubies in the shape of a ball. She placed the instrument on the floor, holding it upright, and it stood nearly a head taller than her helmet.

She then stooped to give attention to the Martian's footwear. "He's wearing shoes with leather-like soles showing uneven wear, meaning he may have walked with a limp from an old injury or a form of arthritis." Looking at Rhodes, she asked, "Don't we have time to open the other sarcophagus? Aren't you curious to see if the other mummy has those gills?"

"We're pressed for time, and I see no need to open all the crypts at once, but if you can't contain your curiosity, let's do it."

Aleksei and Flavio went back for two more stones, and they removed the lid of the beautiful pink granite sarcophagus.

Finding this lid to be more stubborn than the first, Flavio used the crowbar to pry it free, and they saw that a waxy substance had served as a sealant for the crypt. They shifted the lid in the same fashion and let it rest gently on the stones against the sarcophagus.

Now feasting their eyes on what they believed to be the queen, they saw a well-preserved woman with feminine features wearing what was once an elegant gown. Her body rested on white linen that had begun to turn to powder. Her head, supported by a pillow, was slightly leaner than the first mummy's, and she had black skin too, although the artist didn't portray her as having black skin in her image on the pillar. She wore a black, braided wig with tassels. Catching their eyes was the glint of gold and the luster of diamonds, as she wore a captivating necklace encrusted with stunning jewels. The spread of the necklace covered her chest, and her arms crossed over it as if she was embracing it.

"Wow," said Flavio, "what a beautiful necklace! With all of those precious stones, I'd say it must be worth at least a million dollars."

"That may be a conservative figure," stated Far. "I believe the necklace is the same one she's shown wearing in that painting on the pillar."

Gazing at the necklace resting over her bosom, Rhodes noted how those who had prepared her for burial had arranged her arms. "We'll probably have to remove both her arms to get that necklace free, and look," he said, pointing to her cheeks. "She does have those creases too, but they're more subtle. You may be right, Aleksei. Those may be gills they used to breathe through, making me curious about what the atmosphere was like during their time. Or did they have gills because they evolved from aquatic creatures?"

Rhodes began to extricate the necklace from the corpse. Her limbs were brittle, and the first arm snapped off at the elbow when he applied just a little pressure. The other arm dislodged at the shoulder joint, some of the necklace sticking to it, and he was careful when he peeled the stones from her flesh. Her skin was much like cardboard, her limbs lightweight, and he gingerly worked the necklace out from beneath her neck to get it free.

The more effort he put into getting the necklace off, the more the pillow, linen, and gown disintegrated. What concerned Rhodes most was detaching the head from the body. He finally climbed into the sarcophagus and straddled the mummy. He removed the wig and leaned forward to avoid putting any more stress on her neck. As the shield of his helmet hovered above her face, he became quite familiar with her facial features. He eventually freed the chain, and the necklace left an impression on her chest. After replacing her arms in their original positions, he refitted the wig on her head.

He gave Far the jeweled necklace to transport back to the ship, and she carried it in her outstretched arms while Jetha carried the gold staff with the cluster of rubies at one end. They'd stayed beyond their usual working hours but made it back to the ship before sundown, and Rhodes allowed Far and Jetha equal time wearing the necklace before putting it away. They spent part of the evening viewing what Far's helmet camera recorded when they were in the gallery. Fast-forwarding through bits and pieces of the recording, Far mentioned she intended to edit it later to shorten it before sending a copy to Earth, but the original recording would remain untouched. Some of it looked fuzzy, and when they got to the part where Far stood before the statues in the gallery, she froze the picture so they could study the statues' features. The sprawling, winged bat-god and the ruler sitting on his throne in the foreground were captivating.

Rhodes stood and announced, "Tomorrow we'll run a string of electric lights into that grand gallery, or funerary hall. Maybe with the proper lighting we'll be able to see details we didn't notice before. I want at least one more camera with a motion detector set up down there, and an air quality sensor to tell us if there's any poisonous gas seeping into the pyramid that may be life-threatening. We keep going deeper into the pyramid, and it's beginning to affect picture and sound quality, so it's important that we set up an antenna at the mouth of the pyramid to relay clearer signals." The frozen frame showing the ruler and the bat-god remained on their monitor screens, and Rhodes paused to study it. "It may interest you all to know I don't think we're far from discovering the king's resting place. A minute ago I had an epiphany about where his sarcophagus may be hidden."

"Where?" asked Flavio, his eyes opening wide.

"Look at the sculpted figures on your monitors. We've talked about how these beings had a deeply held belief in their bat-god. A statue of this deity stood guard in the offering room before a well-concealed passageway, so doesn't it seem natural that the inner sanctum of the deceased ruler be behind the flailing, webbed wings of their bat-god?"

Flavio's mouth hung open as he stood staring at his monitor, and he managed to say, "Of course! They believed the deity was their protector in the afterlife. They cleaved to the deep-seated faith that their precious god would protect their remains. They may even have imagined that this statue might come to life to attack and slay tomb robbers."

"Before tearing through that wall, I want those other items taken care of," reiterated Rhodes. "To continue exploring the labyrinth, we need adequate lighting down there."

Later, Rhodes sent to Earth a transmission telling of the mission's progress, along with pictures of the newly discovered grand gallery showing those astounding statues. He wondered what impact this was having on the inhabitants of Earth, for the idea that a civilized architectural culture existed on Mars was proof that there was intelligent life elsewhere in the universe.

He stayed up till after eleven to see if any disturbances activated the motion detector in the funerary chamber. From his seat in the ship, he viewed the vacated opening leading down to the gallery, and when nothing occurred after eleven o'clock, he soon shut down his monitor and went to bed. He wondered if the strange orb would appear again in a different location and lead them to discover something else. It was a mystifying experience, and he still couldn't say it had something to do with the paranormal, but neither could he rule that out. . . .

CHAPTER 21

An Unexpected Meeting

The team got an early start the next day, returning to the pyramid to accomplish the duties Rhodes had proposed. Flavio wired the gallery and connecting funerary chambers with lights, and he also moved one of the post lamps from the upper chamber to the gallery to illuminate the newly discovered statues. Rhodes set up another motion detector and a safety device to monitor air quality at an electrical junction box. Far activated her helmet camera to record a view of the ruler's statue, the artistically carved bat-god, and the mummies. Jetha spent a few minutes properly fitting the queen's wig and then searched for markings to identify the male mummy, but he remained an enigmatic figure.

The looming bat-god stood larger than life but didn't look nearly as threatening as it did before, for it now appeared to be shrieking for help to stop tomb raiders. The compelling idea that the remains of the Martian ruler lay beyond the barrier wall behind that statue was nothing more than a guess, but they were determined to find out what, if anything, was there. Flavio accumulated excavating equipment to the left of the deity. The others watched as he began pounding the wall with a sledgehammer to weaken it, hitting it until stones cracked and broke up and an opening formed to expose a rock-cut area behind it. This didn't quell their curiosity, and Flavio went to work on the opposite side of the statue. Soon a few stones collapsed inward, and this time a dark cavity awaited them. Intent on having a look, Flavio peered inside without noticing that some unsteady stone blocks above him were ready to fall. Seeing imminent disaster, Rhodes latched onto his arm and dragged him away just as a cluster of stones collapsed, barely missing him.

As smoky dust turned into a cloud, Flavio turned his head to look at Rhodes through his face shield, saying, "Thanks, Stan. That was close."

The dust cloud lingered to block them from seeing what lay beyond the opening, and a few minutes later they began removing more stones to expand the opening. Another look inside allowed them to see an alcove leading to a short staircase where three, tall vertical stone slabs stood, and they made their approach.

Far aimed the searchlight's beam at a symbol etched in the middle stone, which everyone recognized as the lizard beast. "A last deterrent to tomb robbers," she said. "I'm not sure whether this creature struck terror in those who lived in this region or it represented a mythical deity the ruler battled in legend."

The immense stones blocking the entrance inspired Flavio to comment, "Can you imagine the concerted effort it took to set these three massive stones in place?"

They drilled several holes shoulder high into the center of the middle stone to discover the stones weren't more than twenty centimeters thick. Anxious to see what lay on the other side, they began chipping around the middle stone to dislodge it from the others standing abreast of it, but this became time consuming. They tried pushing the middle stone forward, so it would topple and fall into whatever chamber that lay on the other side, but it wouldn't move, and they thought the top of the stone was up against a drop in the ceiling on the other side.

Stuck on how to get the center stone to move, the next thought was to get this monolithic block of stone rocking to fall in their direction, but this presented the danger of it smashing someone when it fell. Nonetheless, they sought a way to get a hold on the stone for pulling it from the inside of the tomb. Flavio made one of the holes he'd drilled much larger by running a larger drill bit through the hole and then he tied a rope around a smaller drill bit before stuffing it through the hole. After sliding it through, they pulled on the rope until the bit caught the stone from inside the tomb, and they moved back to keep their distance while getting ready to tug on the rope. Drawing slack out of the rope to create tension, they kept tugging until the stone tilted away from the others. Then, feeling it catch, they let it lean back in place. They tried again, pulling even harder than before, the stone leaned outward and then back, and they figured it had to be snagging somewhere or else it would've fallen. Preparing to try again, Flavio jammed his crowbar into a joint on the right side of the middle stone, applying leverage in an attempt to force it free.

"One more time," he ordered, and as they tugged, he dug the crowbar in the joint, prying at it with its flat end, and the stone moved out further before stopping.

"We almost had it that time," said Flavio. "I think it's catching somewhere at the top. Let's give it one more try."

The others tugged with fierce determination as Flavio pried with the crowbar to force the stone to give way, and this time the top of the stone lurched outward a tiny bit farther before rocking back.

Flavio said, "Once more, but this time after it rocks back in place, immediately pull again, and keep tugging with everything you've got to give it momentum."

Pulling the stone until it caught again, they let it rock back before pulling as hard as ever, and this time it moved outward to keep coming, but so did the other two!

"Flavio!" shouted everyone, and he leaped from the stairs just before the slabs hit the floor in a thundering clap. Two of the three slabs broke apart as they came down the steps, but they fell short of causing injury. The crew evacuated the enclosure to escape the dust cloud.

Flavio had just missed getting crushed and was shaken. "Those stones were obviously set up that way to crush anyone trying to bring them down, and it almost worked.

When the dust settled, Rhodes reentered the alcove and climbed over the fallen stones to see what lay beyond the opening. The first thing he saw was a mammoth burial vault with a raised figure protruding from its lid, which depicted the divine ruler resting peacefully. Caught up in this triumphant moment, he turned to face his comrades. "You've all earned a look at his resting place."

The others entered the magnificent tomb to admire the massive crypt of this once-powerful ruler. In a connecting cubicle, they found a large cache of gold, jewelry, and precious stones in four large jars. Rhodes first assumed the jars were ceramic, but their remarkable condition made him think they were made of a material similar to ceramic but more durable.

The walls held colored reliefs glorifying the ruler's life, but their features were hardly distinguishable because they were so badly decayed and covered with an ugly brown overgrowth. Speckled patches of mold blanketed these images, and Rhodes warned the others, "Don't touch this fungus growing on the walls. It's a living thing producing deadly micro toxins. Whatever this mold is, it's not healthy to get on your suits, and bringing it inside the ship may prove disastrous for us all."

Jetha took notice of the growth, adding, "Stan's right. In the tombs of the Valley of the Kings, there are toxic microorganisms living in a lethal fungus called *Aspergillus Niger*. When disturbed, it produces airborne spores that infiltrate people's lungs to bring on sickness and a horrible death."

One color relief was still intact enough for them to recognize the king slaying the giant lizard beast just as the statue in the upper chamber showed. The wall to the left wasn't rock-cut like the others but looked like a stone wall with a bad fracture that occurred from settling or a violent tremor. This wall had pockets or recessed areas that may have once held candles, and the wall's fracture cut directly through an empty, knee-high depression.

They went back to the alcove outside the tomb to remove chunks of the two slabs that had broken apart to make a clear passage. The slab that didn't break apart wasn't an obstacle. While the others began bringing down parts to assemble the lift-hoist to remove the lid to the sarcophagus, Flavio ran electrical wiring and hooked up two lights inside the tomb.

The lid portraying the king in a restful sleep was substantially larger than the others they'd moved by hand, so they configured the lift-hoist to straddle the sarcophagus. Stopping to admire the artistry of the sculptured figure, Rhodes wanted to avoid drilling holes in the lid to preserve its appearance. The rim had enough of an overhang to secure fastening clamps, but after attaching them, he felt apprehensive about their holding ability. Nevertheless, they powered up the compressor to activate the hydraulic system, and the lid rose till it was completely free of the sarcophagus. As soon as they'd moved the hoist out of the way of the sarcophagus, they lowered the lid a meter so the hoist wasn't so top-heavy.

Rhodes warned the others, "Keep your distance, everyone. I don't want to take any chances on this thing falling and crushing somebody."

They wanted to rest the lid on the floor against the wall as soon as possible, but the unevenness of the floor impeded their efforts. One wheel and then another kept catching and binding in open joints between floor stones, and this jerking motion caused the lid to sway back and forth. The next abrupt jerk caused a fatigue crack in the lid to suddenly give way, and the lid smashed into a hundred pieces on the floor! It startled everyone, but no one was hurt. Gazing at the fragmented lid in disgust, Rhodes said, "I was afraid that would happen. I suppose we'll never make it as archeologists."

"Take a look here," blurted Flavio, gazing at the crypt's contents.

When they looked inside the sarcophagus, they were spellbound by an ornate, coffin-like crypt overlaid with gold. Adorned with precious diamonds and colorful gems, the gold appeared bright and shiny as though the sarcophagus had been sealed only the day before. A skillful metallurgist had fashioned the likeness of his ruler, and though the width of the case had left his features distorted, the dazzling eyes made of glass looked so lifelike they had a hypnotizing effect.

"Let's all spread out around the crypt. Aleksei, you get at the feet while I take the head. Everybody else, grab hold of the lid as best you can to lift."

They made a united effort to lift the lid, but it didn't budge, and Rhodes said, "Let's try again."

This time the lid came loose at the foot end, and they managed to raise it out of the sarcophagus. Finding it manageable, they balanced and maneuvered it horizontally, carrying it from the crypt before lowering the foot end to lean it in an upright position against a wall in a corner.

Now gathering around the sarcophagus, they viewed the remains of the ruler, resting in what was once fine linen and shrouded in a dusty, red cloak with yellow fringe. He wore a choppy crown of gold bearing royal insignias, and his face looked gruesomely striking, for his features were crusty and crumbling. A gold chain ran around his neck, connected to a brilliant sunburst medallion lying on his chest, and a ring with an outlandishly large ruby was on the third finger of his left hand.

Far asked, "Why is it we found the other mummies fairly well preserved, but the king shows so much deterioration? Shouldn't the king have had the best embalming methods available?"

"The mold in this tomb may have caused decomposition," said Aleksei, "or they may have tried a new technique of mummification that simply didn't hold up against the ages."

They heard a faint, repetitive beeping sound they thought was the device monitoring atmospheric conditions in the gallery, and Rhodes went to investigate. He went to an oversized electrical junction box anchored to the wall and lifted a small door to view a miniature, computerized panel inside. He entered a code that stopped the signal and then read a printed message. What the sensor detected surprised him.

"It says there's a high level of water in the air. The last compartment to be opened was the tomb, so I imagine that's where it's sensing moisture from. The growth on those walls is found nowhere else in the pyramid, making me wonder if that mold is extracting water from the bedrock to help it grow."

Far then commented, "We have devices designed to be inserted into Martian soil to read its moisture content, and they can be jammed into the wall's cracks to read the amount of moisture in the bedrock."

"Good. Let's try to remember to bring them with us tomorrow."

Then Alek said, "There's a bad fracture in the stone wall that has recessions in it, and that wall may lead us to another passageway. What's most interesting is that at the depth we've gone beneath the surface of Mars, we may be nearing the water table."

The idea of finding water drew them to examine the tomb's fractured wall. The crack's widest opening was at floor level, and then it narrowed and nearly closed at the top. Aleksei knelt to study the fracture and offset recession. Whatever had occupied these recessions had long ago disintegrated to dust. Other hairline cracks running off from the main fracture made it easy for him to dislodge loose stones, and pulling two free, he placed them on the floor. Catching sight of a wedge-shaped stone that had fallen to the floor, he picked it up and used its flat side to knock off chunks of the ugly mold. He commented, "It seems odd they'd stone up this one wall in the tomb, making me wonder if something of great value lies on the other side."

Removing enough stones to create a small hole, Aleksei saw nothing but darkness on the other side, but dislodging more stones expanded the hole, and he peered inside the cavity. Far moved to hand Aleksei the searchlight, but instead of taking the light, he extended his right arm to reach inside. He immediately made a jerking motion and cried, "Something's got a hold of me!"

Thinking he was kidding, Rhodes ignored him. A sharp piercing pain in his right hand resulted in a strange feeling washing over his entire body, and he braced his left hand against the wall while trying to pull his right hand out but couldn't.

"I'm not kidding! Something's clamping down on my hand and won't let go!"

The urgency in Aleksei's voice told Rhodes he was in trouble, and he took hold of his arm and began pulling, but he couldn't get the hand free.

"Be careful," said Far. "Don't lose your glove."

"Try making a fist so you don't lose your glove," Rhodes told him.

Shaking his head no and grimacing, Alek sucked air through his gritted teeth. "My hand feels like it's on fire."

"Everybody, glove or no glove, get a grip on him and pull!"

Each of them caught hold of an arm, a shoulder, or a piece of his suit, and then they yanked and pulled Aleksei free from the wall. More stones broke loose as he fell on his side. A frighteningly repulsive reptilian creature had sunk its long, canine teeth into his right hand! Its head looked like a goat's, with two spikes projecting as offensive horns. Two larger horns were located on the back of its skull, facing backwards, and a row of short spikes ran down its tailbone. The gruesome creature had long, clinging claws and a whipping tail that wrapped around Alek's arm! A jutting brow ridge and stark, staring, brownish-orange eyes with yellow, catlike pupils reminded Rhodes of a viper.

Aleksei lay on his right side, holding his right arm extended, and grabbing his elbow with his left hand, he gasped in torment, "Get it off me!"

Gawking at the unbelievable, Rhodes feared touching the nightmarish thing's wedge-shaped head and dirty-brown, scaly skin with amber spots. Aleksei convulsed in agony, slumping until his helmet touched the floor, and at that moment, Rhodes grabbed hold of the horns projecting from the creature's head. He tried twisting its head to pull it free from Aleksei's hand, and Flavio squatted to grab its neck in a stranglehold, but seeing its sharp teeth sink deeper as its jaws clamped down, they stopped.

When the animal's eyes began twitching, Rhodes said to Flavio, "Grab hold of its horns here." Flavio traded places with Rhodes and they pushed the left side of the animal's head firmly against the floor, trying not to put pressure on Aleksei's hand. Far and Jetha closed in around Aleksei to hold him still. The creature's eyes shifted as its claws clutched Aleksei's hand tightly, and then its tail began whipping about.

Rhodes grabbed a stone that had fallen from the wall, taking aim before sending it crashing down on the animal's skull, breaking its jawbone. Raising the stone again over his head, he brought it down with enough force to crush its skull, and it fell limp, lying in a pool of red blood, more draining from its mouth.

Aleksei pried his injured hand from the animal's protruding fangs and held it protectively close to his chest as they whisked him away. Walking briskly, Rhodes pulled Aleksei gently by his left arm. "Far, can you think of anything that might help in this situation?"

"Alek, it may have injected a type of venom. Fear causes the heart to pump faster, resulting in the spread of poison, so try to remain calm."

Giving no reply, Rhodes led the way at a rushed pace, but they had a long way to go before reaching the end of the labyrinth and the upper chamber. In the minutes that flew by, Aleksei for the moment seemed to be doing fine as he walked, but looked worried, and they passed through the funerary room and pillared hall to follow the passageway quickly.

When they came to the pit, Rhodes motioned for the others to climb the ladder and asked Aleksei, "Can you climb this ladder using just one hand?"

He nodded and began climbing with Rhodes close behind to lend support, but when he neared the top he swayed, losing control of his muscles. Far and Jetha steadied the ladder at the top as Flavio stooped over to grab hold of Aleksei's left arm to pull him the rest of the way to the upper chamber.

Aleksei became lethargic, saying in a raspy voice, "I've never known such pain before. It's channeling through my entire body, and my right arm feels like I've stuffed it in a bed of red-hot coals."

Far now spoke in a commanding voice. "We've got to get him out of here fast. He may not be able to remain on his feet much longer."

Rhodes guided him out of the pyramid and onto the decking, ushering him to the steps. He and Flavio each gripped an arm to guide him down one step at a time, and he stayed on his feet, but at ground level, he slouched over, succumbing to his condition. He nearly collapsed before they placed him in the rover's front passenger's seat, and on the way back to the ship, Aleksei slumped over, but Flavio clung to him from behind the seat. Knowing every second counted, Rhodes sped toward their ship, worried about his friend's condition and fearing the worst.

CHAPTER 22

What Do We Do to Treat It?

When they arrived at the ship, Rhodes and Flavio practically had to carry Aleksei inside the cargo chamber, and after closing the access door, they went through decompression. Far and Jetha did what they could to get him situated on the floor before the giant eye, and once atmospheric conditions evened out in the chamber, they removed his helmet and suit. He now lay limp, wearing a T-shirt and boxer shorts, as the rest of the crew moved frantically to get out of their suits. Far and Flavio quietly conferred while observing that Aleksei's right forearm had swelled enormously.

Rhodes examined the fang marks on the back of Aleksei's hand. To merely touch his skin made him flinch in pain. Rhodes wadded up part of his suit to use as a pillow to elevate Aleksei's head.

"Far, what can you do for this type of wound?"

"I'm not sure, but we can't let him inside the ship's cabin. It wasn't wise to even let him in the decompression chamber, but I guess we had no other choice."

He turned to face her. "What do you mean we can't let him inside the cabin?"

Far raised her voice, saying, "I know you're concerned about him, Stan, but I'm the medical officer, and we can't risk letting him inside our living quarters without endangering ourselves."

Rhodes stood to confront her, and Flavio grabbed hold of his arm. "Listen to her, Stan."

Trying to shake loose of him, Rhodes demanded, "We've got to give him medical attention! Look at the size of his arm!"

Far latched onto his other arm to shove him against a wall, and while Rhodes fought to get free, the erupting violence caused Jetha to back away. Clinging to his arm, Far shouted, "Listen to me! We'll do what we can for him, but we don't know what we're dealing with here. I think the bite from that creature delivered a massive dose of fast-spreading venom, and as much as I hate to admit it, I think we're going to lose him. Is what it injected into him a lethal poison that kills quickly, or is it an infectious virus that feeds off the body before killing it, potentially going through an incubation period, mutating while turning the body into a pathogen-replicating factory? Whatever it is, it's had plenty of time to course through his veins and attack vital organs."

"You haven't even examined him yet, and you're condemning him to death!"

"As the substance assimilates into his body, Alek may be the host for a deadly virus that has the ability to transmit to others in many ways. This could be a virus that attacks the nervous system. Are we dealing with a new form of rabies? The possibilities are endless."

"She's right, Stan," began Flavio. "We must follow strict quarantine procedures and not allow him in the cabin. We can't take any chances. You know that if you let him inside the ship, you'll be endangering your crew. You're letting your emotions override common sense."

Far remained insistent, "We have no choice but to keep him in the cargo bay. An infectious outbreak on this ship will kill us all!"

"I love Aleksei like a brother," said Flavio, "but I have to agree with Far. Right now, he poses a danger to this ship, and Far is the one best qualified to decide how to proceed. If Aleksei were in charge here and you or I had been the one bitten, he'd go by the book."

"Okay, okay, we'll keep him here, but what can we do to help him?"

Sweating profusely, Aleksei had curled up in the fetal position, holding the injured arm away from him, before losing consciousness.

Far knelt down to examine the puncture marks on the back of his hand, saying, "Before examining the wound, I want to get a surgical mask and gloves on and antiseptic to clean the wound. What bit him had tubular fangs, and we don't have any idea how the substance it injected into his system will react in his body. Is it going to flourish on nutrients in his blood as it evolves, whereby his breath may contaminate our air with an airborne virus? While we're in this room, we must wear face masks and gloves for our protection. Meanwhile, we need to gather some bedding and keep him as comfortable as possible."

"I'll help you with medications," said Jetha.

Rhodes followed Far inside the ship's cabin, hoping to hear the situation wasn't as bleak as he believed to be, and the others followed to gather supplies. Far entered a medical station, positioning a handcart and handing Jetha a medical kit, and then she placed a box of rubber gloves and a box of face masks on the cart. She wheeled the cart toward Jetha and looked her in the eye. "I can't stress enough the importance of wearing a mask and gloves before coming near him."

Collecting bottles and a syringe on the counter, Far explained, "I need time to see what treatments are available. The first rule about a venomous bite is to identify what bit you, and we don't even know how to categorize that creature. Is it a lizard, an iguana, or a form of dinosaur? When I looked at it, I thought lizard. Lizards have been on Earth for millions of years. On the Galapagos Islands off the coast of South America, you can find twenty-three species of land reptiles, including three species of iguana and seven land lizards, and some have spiked horns. I don't think their bite is venomous or believed to be fatal, but anything that has fangs has the potential to inject poison. You saw its eyes, and when you see eyes like that on a snake, you can bet it's venomous.

"So how can I recommend a treatment when we don't even know how to classify that creature? Even though it was hairless, its physical build reminded me more of a wolf, a dog, or a goat, but we can't even begin to imagine how that creature developed from the evolutionary chain on this planet. One thing is for sure:

It's a completely new class of reptile, and judging by the swelling of Aleksei's arm, it's delivered virulent, fast-acting venom. The questions we face are these: What is its potency, and what is the progression of the disease? We don't have those answers."

"Can you give me in simple terms what his chances are without all the technical jargon?" asked Rhodes impatiently.

"Yes, I can. His chances for survival aren't good, and my gut feeling is that we haven't much time before he dies. I'm going to try to extract the poison from the wound, but that's not going to be a simple procedure, and it's probably too late to make a difference anyway. My experience with snakebites is limited, as over the course of my career I've treated only one case. Having witnessed this attack, I would not describe Aleksei's injury as snakebite; fangs were merely the method by which the animal transferred the secretion. I'm no expert on venomous creatures, but I once made a study of venomous snakes, and it's thought that sea snakes are the most poisonous. I know the king cobra carries predominantly neurotoxic venom, while the Eastern diamondback rattlesnake has predominantly hemotoxic venom, so what treatment works on one isn't likely to work on the other."

Rhodes looked at her disdainfully.

"Don't look at me that way. What? Do you want me to perform a miracle? I don't know if we even have antivenom to counteract snakebite, so how can we hope to help him? I'd like to make a better prognosis, but any blood work will require at least forty-eight hours to show results, and that would be a waste of time because it's not likely he has eight hours to live. As terrible as it sounds, I think the only way we could've saved him was to immediately amputate the arm, but the time to do that was lost before we even got him back to the ship."

Slamming cabinet doors while rifling through others in search of medical supplies in the form of a specialized hypodermic Far knew she'd need, she kept blabbering breathlessly. "As long as that hellish creature's existed on this planet, this is the first time one's bitten a human, so how can we possibly know how its venom is going to react to human chemistry? If nothing else, try to think of it as though a rattlesnake bit him.

Snakebite protein is a complex cocktail of thousands of proteins and enzymes, and some are powerful enough to dissolve bone. However, this venom may be the basis for a newly discovered, biological weapon, a virulent, toxic substance beyond human comprehension, and that's why we can't let him in the ship's cabin. Will it thrive in oxygen-rich blood in our arteries to feed on red blood cells, and then mutate to something else?"

Far turned around to look Rhodes in the eye, saying, "There you have it! The only thing you can be sure of is that I'll do all I can for him and monitor his condition. In the end, I believe the best we can offer is to make him as comfortable as possible until death takes him." She proceeded to place the syringe and bottles of medication on a tray, and checking another drawer, she found what looked like a hypodermic with a plastic suction cup extractor connected to it in a plastic bag. After placing it on the tray with the other instruments and medications, she started back to the decompression chamber.

The idea of Aleksei dying devastated Rhodes, but he shook off the thought to join the others in the cargo chamber. Flavio had prepared bedding, and they placed Aleksei in a restful position on the mattress from the capsule he slept in, covering him with a blanket. He continued holding his right arm extended, and his hand and forearm had swelled up even worse during the past few minutes, fluid seeping from his skin.

Jetha wore a surgical face mask and gloves as she knelt beside Aleksei, and placing the bare back of her wrist against his forehead, she said, "He's burning up. Should we check his blood pressure and pulse?"

Far knelt beside Jetha and looked at Aleksei, who was barely conscious. "I want any of you who've touched him to immediately go wash your hands thoroughly, and don't touch him unless you're wearing a mask and gloves. We may be dealing with toxins that can penetrate skin." She then looked at Jetha. "You just touched him with your wrist. Go wash up, and if you don't want to end up in the same shape he's in, don't do it again."

Everyone went to wash up as Far had instructed, and upon returning put on masks and gloves as she'd recommended. Far had checked his vital signs: His blood pressure had doubled and his heartbeat tripled, and knowing he was in enormous pain, she gave him the maximum dose of morphine. As she touched the bitten hand in preparation to treat the wound, Aleksei's body contorted in agony, and she hesitated, shaking her head. "We've lost so much precious time."

Far removed the hypodermic with the plastic suction cup from its bag, and focusing on the hand's wound, she said, "I have this extractor, but as swelled up as the hand is, I don't think it'll work. I'm going to give him a series of painkiller injections around the wound, and after it's had time to work, I'll need to make a short incision across the wound. My hope is that blood flow will help get rid of some of the poison and lessen the swelling to enable me to use the extractor."

"Let's do it," Rhodes agreed.

She gently touched the swollen hand, examining where the fangs had penetrated. Aleksei winced, and she hesitated. The area around the fang marks was already turning black. Rhodes asked, "Can I help in some way?"

Far nodded. "You can help by holding him still."

They squatted and took positions around Aleksei, who, beleaguered by pain, knew little of what was going on. Rhodes braced him from behind his back, Flavio held his legs, and Jetha held the injured arm still. Aleksei flinched as Far began injecting painkillers into his hand.

After giving the solution a few minutes to deaden the pain, she then used a scalpel to slice open the wound, and Aleksei yelped in pain as a yellow substance oozed from the wound until blood flowed freely. Far caught the fluids with a towel and then administered an antiseptic to clean the wound.

She now grabbed the hypodermic with an extraction suction cup, placing the cup over the wound and surrounding skin. Drawing on the hypodermic created a vacuum, and a yellow substance began entering the cup as though someone were sucking the poison out. She had some success drawing a small portion of fluid, which was more red than yellow near the end of the extraction, and then she bandaged the hand.

"I need time to see what's in our medical supplies to counteract the venom. We may have antivenom…I'm not sure."

Left in a quandary about how to proceed, Far left the chamber to check her computer for a listing of medications onboard the ship. The others watched as Aleksei remained in a tight ball, the blanket tucked warmly around him, and after a surprisingly short time, Far returned with another syringe.

"We have ten vials of heparin, which is the only clinically tested treatment we have to interrupt venomous thrombosis progression. However, as a general rule it doesn't actively resolve the progression." Far turned teary-eyed, saying, "I'm going to give him a series of injections with the solution, but too much of this medication can kill him. A validated regimen to treat snakebite requires a careful dosage adjustment to stay in a therapeutic range. Without toxicology tests to establish a medical evaluation, how do I implement a method of treatment when I don't know what it is we're dealing with here?"

Rhodes knew he'd pestered Far long enough and acknowledged the difficulties in providing treatment. "I understand the risk factors, Far. Just give him the shots and we'll hope for the best."

At one point during the night Aleksei became conscious, calling for Rhodes, and he came to kneel beside him. Aleksei's pale skin had a blotchy, yellowish pallor, and flushed with fever, he looked at Rhodes with beseeching eyes that showed he knew the deep trouble he was in. Desperately grabbing hold of Rhodes' arm with his trembling, good hand, he spoke feebly in a raspy voice. "Stan, I don't want to die."

Gently placing his hand on his friend's shoulder, Rhodes tried to be supportive. "C'mon, now, settle down. You're a tough guy, and Far says you're going to be okay. She's injected into you various treatments to help your body fight this thing, including an antivenom, and the best thing you can do for yourself is to try to get some rest."

Rhodes then turned to Far. "Can we give him something to help him rest?"

"Yes, I'll give him a mild sedative."

Far administered an injection in his left arm, and then he placed his hand to his throat. "Can I have something to drink?"

Far noticed Aleksei had developed a nosebleed, and she quickly wiped the blood streaming from his right nostril. The bleeding stopped shortly afterwards. She then gave him a half cup of water, and after drinking it, he said, "I'm having trouble swallowing."

Far examined his throat, saying, "You need to relax and try to get some rest to conserve your strength while giving the medication time to work."

She coaxed him into lying down, and uncovering his chest to listen to his heartbeat, she discovered a rash had developed on his chest in the form of festering, red welts. Further examination showed that they covered his entire torso, and after listening to his heartbeat with a stethoscope, she covered him back up. She also noticed that the swelling of his arm had not receded, which indicated the treatments had done little to help his condition.

Far set up an IV and then motioned for the others to join her in the cabin. "His vital signs are slipping, and inflammation in his throat is causing his airway to close up. He had a nosebleed and when his chest was bare, I saw a rash, leading me to believe the venom is overtaking blood vessels. Any weak spots in veins can lead to internal bleeding. The next couple of hours are going to be the most critical. If he starts getting better, I may be able to do more for him, but I've done all I can for now."

Thirty minutes later, Far saw the rash fast developing into bleeding sores. Aleksei opened his eyes and stared pitifully at Jetha, who gave him a pleasant gaze from the far side of the chamber. He began speaking to her softy in Russian, and Jetha went to him, her eyes worried and teary. Kneeling beside Aleksei, Jetha took hold of his left hand and placed it against her chest. Then he repeated what he'd said in Russian, and Jetha nodded as tears ran down her face.

Far went to speak to Rhodes in a soft whisper, "That rash has developed into bleeding lesions. The only times I've encountered that condition is when the diagnosis is a contagious and progressive strain of an agent."

Aleksei suddenly went into convulsions, coughing up blood on Jetha, who quickly stood up and remained frozen until Far ushered her away. Then he started vomiting blood, so Rhodes used a towel to catch the fluids he expelled. In the process of cleaning him up, blood spattered onto Rhodes' clothing. Aleksei next went into an uncontrollable hacking, gagging cough, so Rhodes backed off.

Flavio tried to help, but Rhodes stepped in his way. "Keep your distance until he's settled down."

They cleaned Aleksei up as best they could. Now his glossy eyes looked oblivious to the goings-on around him. Occasionally ranting in Russian, he was obviously becoming delusional and reliving past experiences.

Far returned and reported, "His lungs are filling up with blood, and he'll drown in his own fluids."

She took a face mask with a hose attachment connected to a small oxygen tank and fit the mask over Aleksei's nose and mouth, wrapping the attached elastic strap around his head. He now lay limp, taking in pure oxygen in irregular breaths, and she proceeded to check his vital signs. "He's nonresponsive, his heart rate is falling as his body temperature has dropped, and his breathing is down to twenty breaths per minute. I don't know if pure oxygen is helping him breathe any easier, but it can't hurt, unless it's feeding the pathogen, and that's certainly a possibility."

Kneeling beside her, Rhodes asked, "How's Jetha?"

"Oh, she's fine. Right now she's showering. None of it got in her eyes, but she's terribly upset, and I've given her something to relax her. When Aleksei spoke to her in Russian, he thought he was talking to his mother, and Jetha said his words were heartfelt." She then looked at the blood on Rhodes' clothes and cautioned, "I strongly urge you to get out of those clothes and shower immediately. This is nothing to fool around with."

Aleksei began coughing again. Far removed the mask to find blood in it and sadly shook her head. "His condition is deteriorating fast. His vital organs are shutting down, and I expect he'll be gone before sunup, which is only a couple of hours away. His condition is hopeless, and frankly I'm surprised he's lingered for this long, although I don't suspect he's suffering anymore. I know it sounds heartless, but given his condition, the sooner he dies, the better for him—and us."

As soon as Jetha left the shower room, Rhodes placed his clothing in a plastic bag with hers, knowing they'd have to dispose of anything that came into contact with Aleksei. While showering, he thought of Aleksei. Accepting he was losing a crew member wasn't easy, but Far had done all she could to save him. Soon their number would be reduced from five to four, and he was already wondering how Aleksei's death was going to affect the others.

CHAPTER 23

Burying One of Our Own

Rhodes returned to the cargo bay wearing fresh clothes, a face mask, and gloves. He watched Far check Aleksei's condition. His outward signs looked hopeless, and it was agonizing for the others to witness his slow deterioration.

Far said, "His pupils are fixed and dilated. We're are going to lose him soon, and we'll have to bury him outside the ship with every stitch of material that has come into contact with his body fluids. No trace of his blood can be left behind in the ship, for even after it dries, it could become airborne and enter our lungs."

Aleksei's rhythmic breathing halted with a final exhale, and Far pronounced him dead. They had a moment of silence on his behalf, falling into a somber mood until Jetha suddenly broke down in tears and Far came to her side so choked up she couldn't speak. Flavio's sorrow showed on his face, and Rhodes could only feel misery in knowing they'd lost a good man.

Rhodes said to Far and Jetha, "Flavio and I will take care of preparing him for burial, which can take place later this afternoon, so why don't the two of you turn in and try to get some rest?"

Far and Jetha went into the cabin, and Flavio and Rhodes placed Aleksei in a body bag, along with everything that had come into contact with him. As much as Rhodes would have preferred to take his body back to Earth, they simply couldn't risk transporting a body carrying an infectious virus.

It was midafternoon by the time they were all up and moving around. The crew of five was now four. What happened to their colleague was hardly believable, but one look in the cargo chamber reminded them that they really did lose him. Flavio and Rhodes gathered shovels to bury him, placing his body in a sunken area beyond a sand dune where they believed there was little chance of the wind blowing away the soil covering him.

Having made up a marker in the simple shape of a cross, they stood in their spacesuits under a hazy sky, and Rhodes offered a prayer in their dead friend's honor. "Heavenly Father, here lies our fallen comrade, Aleksei Dimitri Polzinov, a good and brave man. He was an asset to our team, and we wouldn't have come as far as we have without him. His loss humbles us in showing us how delicate and fragile life is. We will miss his camaraderie and humor. His presence is irreplaceable. We beseech Thee, Heavenly Father, Creator of the entire universe, to embrace this unique individual and grant him peace. Amen."

Rhodes wasn't sure how they were going to carry on, for Aleksei's death crushed the spirit that drove them to explore the pyramid's labyrinth. The loss of any crew member was a terrible thing to deal with, and he also had to contend with the survival of the living. He understood they needed time to grieve. He knew it bothered Far that she was unable to aid an ailing crew member who died in her care. He thought Jetha had grown especially fond of their favorite Russian, and Flavio had lost a friend.

On the next transmission Rhodes sent to Earth—one he dreaded to send—he delivered news of Aleksei's death. Giving a detailed report about how it happened, he mentioned they expected to bring back the remains of the strange creature. It was an alien life form that required study, and mission planners would insist on their returning with it. Far had entered in her medical journal that the cause of death was the result of a bite from an unidentified creature of unknown origin indigenous to Mars, and he included this in his message.

Rhodes knew he needed to return to the pyramid to collect the creature, and he'd eventually have to see what lay beyond the fractured wall in the tomb. The next day, he asked Flavio to accompany him to the monument. The fact that none of the motion detectors had activated made them confident that nothing else had entered the grand gallery from the ruler's tomb. But knowing more of the creatures could infiltrate the tomb and labyrinth at any time, they sought weapons to defend themselves with. Their best and perhaps only defense were flamethrowers that could shoot a pressurized flame as far as eight meters. An ignition trigger sent out the fuel mixture, spraying a potent, compressed, oil-based liquid fuel, and an auto-ignition spark plug at the barrel's tip caused the fuel to change to fire. Along with these pyrotechnic weapons, they had to haul additional tanks on their backpacks, which made their spacesuits bulkier than they already were. A fuel supply hose went from the compact tanks that hung off their life-support systems to the gun housing, requiring caution when they maneuvered through tight spaces.

As Rhodes and Flavio prepared to leave the ship, Far and Jetha kept a vigil, viewing camera angles in the pyramid from their monitors. They intended to focus on the motion detector in the grand gallery and relay a warning if they sensed movement while the men were traveling to the pyramid.

The first thing Flavio and Rhodes did after they arrived at the Cydonia Complex in the rover was to fit each other with the flamethrower equipment. A short burst discharged from each weapon was enough to show they were in good working order. Rhodes carried additional fuel for the generator, and Flavio carried a tough, plastic bag under his arm which they'd use to place the dead creature in. After climbing the stairs to the platform, they stopped at the pyramid's entrance to refuel the generator and started it up. They briefly searched the upper chamber before descending into the labyrinth and the depths of the pyramid, carefully inspecting the foreboding chasms.

The idea of meeting up with another creature made them wary. When they came to the first junction, Rhodes shot a streak of fire down the corridor leading to the original pyramid entrance. Soon arriving at the pillared hall, he had Flavio stand guard as he went to the heap of Martian remains at the core of the pyramid. Shooting a flaming streak over the mound, he saw nothing move. He used the flamethrower again to shoot a flame that stretched all the way across the funerary hall. Flavio made a fast check of the rooms where the mummies were, and then they stood before the statue of the Martian king sitting on his throne, his bat-god in the background.

Seeing the lights inside the tomb still working, Rhodes entered the chamber with the utmost caution, ready to blast anything that moved. He glimpsed the hideous creature lying frozen on the floor before he approached the sarcophagus wide-eyed, only to see the king inside. Flavio kept watch over the hole in the wall as Rhodes gave the area a look-over, last turning his eyes to the cubical where the treasury jars lay. The decorative lid of the coffin-like crypt stood like a sentinel in the corner where they'd left it. The dazzling eyes in its creepy, distorted image seemed to study them from the very moment they entered the tomb.

Rhodes turned his attention to the creature, nudging it with the barrel of his flamethrower to confirm it was as stiff as a board and examining the lethal fangs without touching them. Then he inspected the fractured wall where the thing came out from, and he tried to think of a way to close up the hole so nothing else could get inside the tomb. He wadded a bundle of plastic packing material from the gallery and shoved it into the hole, jamming it tightly to block the opening. If they saw the plastic missing later, they'd know that something must have gotten through to enter the tomb.

They knew it was more important than ever to keep the motion detectors and cameras working to warn them of an invader in the passageways. If it was their destiny to discover water in the deep recesses of the pyramid, they'd have to investigate what lay beyond the fractured wall. However, it would have to wait till another time, for he felt no urgency to seek out the unknown now.

Carefully handling the creature's stiff remains, they placed it inside the plastic bag, intending to place it in deep freeze upon returning to the ship. Thinking they needed to accomplish something more during their trip to the pyramid, Rhodes considered taking the gold crown and sunburst medallion the king wore. However, believing he'd have to remove the king's head to free the medallion and dreading the thought, he thought it best to leave that job for another day, permitting the king to wear his coveted crown and medallion a little longer.

Taking a moment to examine the jars of jewelry and diamonds in the connecting cubicle, Flavio suggested they take this opportunity to transport the four treasury jars back to the ship. Moving the jars out into the tomb where they were easier to handle, they found them to be quite heavy, and Rhodes went to find the handcart. They managed on the stairs off the gallery, and the handcart enabled them to transport two jars at a time through the labyrinth up to the pit.

Spending more time than they'd anticipated on this job, they set up the lift-hoist to straddle the pit to raise one jar at a time to the upper chamber. After getting the first two up to the upper chamber's floor, they left them there to return to the tomb for the other two. Rhodes checked the plastic he'd jammed into the hole first to make certain it hadn't been disturbed, the bright eyes on the leaning coffin lid silently watching their every move. They transported the last two jars in the same manner, and not forgetting the dead creature, they placed the bag with its remains atop one of the jars on the cart.

After moving all four jars to the upper chamber, they used the cart to transport them along the decking and left them together near the stairs. They then returned the cart to the upper chamber before lugging one jar at a time down the steps of the pyramid. The job was strenuous and tiring.

The contents of the treasury jars raised Far and Jetha's spirits, and they examined jewels and diamonds for almost half an hour in the decompression chamber, making it a worthwhile accomplishment. It took almost two days to photograph and document the jewelry collection, and while this went on, Far studied the venom that killed Aleksei to determine its potency. Ordinarily, encountering any form of life on Mars would be a thrilling discovery, but the crew spoke little about the creature that took the life of one of their own.

Everyone had a different way of adapting to Aleksei's death, and Rhodes closely monitored his crew to see any changes in their behavior. Mission planners had warned about a number of situations that may evolve as a result of psychological trauma pertaining to the death of a crew member. Furthermore, living in such isolated conditions could lead to a form of cabin fever, which may eventually develop into an even more serious mental condition.

Rhodes observed Jetha in particular because he thought she'd developed a close relationship with Aleksei. She spent much of her time deciphering the inscriptions on the walls of the upper chamber. She had become a bit reclusive, leaving Rhodes to wonder if she was becoming depressed. One day she told him she was nearly finished translating the inscriptions but didn't think the timing was right to present her findings to the crew. After another two days passed, he wondered when she would let everybody know what she'd uncovered about the ancient writing, but knowing she was a levelheaded person, he left her alone.

Radiation levels outside the ship ran high for a few days, and during that period, they took turns traveling to the monument in pairs to refuel the generator. The motion detectors and cameras hadn't picked up any activity to make them think something had gotten in the tomb, but Rhodes wondered if the plastic he'd stuffed inside the hole had been disturbed. He didn't want his meager crew to have to face off with another one of those frightening creatures in the confines of the labyrinth.

The thought of finding out what lay beyond that stone wall in the tomb wouldn't leave Rhodes alone, and he didn't want to hold back a touring inspection of the pyramid for too long. They'd have to take the flamethrowers to defend themselves. He now believed they had sufficient water to see the mission through, and as much as mission planners didn't expect to find water on this first mission, he now saw it as a possibility.

As radiation levels subsided, they knew their return to the monument was inevitable. It was strange how a cold, stone edifice could mesmerize the human spirit. Its secrets constantly lured them to it. One day their journey here would seem like little more than a dream, and they'd yearn to touch its stones once more.

CHAPTER 24

The Torrent Age of a Legendary Ruler

They had buried Aleksei ten days earlier. His death had undermined their ambitions while reminding them of their own mortality. The way he died was a wake-up call to how little they know about this alien world. Unable to venture outside for any lengthy period of time because radiation levels were high, they needed some form of distraction to shake loose their sorrow.

They were all up one morning sipping coffee or juices and taking in the never-changing view of this desolate planet when Far's voice broke the silence.

"Jetha, by now you must've deciphered something from that text."

Rhodes watched Jetha as she replied, "Yes, I have completed the text, and you might say it's a telling find."

"Okay, let's have it then," demanded Flavio.

"I can give you a printout or I can let the computer say it or both ways if you like. The inscriptions on those two walls run together to chronicle a turbulent period in the history of this civilization and gives insight into the life of one of its most revered emperors."

"What did you mean when you said you could let the computer say it?"

"The computer is equipped with a variety of different voice impressions, and after completing the translation by inserting key words, I programmed the computer to provide a voice to read to us what the inscription says. I chose a masculine voice for the Martian ruler, and it is he who will be delivering this historical record. There's mention of the eye pyramid and circumstances connected to the building of it."

Jetha produced stacks of papers stapled together and passed them around. "This is a printout of the text, but I'll play it for you now."

Then Rhodes asked, "Did you decipher any other writings besides the text in the upper chamber?"

"A few, on the rose-colored stone in the funerary room were inscribed 'Stone of Wailing Sorrow.' The archway in the grand gallery was inscribed with the words, 'The Hall of Truth—A Calling for Truth, Order, and Justice.' In addition, etched into the ruler's sarcophagus was the phrase, 'Here I remain on guard to protect my loyal subjects.' I tried translating writing from the queen's funerary room where I believe on one wall are parts of a poem, but most of that was painted and is incomplete so I couldn't. However, the queen's name was Adeemah, and she was also referred to as the 'Sublime One.'" She then went to her monitor and, after pressing a few keys, said, "Okay, here goes. The past will actually speak to us."

A stern, powerful voice broke through the speakers with a vibration. "My name is Matusek. You have dared to enter the sacred realm of my resting place, and for this trespass my immortal soul curses you. This is my enduring story.

"For generations my family ruled over the thriving island paradise of Kopel Pikala. We were a simple but proud people who coexisted in harmony with nature, and our world was no more than a gift from the creator of all things. Our ancestors passed down customs and rituals to honor the creator, and as long as we abided by those traditions, we could live in tranquil surroundings that would bring us a rich harvest of plant and seafood. However, if we strayed and became corrupt, the spirits of our deceased ancestors would call on the creator to punish us by bringing upheaval. His rage shown as powerful storms pounded our seashore, and far-reaching unrest disturbed fearsome sea creatures, tenacious predators with a ravenous appetite for flesh that would roam on land to feed upon us.

"East of our island country lay the expanse of a great unexplored ocean, and to our west was the Oborahn Sea, which separated us from the mainland continent. Here was where the power base for the prosperous Mycurian Empire was located in their capital of Gaugamar. Changing wind patterns made the waters turbulent, and heaving waves and strong currents in the Oborahn Sea served as our only protection from the Mycurians. In many respects, they were the highest order of civilization that regarded us as savage barbarians, but they were an immoral and profane race that worshipped pagan gods. Hatchek, their ruling emperor, constantly sought to expand the boundaries of his kingdom, and having conquered nearly all neighboring territories, he coveted our prized island paradise.

"Before my time, our god had twice aided us in repelling invasions by sea, raising his hand to bring forth angry storms and raging waves that sank or dispersed Mycurian vessels bound for our island. The Mycurians eventually succeeded in reaching our shores, however, and viciously attacked us in a blazing path of death and destruction. My people were no match for the well-armed invaders, who slew my grandfather, Petalah. At the moment of his death, my father, Talingra, the reigning prince of Kopel Pikala, became king. The invaders slaughtered many of my people and enslaved many more, whom they took to the Mycurian mainland. My father remained steadfast in his effort to free our island, killing Mycurians whenever he could. He and a band of island warriors went up in the hills to organize a resistance, making surprise attacks against our conquerors.

"The Mycurians had long since dominated the mainland, where their army was undefeated. The only threat to their borders came from the Kamaran nation, but a vast desert wasteland separated these warring kingdoms and greatly reduced the risk of attack by either side. The last time their armies clashed was years ago when the Kamarans suffered a devastating defeat. The Kamaran king led the attack, and in the midst of a bloody battle, the Mycurians captured him; the victorious Mycurians forced the Kamaran nation to pay a humiliating tribute to have their king returned. Since then, the brooding, contemptuous Kamarans held a deep-seated determination to rebuild their army and one day conquer their hated enemy.

"One day, a wayward merchant trader witnessed the Kamarans organizing offensive units to wreak their vengeance upon the Mycurians. He reported this news to a Mycurian lookout outpost, and they alerted the aging emperor. Receiving word that this great foe would soon be crossing the desert, Emperor Hatchek now saw how he'd underestimated the vindictive Kamaran king, who would soon settle for nothing less than Hatchek's head. The Hatchek dynasty had conquered many new territories to broaden an ever-sprawling empire, and Hatchek had grown so arrogant that he believed no nation would dare threaten to attack him. Ruling with absolute power, his successes and the accumulated wealth and resources of those defeated nations brought about the enslavement of many. His policy of expansionism had left Mycurian forces occupying foreign lands, which weakened border defenses and left him ill-prepared for a land-based attack from the west. The citizens of Gaugamar had grown accustomed to an opulent lifestyle that degraded their morality, but they were now nearly panicked about an invasion.

"There was one fort at the edge of the desert frontier that the Kamarans would have to overtake before coming to the outskirts of the capital. Hatchek anticipated this fortress would fall but hoped that the forces defending it would hold out long enough to buy him precious time. He sent out messengers to retrieve additional forces, but Kamaran spies lying in wait killed them before they reached their destination. Having bolstered the city's fortifications, Hatchek turned to his advisers for guidance. His chief adviser, spiritual reader, and head architect, Arkenebus, stepped forward to suggest the emperor send a representative to Kopel Pikala to bring back those forces occupying the island, and he also suggested asking the island people for help. The islanders had proven themselves great warriors and worthy opponents, and if they would give their support by fighting to save the empire, they would be handsomely rewarded. An expeditious treaty forwarded to the island would promise that henceforth the islanders would be able to rule themselves without Mycurian interference. Kopel Pikala would be an ally, only serving as a port to Mycurian vessels. In exchange for the island's participation in fighting enemies of the empire, Kopel Pikala would become a protectorate of the Mycurian Empire. If another kingdom ever attacked the island nation, Mycurian forces would come to their defense.

"Hatchek respected Arkenebus, who had distinguished himself as a brilliant visionary and had a reputation as the wisest man in the kingdom. Hatchek was still reluctant to release his grip on the island paradise, but Arkenebus asserted that all would be lost if this plan didn't work. They'd received more reports of a massive army crossing the desert. If this plea to the king of Kopel Pikala succeeded, Mycurian units would be returning with a large number of islanders to preserve Hatchek's throne. He last cautioned Hatchek there was little time to cross the Oborahn Sea to recover the empire's forces and make a convincing offer to the island king before Kamarans marched on the city.

"Emperor Hatchek was finally moved by the persistence of Arkenebus, who now voiced his concern that the offer wouldn't be tantalizing enough to convince Talingra, king of Kopel Pikala, to come to the aid of the empire. Arkenebus now persuaded Hatchek to give the hand of one of his daughters in a royal marriage ceremony to the island king, thereby forging a strong alliance between the two nations.

"At his wit's end, Hatchek sent Arkenebus to approach King Talingra, who was in a well-fortified stronghold in the hills on the island. Arkenebus arrived on the island in good time and immediately sought to arrange a meeting with Talingra. When presenting the Mycurian Empire's offer, he cautioned that if his efforts failed to unify the two nations, the Kamarans could very well take over the entire empire. Instead of Kopel Pikala gaining a strong ally in the Mycurians, Kopel Pikala could one day face an invasion from the Kamarans.

"Talingra had heard of the warring Kamarans but hesitated to join an alliance with Mycuria. Before pledging his support, he needed the emperor's promise that he'd grant freedom to all native islanders enslaved by the Mycurians and let them return to their homeland. Arkenebus said that as acting representative of the emperor, he had the authority to honor Talingra's request, giving his solemn promise that this would occur immediately after the Mycurians secured their borders.

"The Kamarans had amassed an army at the entrance to the walled capital and were set to do battle. They'd already begun testing the city's fortifications when Mycurian vessels arrived at the city's harbor, bulging with islanders prepared to fight, and they reinforced Gaugamar's defenses. At dawn, a spearhead of Kamarans stormed the city, throwing everything they had at the gates, and as they broke through, alarm and chaos spread throughout Gaugamar. The Mycurians and islanders fought courageously side by side to stem the flow of marauding invaders, but it appeared there was no way to stop their enemy.

"The waters of the Oborahn Sea were still for the king of Kopel Pikala to land south of Gaugamar with three vessels of his own at an area of unpopulated marshland. Hearing the city was under siege, he formed two divisions to launch an assault to start a new front against the Kamarans, diverting their attention. Bloody fighting and stiff resistance were all that kept the Kamarans from overrunning the capital, but Mycurian losses were growing. The onslaught raged on until an exhausted Mycurian line caved in, but as Kamaran commanders saw victory in their grasp, they received word about unexpected fighting south of the capital.

"A communication described a fighting force coming up from the marshes and attacking with ferocity, and the Kamarans were suffering high losses. Kamaran leaders knew they needed to fortify units fighting at the south before taking the city or they'd be smashed in a vice. Just when the Kamarans split their forces, the Mycurians rallied to redouble their efforts to save the city, and Hatchek released an aggressive, imperial guard unit that tore into Kamaran lines. At the southern front, Talingra's forces clashed with Kamarans and the Mycurians gained strength while Kamaran commanders saw their legions crumble, and their glorious victory turned into a disastrous defeat. By the end of the day, one Kamaran general had committed suicide and another had escaped with a small, demoralized force, and many of the survivors had perished retreating across the desert to reach their homeland.

"Among the dreadful carnage, the Mycurians celebrated a great victory as they came together with King Talingra and his joyous islanders. Talingra stood among the crowd, announcing that the victory marked a new beginning in Mycurian-Kopel Pikala affairs. As he pledged his support to the Mycurian Empire, few noticed the stealthy approach of two assassins in Kamaran uniforms who suddenly attacked and fatally wounded him with knives. The crowd slaughtered the two Kamarans.

"The two assassins were rumored to be members of the emperor's own imperial guard, and the guard was quick to execute anyone who dared spread such a lie. Hatchek kept his word that those who fought were well-rewarded, and they returned to their island paradise. However, the emperor's treaty was an agreement specifically made with King Talingra, and now that he was dead, Hatchek cited that Kopel Pikala needed to remain part of the empire for its own best interests. Over objections from senior islanders, slaves who were formerly Kopel Pikala natives remained slaves, and this enraged islanders.

"Hatchek was seen as the embodiment of evil by the islanders. As time passed, Hatchek died, but not before his young queen gave birth to a new ruler, Emperor Horuk. Mycurians commonly believed the last hereditary king of Kopel Pikala was Talingra, but a new king had been born in secrecy to carry on the bloodline. I, Matusek, grew into manhood, and I waited while organizing and planning for the day when I could avenge the deaths of my father and his father before him.

"Young Emperor Horuk had the same giant ego as his father but not his cunning, and one born into dynastic rule over a sprawling empire needn't be as clever as his father was. This emperor wanted to build a magnificent pyramid to feed his self-exaltation, and this great shrine would entomb his remains while immortalizing him.

"While clearing and leveling land at the designated site for the pyramid, excavation crews experienced an unexpected cave-in that exposed a cavernous, subterranean region. This cavity was the lair of extraordinary, flesh-eating monsters that, once disturbed, began emerging after sundown to devour workers and unsuspecting citizens. They were nocturnal animals, as their eyes were sensitive to light, but work at the site drew them out during the day as well, and construction on the pyramid halted. These ferocious, predatory beasts terrified the population, and even the army was powerless to stop them. Their skin was tough as armor and not easily pierced, and they had a voracious bite that could cut a man in half. Some brave soldiers died facing off with them. The entire population was alarmed, for the beasts had broken into homes and eaten the residents, leaving Horuk hard-pressed to calm the fears of his citizens.

"Horuk summoned his chief adviser, Arkenebus, who was also the architect of the pyramid and the same man his father had relied on in troubling times. Arkenebus had but one idea for dealing with these creatures, and it concerned a legend connected with the island of Kopel Pikala. According to this legend, fearsome beasts periodically came out of the sea to overrun the island, and those beasts were strikingly similar to the creatures at the pyramid site. If stories he'd heard were true, the islanders had developed methods to combat the beasts, for nowadays there were rarely any fatalities when they came ashore.

"The viceroy governing Kopel Pikala arrived in Gaugamar to honor Emperor Horuk and confirmed there were such terrifying beasts. After glimpsing one of the flesh-eating creatures at the pyramid site, he said they were the same species as those on the island.

"Arkenebus warned Horuk that should he employ islanders to combat these animals, he sensed danger in dealing with them. They resented the takeover and occupation of their island paradise, and he told of a new reigning king on the island of Kopel Pikala. High priests disputed this claim, insisting the island's hereditary line had ended with the death of Talingra. However, Arkenebus argued that he had a premonition that such a person did exist, and stressed that if the opportunity presented itself, this person would kill Emperor Horuk. Sometimes the predictions of Arkenebus seemed so outrageous that Horuk had little faith in their veracity, and there'd been little resistance from the islanders during the last few years. He wanted to see his pyramid built, and a meager force of natives coming to the mainland hardly presented a threat to him or his empire. Therefore, Horuk sent a high-ranking official to Kopel Pikala to seek help from the islanders to kill the terrible beasts.

"When I received word that Emperor Horuk sought help ridding his capital of these fearsome creatures, I at last saw my opportunity to settle with the dynasty that delivered oppression to my people. This was a day ordained by the heavens, and soon blood would run in the streets of the Mycurian capital. . . ."

Jetha stopped the text. "There's a lot to take in, and the best is yet to come. The text didn't have a break in it, but this is where the historical record shifts to the wall behind the statue depicting a man battling the lizard beast." She refilled Rhodes' coffee cup while the others went to grab refreshments and something to nibble on before resuming the text.

CHAPTER 25

Beasts of Mycuria

Jetha pushed the pause button, and the voice began speaking again.

"Acting in the capacity of a tribal lord, I met and bargained with the official sent by the empire, and being familiar with these beasts, I knew they'd be willing to pay a high sum for our services. After quietly listening to his offer, I boldly demanded the Mycurians pay double what their emperor was offering. I reasoned that with one bite, these animals could sever a leg, and I would need a large force to kill them all.

"The official huddled with his delegation before agreeing to pay the sum, but then his advisors cautioned him to set a limit on how many warriors I could bring into the city at one time, which I agreed to. The rest of my tribe would have to remain on our vessel unless it became evident they were needed.

"A large population of slaves residing in the Mycurian capital had prayed for the death of the tyrannical Hatchek, but after he'd perished, they saw no change under his son's reign. I had long been in contact with a network of slaves, sending ahead a dozen spies to infiltrate Gaugamar and conspire with them. These spies communicated a password to let them know the hour was near for them to revolt against their masters. They had my solemn promise that with the overthrow of Horuk a new order would be set in place to govern the empire, where slavery would be banned.

"I arrived on Mycurian shores to see the towering pillars of the offering temple at the edge of the peninsula. Horuk ordered my presence at his palace just south of the site designated for the new pyramid, and in the grandeur of a majestic pillared gallery

I stood before him. I bowed before the youthful emperor, who pompously issued his expectations, announcing that my followers and I should slay the abominable beasts in no more than seven days. I astounded him by replying that after two nights all the creatures will be dead. He then stated that he must see their carcasses before making payment, and I proposed that my tribesmen would honor him by displaying the dead creatures before him. I last suggested that he issue a proclamation for his citizens to keep off the streets for the next two nights, for their own safety, which he did.

"I'd heard the young emperor was as profane and arrogant as the father he had replaced on the throne but lacked his father's ruthless cunning. I hadn't as yet taken him for a fool by allowing us free reign so close to the palace when he then addressed me by saying he'd appointed a unit of his imperial guard to oversee our progress at the site. He went on to say that he'd personally reward me if I succeeded in slaying the monsters in only two nights, and I replied that nothing would please me more.

"I had devised a daring plan to seize the capital and overtake Horuk's forces, but success depended on total secrecy. Facing a host of problems keeping our enemy in the dark, we said little to the slave class living in Gaugamar, biding our time until the moment was right. Determined to strike fast, I scheduled our invasion forces to come in two waves. The first wave consisted of the legion accompanying me to the Mycurian port, and the vessel we'd arrived in swelled with warriors. Crowded conditions aboard the vessel were relieved once I directed a column of islanders off the ship to the nearby pyramid site, located in the midst of a necropolis and monuments built in the memory of previous Mycurian rulers. The rest of the crew would remain aboard ship until the following night, when they'd move stealthily of their own accord. The second wave would come from two ships scheduled to depart from Kopel Pikala to arrive the following night south of the city at an area of unpopulated marshland.

"This force would land where islanders had landed under my father's command many years before, and much depended on the sea being calm for their departure from the island. Those spies who'd landed earlier would meet them and lead them to designated hiding places arranged by the slave underground movement. This was indeed an ambitious plan, and there'd be little chance of Mycurian citizens spotting our movements. In addition, those in charge of protecting the empire would undoubtedly have their eyes focused on the goings-on at the pyramid site.

"On the first night, we prepared to battle the flesh-eating beasts, quietly setting up to defend against them as they came up from the bowels of the planet. We waited for them at an outdoor dugout area where tunneling had been done.

"Members of the imperial guard watched us set up at the mouth of the passage, studying our procedures to see how we took down such formidable beasts their own army couldn't stop. They knew the dangers of tangling with beasts easily whipped into frenzy, and they'd witnessed the creatures' vicious attacks on soldiers and citizens. They'd seen limbs severed and chunks ripped out of victims. They'd heard screams from those dragged away to be eaten alive.

"The beasts' true vulnerability was a soft spot at the base of the neck. We had a technique to avoid their jaws of death, designating a single warrior to jump onto a creature's muscular back and inflict the first wound. I was first, and as all the others watched, I stood ready above the opening with my spear, prepared to leap on the first one that appeared. Our handheld torches lit the opening from which they'd emerge, and we lay in wait for a lumbering, dark shadow.

"Its breathing was fierce as it moved out from the opening, snapping violently with its jaws. The creature hesitated as our torches distracted it, and I pounced on its back, plunging the head of my spear deep into the base of its neck. The beast tried to turn its head to lunge and take a bite out of me, but the location and depth of the spearhead made it difficult for the agile creature to turn its head, leaving it incapacitated. Now the warriors encircling the opening made their assault, ramming spears into the beast's torso and ribcage to finish it off. After we'd slain the creature, we used hooks to drag the carcass away.

"These monsters weren't much different from the sea creatures that were stirred by violent storms to come to our island. Both had huge jaws and sharp teeth, webbed feet, and a long, whipping tail. We kept our bodies conditioned, as we were athletic tree climbers who built our huts above the ground to avoid them on their unexpected visits to prey upon our livestock. With our well-trained eyes for throwing spears, we were quite accurate, hitting our mark at the base of their necks.

"At the pyramid site, they came out in single file, and the imperial guard was astonished at how we bravely took the creatures on. Throughout the night, we used torches to draw their attention, taking turns volunteering to lead the attack by pouncing on the creatures from above. Our successes mounted as we stacked their carcasses in a heap. The last two came out as a pair, which made for a much more challenging encounter. In their cramped surroundings, they couldn't put up much of a fight, making a growling roar while snapping at us, but we dealt with them swiftly. Prodding and poking with our spears and torches, we concentrated our attack on the lead one first, managing to avoid the snapping jaws, and killed the two off in a short period of time.

"By morning, we had slain a total of six of the beasts, and a gang of Mycurian slaves carted away their carcasses. The facial features of the oldest slave told us he was a native islander. Some of the imperial guard anticipated their emperor's arrival at the site and wanted to learn our ways of attacking and slaying the creatures to prove their bravery. We spent much of the next day training them for the coming night's confrontation.

"We won the trust of the imperial guard in many ways. We helped them formulate different strategies to attack the beasts. We showed concern for their safety by telling them that to boldly jump on the back of a creature was a tough balancing act, and one misstep could mean certain death.

"I believed the beasts' numbers to be fewer the coming nightfall. After sundown, the first creature appeared, and I leaped upon its back, spearing it in the same fashion. As my warriors drove spears into its ribcage, members of the imperial guard joined in to finish the kill. This would be the only beast I'd assault on this night, as I received a signal that the second wave of islanders had come ashore from the marshlands south of Gaugamar. A small force went on ahead to kill and replace sentries at the city's gates, allowing those forces to infiltrate the city, and they kept hidden, waiting to hear the signal to attack the next morning. At the same time, those forces that had originally arrived with me on my vessel moved to overtake guards keeping watch along the shoreline. Under the cloak of night, they made their way to the pyramid site, one by one taking out sentinels on the outskirts of the necropolis. Guards who should have been keeping watch were caught up in the goings-on at the site and were easily killed and replaced by my forces, who now wore their uniforms.

"After eliminating four of the beasts, a crew of my islanders entered the cavity with torches and later returned to declare they had killed off all the beasts. A small band of imperial guard escorted a slave gang into the cavity to seal off the monsters' domain, and their commander sent word to the palace that the beasts were disposed of.

"At the first hint of sunlight at daybreak, I stood and raised my spear above my head with hands outstretched to signal my forces to take down the outnumbered imperial guard. We quickly silenced cries for help, and the clamor of shouts and applause made throughout the night while the beasts were slain masked this surprise assault. The unsuspecting guard put up little struggle before we either killed or disarmed them, and under the threat of death, those who lived complied with my order to exchange their uniforms for garments worn by my forces. We then directed them to go into the dugout where the beasts had come from, and since they had no weapons, a small band of my compatriots easily held them at bay.

"Horuk had received timely reports of our progress, and believing the site to be safe, at dawn he came to see for himself the carcasses of the fearsome beasts. This is exactly what I'd counted on. He came to honor us with his presence, and participating in the pageantry of his grand entrance was another squad of his elite imperial guard. Elevated in a throne-like chair carried on the shoulders of slaves, the emperor wore a crown of gold with royal insignias and a bright red robe with fine yellow tassels. A gold chain with a dangling starburst medallion shone brightly on his chest, and we bowed before him in royal welcome.

"Servants placed his carrying chair down gently, and Horuk stepped forward with a gold staff capped off with precious stones. Examining the carcasses of two beasts, he used his staff to poke and prod their lifeless bodies as if he was their slayer, prying open the mouth of one to study its teeth and huge bite. Horuk then inquired as to whether the dwelling place of the creatures was securely sealed. My islanders, now wearing the uniformed dress of the imperial guard, were reluctant to reply, and finally one firmly nudged a slave stonecutter, who bowed while acknowledging the work was finished.

"The young emperor acted pleased, and I seized the moment by waving my spear to signal my followers to act. They boldly charged the emperor's entourage to smash the elite imperial guard. Quickly killing or disarming them, we prevailed in overwhelming strength, and I had the few survivors placed in the dugout with the others. I now held the shocked emperor as my prisoner. Fearing for his life, he was anxious to accommodate my every wish.

"I had the guard's chief commander, Jamalek, spared and brought before me. I then instructed the emperor to order Jamalek to summon the army's generals and their staff stationed at the outskirts of the capital, and I demanded the presence of all the emperor's advisers. I told Jamalek that a detachment of six of my tribesmen would accompany him as uniformed imperial guards, and I emphasized that these high officials mustn't know the emperor was my captive. Should he or any of the squad of six sent with him fail to return promptly, the emperor would die and he would be responsible for his death. The emperor exerted his will over Jamalek, and he reluctantly submitted, assuring Horuk that he wouldn't fail him.

"It wasn't long before Jamalek returned with the party I'd sent with him, and my followers said they expected those whom I'd summoned to arrive at the site soon. Shortly thereafter, they began assembling at the site before their emperor. Advisers stationed at the palace arrived first, and the generals and their staff arrived soon after that.

"I had the emperor's chief adviser, Arkenebus, a tall but meek man, singled out to stand alongside Horuk and Jamalek. The emperor feared for his life now more than ever before and fell to his knees, pleading for mercy. I replied that I'd return the same measure of mercy his father had afforded my father, my grandfather, and my island's people. I gave the signal for swift death, and the thrust of spears slaughtered the high-ranking officials gathered there. Some tried to run but were cut down in stride. Not one escaped.

"Though I sought to bring down the Mycurian dynasty, I temporarily spared Emperor Horuk, Arkenebus, and Jamalek. Witnessing the slaughter of the officials gained the submission of the three survivors, and so long as they were useful in hastening my will, they would live. I gave another sweeping signal with my spear, and horn blasts started a chain of events designed to lead to our takeover of the Mycurian Empire from its power base at the capital.

"Intending to act fast to retaliate for the years of oppression suffered by my people, I left behind a unit to hold the imperial guard in the dugout. I then instructed Emperor Horuk, Arkenebus, and Jamalek to lead the way to the nearby palace and royal court, and they did so without question. I walked behind them, my forces marching behind as though they were the emperor's imperial guard. Before reaching the palace, I saw a black plume of smoke, giving evidence that my islanders were laying siege to Gaugamar. Slaves were in revolt, and distant wails and screams told of panic and confusion sweeping through the capital.

"As we entered the pillared palace court, any guards who weren't part of my forces were overtaken and killed. I wasn't taking any chances, insisting that only warriors whom I knew on a first-name basis should accompany me in the palace.

"The young emperor wore a look of horror and disbelief, and to prove to him there was no turning back, I had blood relatives of the royal family rounded up and prepared for execution. In order to claim power and still take control of the dazed and confused Mycurian army, I had to keep the emperor alive a little longer. I then arranged entertainment by holding a mock ceremony, choosing Arkenebus to administer proceedings. I added further humiliation to the emperor by having him voluntarily remove his crown, fine jewelry, and robe.

"Horuk then assisted Arkenebus crowning me emperor, and afterwards they placed other auspicious attire on me. After I announced that death would be delivered to anyone opposing my will, all Mycurian subjects paid homage to me, the new emperor of Mycuria. After the dethroned emperor suffered this indignity, I had him and his family shackled in chains and imprisoned within the palace, where my most trusted compatriots saw to their care.

"I now sat on the emperor's throne in all the majesty and garb Horuk formerly possessed, determining the fate of those citizens who refused to take an oath to serve me. My forces were in control of the capital. I'd succeeded in chopping off the head of the Mycurian military to leave no chain of command, and the Mycurians were unable to organize their stifled army. Should any remaining military officers attempt to rally forces to retake the palace, their emperor would be the first to die. They had little choice but submission, but I knew I must achieve more to ensure my hold over the Mycurians.

"The commander of the imperial guard, Jamalek, had unwittingly served my purpose well in luring high-ranking officials to their demise, and I chose to have him stand before me. He'd seen his family members rounded up in the palace and placed as wards under a new court established under my rule. I then informed him that I'd had every member of the imperial guard executed, for I could not trust their devotion to a new ruler. I told him he could die like the others who'd fallen before him or swear his devotion to me, and his family would most assuredly share in his chosen fate.

"After he swore an oath to honor and obey me, I pointed out that he was the highest-ranking official left with military experience. I then explained that any army officers attempting to rally Mycurian forces should respect his rank by allowing him to take over command. I expressed my desire for him to use his influence to quell the army. His first duty would be to get all remaining officers to pledge their loyalty to him and to their new king, delivering death to any who refused.

"I announced, 'I am now emperor of Mycuria, and Jamalek represents the force that will deliver my will. The loyalty of the army will come later, but for now he will be consul in charge of the army.' Afterwards, I made clear how things stood, and until the day came that he could prove himself worthy of my trust, the same staff of six guards would accompany him both day and night. Believing he'd submitted, I allowed him a short moment with his family before he left.

"My followers continued to lay siege to the capital as the Mycurians either yielded or faced massacre. I summoned Arkenebus, and he stepped forward. My perception of him was that he was a very astute individual whose accomplishments had given him an honorable reputation. Choosing to exercise discipline and restraint, I believed the death of such a man might later be a regrettable mistake. I thought he could be useful as a diplomat to restore order to the empire and help the Mycurians accept a new emperor. He had not shown any outward signs of fear, nor did he have a family by which I could apply leverage to convince him to swear allegiance to me.

"Wanting to reason with him in an unthreatening manner, I asked Arkenebus to accompany me on a walk. From the court, we strolled beside a pool in another section of the palace that had been a private retreat for royalty. I told him I knew of his reputation as a wise statesman, and I didn't want to deal with him in the same manner as the others. I explained how the Mycurian dynasty had persecuted my islanders and that such an evil empire had to go through a cleansing and the royal bloodlines be killed off, just as Hatchek had tried to dispose of my family.

"Before I finished speaking, I said that I was normally a tolerant individual, and while I sought compliance from others, from him I was looking for cooperation. I wanted him to willingly join me in a great adventure by which we could work together to enrich the lives of everyone in the empire, not just the Mycurians. Only an empire governed with a sense of justice can withstand the test of time, and if he stood by me and his contributions pleased me, he would reap rich rewards for his services. I patiently waited for his response.

"Arkenebus replied that he was not one to adorn his body with gold, nor did he want to own property. He simply said that if I wanted his cooperation, the massacre had to stop immediately.

"I told him I detested bringing my wrath upon the capital, but the events of this black day had afforded me little patience for those devoted to Emperor Horuk. I then warned him not to provoke me by pleading for the lives of the emperor and his family. If the emperor's father, Hatchek, hadn't been an evildoer, this day would not have come to pass. Who listened to the pleas of my people when Mycurian soldiers slaughtered them on the emperor's orders? I had long since vowed revenge for the sins of the father to avenge the deaths of my father and his father before him, and this meant no less than Horuk's execution. I wasn't foolish enough to allow any survivors of this dynasty to prosper and return to power. To exterminate them was to wipe out any threat of conspiracy against me. The entire dynasty had to perish.

"In a calm voice, he then asked how long I intended to punish the entire population for the actions of one who had died years before. Would the suffering of a great multitude be enough to satisfy the rule of vengeance? Exactly how many had to die to equal the wrongs of the past?

"I began to see the wisdom in Arkenebus, who was not asking anything for himself, only mercy for those who were being cut down in the streets. I saw why others had sought his advice. What he'd said convinced me that he cared about the welfare of the common citizens. Promising to be a fair and just emperor and informing him that I'd already given my word to end slavery, I then led him back to the palace court, where I gave the order for all hostilities to cease.

"Arkenebus later disclosed that he was a slave by birth, and he'd always thought slavery was an abomination. He could've had great wealth but instead asked for nothing but justice for all. He would be an asset to lead our nation to greatness. I no longer pressed Arkenebus to swear his allegiance to me, and he and I traded ideas and philosophies until sunup the next day. He said that if I kept my word about how I'd lead the country, this would be enough for him to swear his devotion. Even though he understood my reasoning in wanting to execute the royal family, he used many theological phrases to sway me in sparing their lives, but I would not waiver. Jamalek served me well too, and after only a few years did an up-and-coming officer earn promotion to commander of the army—my eldest son, Kurn.

"Arkenebus arranged for a ritual ceremony that placed me as an exalted deity over the Mycurian people, and this in turn helped to solidify my standing as emperor of Mycuria. Recognized as a wise and pious king, I learned a great deal from Arkenebus, and he counseled and inspired to me to be an honorable leader whom my subjects and citizens revered. Arkenebus became a trusted and dear friend, and through the covenant we shared, we shaped a great nation.

"Over time, I won the devotion of my citizens, and they raised this magnificent monument in my honor. Arkenebus was the designer who oversaw its construction, and he lived to see its completion. Before his death, Arkenebus used his mystical powers to foretell that I would live a rich, full life and that under my leadership the empire would prosper. He prophesied that after my death, the empire would fall and this civilization would cease to exist, and a doomsday would make all life on this planet extinct. The pyramid would stand until the end of time, but one day distant travelers would arrive to breach these walls, starting a new beginning.

"If you are those distant travelers who've come to disturb my eternal resting place, you will feel my wrath, for I will resurrect the beasts of Mycuria to prey upon you, and they will devour your flesh and bones."

When it ended, the crew was stunned, and Far said, "It was as if he directed the final part of this historic text to us. Are we the distant travelers the ancient record is referring to?"

Afterwards, there was silence as they pondered the exploits of a legendary ruler for whom a race of Martians had erected the great eye pyramid.

CHAPTER 26

Returning to the Pyramid

Following a period of silence, Jetha expressed her thoughts. "The era during which this culture came into being may well have compared to biblical times on Earth, in that it was a period of contentious rival nations. Matusek mentions changing wind patterns that caused the waters to turn turbulent, and this may have come about as their planet was going through radical climate change. Maybe a periodical weather phenomenon was impacting their ocean currents, or they may have had an unstable jet stream that for reasons unknown was constantly shifting in this coastal region."

Rhodes said, "While listening to the text and trying to put the geography into perspective, I imagined the island kingdom to possibly be the landmass we've designated as the face. There are strong indications this outcrop of land was actually an island. Even the computer graphics generated an image showing it as an island paradise."

Flavio then said, "I was thinking the same thing myself, but the translation may not be entirely accurate. I'm not knocking the job you did, Jetha, but when you use the term 'island paradise,' you could be describing more than just one island. There are other protrusions of land east of the face that may have been part of this island nation. Hawaii and Japan were once island nations, even though they consist of more than one island."

Rhodes remarked, "The text talked about how excavation at the pyramid site resulted in a cave-in opening to an underground subterranean region, and diggers disturbed the beasts from their lair."

"Yes," blurted out Far, "some sort of a cave-in disturbed these extraordinary flesh-eating monsters, and similar giant beasts periodically overran the island paradise. The text described Matusek leaping on a beast to spear it in the neck as other islanders assaulted it with spears to kill it, and that must be what the statue in the upper chamber depicts. Before recorded history on Earth, there were still giant monsters running about, such as the saber-tooth tiger, the woolly mammoth, the giant sloth, and the giant lizard 'Megalania prisca' that lived in Australia. When I look at the picture as a whole, life on Mars may have been of a shorter duration, in that it's possible these beings advanced more rapidly than humans did."

Rhodes added, "Okay, but if they were digging out the labyrinth when this cave-in occurred, where inside the pyramid do you think they happened upon this cavity they described?"

Flavio pointed at Rhodes and said excitedly, "The wall in Emperor Matusek's tomb!"

"Of course," said Far. "They were tunneling to create a dug-out tomb for the Mycurian emperor, but when they went deep enough to hit an open cavity that disturbed those creatures, the project had to be stopped. That's when the Mycurians sought help to destroy the beasts. The next question is do we tear an opening through that fractured wall to see what's beyond it?"

Flavio replied, "I believe there may be something of great importance on the other side of that wall, perhaps not anything in the way of gold and jewelry, but something worthy of discovery just the same. These beasts had terrorized a city, and Matusek's slaying of them must have helped win him favor in the eyes of the Mycurians. He achieved something that even the mighty Mycurian army couldn't do, thus making him a heroic figure, and this must have in part helped to galvanize the country behind him."

Far looked at Jetha, saying, "You mentioned that on his sarcophagus is etched, 'Here I remain on guard to protect my loyal subjects.' Does this mean that he watches eternally over the cavity from which those beasts arose?"

Far then turned to Rhodes. "You told us you blocked off the hole in the tomb where that animal came through?"

"Yes, I stuffed a big wad of plastic into it. Should we return to find that plastic missing, we'll know something got into the tomb and could be anywhere in the labyrinth. However, the motion detectors and cameras haven't picked up anything."

"I don't know if I want to go back down there again," said Jetha, looking at Far with a fearful expression. "It's too dangerous. I don't want what happened to Aleksei to happen to another one of us."

Then Flavio asked, "Aren't you the least bit curious about what's on the other side of that wall?"

"Not if it means going up against another one of those reptilian creatures that killed Aleksei. There could be hundreds of them on the other side of that wall waiting for us."

"There are risks in going back inside the pyramid," said Rhodes, "and if we learn the plastic's been disturbed then we'd better get out of there and stay out so we don't fall into a nest of them. We'll have to take the flamethrowers with us as protection to make a thorough inspection of the labyrinth, but I'm not forcing anyone to go. I think Flavio's flair for exploration makes him a candidate to return, but I don't want to put words in your mouth. Do you want to go back or not?"

"I don't want be the only one pushing for this, but yes, I'm willing to go."

"Far and Jetha, understanding the risks involved, what do the two of you think about going back down inside the pyramid?"

Far replied, "I don't mind saying I'm afraid of coming across more of those things. Our suits do nothing to protect us against them, as its fangs cut right through Aleksei's glove. We have only two flamethrowers, but if the two of you go, I think I ought to come along because it's my place to be there with you. An extra set of eyes could make the difference between life and death. I can warn you if I see anything stirring."

"Knowing what those things are capable of, I think the three of you must be out of your minds," said Jetha. "There's a high probability that there are more of those devilish creatures inside that cavity, so why do you want to take the chance of one of them attacking you?"

Rhodes replied, "I've been squawking all along about the chances we're taking, and in all honesty, I don't believe it's a good idea to tear into that wall. What can possibly be in there that's worth endangering our lives for? However, the prospect for finding water on Mars dictates that we investigate. I see it as a mission requirement. If that sensor in the gallery didn't give off readings indicating the presence of water, I'd be reluctant to go back, but because it did, I have an obligation to return to the tomb. The discovery of water on Mars will be vital to future missions to the red planet."

Flavio then said, "That hole in the wall was left open for quite some time after Aleksei was bitten and nothing got through, so that's in our favor. The plastic you shoved in there wouldn't stop an animal from getting in—at least not one of those creatures—so if there are more of them, why haven't they gotten into the tomb? It suggests to me that this reptilian creature was the last of a dying species that climbed or crawled up into that niche and became dormant in a state of hibernation. We won't know unless we go back and investigate, but it remains a possibility that there are no more of them in existence. I know I'm always eager to dive into adventurous situations, but I don't want anybody losing his or her life doing this, and that, of course, includes me."

They were all in deep thought, and then Far said, "Why not take another day or two to think this over? We don't need to make a decision right this very minute. I'm working on receiving a signal through my helmet so we'll have a warning in case something sets off a motion detector while we're traveling to the pyramid. The equipment has the capability; I just have to figure out how to do it."

Rhodes spoke up, saying, "You know, we've taken a lot out of that pyramid, but there are still a few articles I'd like to get—the decorative lid of that coffin, for instance. It's not that I'm getting greedy; I just think it's my duty to bring back whatever I can to prove this Martian civilization existed. The text described the Mycurian emperor, Horuk, wearing a crown and sunburst medallion on the morning when he went to inspect the beasts' carcasses. It may be that Matusek's mummified remains now wear that same crown and medallion, which links them to a historical event. One thing is for sure: If we go back, God help us if we come upon any more of those savage creatures like the one that attacked Aleksei!"

This ended their discussion about returning to the pyramid, but even though Rhodes was committed to going back, he could imagine himself and Flavio engaged in a firefight, using flamethrowers to defend against a horde of the lethal creatures. Fighting for their lives within the confines of the labyrinth was something he didn't want to consider. His instincts were telling him not to go back, but his responsibility as commander of the mission made it an obligation he couldn't shirk.

They needed to return to the pyramid within the next twenty-four hours to refuel the generator. Rhodes didn't want to lose the advantage of keeping the motion detectors, cameras, and other devices working inside the labyrinth, and he decided they'd return to the monument the next morning. Though Far said she was willing to go along, Jetha strongly objected to the idea, so she would remain behind.

The following morning, they ensured that none of the motion detectors had activated their cameras during the night. Far had accessed the main computer and figured out a way to receive a signal whereby she could view the camera angle in the grand gallery from a tiny television in her helmet. In addition, she could pick up an audio signal if something triggered any of the motion detectors.

Rhodes, Flavio, and Far were riding in the rover on their way to the pyramid when they received a communication from Jetha asking that they come back for her. The request came as a surprise, and they returned to the ship to find her suited up and waiting outside for them.

Rhodes was driving and listening as Flavio asked Jetha, "So what was it that made you change your mind?"

"I got to thinking about what I would do if something happened to all of you and what life would be like here on Mars if I was all alone. Such a solitary existence could drive a person mad, and when it came time to leave, I don't know if I'd be able to launch and operate the ship by myself. So I may as well join the expedition and die with the rest of you crazy people!"

Flavio replied, "There's something about a woman with that old, pioneer spirit that turns me on!"

Far rode in the front passenger's seat next to Rhodes, and at a glance he could see her grinning, but there was nothing funny about what they were doing, as the danger and risks ran high.

Inasmuch as Rhodes was glad Jetha had overcome her fear by joining the expedition, he dreaded the idea of encountering another one of those creatures. Normally he thought there was safety in numbers but not in this case, for he had no way of knowing how many of those things they'd be up against. Even with the motion detectors monitoring the grand gallery, he couldn't be sure if any of them had slipped through to enter the labyrinth. . . .

CHAPTER 27

What's Beyond the Wall?

Arriving at the pyramid, Rhodes and Flavio were fitted with the flamethrowers, and the team of four started up the steps to the platform, Far and Jetha carrying containers of fuel for the generator. They filled the generator's fuel tank and fired it up, and then they entered the breaker compartment in the upper chamber. Readings on atmospheric conditions showed oxygen levels were higher than ever before in the chamber, so putting a door at the labyrinth's opening had worked to seal off the area.

The miniature monitor in Far's helmet allowed her to keep watch on the grand gallery. She'd arranged to monitor all the motion detectors through audio signals transmitted from the ship and acknowledged receiving a series of three faint beeps. Their entrance into the pyramid had triggered the first motion sensor, and she mentioned that when she heard the signal, she lost all other audio for those two or three seconds. Standing before the pit and gazing down at the labyrinth's door, Far heard three more beeps as the next motion sensor aimed at the pit caught their presence.

Rhodes turned from the pit and looked at the pentagonal shape of the bust's base. Then he looked up at the ceiling and the stars in a painted night sky. He then glanced at the peeling aqua-blue paint covering the upper chamber's floor. He went through the breaker compartment to the entrance door of the pyramid that previously held the giant eye. Opening the door, his eyes traveled in the same pattern as they had inside. He looked out at the skyline and realized the distant landmass he could barely see on the horizon was that of the "face on Mars," which lay straight out to the northeast. Having determined that the face may have been the island paradise of Kopel Pikala, he also saw significance in the pyramid's design.

"How about this," Rhodes began, closing the door and walking back toward the pit, "we have a night sky above us, and this blue on the floor represents water. The bust represents Matusek, and the diamonds it held were his eyes, but I also see the shape of its base is a five-sided pyramid. Is it possible that this bust is a representation of this pyramid monument, with the night sky and water as it would've been when life thrived here?"

They all moved back toward the entrance to the pyramid, and Rhodes opened the access door so they could see out across the land. "The bust is facing the entrance to the pyramid that contained the eye. When we look straight out across the skyline in the same direction as the eye, we're looking to the northeast. Out there, you can barely see an outcrop of land on the horizon that would in most likelihood have been Kopel Pikala, which, of course, is the face seen in satellite photos. I first thought the pyramid's eye may have been pointing at some star system, but now I'm convinced the eye and the bust are aligned to point to Matusek's island home."

Jetha remarked, "I see what you mean. The aqua blue represents the Oborahn Sea, which would've surrounded this peninsula. Even though Matusek became emperor of a sprawling empire, his heart belonged to the island paradise of Kopel Pikala, his beloved homeland."

"We're merely speculating, of course," said Rhodes, "because the pillared temple was already erected below, and the pyramid overlooked that structure. However, Arkenebus may have added the eye as a way to pay homage to Matusek, and I believe the male mummy we found in the funerary chamber opposite the queen's is Arkenebus. The text praised Arkenebus for his devotion to Matusek and told how the two formed a close friendship, and that is why Arkenebus earned a place of honor inside the pyramid. What greater way to pay him back for his loyalty and devotion than to give him a place where their bond of friendship could carry on in the afterlife.

"The reason there weren't any inscriptions connected with the other tomb was because Arkenebus preferred it that way. Again, I'm only guessing, but the text also told of the day when Emperor Horuk came to the pyramid site to examine the beasts that Matusek and his islanders had slain. Horuk used his staff, capped with precious stones, to prod at the beasts' bodies and pry open their mouths. We didn't find such a staff with the remains of Matusek, but we did find one with the remains of the first male mummy. Far said that first mummy showed signs he had difficulty walking. Arkenebus must've lived to a ripe old age before passing away, and maybe Matusek gave him the staff to use as a walking stick. Arkenebus may not have placed much value on gold and jewelry, but to use a gold staff capped with rubies as a simple walking stick would've been acceptable to him."

Rhodes and Flavio cautiously descended the ladder with the flamethrowers. They then led the way into the depths of the labyrinth with Far and Jetha following, and the lights inside the labyrinth allowed them to see a good distance ahead. Combing the passageway for signs of reptilian creatures, they reached the junction leading to the original entrance, and Rhodes shot a streaking flame down it. They eventually came to the pillared hall, and Far mentioned that she caught another signal from the ship as the third motion sensor picked up their movement.

The others waited as Rhodes shot a flame across the heap of deteriorating bones to stir anything that may be alive, but he saw nothing move. They proceeded to enter the funerary room and passed through what was formerly the offering room, and Far let them know she received a timely signal from the motion detector stationed there.

Continuing down the last leg of the labyrinth, they descended the stairs leading to the grand gallery, and Far told them she heard the signal there. Rhodes saw that the lights inside the tomb were still working and shot a streak of flames across the gallery to the entrance of Matusek's tomb. He stood watch while Flavio inspected the vaults holding the mummies, and then they approached the statues to enter the tomb.

Coming through the alcove ready to blast anything that moved, Rhodes stepped into the tomb and immediately checked the fractured wall to see the plastic still stuffed in the hole. It looked exactly the way he'd left it, and this was about as good an omen as he could have hoped for. Discovering the plastic missing would've sent his mind racing with fear. However, he was still hesitant about opening up the wall to see what was on the other side.

Rhodes went to Matusek's sarcophagus to glimpse his mummified remains, seeing the gold crown positioned on his head and the sunburst medallion resting on his chest. "I don't know if we're ready to open up the wall because once we've opened it, we'll have difficulty closing it off securely. Right now, I'm confident that nothing has gotten into the labyrinth, but once we open the wall up enough for us to pass through, what's stopping anything from infiltrating the labyrinth and surprising us? If I understood the text right, it made mention of a cave-in that opened into a cavernous region. We don't know how big the space is behind this wall, and I don't want to go through this same nerve-racking inspection every time we come down here."

"So what do you suggest?" asked Flavio.

"If we're going to explore what's beyond this wall, we should first install an access door here at the tomb's entrance. The opening is a fairly squared-off space so fitting it with a door shouldn't be a big job, and by doing that we'll isolate this area. The lab door from our ship should work. We should also install a motion detector and camera inside the tomb, aiming it toward the hole in the wall. It'll work as our watchdog to let us know if there's any activity later, and, of course, it will photograph it so we'll know what it was."

"That makes good sense," said Far, "and all that work should take no more than a day or two. We also now have breathable air inside the upper chamber in case there's an emergency here in the pyramid."

With that settled, they left the labyrinth the same way they'd entered it. Rhodes didn't remove the gold crown from the Martian ruler or take his brilliant medallion since he knew they'd be returning soon to spend more time in the pyramid. Returning to Matusek's tomb had reinforced their courage to come back the next day. Flavio would construct the door enclosure, framing it with leftover materials they had available.

They came back the next morning, following the same procedure as the day before. The plastic in the hole remained undisturbed. Jetha stood guard, holding a flamethrower while keeping watch over the wadded plastic in case something tried to get in the tomb, and Far helped Flavio install the door. Rhodes focused his attention on wiring up a motion detector and camera in the tomb but soon realized there were no motion detectors or cameras left. He'd have to remove one of the two in the upper chamber to use inside the tomb.

Rhodes removed the motion detector and camera viewing the pit and returned to the tomb. He eyeballed the plastic jammed in the hole and noticed the others were just as vigilant.

The plastic remained undisturbed while they worked, and Rhodes had the newly installed motion detector and camera facing that spot before Flavio finished with the door. Far tested the newly installed motion sensor to ensure the ship's computer was picking up the camera's signal. Flavio had installed the door to open into the tomb, and he last connected a screw-fastened strike plate to catch the latch when the door closed. With the door intact, they prepared to enlarge the hole in the wall.

Rhodes and Flavio were both now equipped with flamethrowers, as Jetha had given hers to Flavio, and Far and Jetha stepped into the alcove outside the tomb. "Flavio," Rhodes began, "I want you positioned behind me with your flamethrower ready. If something pops up, jam your weapon in the hole and blast away."

Rhodes struck the wall with the sledgehammer numerous times until cracks began to form, and then he left the hammer on the floor. Keeping the flamethrower's triggering device and the searchlight close by, he stooped to pull the wad of plastic from the hole and tossed it aside. He then began to free up fragmented stones that dislodged with little trouble as the mortar crumbled into dust, and in no time created sufficient space for someone to enter the cavity.

His helmet light hardly pierced the pitch blackness, and he projected the searchlight's beam but still couldn't size up the area beyond the wall. He poked the flamethrower's barrel through the opening with his finger on the trigger. "The expanse of this recession must be large because I can't make out anything."

Far said, "Why don't you fire a blast from your flamethrower first to scare off anything on the other side?"

"I'm going to use the flamethrower only as a last resort because I don't know if any gas clouds have settled in there. If I shoot a flame that hits a pocket of methane gas, this entire pyramid might explode. I don't think that's what'll happen, but it's a possibility we can't afford to overlook."

Flavio stood ready, his finger on the trigger of his flamethrower, watching as Rhodes moved forward to enter the cavity. With the flamethrower's barrel protruding before him, Rhodes barely had enough room to get through the opening, and he scanned with the searchlight's beam until his eyes focused on a subterranean cavern. The naturally formed rock ceiling and walls of its mammoth interior looked like the inside of a huge, open mouth, with a crooked roofline that tapered as it ran back into endless blackness.

Holding the flamethrower's barrel snuggly, he continued directing the searchlight in all different directions. The searchlight's beam faintly reflected off dark walls, making it hard to gauge depth and distance, and then he saw a smooth, sandy beach that pitched as it ran down to a spacious, black pool. The air looked clear, and although many gases were colorless, he thought that not seeing any clouds indicated there weren't any flammable gases.

Standing on a broad stone ledge supporting the tomb wall that had fractured some time earlier, causing the wall to crack, Rhodes said, "Okay. It appears safe. Come and have a look." Rhodes stepped down from the rock ledge into the sand, searching for any signs of life, occasionally glancing at the water about thirty paces in front of him. The others came through the hole to behold the marvelous cave while Rhodes and Flavio shot streaking flames into the air. Fire sprayed all around, and the line of flames crisscrossed a few times.

Seeing how nothing stirred, Rhodes unplugged the searchlight to hand it to Jetha, who plugged it into her suit before pointing its beam at the murky pool of water.

"That is water out there, isn't it? Or am I imagining things?" asked Jetha.

Then Far commented, "Liquid water in a natural reservoir on planet Mars. We'll need a sample of it for testing. What do we have readily available that will hold water?"

"There are plastic cylinders that held electrical components back in the grand gallery," responded Flavio. "I'll get one."

"No," Rhodes said. "Let Jetha get it."

Jetha handed Far the searchlight, and she plugged it into her suit to continue scanning the cave. Returning with a half-liter plastic cylinder with a lid, Jetha stopped to stare at the water, reluctant to get any closer to it. "There's no way I'm going to the water's edge to get a scoop. What if the thing that attacked Aleksei was an aquamarine animal and there are more of them in the water waiting for us?"

"Stan," began Far, "there's little use comparing that creature to anything on Earth, but I thought it similar to iguanas of the Galapagos Islands, which are seagoing creatures, able to hold their breath for fifteen minutes and dive to a depth of fifty feet."

"We'll go together," Rhodes said to Jetha. He then glimpsed at Flavio. "That creature didn't look aquatic, but if you see anything moving in that murky water, blast it with your torch."

They moved cautiously to the water's edge, and Jetha peered about. "I don't like this place one bit. The hair on the back of my neck is standing on end."

With his left hand, Rhodes reached out to Jetha, who removed the lid from the cylinder before handing the container to him, and he knelt to scoop up enough water to nearly fill it. Continuously looking about, he handed it back to her, and she replaced the lid.

They began returning to the cave's opening, Rhodes and Flavio the last to back away from the water, watching carefully. Far stopped to shine the searchlight's beam across the water and said, "Look, the water appears to have a current."

Light glistening on the water allowed them to see a subtle current, and Rhodes commented, "That may be, but let's get this cylinder back to the ship so we can analyze the water."

"You sound a little nervous, Stan," said Far. "I thought you'd be the one most excited about the discovery of water."

"I'm plenty excited about it, but I haven't yet forgotten that hellish thing that attacked Aleksei. It may have been the last of its kind in existence, but I don't want to risk meeting another one."

On their way out of the cave, the motion detector in the tomb triggered the camera and light attached to it. Rhodes was last to leave the tomb, closing the door behind him. They returned to the upper chamber to check oxygen levels to be certain the readings showed this area to have breathable air, and Rhodes said he wanted to test it only in an emergency.

After they returned to the home ship, Far immediately began to analyze the water sample they'd taken from the cave. Rhodes sent a transmission back to Earth to let them know they'd discovered water. Flavio and Jetha brought up satellite photos on a monitor to check the alignment of the pyramid's eye to confirm it looked to the so-called face, revealing that what Rhodes thought may be true. Even though the eye pyramid and the bust aligned with this land mass, they had no evidence to positively conclude that it was the island of Kopel Pikala. Scholars would have to study this supposition for years to come before it became a well-founded conclusion.

CHAPTER 28

A Beast Surfaces

Later that same evening, Rhodes approached Far in the lab as she pressed her eye to a microscope studying microbial life forms in a small dish. A portion of the water from the cave was in a glass flask on the counter, a dark emulsion with sediments floating in it.

"I was curious to find out what you learned about the water from the cave."

Far lifted her head, and turned to Rhodes to say, "Water inside that cave is teeming with diverse life forms—a soupy ecology rich in microorganisms. There are diatoms and bacteria in a rich stew of algae and high concentrations of parasitic enzymes, phosphorus nutrients, and proteins. In addition, there's an abundance of naturally enriched, carbonized molecules stirring in it. This mixture provides constant strife in a continuous chain of events, as life forms are thriving in a repetitious cycle of bigger things feeding off smaller things. Based merely on this one container of water, it's difficult to gauge how far the food chain may go, but there may be eels or a new form of crab down there.

"I'm not an evolutionary biologist, but in this abundance of species, I can't help but wonder what the catalyst is for making it all flourish. Solar energy can be a good energizer for producing life, but we don't need sunlight to spawn life. Maybe there's some kind of geothermal energy at work, such as hydrothermal vents creating a heat source that allows life to take root and reproduce. This is what enables life forms to exist on the Earth's deepest ocean floors, meaning there may be volcanic activity warming up Mars' core, which may explain why the water wasn't frozen.

"However, if this isn't what's happening, then there must be some type of upwelling disturbance driving microbial life to unceasingly churn to keep the food chain replenished. If the planet Mars is dead, then life itself has found a way to reproduce. The decomposition processes of aquatic animals could be causing an upsurge to keep sedimentary layers bubbling while stirring a constant mixture to allow recycling, beginning with microbes feeding off the molecular remains of other minuscule life forms. Even though these all appear to be basic life forms, it proves how tenacious life really is. Life has managed to exist in a world that on the surface appears lifeless and barren."

"If we send the water through a filtering and purification process, can we drink it?"

"There are too many microbial contaminants in it. Just to be on the safe side I'd strongly recommend boiling it first."

They knew they needed to find a way to transport the water from the depths of the pyramid to their ship. The water was so deep beneath the surface of Mars that temperatures remained above the freezing point, and this worked to their advantage. They concluded it was best to run a hose from the water inside the cavity through Matusek's tomb and into the grand gallery using an electric siphoning pump. No one wanted to enter the cave any more than was necessary, and, in addition, by channeling the water through a hose, they avoided contamination from the mold growing on the walls of the tomb. They weren't sure, but they believed the mold could be a lethal strain.

Over the next five days, replenishing their water supply became a priority. They used easy-to-handle lengths of a slinky, interlocking, corrugated pipe as their pipeline, running it from the water, through the tomb, and into a large, plastic container in the grand gallery. To keep the pipeline from interfering with the operation of the new door, Flavio cut a hole in the doorframe for the pipe to pass through. They ran the pump once a day, just long enough to fill up the drum. It didn't take long to fill it. The empty blue canisters they'd accumulated served as containers to carry water to the ship, and they transported them up through the labyrinth in the wheeled handcart.

They stored the canisters in the cargo bay until they boiled the water, and after that, they ran the water through a filtering system before returning it to the canisters, which they sterilized first.

They had problems with the pipeline twice, when the opening at the source clogged and organic matter had to be cleared away for water to flow. It was a simple job for a pair of crew members to go into the cave and clear away the debris. One person stood guard with a flamethrower while the other cleared away the pipe's opening, sometimes pulling the hose out of the water to do so.

They'd gathered a considerable amount of water, and Rhodes didn't see this process going on for much longer, for there were other mission requirements he'd let go for the sake of water. He knew he'd have to enter the tomb at least one more time to obtain Emperor Matusek's crown and medallion, and there was also the decorative coffin lid that contained precious jewels. That peculiar image of Matusek with his bright eyes attracted Rhodes' attention every time he entered the tomb. They would've obtained these pieces the day before, but the generator that had been so reliable finally broke down, and Rhodes wanted to get it running as soon as possible to avoid losing power in the pyramid.

On this particular morning, the climate control device was in need of service and a maintenance check, but if nothing else cropped up, there'd be plenty of time to get the articles they wanted. There was no longer a demand for water, and they went to the pyramid intending to draw it for the last time from the drum in the grand gallery. They'd grown tired of transporting water to their ship and were looking forward to catching up on other items of interest.

Flavio led the procession up the staircase, and he and Jetha carried two empty canisters each. Rhodes grabbed a carton of air filters for the climate control unit and started climbing the stairs with Far. It was Flavio and Jetha's turn to collect water, and they took the flamethrowers with them. They kept the weapons and a few tanks of the flammable mixture in the upper chamber, and the two fitted each other with tanks before starting down into the labyrinth.

Rhodes and Far began servicing the climate control unit, cleaning it and changing the filter, and the device was working perfectly to provide breathable air in the upper chamber. They'd yet to test it, but it was comforting to know that such a safety zone existed in case of an emergency.

When he was nearly finished with the maintenance procedure, Rhodes said, "I just about have this wrapped up, Far, and getting the unit operating is simple. Before leaving today, I want to get Matusek's crown and medallion, so why don't you go down to the tomb and see how difficult it's going to be to obtain them. When I removed the necklace from the queen, I heard a crackling sound as though her head was ready to snap off, and I don't want to damage this mummy."

"Okay, but I don't intend to lay a finger on him, as I prefer to be strictly an observer. You can have the honor of removing the king's jewelry and the responsibility that goes with it."

Far started down into the labyrinth, and after a few minutes Rhodes had the climate control unit operating. He heard the chatter of fellow crew members through his helmet's communications and got the impression that Flavio and Jetha were already in the grand gallery. They'd started using the siphoning pump to fill the drum with water, and it sounded as though the pump was giving them trouble.

Jetha commented, "We ought to be seeing water by now, but nothing's coming through."

Then Flavio remarked, "We'll have to go into the cavity to clear the hose at the other end."

Rhodes started to warn them to be careful, but he'd already cautioned them so many times before, and he felt assured when Flavio said, "Be prepared to use your flamethrower." A minute later, he added, "All clear. You can pass through the opening now."

Soon afterwards, Rhodes thought they must have entered the cave, where they'd pulled the hose out of the water to clear the opening. It usually didn't take long to perform this task. Having finished his work in the upper chamber, he'd just begun descending the ladder into the pit when a strange commotion made him stop. It sounded like Jetha making a muffled, breathless whimpering.

Suddenly he heard, "No! No!"

A spine-chilling screech rattled his eardrums, and he dropped into the pit, yelling urgently, "Jetha! Flavio, what's happening?"

He next heard a deep, guttural grunt, a gasping groan, and then rustling followed by chomping and bone-crackling sounds. Flavio had just stepped into the grand gallery and replied, "I don't know. Jetha was right behind me only a second ago. I'm going back to the cavity to see what's happened."

"You should've never left her alone!"

"I'd opened up the clogged hose, and when I was coming back into the tomb, she was right behind me, carrying the flamethrower."

Fearful for Jetha's safety, Rhodes raced through the labyrinth as fast as he could. "You have your flamethrower, don't you?"

"Yes, I have it with me. Jetha has the other one. I'm back inside the cave now, but I don't see her, although the hose is in the water the way I left it only a minute ago."

"I'm almost to the tomb, Stan," said Far.

A minute later, Rhodes heard Far say, "I'm inside the cavity now with Flavio, and I don't like this at all. There's no sign of Jetha."

"I see a disturbance in the sand," said Flavio, "but it's difficult to make out tracks. It appears she started back with me to leave the cavity when she may have paused before backing up into this other area, and look . . . there's the barrel and trigger mechanism for her flamethrower."

Puffing on oxygen, Rhodes said urgently, "I want you to start back this way now! Don't wait for me in that cavity! Do you hear me?"

"No, wait, there are her tanks and parts of her backpack life-support system," remarked Far. "And what's that? She lost one of her boots, but what is this mess?"

Flavio's voice changed to a tone of sickened disgust. "Her foot's been bitten off!" There was a rustling sound, and then Flavio said insistently, "Don't vomit in your face shield!"

Darting down the labyrinth and through the pillared hall, Rhodes shouted, "Get her out of there, Flavio!"

Flavio now sounded breathless. "I'm trying to get Far back into the tomb . . . What . . . What's that?" Seconds later came a loud crashing sound, and Flavio yelled, "Run, Far!"

Hearing a loud shriek followed by bone-crushing sounds, Rhodes raced down the last leg of the labyrinth, and his heart slumped in fear that his entire crew may be dead. Darting through the last stretch of passageway, he found Far crumpled on the steps at the entrance to the grand gallery. He grabbed her by her arm, and she turned her tearful face toward him. He moved to see if he could help Flavio, but Far latched onto his arm to stop him.

"He's dead, Stan. . . . They're both dead."

Against his better judgment, he pulled away from her grip, switching off the light on his helmet as he peered around the corner to witness a terrifying beast feeding on a headless body! How bizarre to know the limp body belonged to Flavio. Sharp, serrated teeth and powerful jaws savagely ripped into a shoulder, severing an arm with one voracious bite and devouring it whole. Webbed feet and long claws held the body of its victim in place as its teeth sank into it again, tearing loose a dangling chunk of tattered flesh with part of a spacesuit hanging from it.

The creature showed an amazing likeness to the reptilian beast portrayed in the statue in the upper chamber, a formidable figure with broad, muscular shoulders and front legs that were longer than the rear. As he watched in horror, the fearless creature raised its head up, chewing as bloody saliva oozed from its mouth. After swallowing, it slung its slithering tongue out as if whetting its appetite for more, and its tail whipped about, but as long as it was in this feeding frenzy, he didn't expect any aggression directed at him. Sickened by the sight of it gnawing on his friend's chest cavity, he turned away, unable to bear the grotesque scene any longer.

Returning to Far in a stunned state, he helped her to her feet, leading her away from the grand gallery as they started back up through the labyrinth, walking without speaking a word.

Entering the pit, Rhodes closed the door behind him, and they removed their helmets to breathe oxygenized air conditioned by the climate control unit. Drained and stupefied by what had happened, he helped Far up the ladder, and she lost her footing near the top, collapsing on the floor of the upper chamber. He was right behind her to pull her away from the edge of the pit, and she came to lie on her stomach facing Rhodes, looking pale and visibly shaken.

Lying still with beads of sweat running down her face, she spoke in a jittery voice. "We discovered Jetha's tanks and life-support system in a pool of blood. When Flavio picked up Jetha's boot, I saw bloody, raw meat and bone inside. Something bit her leg off!" Starting to get her breath back, she continued. "Flavio tried ushering me out of the cave, and that's when a black shadow emerged from the water. We ducked inside the tomb, darting into the grand gallery, and the beast broke through the wall into Matusek's tomb like a cannon shot, shoving the sarcophagus out of the way in its pursuit of us. Flavio shoved me, shouting at me to run just before firing a blast from his flamethrower at it, but it was so hell-bent on getting us that fire had no effect on it. I'm sure the heat must have cooked its outer layer of skin, but if a flamethrower can't stop it, what can? That thing shredded him to pieces, and if Flavio hadn't gotten me out of that cave when he did, I'd be dead too. I owe my life to him."

Rhodes felt bewildered by the loss of Jetha and Flavio. "In a matter of minutes, we lost two fine people, and I wasn't there to save them. They're gone now, and what's almost as hard to believe is that a descendent of an ancient, reptilian creature killed them." He gazed at the statue of the beastly creature, Matusek riding on its back. "Its ancestor was this incredible, giant lizard. How is that possible, and how do I tell their families what happened?"

Sitting at the edge of the pit with his legs hanging over the edge, their deaths left him crushed, and he let his head fall into his hands. The shock of what had just transpired caused him to lose the ability to speak. He felt as if he'd failed in his mission, and he didn't see how to carry on without them. He couldn't imagine anything more horrible than if the animal had killed everyone, and right now that would've suited him just fine.

Far rose to sit next to Rhodes, who finally found his voice. "If there's any way to get off this damn planet and get started back to Earth, we're going. What's the use in trying to carry on without them?"

Squirming away from the edge of the pit to stand up, Rhodes helped Far to her feet, and they put on their helmets to leave the pyramid. Walking out onto the platform and into sunlight, he felt like a shell of a man, as though what happened to Flavio and Jetha had sucked the life out of him.

After they'd gotten back to the ship, he continued to grow despondent over losing three wonderful people whom he'd grown extremely fond of. Seeing his dejection, Far sat down next to him at the bridge, saying, "Stan, there's nothing you could've done to save them. We know so little about life forms on Mars and the evolutionary processes that shaped them. How could we have known such menacing creatures still existed on Mars? Even after a mass extinction from an asteroid collision, these reptiles lived on to repopulate, possibly even feeding on each other.

"I guess the next question is, can you and I run the ship to get us back to Earth? Perhaps it's too late to attempt a return trip home, and we'll have to go the distance and live here for at least another year."

"I need time to charter a course home," responded Rhodes, "but right now, all I keep seeing in my mind is that creature devouring Flavio. He was so young and had such a bright future.... In the morning, I'll see if there are any workable routes, but the weeks we've stayed here have significantly reduced our chances of scheduling a flight home. Even as we speak, Mars and Earth's orbits are causing them to distance themselves from each other, and we may have no other choice but to stay on here. I believe we have just one slim, outside chance, but if we later fail to rendezvous with Earth once we go into space, we're doomed."

Far saw Rhodes was in no shape to consider a launch sequence and said, "We'll talk about it more tomorrow after you've had some rest."

Far and Rhodes consoled each other and coped as best they could. Mission planners had calculated that they might lose one crew member on this trip, but losing three people in such a short period of time was devastating. Feeling miserable, Rhodes didn't know what to do and couldn't help dwelling on the fact that he was their captain and the one solely responsible for their safety and well-being—and he'd failed them. Rather than making plans to blast off from Mars, he was stuck pondering the last minutes of his friends' lives.

Late that same night, it occurred to him that the motion detectors in the tomb and grand gallery would have triggered the cameras to record what happened to Flavio. He knew Far wouldn't be able to stomach watching Flavio's death, and as much as he hated to see it, he considered doing so. He waited until long after she'd gone to sleep to watch how bravely Flavio had died, trying to save her.

The camera inside the tomb showed them reeling to escape the cave. Flavio was the second one to squeeze through the opening, and then everything turned black. He played the recording again, watching it frame by frame to see the wall bulge, then the stones flying as if from an explosion. Then a black shadow appeared before flying stones took out the camera.

He next watched the video from the camera in the grand gallery. Flavio and Far came running out from the opening next to the statues of the bat-god and Emperor Matusek. The fierce creature charged after them out of the tomb like a rampaging rhinoceros, and, as Far described, Flavio pushed her away while taking aim and firing at it. He was surprised at what little effect the discharge of streaking fire from the flamethrower had on the beast, as it closed its eyes and swatted Flavio to knock him down. The beast's scaly skin must have been like armor, which wouldn't allow the fire to penetrate. Its wide-open jaws caught Flavio's helmet, neck, and shoulders to lift him into the air, jerking him about as if he were a rag doll, and his arms and legs shook loosely in the air. The wounds inflicted on Flavio from then on were horrifying to watch, and he'd never seen anything so obscene and pathetic. When the animal finished feeding, there was little left of Flavio's ravaged remains, and then it turned to walk away. Taking long, sluggish strides, it then stopped and stood still for a moment and regurgitated the helmet and parts of its victim's suit. Then the creature returned to the tomb, presumably to return to the body of water from which it came.

In his despair, Rhodes remembered his lost crew members, and the person he thought about most was the good-hearted and high-spirited Flavio. He cried for the loss of the young man who was nothing less to him than a younger brother. He shed tears for Jetha as well and thought of his good friend and comrade Aleksei. He was their captain, and he just couldn't believe how they had died such terrible deaths without his being able to do anything to help them.

It occurred to Rhodes that the way those tenacious things lived on after asteroids incinerated Mars' surface in a catastrophic firestorm is an amazing story. When an asteroid killed off the dinosaurs on Earth, the crocodiles survived, and these creatures' chances for survival may have been even better than the crocodiles' because they already lived underground. The devastating heat embroiling the planet above ground vaporized oceans and rivers, but did not go deep enough to completely extinguish life in the bowels of the planet. They may have been a carnivorous marine creature that made the transition to land roamer, or the other way around, but in either case, it adapted to dominate a subterranean world, holding the hierarchy of the food chain as an apex predator . . .

He saw no use in staying on the red planet. He began preliminary work to charter a course home and fully realized that a return flight to Earth at this stage would be a gamble. This work took him late into the night, and growing quite tired, he thought he heard the faint sound of one of the motion detectors going off inside the pyramid. The day's events left him exhausted, however, and the signals were so faint that he thought he'd only imagined them, so he went to his pod and soon fell asleep.

CHAPTER 29

A Late-night Visitor

A loud thumping disturbed Rhodes from a deep sleep in the dead of night, and he sat up to peer from his pod to survey the cabin. Dim light from the bridge enabled him to see Far's pod, and he saw her head pop up, her eyes squinting to look back at him.

"What are you doing up?"

"Did you hear something?"

"Yes, I thought it was you," she said, and she turned to look at the bridge. Her eyes got big, and she pointed in that direction. He followed her gaze and saw an immense, dark figure and a set of large, piercing eyes looking back through the windshield! Apparently standing on its hind legs, the creature was leaning on the nose of the ship with cold, dead, wanting eyes. A forked tongue slithered out of its snarling mouth, smearing the glass and exposing serrated teeth and gooey saliva. Its jagged incisors were at least nine centimeters long, and a pair of shorter incisors was set closer together on the lower jaw.

Hearing its claws scratching against the windshield, they bolted from their pods as Far asked Rhodes, "Stan, can the glass withstand that stress?"

Thinking it couldn't but not wanting to say so, he replied, "I don't know, but just in case it can't, we'd better get into our suits."

"But if it breaks through the glass, what do we have to kill it?"

"We don't have anything, but I think our best chance for survival is to get into the cargo bay. It's the strongest, most reinforced cubicle in the ship."

"If it gets in here, it's going to tear this ship apart. We can't stay in the cargo bay forever."

"I know, but let's start by getting into our suits and hope that it doesn't break through the windshield—or we're finished."

Rhodes kept a watchful eye on the beast until it slipped away into the night. They moved to the storage compartment where the spacesuits hung and while they got into their suits, Far said, "Do you think it saw us?"

"It may be completely blind, but it has a keen sense of smell."

"I'll bet that's what it is! It tracked us to the ship by our scent, but how did something so big get through the labyrinth?"

"We're talking about an extremely agile creature motivated by the scent of a new food source. I don't see it having any trouble getting through the labyrinth. What surprises me is that the platform we built supported it. The framework must be stronger than I'd thought. I can't think of any other way it could've gotten out of the pyramid."

They were in their suits but hadn't yet put their helmets on, and they took refuge in the cargo bay, where they stayed for some time. Suddenly there came a loud pounding against the side of the ship! The beast was right outside the cargo door, trying to force its way in, and the reinforced door began to creak from the force applied against it, making Rhodes wonder if the creature was going to burst through.

They moved away from the door to sit with their backs against the giant eye, and Far clutched Rhodes as hard as she possibly could, crying, "It's going to get through!"

"I don't think so, at least not this way," he said, and then the creaking stopped. The door took another pounding, but it withstood the impact, and Rhodes wondered if these forceful jolts were damaging the door or the ship's heat shield.

Wearing a blank stare, Far sat up with her arms folded tightly around her. She started rocking back and forth. Noticing her shivering with fear, Rhodes pulled her close. "I think if the creature gets in, it'll be through the windshield. If that happens, we're doomed."

"Stan, I don't want to be eaten alive."

"Maybe it won't come to that."

Hearing nothing outside for an hour raised their hope that the creature had given up on breaching the ship and gone away. Watching Rhodes open the cargo chamber door to enter the cabin, Far gave him a frightened stare.

"There's no hint that it's gotten into the ship, so don't worry."

"Maybe it's given up and gone away."

"I think it's going to mosey around outside the ship until daybreak, so if we can hold out till then, maybe that's when it'll start back to the pyramid."

Rhodes entered the cabin to find that everything in the ship looked undisturbed, and cautiously moving to the bridge, he looked out the windshield. One of Mars' moons illuminated the landscape, and gazing about at the Martian terrain, he saw the creature squatting in the soil, its tail casually snaking about as it appeared to be gnawing on something, but what was out there that could be edible?

Far came to Rhodes' side. "It looks like it's eating something, but what can it be?"

"I was wondering that too, but as long as it's found something to amuse itself, it's leaving the ship alone."

Far and Rhodes sat at the bridge, losing visual contact with the creature for a time. Then it suddenly pounded on the glass to startle them. The creature snarled at Far, and she jumped out of her seat to retreat to the rear of the cabin. Rhodes followed her into the cargo chamber, where they sat down together, and there came more threatening jolts at the access door. Far sank to a curled-up position on the floor, leaving Rhodes to think she'd fainted, petrified at the thought of the creature eating her alive.

Before long, all turned quiet, and they remained still until dim sunlight came through the cargo door's fish-eye window, giving them hope that the animal's assault was over. Returning to the bridge, they saw no sign of the creature roaming about on Mars' sunlit landscape, and though Far warned him not to, Rhodes suited up to inspect the outside of the ship. When he closed the cargo bay's compartment door, he saw claw marks on the ship's body. But the door opened and closed perfectly, leaving no signs that the attack had damaged the heat shield.

Next, he tracked the creature's movements during the night. Upfront near the windshield, there were prints in the sand from its hind legs, and a long, smooth impression made him think that it used its tail as added support when it stood upright. He saw how it then circled the ship numerous times before nosing around the rover, but it did no damage to the vehicle that he could see outright. Tracks leading away from the ship went off in another direction, and, following them, he soon discovered what the creature had been feeding on the previous night.

Rhodes came across a large, lumpy spot in the sand, and as he approached it he saw regurgitated parts of the body bag they'd laid Aleksei to rest in. There was no doubt the animal was after a meal when it came out onto the Martian surface, but the fact that it was no longer in the area made him think it was sensitive to sunlight. It lived its entire life underground, so it stood to reason that sunlight was something this nocturnal creature may not have even seen before. This was the pattern these beasts regularly followed in the ancient times of Matusek's reign too. Expecting the beast to return again that evening after sundown, he knew this time it wouldn't have Aleksei's body to feast on. The animal would be more determined than ever to get inside the ship to get at them.

Returning to the ship, he removed his gear and began studying the cameras in the pyramid. He was able to watch its movements from different camera angles as it returned, and the camera in the gallery showed it reenter Matusek's tomb just a short while earlier. They'd lost the camera they'd set up inside the tomb, but he thought it safe to assume that the beast had gone back into its watery home inside the cave.

While he was watching the view in the grand gallery, something caught his eye. Lying on the floor was the flamethrower Flavio had dropped at the moment the animal attacked and killed him, and the sight of it sparked a glimmer of hope. The creature's slicing teeth had cut the hose connecting the flamethrower to its tanks, but he had extra hoses and tanks of fuel. In his desperation to find anything to combat the beast with, he wondered if he should risk returning to the grand gallery for the weapon, for even though the flamethrower proved useless thus far, it was the only thing they had available.

Far interrupted his thoughts when saying, "Stan, that giant lizard has similar characteristics to the Komodo dragon. They both have thick skin that's like armor. The Komodo dragon senses odors up to seven miles away with its tongue. As its tongue lashes in and out, sensory organs in the roof of its mouth pick up scents, and maybe this beast has sensory receptors that work the same way. Genetic tests suggest it's possible for Komodo dragons to reproduce without outside fertilization, so perhaps these animals can store sperm for a lifetime after an earlier sexual encounter with a male. Komodo dragons have virulent bacteria in their saliva that drools from their mouths, and this creature constantly has a substance drooling from its mouth too."

Resolved to retrieve the flamethrower, Rhodes wasn't sure how to approach Far about the idea, as her fear had nearly driven her to the breaking point. He kept a cool head as he said to her in a calm voice, "You've done your homework well, and some of that information may prove useful to us. I've been sitting here, monitoring recordings, and I've been able to track the beast's movements back to the tomb, presumably back to the water. Last night it dug up Aleksei's remains, and that's what we saw it feeding on. This creature's found a new food source, and it's likely to come back to the ship for more tonight. The point is that we don't have any weapons to combat it with, and the only thing I can think to do is go back to the pyramid for Flavio's flamethrower, which is still in the grand gallery."

"To go back inside that pyramid now is nothing less than suicide, Stan," said Far. "Let's just launch and leave this place. We can orbit Mars for a year if we have to, but we need to get off this damn planet."

"We need almost twenty-four hours to program and schedule a launch, and that means we'll have to spend at least one more night here with that creature assaulting the ship. I've mapped out a course to take us back to Earth, but there are still a few things I need to work out." Rhodes kept pushing his point, adding,

"Our problems lie in the here and now, and to have a fighting chance to get through the night I want to get my hands on that flamethrower. The risks may not be as bad as they appear, as the cameras will show us what's going on inside the pyramid." He brought up the gallery camera's view, pointing out the weapon's location. "It's only the barrel and trigger piece, but that's all we need. I can replace the hose, and we have other fuel tanks."

"You're not asking me to go back down inside the pyramid, are you?" she asked with her eyes wide open.

"No, I want you to stay here and watch the cameras in the pyramid, the one inside the grand gallery especially, to warn me the giant lizard is coming out of its lair. I imagine it must've smashed up the generator and climate control unit when it left the pyramid, but the generator's energy cell is supplying power to the pyramid so it's still connected. We need some line of defense, and I want to get in there to get that weapon before the power runs out and we lose the lights, sensors, and cameras."

"But the flamethrower didn't stop the creature when it charged Flavio. It was useless to him."

"I know, but that flamethrower is our best chance to put up a fight, and we have this one opportunity to get a weapon that might fend off that creature. Once the juice runs out and the lights and cameras become inoperable, we can forget about entering the pyramid."

"I say no. You're going to get yourself killed. That thing will eat you alive just as it did the others, and where's that going to leave me?"

"Listen to me carefully. We lost the camera in the tomb, but we still have the view of the grand gallery, and we've got to seize this chance now, or we won't have anything to defend ourselves with. By staying here, you'll be my eyes, and with your help, I'm sure we can do this. If you see any sign of that creature, you just tell me, and I'll fly out of that labyrinth like a bat out of hell. You're a smart woman, and you know having that flamethrower will make us both feel more secure. It'll give us confidence to know we have a weapon to fight that thing."

"Maybe it won't come back."

"Maybe it's gone deep into the water where it came from, but if it does come back again tonight, this time we'll have some way to defend ourselves, whereby last night we had nothing. With you watching the camera in the gallery, there will be very little risk involved. Now, can I count on you?"

Far reluctantly nodded yes, and even though she knew how to work the system of cameras to track his movements in the pyramid, Rhodes showed her how he'd tracked the creature back to its lair. She understood the importance of watching the camera in the gallery, as the other camera angles held little significance, and she could also watch the camera angle from his helmet.

Rhodes hadn't even left the ship when he began to wonder if he was kidding himself about defending the ship with the flamethrower. He only knew he wanted some weapon available for when the beast returned. He thought of how Flavio used the last few seconds of his life torching it before being eaten alive. He hadn't forgotten about the emergency ascent vehicle, but it would take the same twenty-four hour period to launch that vehicle, and it hadn't had time to create enough fuel to take them home.

Rhodes was exhausted from lack of sleep. His whiskers were growing out, and the stubble was starting to itch. His main concern was the creature showing up while he was in the gallery, and if that were to happen, he knew he'd never be able to outrun it. Now ready to leave the ship, he attached his helmet and made certain the monitor could pick up the signal from his helmet before he said good-bye to Far. She had the sad eyes of an abandoned puppy, but Rhodes saw little choice in leaving her.

He had no idea how long the cameras would operate, and he picked up speed in the rover. Along the way, he slowed down when he caught a glimpse of *Endurance II*. He saw the windshield free of glass and the cargo bay door open, leaving its dark interior exposed, but he and Far had no need for those few provisions left inside. However, he thought about how their home ship was nearly identical to that one, and if the animal found it could enter through these openings, it may become more determined than ever to break into their ship.

Arriving at the pyramid, he saw the beast's footprints in the sandy soil at the base of the staircase where it had come down and later returned. The prints tracked along the causeway leading to the northeast face of the pyramid and temple ruins. Standing at the base of the pyramid, he saw that the handrail was down. Looking up at the platform walkway, he noticed that it looked intact, but a portion of the cable was loose and drooping.

"Far, are my video and audio signals coming through okay?"

"Yes," she said. "I'm following your every move, and nothing has changed inside the gallery. I haven't detected any sign of movement."

"I believe you were correct in thinking this animal has a keen sense of smell to be able to track us. It's been to the storage depot and ravaged it."

Rhodes started to climb the long staircase as he'd done so many times before, and when he approached the platform, he saw that some of the supports for the handrail were broken. There were sunken areas in the decking where it had given way under the creature's weight, but the framework had somehow held up. Passing the first corner of the pyramid, he saw much of the same: the handrail bent out of alignment and slumping dips and indentations in the decking. At the pyramid's entrance, he saw that the creature had torn through the doorway when it forced its way out, and now there was just a big hole where they'd removed the eye. The generator lay crushed, but a line remained hooked up, and its stored energy was what provided electricity to the pyramid for the time being. He saw no sign of the climate control unit, which the animal may have flung out of its way.

The upper chamber looked like a cyclone had ripped through it. Not much remained of the flimsy enclosure they'd built as a breaker to help trap oxygen inside the pyramid. The first motion detector engaged to record his movements. The post lamp tree of lights near the pit rested on its side near the bust; only two bulbs were working. The bent and twisted ladder at the pit gave evidence that the creature had struggled to climb out, and the animal had flattened the door they'd installed at the entrance to the labyrinth. Realizing the animal must have had a hard time getting out of the pit, he wondered if this might be the best place to take a stand and fire on the beast with the flamethrower. However, that would mean getting the weapon operable and then waiting there for the creature. Getting the flamethrower's barrel and getting out of there with his life was challenging enough.

After resituating the ladder, he found it could support him. Fast losing the courage to go through with his plan, he stood at the entrance to the labyrinth, knowing that once the beast sensed his presence, he'd be running for his life from a meat-grinding machine. Entering this passage could be his final journey in this life, and an unceasing wave of fear kept him from moving forward.

CHAPTER 30

Threats to Our Survival Increase

Stalled by indecisiveness, Rhodes finally moved forward with grim determination to obtain a weapon to defend against the creature when it returned. There was no doubt that it would come to the ship after nightfall, and this time it wouldn't give up so easily. However, finding a way to use the flamethrower without setting the ship ablaze was going to take some thinking, for he'd have to lure the creature away from the ship before using the weapon on it. If the animal got into the ship, maybe the flamethrower could serve as an ignition source to blow the ship to pieces before it devoured them. In that case, there'd be no winner, but at least he'd have killed it.

He entered the labyrinth wide-eyed, scanning what lay ahead with fearful anticipation. Some of the lights weren't working, but enough were for him to see the way ahead. Avoiding switching on his helmet light, he followed the labyrinth. When he passed the first junction, he didn't bother looking down the dark passageway. Moving along, he approached the pillared hall, setting off a motion sensor. Having no reason to inspect the heap of sacrificed Martians to his left, he turned right and went through the funerary room, activating the next sensor, camera, and light.

Continuing his descent to the grand gallery, he followed the rock-cut walls leading deeper into the pyramid. Thinking he'd never be able to outrun the beast in this labyrinth, he moved ahead cautiously until he passed under the archway. His throat getting drier by the second, he spoke softly, "Far, I'm sure you're aware I've reached the gallery. Can you give me an 'all clear' before I proceed?"

"I haven't seen anything move, Stan. Please be careful."

Peering wide-eyed around the corner to view the open gallery where all was still, he held his position as he surveyed the area, his adrenalin pumping. A few of the lights in the gallery reflected off the statues of the bat-god and Matusek seated on a throne. Matusek's gloating, smug smile seemed to say, "You were warned." It was as if the king was blissful knowing that three people had lost their lives exploring this pyramid. Matusek had gotten revenge for their breaching his shrine, and he was having the last laugh.

It was easy to find the barrel and trigger devise for the flamethrower, since he already knew their approximate location from the camera's view of the gallery back at the ship. He bent over to pick up the weapon, and the sensor activated the camera and light. When motioning to return to the passageway, he caught sight of Flavio's helmet in a bloody mass of gunk on the floor: It was what the animal had regurgitated after attacking Flavio and all that remained of the young man.

Momentarily absorbed in thought, Rhodes looked at Matusek's statue once more, and even though it was nothing but an image carved in stone, he resented the sight of it. The grinning representation of Matusek provoked him. Feeling an urgent need to do something to avenge his crew members' deaths, he decided that he must enter Matusek's tomb to acquire his most prized possessions: the precious gold crown and the sunburst medallion.

The danger and risk of meeting up with that creature made these thoughts insane, but he quietly placed the flamethrower down at the base of the stairs. He leaned it vertically against a wall with the barrel upright to make it easy to grab when he moved quickly to leave. Then he crept toward the opening in the wall next to the bat-god as if sneaking up on Matusek's resting place.

Far's fearful voice startled him. "Stan, what are you doing? Get out of that pyramid right now before that thing senses you're there!"

"Shhh, I'm going to leave in one minute. Just relax."

She asserted, "You're going to get yourself killed! Remember that creature has a keen sense of smell. Even now it may be lying in wait."

He hesitated, thinking she may be right, but he felt sure that the animal was in the murky water and couldn't catch his scent. "Just keep quiet," he said.

His tortured soul wouldn't let him forget his fallen comrades, and he couldn't quell the temptation to go through with his crazy plan. A strange calm came over him as he rallied the courage to push forward. He saw that the door they'd installed at the entrance to the tomb was gone and only one light was still working inside the burial vault. Staring wide-eyed at the way ahead, he moved up the last few steps to the opening.

He saw where the creature had shoved the sarcophagus out of the way when it first crashed through the wall in pursuit of Far and Flavio, and debris lay scattered about. The lid to the crypt still leaned in the corner, its odd, distorted image of Matusek with its shining, glass eyes staring in his direction, as if daring him to come one step further.

Breathing shallowly, Rhodes could barely see the cave's opening from where he stood and was unable to view the cavity's interior without moving deeper into the tomb. His desire to obtain the crown and medallion drove him forward, and he saw that the opening in the fractured wall had grown since he'd last seen it. The cavern that lay beyond was pitch black, and he approached the sarcophagus with the utmost caution, noticing that Matusek's body had changed position when the animal pushed the sarcophagus out of its way. A thin crust of dust covered Matusek's facial features and red cloak as he lay partially turned in the crypt, the bold crown tilted and loosened from his head. After removing the crown, Rhodes ran his right forearm through it as a handy way to carry it.

Rhodes glanced at the blackness in the cavity before trying to remove the brilliant medallion. He had no patience with the chain around Matusek's neck. Getting a firm grip of the head, he made a quick, jerking twist, snapping the brittle neck. The head popped off. With the prized medallion and gold chain in his possession, he carefully raised it over his helmet to wear.

He looked at the emperor's face and thought about taking the Martian king's head back to Earth, but then he caught sight of the ring with a large ruby on the third finger of the mummy's left hand. Acting as nothing less than a tomb robber, he grabbed hold of the finger and twisted it until it tore free, then stuffed it in the zippered pouch of his pants leg.

Rhodes turned to leave the tomb. Moving abruptly without looking down, he clumsily stumbled over a loose stone lying on the floor but remained on his feet and froze. Then he heard a ferocious roar, greatly amplified by the cave walls! His heart jumped and his knees knocked before he ducked and ran for his life, darting through the gallery and snatching the flamethrower as he began his long ascent to freedom outside. Another roar made him think he didn't have a chance at getting out alive. His heart pounding, he wasn't certain if he was being chased or not, but then the lights in the pyramid suddenly began blinking before power was lost!

Oh, no, please don't let this happen now! thought Rhodes.

The pitch blackness surrounding him drove him to panic, but he kept moving and flipped on his helmet's light to see where he was going. Racing through the labyrinth, he finally reached the pit's enclosure and climbed the twisted, rickety ladder to see daylight showering the upper chamber from the entrance. He let the ladder fall into the pit before kicking the post lamp in as well and dashed out of the pyramid into the sunshine. Walking fast across the decking, he glanced back several times to see nothing following him. He was careful as he hurriedly descended the steps so not to fall down.

When he reached the rover, he looked up at the platform walkway, and seeing no sign of the creature, he felt vindicated for having acquired what may have been most precious to Matusek. Placing the emperor's crown on the passenger's seat, he then let the flamethrower rest on the floor against the back of the passenger's seat.

Glimpsing the medallion dangling from his neck, Rhodes heard Far say, "You're one crazy fool, and you very nearly scared the life out of me."

"I hadn't gone to the pyramid with the intention of taking these things, but the gloating expression on the emperor's statue kept daring me. Once I made the decision to go through with it, I couldn't stop myself, and I'm glad I did, for these were probably his most prized possessions. I'll be back to the ship shortly, and then we'll program a launch sequence so we can get off this godforsaken planet."

When Rhodes returned to the ship, Far met him in the cargo bay and gave him a big hug, squeezing him tightly to express her joy at seeing him again. At first she wasn't thrilled that he had taken the items, but then she examined them and could appreciate their value. Rhodes was at first hesitant about showing her Matusek's ringed finger, and when he did produce it, Far looked almost offended. She then studied the ring closely before placing it in a plastic bag to store with other articles collected from the pyramid.

Expecting the creature to return that night, Rhodes and Far initiated procedures to blast off from Mars, but finalizing this sequence was no simple task. There were only two of them to complete a list of systems checks and tabulations needed for launch. They consulted with each other throughout the day, trying to hasten the process, but as the day progressed, he couldn't see their launching from Mars until sometime the next morning at the earliest.

Rhodes felt unsure about what to do, and as time went by, he became desperately aware of his mortality. He ran through all kinds of scenarios, hoping to figure out a way to detonate an explosion after the beast had crashed through the windshield, giving them time to escape out of the ship's outer cargo door before it went off. They'd still have the emergency escape vehicle, but a ship equipped with a nuclear reactor was essentially a nuclear bomb, and the explosion would kill any living thing within a radius of a few kilometers. He preferred not to linger on the possibility of a confrontation with the monster, but as the sun drifted westward on the horizon, he saw time running out.

Rhodes hadn't notified Earth about the deaths of Flavio and Jetha, and just in case he and Far shared the same fate, it was imperative that mission planners know what dangers they had faced on Mars. Flavio and Jetha had shared worldwide popularity, and many would mourn their loss. People would want to know details about how they died. Rhodes sent still images of the creature to show what killed Flavio, and Jetha. In addition, he sent recordings of the animal passing through the labyrinth, as the existence of such a giant reptile would surely intrigue scientists.

He also let mission planners know of their plans to launch the following day so they could track their movements. However, he informed them that after sundown, their ship may be under attack by the giant lizard beast, and if they didn't launch it was because the creature had penetrated the ship and eaten them alive. He wasn't sure if Jetha had sent a copy of the ancient text she'd deciphered, so he went ahead and sent one.

The idea of the creature returning to the ship never left Rhodes' thoughts. As the sun set, he saw the sky turn from a hazy gray-blue to a dull gray. While shadows of night fell across the land, he realized that losing electrical power inside the pyramid had cost them the chance to see the creature leaving its lair. He'd put a new delivery hose on the flamethrower and hooked up fresh tanks full of a flammable mixture. He placed the weapon and the harness carrying the tanks in the cargo bay, where he expected they'd be bracing for making a last stand.

Darkness engulfed the outside world, giving way to a twilight sky, and not knowing when or even if the creature would return, he thought he'd better try to get some much-needed rest. Finally giving in to the urge to lie down, he encouraged Far to do the same, but she stayed up to keep watch.

Rhodes awoke sometime later to see Far standing at the bridge. He crawled out of his pod to join her, and she turned her deeply distressed eyes to him.

"There are at least three of them prowling outside the ship. They haven't been out there long enough to threaten the ship, but they're becoming more active, as if agitated or growing anxious to attack."

"A lot of good that flamethrower's going to be. I'd planned to face off with one beast, but I've got no chance against three of them. After they've crashed through the windshield, it's the end for us. I couldn't do anything to save the others, and I have no means to protect you."

Rhodes saw the three beasts lumbering about in the moonlight, stalking the ship. He believed they were sizing up the spacecraft, knowing there was food inside. He saw by the way they circled the spacecraft that they were growing eager to make an assault but weren't quite certain how to carry it out. Their primary motivation was instinctive, although he thought them smarter than most people would've given them credit for.

He and Far were no match for these creatures' size and brutal ways, and only the ship's strength would determine whether they would live to see the next sunrise. Most vulnerable was the windshield, as even this glass had its limitations.

Now seeing only two monsters lurking outside, Rhodes was startled when the third hit the windshield with a loud thump while standing on its hind legs, and Far let out a gasp. Watching its tongue licking the glass sent Far to the brink of panic, and she backed away from the bridge. "If another one of them leans against that windshield, it might give way. What are we going to do?"

"There's nothing we can do. The only thing stopping them from eating us alive is this ship's construction."

"Shouldn't we be moving into the cargo bay?"

Rhodes stood still, unable to take his eyes off the creature.

A second one slammed into the windshield from the other side, and she clutched his arm to pull him away from the bridge. "Stan, let's get inside the cargo bay."

They went into the cargo bay, where he'd placed their life-support equipment and the flamethrower, and the giant eye from the pyramid stared them down, as though looking forward to seeing them devoured.

Rhodes sealed the door, saying, "I see no reason to put on our helmets and life-support units until we know they've broken through the windshield."

Far watched Rhodes pacing, her voice sounding insecure when she said, "Stay clear of that fish-eye window. They might see your shadow."

A sudden crash against the cargo bay door rattled the ship as the creatures tried to break in, and Far latched onto Rhodes, her body trembling as they held each other close. Skeptical about the door's ability to keep the creatures out, they moved into a corner where they sat on the floor with their backpacks resting against the wall, the flamethrower within arm's reach.

A minute later, another unexpected jolt jarred the door, as they'd begun ramming the ship, and a set of claws ran across the fish-eye glass, making a screeching sound! Death was at their door, and they watched the door's framework bend inward from outside pressure. Rhodes' mouth dropped open as he watched the reinforcing crossbars move inward and heard the metal groan, making him wonder how much more punishment the door could take. The fact that the door opened outward and not inward was probably what was making all the difference, but he was also afraid the door's bulging fish-eye window would explode from the stress.

The door returned to its normal position before suffering another crashing boom, and it groaned as if giving its last ounce of strength to hold! Far's fear the door would rupture made her nauseated. Unable to watch the door any longer, Far clutched her partner tightly. "Stan, I'm so afraid we're going to die."

At this bleakest, blackest moment, he embraced her, and with the next crashing jolt, Far's head sank against his chest as she looked at the floor. Everything turned quiet, and he studied Far's expression for as long as five minutes. He was concerned for her welfare, believing she may be on the verge of a mental collapse, unable to deal with the hopelessness of the situation.

It seemed like Far and Rhodes were sharing their last breaths of life together, as though they were the only two humans left in existence, and he could no longer sit still. He got up and reached for the flamethrower, grabbing hold of the barrel and the harness holding the tanks to carry the weapon around with him. Moving about the cargo bay restlessly, keeping his finger on the trigger mechanism, he wondered if they would survive the night.

The creatures had apparently given up on getting in through the cargo bay, and he feared they may have turned their efforts toward breaking through the ship's windshield. He opened the door to check the cabin, and approaching the bridge, he saw one of the monsters with its face at the window, clawing at the glass. Then another pounced on the windshield from the other side, its jaws open wide, and Rhodes squinted his eyes at the thought of the glass breaking. Once the glass shattered, they'd be able to pull themselves up inside the ship, and it wouldn't be long before it was all over.

Standing ready to ignite the weapon and blast the creatures the second they got inside the ship, he watched as one of them tried climbing onto the back of another, clearly attempting to make its way up and on top of the nose of the ship. This resulted in a fight in which neither came out the winner. The beasts returned to the window and scuffled with one trying to overtake the other, and again, their battle for domination ended in a draw.

Rhodes knew that if one of them were to climb up onto the ship's nose, the danger of the windshield collapsing would drastically increase, for it would be able to put its full weight against the glass. Hoping the glass would hold, he watched on with his insides all knotted up, while keeping the flamethrower's barrel aimed at the windshield.

Not wanting to watch them any longer, he returned to the cargo bay just as the access door suffered a series of crashing jolts, and Far passed out on the floor. This same nerve-racking scenario went on throughout the night, as the determined creatures continued to assault the ship by pounding at the windshield or at the cargo bay door. In his desperation, Rhodes tried to think of different ways to escape, but there was no escaping three of the beasts, and the flamethrower he'd risked his life to get was useless. All he could do was wait them out and hope something didn't give way to allow them entrance into the ship.

At the first sign of sunlight on the horizon, the animals gave up and went away, presumably returning to the pyramid and their watery home. The ship had provided refuge and protection from the rampaging beasts, but Rhodes didn't know how much more punishment it could've taken. Thinking about it, he realized that their ship sat higher off the ground than the cargo ship, which had crash-landed, its landing gear collapsed. Had one of the creatures been able to climb up onto the ship's nose to put its full weight against the glass, the outcome may have been different.

With the light of day, they would use this precious time to ready the ship for launch, and Rhodes went to check on Far, who was awake but unresponsive, appearing frail and drained from the terror they'd endured. Seeing no expression on her face—only a faraway look in her eyes—he believed she'd suffered a breakdown. He helped her to the bridge and placed her in a chair.

Rhodes had no intention of resting until he had the ship in the air, and he estimated that in less than two hours he'd be able to start countdown. He tried getting Far's attention once more, saying, "We have to launch sometime today or risk more of the same, but we aren't far from programming a launch sequence."

Far's eyes finally turned to him, and words tumbled from her mouth. "Were you able to chart a route to get us home?"

Glad to get a reply from Far, Rhodes said, "Take a look at this," and he brought up on her monitor a computer-generated sequence showing the flight path they'd use to get home. Animation came up representing the solar system, showing Mars, Earth, and Venus in their orbit around the sun. By the ship's projected motion and movement, it was orbiting Mars before breaking away from its gravitational pull.

He described the simulation. "In plotting a flight path, the alignment of the planets dictates there's only one route we can take, and after launching from Mars, our propulsion will begin taking the ship toward the sun. We'll actually cut across Earth's orbiting path while at the same time targeting Venus, using its gravitational pull to realign with Earth's orbit. In short, it's a long shot, as we'll be trying to play catch-up to Earth, and the timing must be perfect. Missing our trajectory will mean an infinite trip into the cosmos."

Watching the animation played out on her monitor, Far said, "Our chances for survival out in space have to be better than what we have staying here on Mars with those giant beasts prowling about every night."

David Gatesbury

Exhausted, Rhodes strove to accomplish liftoff, and all preliminary systems checks were positive. He didn't want the ship to take another battering from the giant predators, and he thought of a new problem: He suspected they'd try to get in through the undercarriage where the landing gear was stored. There was no doubt in his mind that they would eventually find a weak spot, so he wanted to launch as soon as possible, preferably before noon.

CHAPTER 31

A Last-ditch Effort

Rhodes and Far hadn't gotten any rest since the giant beasts had appeared outside their ship the night before, and since dawn, they'd been preparing to achieve liftoff. Rhodes inspected the exterior of the ship, and the heat shield and windshield looked intact. Having seen evidence that at least one of the creatures had given attention to the ship's undercarriage where the landing gear stowed, he checked the equipment once more but found no damage to the spacecraft.

Returning to the ship, he kept his helmet on as he finalized data checks through the computer. He addressed Far, who sat next to him, fully suited. "How is data reading on your end?"

"All systems check out here."

Rhodes then addressed the computer, saying out loud, "Abe, we're finalizing liftoff procedures. Do your data readouts coincide with ours?"

"Affirmative. All ship's systems are ready for launch."

He settled comfortably into his seat. "Far, let's finish running the countdown sequence."

"Ten, nine, eight, seven, six, five, four, three, two, one, ignition," she said, but when she flipped a switch, nothing happened.

Rhodes' shoulders slumped in disappointment. "Hit it again."

Far flipped the switch again, but still nothing happened.

"This can only mean I'm living a nightmare." He took a deep breath and calmly asked for assistance from the computer, saying, "Abe, engines didn't fire. Do you have a clue as to why they didn't fire?"

"There's indication of a short in the ignition system."

Rhodes raised his head. "Some time ago, we replaced an automatic relay switch that blocked the engines from firing. Is there any way to electronically check that replacement part to determine if it's defective or faulty?"

"No, Stan, but signals I'm reading in the system are telling me the problem is of a different nature."

Rhodes shook his head. "It's going to take hours to run down the problem, and after repairs are made, if the systems tabulations don't hold, we'll have to start the launch sequence all over again."

A wiring diagram popped up on Rhodes' monitor showing how the electrical system ran to an array of different components. It was the same diagram the computer showed the last time the engines failed to fire. He dreaded racking his brains, trying to determine what's working and what isn't, and he wondered if he could make liftoff before sundown. Removing his helmet, all he could think about was the terror they had endured and how much more stress the ship could take.

He looked disgusted as he said, "Someday they're going to develop a computer that can do a far better job of isolating problems, but in the meantime, we're going to die here on the red planet."

Far removed her helmet, and then turned to ask Rhodes, "Stan, couldn't we use the emergency vehicle?"

"It hasn't had sufficient time to produce enough fuel to launch and get us on a trajectory for home, but even if it had the fuel, we'd still need twenty-four hours to prepare to launch. I consider the emergency ascent vehicle small compared to this ship. Since its vertical, two or three of those powerful beasts could possibly topple it and bring it down, and then what? Besides, if we went to it, I imagine the creatures would be able to track our scent.

"So what are we going to do?"

"I've got only one idea, but you're not going to be thrilled about it. I believe you're capable of running down the ignition problem here, so I'm going to open up some of the floor panels on the bridge to allow you to begin systematically testing components. Just do what you can, and when I get back we'll see what can be done about getting this ship off the ground."

Her expression turned to disappointment. "Oh, no, Stan, don't tell me you're thinking about going back to the pyramid again! Are you?"

Rhodes took a deep breath. "Ever since yesterday when I went up to the pyramid to get the flamethrower, I've been thinking about how we came to be endangered by these beasts. The platform decking bridges the pyramid entrance to the staircase, which makes the way accessible for them. The platform was showing signs of weakening that night from when the first beast crossed it, and we know that at least three of them made passage to and from the pyramid last night. Unless I go back and find the platform has collapsed, they're almost certain to be back again tonight, and judging by what I've seen, they just might succeed at getting in here.

"I don't feel the least bit comfortable relying on the integrity of this ship to protect us for another night. That windshield is not designed to take the punishment they're dishing out. If the windshield shatters under the weight of two of them leaning against it, it's over for the two of us. They were trying to climb over each other to get up on the nose, and if one makes it, I'm afraid they'll cave in the glass. You saw that cargo door flexing against the pressure they put on it, and they've begun looking at the landing gear and undercarriage for a way to get in."

"Okay, but I don't follow what your plan is. Are you considering taking down part of the platform or what?"

"No, I'm simply going to weaken part of the structure by removing a number of key fasteners anchoring its framework to the pyramid. If those creatures leave the pyramid again tonight, their weight will collapse the platform. I don't know what else to do. That's the only sure way I know to stop them. There's a slim chance we'll get this ship off the ground before nightfall, but I doubt it, so the intelligent thing to do is to find a way to keep them from leaving the pyramid."

"If you're going back to the pyramid, I'm going with you, because if something should go wrong while you're climbing around, I want to be there to help."

"There's little risk in what I'm going to do, and I shouldn't be much longer than a few hours, which means I'll be back about midday, hours before dusk. Failure to accomplish liftoff is going to lead to another confrontation with these beasts. So look at it this way: With my weakening the platform and your focusing on the ignition system, we're approaching the situation from two different angles. First, it's just possible that we might locate and correct the problem before dark, and if that's the case, we won't have to contend with the threat of the beasts trying to get inside the ship. However, just in case we fail to launch by nightfall, I'll have accomplished weakening the platform, and that may be enough to stop them from leaving the pyramid. One way or another, we just might avoid dealing with the same threat we've had the last two nights."

"I've got a bad feeling about this. I think you're asking for trouble by going back to that pyramid. We've lost the use of the cameras inside. What if they're in that upper chamber, and your working on the platform draws them out?"

"I'm relying on these creatures' instincts to make them stay in their lair during the day. Judging by the pattern they've followed thus far, they won't come out until after nightfall. Even back when this Martian civilization existed, the creatures always instinctively returned to their lair. They don't like sunlight; their eyes must be sensitive to it."

"Okay, they don't like sunlight, but remember that the text also said they came out in the daytime if something disturbed them."

"Far, I'll be working on the side opposite the opening to the upper chamber, and it's unlikely they'll sense I'm there. Let me accomplish what I want to do, and when I get back we'll give these technical problems our full attention."

Believing he'd convinced Far that what he wanted to do was worthwhile trying, he removed panels in the floor at the bridge so she could begin tracking down the source of their ignition problem. She wouldn't be much help out there on the pyramid, and he knew that testing components linked to the ignition system was simply a matter of following the leads from the instrument panel.

Rhodes quickly made preparations to return to the pyramid. Taking the flamethrower and harness strap holding the tanks, he grabbed a length of nylon rope as well and left these items in the cargo bay before going to look for Far. He wasn't comfortable about leaving her in an emotional state. He hadn't seen her for a short while and she wasn't on the bridge, making him wonder what had become of her. He finally found her in the lab, sitting at the counter, and she was obviously upset.

"Stan, I'm so afraid we're not going to be able to leave this planet, and those terrible creatures are going to get us, and what if you don't come back?"

He sat down next to her and spoke reassuringly. "We've come a long way and overcome so many obstacles, and God willing, we're going to return to Earth."

Rhodes gave her a moment to squeeze him tightly and then pulled free from her clinging hold. "I'll have my camera turned on, and you can sit and watch the view on the monitor if you like. I'll try not to be any longer than two or three hours. If this works, it'll remove the threat the creatures pose against us."

He waited for her to acknowledge his comment, and when she didn't, he walked away, knowing their deadly circumstances were becoming too much for her.

Before leaving the ship, he switched on the camera in his helmet and then made sure the toolbox containing wrenches and a socket set was in the rover. He intended to remove fasteners from the bottoms of the last three or four leg assemblies. The framing would lose strength without these low mounting brackets anchored. Under the weight of the creatures, the framing legs should shift, sink, and collapse, and this was his goal.

Along the way, Rhodes slowed down to look at the storage depot, noticing the midsection was on the verge of collapsing. The beasts must have consumed whatever rations they'd left inside the ship to quell their appetites. Perhaps they had exhausted the food supply in their watery underworld, and even if they had a low metabolism, as many reptiles do, it would still take a tremendous amount of food to sustain them.

When he arrived at the pyramid, Rhodes saw that the platform was still standing, but there was no sign of the handrail cable. The trampling footprints of the beasts had disturbed sand and soil at the bottom of the stairs, but for the most part everything appeared much the same as he'd last seen it. Grabbing the looped rope and toolbox with his left hand, he then picked up the flamethrower and harness with his right. Glimpsing the platform one last time and seeing no sign of the giant lizard beasts, he began climbing the steps at a steady pace.

Noticing that the platform's construction had held up against the weight of the creatures, Rhodes thought it looked intact. He finally reached the platform to approach the framing legs supporting the decking. Many of the outside uprights had bowed in the middle, and only short, bent nubs were left of the posts that had held the handrail. The cable must have fallen somewhere below.

He climbed a few more steps to leave the flamethrower and tanks resting on the decking. This view enabled him to see indentations left when the giant lizard beasts walked across it, and this told him the platform had withstood a lot of punishment. If the decking and supporting framework didn't have elastic properties to absorb shock, the entire assembly would have certainly collapsed under their weight.

Before attempting the work, he scrutinized the anchors at the bottom of each leg assembly. There were two levels of anchors, and those at the lower level fastened to the pyramid in plain view, while the set at the top sat where the decking met the pyramid.

By moving out onto the pyramid's slanted face, he could reach down to unscrew the hex-headed fastening screws at the low end as he backed up to return to the stairs. Intending to use the rope as a tether in case he fell, he tied it to the first leg frame and then secured the other end around his waist. He examined the socket sizes available in the toolbox and remembered he had needed the largest size, 17 millimeters, which he fitted to the socket wrench. Tucking the socket wrench into the pocket of his pants leg, he then grabbed hold of the first leg frame support assembly and moved out from the stairs.

Stepping from the wedged section at the bottom of one leg frame to another, he managed to climb out underneath the decking, and he avoided looking down. Creating distance between him and the stairs, he planned to go out as far as his tether would allow. He'd moved one third of the way toward the next corner of the pyramid and squatted to remove the first hex-headed fastener. It loosened slowly and smoothly, the threads turning in the plastic sleeve.

He let the fastener screw drop down the pyramid face, and it pinged as it made its way to the ground below. The hole in the leg assembly where the screw had gone through didn't move, but this was only the beginning. He backed up, moving toward the stairs to remove the lower screw from the next leg assembly.

After the removal of this screw, it appeared the hole in the framing hadn't shifted even a mere fraction from its original alignment position. As long as the high anchors fit snugly with no weight on the platform, the legs weren't likely to sink. However, when the beasts lumbered across it, the low end of the assemblies were sure to shift and twist.

Rhodes had removed four anchors so far. Leaving the next fastener in, he then removed the next three, thinking that seven missing fasteners would significantly reduce the platform's load-bearing strength. He crouched on the stairs and breathed deeply, relieved at having accomplished what he'd set out to do. Wanting to get off the red planet as soon as possible, he untied the rope from his waist, secured his toolbox, and gathered up his equipment.

CHAPTER 32

Jaws of Death

Standing on the pyramid steps, viewing a desolate region stretching to the far horizon, Rhodes loosely looped the rope and hung it over his helmet to rest diagonally across his chest from his shoulder to his waistline. Glimpsing the sun's position, he thought he might still have time to find out what was wrong with the ship and launch before sunset. He began to reminisce about his fallen comrades. He could see Flavio poised on the pyramid's face, anchoring the framing assemblies. Rhodes hadn't put much faith into their being able to build the platform in the beginning, but Flavio never once wavered from his belief that they could do it. Not only did the finished platform emerge as a sturdy piece of construction, but they'd built it strong enough to support the three giant lizards as well.

Picking up his gear, he began descending the stairs while continuing to reflect on the recent past. Aleksei's idea to use the climate control unit to pump oxygen into the pyramid had worked surprisingly well. Alek had been such an asset when they assembled the legs of the platform, and he always had good advice for others. Jetha was a good friend to everyone, and who else would have had the patience to recreate the Martian text to help the computer decipher it? She'd been a fine assistant for Far, helping with some of the gadgetry supplied by mission planners, and the computer graphics she and Far had produced were highly entertaining.

If he'd lost only one crew member, as bad as it would have been, he'd still be able to see the mission as a success, but right now, he didn't think they'd accomplished enough, considering they had lost three people. They had discovered an ancient civilization and found water, but he still couldn't say in good conscience that their gains had made this a worthwhile trip to the red planet. Perhaps it would be up to historians and future space travelers to say whether this mission was a great achievement. In Rhodes' mind, those who thought they had fared well would have far more difficulty believing that if they'd known Flavio, Jetha, and Aleksei.

Rhodes was only about two stories from ground level when he saw one of the giant lizards prowling around the rover! He froze, hardly able to believe he was watching the creature circling the vehicle with its nose to the ground. Its presence defied logic, for he believed the animals returned to their lair to shun sunlight. What was it doing out here?

The predatory beast's tongue slithered in and out of its mouth, and then it momentarily stopped as if catching a scent before turning its head to look directly at Rhodes! Its posture changed when it made eye contact with Rhodes, ratcheting his fear up to sheer terror, and now it lumbered toward the steps of the pyramid with its tail whipping about. He knew it was capable of making a fast-moving charge, but for now, it crept toward him slowly as if it knew he had nowhere to run.

Snarling like a bloodthirsty prehistoric dinosaur, the monstrous creature advanced, its penetrating eyes targeting him as easy prey! Sidestepping up the stairs, he tried to keep pace with the powerful predator, but it gained on him and followed him up the stairs. Its broad shoulders tipping to one side and then the other as bones and muscles shifted in its steady climb, and its webbed feet and long claws pulled and pushed to ascend the stairs.

Watching it move up the staircase gave him a sick feeling in his gut, and he was terrified at the prospect of dying in the creature's jaws. Taking his eyes off the formidable beast was almost impossible, and maneuvering in his spacesuit was proving to be a challenge as he continued to back up the steep steps clumsily, stumbling before catching himself.

Turning to look up the staircase, he realized the monster had cornered him, for to keep going meant eventually he'd be trapped at the pyramid's summit. His mind racing, he knew he'd have to take to the platform's decking, but he wasn't sure if the weakened structure could support him now. He turned the flamethrower's barrel to take aim on the creature, and pulling the trigger powered a streaking flame. When he took his finger off the trigger, he saw its head slumped and its eyes closed, but it was still coming! He stared in disbelief at fiery patches on its hide that were still burning, and then it reopened its eyes! In a fit of desperation, he threw the toolbox at the animal but missed. The beast's eyes remained fixed and focused on him, and it kept coming.

Fast running out of time, Rhodes had risen as high as the platform and backed up one more step, but there was no use in going up higher on a staircase that led to nowhere. He'd fallen into his own trap! He shot another streak of flames at the creature, and it reacted much the same as before, closing its eyes and bowing its head but never missing a step. As much as he wanted to fire on the creature once more, he saw the beast fast approaching, and knowing the decking might not hold him, he started across it anyway.

Flushed with sweat, Rhodes leaned against the pyramid, the gloved knuckles of his right hand sliding against the pyramid's slanted stone as he gripped the flamethrower, his left hand clinging to the harness holding the flamethrowers tanks. Gritting his teeth as he moved awkwardly across the decking, he kept his boot's toes close to the slanted face to keep stress off the high anchors supporting the leg assemblies.

His face shield limited his viewing angle, and he kept turning his head one way and then the other, seeing the creature's approach as it rose to the platform and then viewing his feeble progress. The animal was deliberate in how it stepped onto the decking and he frantically sidestepped to avoid its advance. He soon calculated that he'd gotten past the point where he'd removed the fasteners from the platform's framework. Now believing he stood on stable decking, he changed to an audacious, surefooted stance, raising and leveling the flamethrower's barrel as he turned to face his enemy!

The creature took a vicious lunge at Rhodes, its fiercely snapping jaws coming together with a loud clap, and looking into its wide bite radius and prominent incisors, he saw jaws of death. The beast acted as though it had Rhodes exactly where it wanted him, taking a menacing stance as though preparing to pounce on him. Rhodes stooped to one knee, letting the tanks rest on the decking while taking steady aim with the flamethrower and when putting his finger on the trigger, the creature's next step caused the level platform to shift and slant downward!

As the decking sank beneath him, Rhodes leaned to shift his weight to the pyramid side that remained anchored. Releasing the harness holding the tanks, he held his position while keeping his balance with the flamethrower aimed at the creature. He placed the gloved fingers of his left hand on the decking to resist tipping toward the edge, but the decking continued dipping to the outside. He saw the giant lizard sinking with the slant of the decking, clawing as it began to slide, and as the platform's framework sank, he feared the entire section could pull loose and fall!

Rhodes fell frightfully forward headfirst to land sprawled on his stomach and losing his grip of the flamethrower, he tried to create as much drag as he could with his flattened body. Witnessing the platform falling down around him, he kept sliding toward the edge! The weapon and its tanks slid until the animal caught them with its scratching claws and with one swipe flung the flamethrower assembly from the decking.

Hearing the loud clapping of creature's snapping jaws through his helmet, he looked into its gaping jaws to see stringy saliva oozing between its teeth and saw the end coming. He could do nothing to save himself, and the beast kept violently snapping at him as if it cared little about the collapse of the decking. He clutched wildly for anything to stop his slide. If the creature didn't eat him alive, he would fall to his death off the sinking platform!

The platform kept collapsing, he reached to catch hold of a short piece of bent handrail sticking up from the edge to stop him from falling off the edge, and the creature finally fell from the decking! This took stress off the supporting framework, and the sagging structure sprang upwards with Rhodes hanging on for his life! The platform's bobbing action left him throwing an outstretched arm and leg to the pyramid to keep from sliding off until the decking finally settled and held steady.

Rhodes crawled on his belly to the edge to look down the pyramid's slanted stone face. Down below, he saw the creature's carcass lying lifeless in a cloud of dust. Then he scooted away from the edge to sit cross-legged, thinking how the anchors he'd removed worked to deliver a swift death to the beast. The anchors he'd left untouched at the higher level remained intact, and they were all that had kept the weakened platform from pulling completely free from the pyramid.

Seeing those snapping jaws in his mind, he took a deep breath while gaining his composure. The terror of falling into that meat grinder had nearly given him a heart attack. Surveying the sagging platform, he saw danger in attempting to cross it to reach the stairs, and he had no way of knowing if there were more creatures running loose on the Martian surface.

He now heard Far's familiar voice. "Stan, I saw everything as it happened, but I couldn't say anything! Are you okay?"

"I'll be okay in a minute. At least I'm still alive. I certainly wasn't expecting one of those creatures to be roaming around out here in the light of day. I'm guessing it must've eaten its share of rations in the storage depot last night and then fallen asleep. The wreckage of the ship provided shade and shelter from daylight until the sound of the rover disturbed it."

"Are you going to be able to get back to the steps?"

"I'll manage somehow. I just hope there aren't any more of those creatures running around out here. I don't think I've ever been as scared as I was just before it fell off the decking."

After resting awhile, he stood up and eyed a short, metal nub protruding from the platform's framework near the stairs. The stubby metal had been a support for the handrail, and he knotted the end of the rope for forming a lasso. Holding the drooping rope loosely in his hands, he swung his right arm in a circular motion to give the rope momentum before tossing the looped end. Falling short of his mark, he repeated the move again and again until the loop caught the upright metal piece, and then he pulled the rope tight to make certain it would hold.

Wrapping the other end around his waist, he then mustered the courage to begin working his way to the stairs. Leaning against the pyramid with his hands and arms spread apart to keep as much of his weight off the decking as possible, he perilously inched his way toward the staircase.

After making it to the steps, he stood erect to take a full breath of air, and by the time he got down from the pyramid, he felt the ordeal had taken something out of him. He got into the rover and started back to the ship feeling exhausted. As he drove past the storage depot, he slowed down to give it a long, hard look but saw no signs of the predatory creatures.

When he returned to the ship, Far greeted him joyfully, but the confrontation with the beast had left him fatigued, and he went to lie down. He felt downright ill from his encounter with the beast, and it wasn't long before he fell asleep.

Awakened by screams, Rhodes poked his head out of his pod to see a lizard beast crashing through the windshield! Far kept distancing herself from the creature, screaming at the top of her lungs and he looked around frantically for the flamethrower, only to recall they no longer had one! The monster tore through the cabin, wrecking everything in its path, and he grabbed hold of Far to pull her away, but it was already upon them, its jaws opening wide. . . .

Rhodes sat up in his pod in horror and realized he'd been dreaming. Placing his hand over his chest, he felt his heart pounding. The ship was quiet, and he looked up at the bridge to see Far sitting in her chair, keeping watch. Concern that the ship might again come under attack prompted him to climb out of his pod and rush to the bridge to survey the Martian landscape.

"See any sign of them?"

"Not a one."

He sat down next to her. "I keep seeing that creature coming at me. That incident on the pyramid may have taken a few years off my life."

"You looked awfully pale when you first returned to the ship. I still haven't located the problem with our ignition system, and if we can't get this ship to launch, we may have to consider using the emergency ascent vehicle after all."

Using his computer, Rhodes brought up conditions transmitted from the other ship and briefly studied the figures. "Readouts from *Endurance I* show it may be months before it produces sufficient fuel to launch and deliver a trajectory to send us home. However, I don't think there's anything serious causing this ship's malfunction. Since I'm feeling much better now, I'll check the ignition system."

Neither Rhodes nor Far could sleep now, their fate still uncertain, and they remained watchful for predatory creatures lurking outside the ship. The expectation of launching and beginning a long journey home was also making them restless, but with the passage of time came morning, leaving them more at ease. At the first hint of sunlight, Far went to her pod to get some sleep, and Rhodes later suited up to give the ship's exterior one last inspection.

CHAPTER 33

Homeward Bound

It wasn't until hours later that Rhodes located a bad ignition module. Changing it out was a simple job, and when Far woke up she began programming the system for a scheduled launch. Rhodes got a few hours' sleep before they ran through a round of systems checks to confirm the ship was ready for liftoff.

Sitting at the instrument panel, gazing out across Mars' desert landscape, Rhodes thought about his lost colleagues, and he knew memories of them would haunt him for the rest of his days. Their deaths were the one great disappointment about this trip, and even though there was probably nothing he could have done to save them, he had trouble accepting their fate. Before liftoff, he sent a transmission to alert mission planners that they were preparing to launch and briefly updated them on every aspect of the mission. He last gave them the planned course they'd use to aid the technicians tracking their progress.

Far initiated countdown and they ran through ignition and liftoff without a hitch. It was a relief when the ship's rocket engines powered them to hover level with vector thrust over the Martian surface. An explosive burst took them into forward flight to make a steady climb, and the landing gear retracted into its compartment. Once the spacecraft was cruising at a tremendous speed, the computer took over to maneuver the ship and gain altitude, and they soon took a vertically bound sweep to rocket their way into outer space.

As soon they broke through the Martian atmosphere to enter the twilight infinity of outer space, Rhodes removed his helmet and checked their course on the computer. They would orbit

Mars once before beginning a six-month return flight to Earth using a flight path programmed by computers.

As they ate their first meal in space, Far said, "It's not the same without the others. Their absence is going to make for a long trip home."

Rhodes replied, "I'll never forget those people as long as I live, and I don't know if I'll ever be at peace over their deaths."

Over time, the two spoke little. Far performed tests on soil and rock samples they'd collected while Rhodes studied the sacrificial Martian skulls. The skulls had characteristics similar to that of early man, and he laser-scanned one of them to get a 3-D computer image, which enabled him to give it a face.

Far complained that sleeping in the pod made her cramped and hurt her back. She set up bedding on the floor next to the pods. This was against regulations, but Rhodes said nothing about it. He often had difficulty finding a comfortable position in his pod.

He began noticing that Far often went out of her way to bump into him or briefly block his way to make eye contact with him. She was undoubtedly doing it deliberately, as there was little interaction between them. It wasn't like he was trying to ignore her; he was just keeping himself occupied to make time pass. When the last incident occurred, Far had a strange glint in her eye, and her complexion was unusually aglow.

Rhodes spent hours examining the skulls, and one particular skull held his attention. The skull had a well-rounded cranium and pronounced brow line, and while examining it closely, he envisioned Matusek's facial features superimposed over the shape of the skull. He saw those eyes, the jutting brow, and the distinctive, sinister grin with those pronounced creases in his cheeks. For a moment, he became engrossed in the hauntingly real image. Suddenly and unexpectedly, he saw the skull come to life.

He winced at the thought, and a buzzer signaling that a laboratory experiment was completed unnerved him. Settling down and thinking the experience was funny, he realized he'd gone without rest for a long time. Rubbing his eyes and leaning back to stretch, he thought it was time to get some sleep, and he gave the skull one last glance before putting it away with the others.

Entering the cabin, he found the lights dimmed, and Far was lying on the bedding she'd arranged, holding a provocative pose. A sheet neatly pulled up to her armpits followed the shape of her slender body. The sheet left her arms and shoulders bare and revealed her cleavage. She looked exotic with her long, silky black hair draped about her.

Far turned to look at him with seductive eyes, and spoke softly, saying, "I'm terribly lonely without the others, Stan, and I want you to lie with me for a while."

Far reached over to pat the bedding, as though inviting him to lie down beside her, and watched him shed his uniform before slipping beneath the sheet to lie on his back beside her. She turned and shifted to place her head against his shoulder and said, "For the next six months we're going to be the only two people in existence, and I hope you're not going to pretend I'm not here."

In an understanding tone, he replied, "Chances are that after we return to Earth, we're going to drift apart. Are you going to let this time that we're stuck together influence the rest of your life?"

She raised her head to look into his eyes. "I feel terribly lonely, partly because others who came on this trip are gone forever, and their absence is a void. It's their loss that makes me cleave to life all the more, feeling a longing to share closeness with another, proving I have human instincts. Trapped in this ship for months to come, circumstances as they are, am I wrong to have desires that constitute life and living? Feeling uncertain about tomorrow—if there is a tomorrow for us—should it come out that we were intimate, I don't see how people can ridicule us."

Whipping her hair back, Far turned on her stomach, using her arms and elbows to prop her shoulders and head up, her warm, slender body rubbing against Rhodes. "I grew to love those people, and to know they're gone leaves me with a sense of mortality. Perhaps this emotion is something God or Mother

Nature has instilled in me. I'm very fond of you and have been for some time, and I don't know how you feel, but if I had to choose one other person to survive this trip with me, it would be you. Had that creature killed you, I think I may have killed myself rather than die of loneliness and despair, for losing you would've been too much for me to bear." She looked at him. "Does anything I've said mean anything to you?"

"Yes, I suppose it does."

Far had opened her heart by sharing her feelings and Rhodes pulled her close to give her comfort, although still feeling beset by guilt for having failed his comrades.

Kissing him ever so tenderly on the lips, she then said, "Are we to coexist over the span of our trip home and ignore the fact that you're a man and I'm a woman?" She kissed him again and ran her fingertips over his arm and chest, saying, "I hope you're not finding this repulsive."

Trying not to grin, Rhodes replied, "Not at all, but over the course of this trip I've tried to put the allure of the opposite sex out of my mind, and maybe it's not going to be all that easy to focus."

Far couldn't help smirking, and said, "Well, if that's all that's holding you back, leave it up to me to get the fire going."

With that, she lovingly curled up against him, caressing, and kissing him passionately, as though unleashing a tiger within her, and they fell into rapture.

CPSIA information can be obtained
at www.ICGtesting.com
Printed in the USA
FFOW041442010313
941FF